VENUS' VENGEANCE

ASHLEY WEISS

First Edition: August 2025
For more information contact:
Ashley Weiss
www.ashleyweisswrites.ca

ISBN 978-1-7389347-5-1 (hardcover)
ISBN 978-1-7389347-3-7 (paperback)
ISBN 978-1-7389347-4-4 (e-book)

DEDICATION:

To all the readers who finished Cupid's Compass *and cursed my name, we're not done yet.*

DAY 1

WITHOUT COMPASSES

Pain, grief, torture, and death,

That is what mortals have come to expect.

Of the panel of gods and goddesses so cruel,

The Pantheon sees humanity as theirs to rule.

Beware the divine's gifts, blessings, and boons.

They've mastered deceit over millennia of moons.

—The Pantheon

CHAPTER I

"Somebody help me!" Blake's voice pitched into an unnatural octave as panic shifted her systems into overdrive.

Curling smoke and the scent of something sharp and earthy filled the clearing. Tree trunks bowed away and branches scattered the ground where the circle of salt had been. Though the bronze table was unscathed, every item that had sat on the altar smoldered, cast across the charred grass. And then, of course, there were the bodies.

In Blake's tattoo-covered arms, a woman convulsed. Psyche's golden skin paled as her usually bright blue eyes rolled back to white. Her back arched and her fingers raked at the dirt. Blake grasped Psyche tighter and tried to keep the woman's head of black curls from slamming against the ground as visceral fear thundered in her chest.

"Please! Somebody help me!" Blake tore her gaze from Psyche and searched the meadow for any movement from her other companions.

She found Nessie's stunned face first. Nessie stared up at the sky, knocked back on her elbows. A trickle of blood ran out of one nostril, and dirt streaked the girl's face and denim jacket. Her long blond ponytail lacked its usual composure, ruffled by the wild winds Venus had released with her curse before she vanished.

Venus. Could it be possible Blake had really just been kneeling before the goddess of love and beauty? The mother of Cupid?

The gods are real… A shiver ran up Blake's spine as her reality shifted. Psyche hadn't been making it up. The truth gave Blake vertigo as she recalled every time she'd sworn up to the skies.

Nessie pressed her eyes shut, gave herself a shake, then crawled toward her mother. Charity was curled in the fetal position, her arms clasped tight around her knees. A haunting wail wrenched itself from the older woman's chest.

"Mom," Nessie whispered, her own voice shaky. "Mom, are you okay?"

Blake scanned the clearing as another worry arose. There was something missing. No, not something—someone.

Where is Jaylynn?

As the other person connected to Psyche through Cupid's soulmate link, Jaylynn should have been here by Psyche's side with Blake. But no traces of auburn braids or a face of spattered freckles could be found. Psyche jolted awake with a gasp, her chin tilted up to the afternoon sky. Willing herself to breathe, Blake wrapped her arm around the woman's slender waist to support her.

"Psyche, I'm here."

Blake's supposed soulmate turned slowly to look into her eyes, horror woven in the icy flecks of her irises.

"What have I done?" Psyche whispered.

Before Blake could answer, the woman's eyes rolled back, and her body slumped in Blake's arms again.

No, no, no…

"Nessie, I need you!" Blake cried, hating how weak she sounded.

Nessie caught her gaze. For a second, fear flashed in the girl's eyes before settling into resolve. She dragged the back of her hand across her face, smearing a trail of blood along her cheek.

"Mom, come on. We need to get up." Nessie wrapped an arm under Charity's torso, pulled her to standing, and staggered over.

"Where is Jaylynn?" Blake asked.

Nessie shook her head. "I don't know. I'm not even sure I understand what just happened…"

Blake did. They'd summoned a *literal god* to the clearing in the forest. They'd asked for Psyche to be freed from her curse to live forever without her soulmate. But everything had backfired. First, despite calling upon Cupid—the god of love and Psyche's soulmate—his mother had shown up.

The second thing that went wrong was the request. When Psyche had begged Venus' forgiveness, the goddess had refused. Well, *refused* would be the light way of putting it. Blake looked down at her left wrist. Three years ago, she'd covered her compass-clock with a mess of black rose tattoos. Now, without the underlying compass, the sloppy linework of her cover-up didn't look any better. Compasses were really gone, exactly as Venus had promised. A flicker of joy lit in Blake's chest as she realized she was free of the Fates' games, but it evaporated as Nessie and Charity collapsed next to her.

"Is she okay?" Nessie asked, nodding to Psyche. She held her mom up with a protective arm.

Blake shook her head. "I don't know. One minute Psyche was convulsing, then the next she passed out."

Nessie bit her bottom lip. "We should get out of here. I don't want to be here if that psychopath comes back."

Blake hadn't considered Venus might come back. Suddenly the blown-apart salt border felt even more ominous. "I don't think she'll be coming back, but you're right. We can't stay here." Blake assessed their options, pausing at Charity's trembling form. "Charity, can you walk on your own?"

Charity's eyes were pressed closed against the streams of tears flowing down her dirt-covered cheeks, but she nodded. It would have to do. Blake rolled her shoulders back, conscious how every muscle burned and ached.

"Ness, help me with Psyche."

Nessie stood and reached out for Psyche's arm, then sucked in a gasp and withdrew as if she'd only just noticed she was injured. Blake stared at Nessie's palms. The skin glistened red-hot with a white sheen of blisters.

"What happ—" Blake broke off as she reached up to take Nessie's shaking hand, realizing her own palms looked exactly the same. She hadn't noticed in her panicked state, but now the sharp throbbing pain demanded its audience.

Nessie gaped. "What…?"

Blake flexed her fingers to test the extent of the pain, suppressing the urge to flinch. The strange burns covered her palms and the length of each finger, rounding to cover part of the back of her hand.

"I think—" Nessie shuddered. "I think they're our handprints."

She was right. Blake could now make out where Psyche's long fingers had wrapped around her left hand. Blake and Nessie met each other's eyes, both slowly reaching for the other, mirroring exactly how their hands had been clasped during the ritual. The burns were a perfect match to every point their skin had touched.

"Venus," Nessie muttered. "What a nasty, vile piece of—"

"Nessie," Blake interrupted. "You're not wrong, but we need to move."

The hard tone broke whatever angry spell had taken Nessie over. Blake stood, using the crooks of her elbows to distribute Psyche's weight instead of her burned hands. Nessie and Blake managed to span Psyche's arms across their shoulders, and Charity held the sleeve of Nessie's free elbow.

The walk back to Psyche's cabin was hard. Every few steps, Psyche's limp arms would slip, but they made it to the small wooden cabin, staggering through the doorway to the smell of crushed roses and lavender. In the common space, they laid Psyche out on the cot as gently as they could. Blake drew a heavy quilt to cover her frighteningly still body.

Psyche said she could never die. She's just passed out from shock.

Blake swallowed hard, the panic and fear from the clearing bubbling back up.

Across the room, Nessie draped a yellow quilt over her mom's shoulders as Charity settled on the ground next to the fireplace. Charity's vacant stare fixed dead ahead at the flames. Despite sporting the same burns, the woman didn't flinch the way Blake and Nessie both did with each small task. It was like she'd left her body.

"It's okay, Mom. You're okay." Nessie's forehead creased in concern. Blake moved to her side.

"Nessie. I need to go find Jaylynn. I don't think Psyche will go anywhere. Can you handle this until I get back?"

Nessie nodded, her thick blond eyebrows heavy. "Yeah. But hurry."

How one nineteen-year-old and one fifteen-year-old were the ones in charge amid all of this baffled Blake, but she simply nodded back and went to find their missing accomplice.

The meadow was still smoldering when Blake arrived back to ground zero, but the heavy haze had lifted, and a soft white filter had settled over the greenery. She searched for any sign of where the missing redhead might have gone. Blake passed the spot where Psyche's nails had clawed into the dirt, then she turned left, toward where Jaylynn would have been in their circle. As expected, the clover flowers were crumpled in an outward direction from the middle, and an imprint of a warm body was pressed into the ground ten feet away from the bronze table. Blake knelt and brushed the spears of grass with her fingers.

Where did you go, Jaylynn?

Blake stared at the trees outlining the clearing. Venus' winds had torn through their branches, leaving jagged fractures in their wake. Blake retraced the direction Jaylynn's body would have slid from the middle, and at the tree's edge, she found the telltale scuff of a muddy footprint.

Gotcha.

Jaylynn had left the clearing. But why? Luckily, tracing her path was as easy as following an elephant's path through a field of barley. Unnatural streaks cut into the earth where the girl must have stumbled and fallen. Even when Blake came up to a rocky bit and the footprints were less discernible, branches twisted away and beckoned her forward in an obvious path of least resistance.

When Blake broke free of the brush at the edge of the river, she stopped dead. Jaylynn knelt at the side of the creek. Tiny twigs clung to her usually neat double braids, and mud caked her knees and elbows. Her disheveled appearance couldn't compare to the absolute heartbreak on her face, though. Jaylynn was hyperventilating, her palms planted in the water and her freckled cheeks swollen with purple blotches.

"Jaylynn?" Blake hovered at the edge of the trees as she tentatively called out. She'd never been great with crying, and Jaylynn's raw grief made Blake's skin prickle. The hysterical girl didn't answer. Blake ground her teeth together and marched forward. Cold water sloshed through the holes of her worn combat boots as she sank into the soft riverbank. Blake grabbed the shoulder of Jaylynn's shirt, banishing her own pain.

"What do you think you're doing?"

Tears streamed from Jaylynn's bloodshot eyes to the corners of her trembling lips. Her words came out in a slurred mumble that Blake could hardly make out.

"It's all my fault—" Jaylynn confessed. "I agreed. I told Psyche I would do it. I should have said no. I should have stopped her." Her words dissolved into another fit of sobs.

Blake couldn't put a finger on why seeing Jaylynn like this made her so furious. Maybe it was because she'd wanted to run away herself but couldn't. Maybe it was because Jaylynn should have been the one holding the group together. Either way, Blake leaned into the anger. As it built, it supplanted Blake's blooming fear that the gods were real and they were coming for her. Blake hated fear. She hated the way it made her heart race, the way she couldn't catch her breath. But above that, she hated watching Jaylynn cry.

Blake's hands softened. She let go of Jaylynn's shirt as she stepped back. Then her hand cut through the air, and she slapped Jaylynn across the face. Screaming pain lanced up Blake's wrist and renewed the fiery burns on her hand, but she didn't care. In fact, as adrenaline rushed through her veins, Blake almost felt like she could breathe again.

The blunt force of Blake's attack seemed to reset Jaylynn's whirl of emotions. The woman fell back on the riverbank in stunned silence. Her fingers grazed her cheekbone in shock. A shred of guilt joined the satisfaction in Blake's chest as she towered over Jaylynn. At least the crying was done.

"You don't get to do this," Blake bit out. "Do you hear me?"

Jaylynn's chin wobbled, her pale blue irises wide and terrified. Their innocence did nothing to cool Blake's boiling frustration.

"I get it," Blake continued. "This all sucks. But that doesn't mean you get to run away and have a pity party for yourself when everyone else is also falling apart."

Jaylynn shrank into the tall grass, the bright red imprint on her cheek flushing a furious scarlet.

"Blake, I—"

Blake threw her arms up to the tree line. "What about Psyche? What about Charity? You think they aren't hurt? That they aren't struggling?"

Jaylynn's eyes watered anew. "Is Psyche—"

"She's fine," Blake snapped. "No thanks to you."

The roar in Blake's chest shifted, and she knelt down closer to Jaylynn. "Now, you're going to listen to me. We are going to go back to that cabin. You are going to tell them you were in shock and wandered away. You are going to do what a good soulmate would have done—you are going to tend to Psyche."

"What are you going to do?"

Blake glared. "I'm going to figure out how to fix this, because apparently everyone else has lost their minds."

CHAPTER II

LACEY

Damien. My soulmate's *name is Damien.*

Lacey's heart skipped against her rib cage in stunned glee. As they sat side by side on the steps of the café, the surroundings faded away. All Lacey could see was Damien. She'd found her perfect match, chosen by Cupid, and he was here, holding her very sweaty hands, looking equally in awe.

The rich, sweet tang of Damien's cologne made Lacey sigh as she leaned even closer. She couldn't explain the ache she had to trace her fingers over his bronzed skin and the dark beauty spots that dashed his face. But what took her breath away most was Damien's perfectly lopsided smile. It hitched up higher on one side, playful and beautiful.

This is the face I get to stare at for the rest of my life.

Lacey couldn't help the happiness that pulled her mouth into a giddy smile. Damien wore his hair longer on top and buzzed short on the sides, the front curling over his dark eyebrows. His dreamy eyes swept over her own features, his eyebrow arching.

The tiniest knot of apprehension cooled Lacey's high. Was she what he'd expected? There hadn't been time to sleek down her hair or touch up her lip gloss. Everything had happened so fast, but now it was as if time stood still. Damien's gaze danced over her round cheeks and the rapid rise and fall of her chest.

"I can't believe—" she started.

"It's mad, isn't it?" Damien's English accent made her split into a fresh grin.

"Totally mad." Lacey sighed and planted one elbow on her knees for stability. Damien still held her hand in his, their palms hot and slick together. Lacey never wanted to let go.

"I tried to come find you—" Lacey started to say, but she was cut off as Damien spoke at the same time again.

"You live here in Toronto?"

Lacey nibbled at her lip, the grin on her face permanently etched in place. "Sorry."

Damien shook his head. "You first."

"I take it you're not from around here."

His crisp black jeans and baggy gray shirt hung over his frame, giving him an edgy, urban look. Compared to the boys from her high school, he seemed so mature.

"My flight from England landed less than an hour ago." Damien grinned that perfect crooked smile back at her.

And he came straight to find me… Lacey's entire being melted further into romantic oblivion. She'd spent the last six days trekking across the eastern provinces of Canada to find her soulmate, and in the end, he'd been the one to find her.

From the UK of all places. So much for Nessie's theory he'd be a French boy from Montreal.

The thought of her best friend and their last fight soured her mood slightly, but Lacey pushed away the pang of guilt. She had too many questions to worry about Nessie right now.

"Is your family here too?" Lacey asked.

"No, my folks stayed back home. I came down with my football club for a monthlong exchange."

A month.

Lacey knotted her fingers together. Her excitement bled into a quieter hum.

"Oh." She wasn't sure what to say to that, or what it meant for their future. Would he move to Canada? Or would she have to move to England? When would that happen? Would they have a long-distance relationship once his trip was over? The silent moment stretched on as their eyes met and flitted away.

Despite being on a small side street in Toronto, the blaring sirens from the adjacent and busy York Street pulled Lacey from her reverie.

"It sounds like the world is falling apart over there," Lacey whispered. It seemed on every street, people were laying on their horns, urging one another to go faster while simultaneously becoming more and more clustered.

Damien leaned forward. He reached out, gently tucking a piece of Lacey's hair behind her ear. Her worries dissipated at his touch. "And yet, somehow we still found each other."

Lacey fought the prickling urge to cry from the overwhelming relief and happiness. Damien's hooded eyes flickered down to her lips, and his shoulder dropped as he closed the space between them. Understanding dawned on her and Lacey pulled back, conscious of how horrid her own breath was at the moment.

Why on Terra Mater's green earth did I have to puke?

It made sense, of course. The shock of her compass being stripped from her arm completely justified her body failing her, but now Lacey couldn't seal this first moment with the kiss of her dreams. The momentary reminder that her compass was gone left a new heaviness in her heart. Less than five minutes ago, she'd been crying on the floor as pain racked her bones. Now, as she searched for it, she could feel the cold emptiness her compass had left in its wake. A body without magic, without a tether. Lacey's spirits sank as she realized she and Damien wouldn't have the classic love story. There wouldn't be a magical link that always led them home to one another.

But at least we found each other.

Grief wove with her gratitude, and Lacey gave an apologetic smile.

We can wait. We'll find a perfect moment for our first kiss. It'll come.

Damien's grin faltered, as though he was surprised by her gentle rejection. Before Lacey could explain, the door chimed and opened behind them, prompting them both to stand. As an elderly couple came out, Lacey caught sight of the barista.

Lacey had been to this Toronto coffee shop a few times before with Nessie, so the café employee was familiar. Though Lacey didn't know the worker's name, she remembered the bold hand-scrawled they/them pronouns on their nametag and their choppy red bangs. Behind the barista's oversized glasses, though, any prior cheerfulness was replaced by a predatory glare, targeted straight at Lacey.

They're just jealous, Lacey reasoned as the door swung closed. *They probably didn't find their soulmate in time and wish they were us.*

Us. Warmth flooded Lacey's belly as she considered the new prospect. She wove her still-sweaty hand back into Damien's and smiled up at him.

"Can we get out of here?"

He smiled, nodding his chin forward. "Lead the way."

Lacey headed back toward the main road in a semi-trance. The blare of the emergency sirens had her curious, despite hardly being able to pull her gaze away from Damien. They walked the block hand in hand as pedestrians scrambled like ants on a hill doused with acid. In her pocket, her mom's phone rang. The unfamiliar buzzing pattern was a sour reminder Renee had given Lacey her own phone after losing hers on the train to Montreal. Hardly sparing the screen a glance, Lacey dismissed the call then squinted against the sun as she glanced up at Damien.

"How tall are you?" she asked.

Damien let out a surprised huff of laughter. "Six foot one. And you?"

"I'm five foot five and three quarters."

Damien smirked. "Why not just say five foot six?"

"Feels like a lie."

"And five foot five isn't tall enough?"

"Exactly." Lacey smiled a wide, toothy grin.

The next street was a gridlock of stopped cars. An ambulance wailed as it tried to get by, and vehicle bumpers crept up the curb on the sidewalk to make room. Lacey's blossoming joy wilted as they both silently took in their surroundings.

"What do you think caused it?" Damien asked.

"I have no idea. I can't imagine Cupid's magic just ran out." Lacey swept a wary look at her soulmate, reminded of how little she actually knew of this person she was going to spend the rest of her life with. He could be an atheist for all she knew. "You do believe in the gods, right?"

Damien laughed and squeezed her hand, pulling her close. Their shoulders bumped together. "Of course. Back home, church is everything. My dad warned me only the Capitoline Triad and Cupid have any real presence here in Canada, but where I'm from, we pray to all the gods—major and minor alike. Every meal and every night."

"Huh," Lacey said, considering her own limited religious knowledge. "I guess that checks out. I've only ever really prayed to Cupid."

The corner of Damien's mouth tugged down, and Lacey suddenly wondered if she'd answered wrong.

"Today alone we can thank Cupid, the Fates, and even Fortuna for our luck."

Lacey nodded emphatically when in reality she'd never considered people might pray to the Fates, let alone some minor goddess of luck and fortune. She gave Damien's hand a reassuring squeeze. She wasn't going to let this small difference cause a rift between them on their first day together. Lacey would give offerings at meals for the rest of her life if it was important to her soulmate. It wasn't like she had anything to actively pray for anymore.

The ambulance that had been trying to get by crept closer, making conversation next to impossible. Lacey winced as the octave of the siren pierced higher. She shut her eyes, willing the truck to pass quickly. Suddenly, the breath was knocked out of her. Lacey gasped as Damien swept an arm around her waist and crushed her up against a brick wall. At his heels, a car screeched to a stop where it had swerved up and onto the sidewalk. Heat crept up Lacey's neck as Damien pinned her against the wall, his arms a protective shield around her.

"Are you okay?" Damien searched her face, and Lacey sucked in a breath against the pain in her shoulder.

"Yes." They stood taut for a minute, a hairbreadth apart. Damien's gaze lingered on her lips, and she realized what he was thinking instantly. Lacey tucked her chin and hugged him closer, fending off his second attempt at a kiss. To her relief, Damien hugged her back, his arms closing around her back.

The sirens softened as the emergency vehicle made its way by, and Lacey pulled back, torn between standing in this moment forever and her fear that she smelled like puke and sweat. As she and Damien parted, Lacey stared dumbstruck at the closeness of the car that had almost taken them out. She noticed the driver had a panic-stricken face, and her annoyance fizzled.

We're okay, but clearly everyone is losing their minds. We need to get off these streets.

Lacey considered where to go.

I need to find my mom.

They'd talked about meeting at their favorite Italian restaurant by the CN Tower at one o'clock. While it wasn't close to one yet, Lacey figured they may as well head there to wait.

Lacey was much more cautious of straying cars as they walked on, her fingers laced together with Damien's. Unfortunately, the ambulance had been heading in the same direction, and the wailing sirens only got louder. She was about to steer them away from the noise when she glimpsed what had drawn the emergency vehicle in the first place. A very familiar black SUV with tinted windows sat less than ten car lengths ahead, its front end wrapped around a traffic light post like it was made of tinfoil.

Dread dispelled everything.

"Mom?" Lacey dropped Damien's hand as she drew her fingers up to her mouth in shock. "Mom?!" She burst into a run. Another vehicle jarred into her path as Lacey rushed into the intersection. Her hands slammed on the hood of a car as she stumbled, but she didn't stop. She couldn't. Damien let out a torrent of curses at the driver as he followed hot on her heels, but Lacey didn't look back. She ran to the wrecked vehicle, the bellowing alarms echoing her own terror. The SUV's front windows were shattered, and broken glass glittered on the ground in the afternoon sun. A small group of people anxiously lingered around the car—all of them with phones pressed to their ears.

"Mom!" Lacey cried. She coughed against the noxious fumes as she fought through the bodies to get closer. The sight of the driver was like a spear through Lacey's heart. She would recognize that braid anywhere: the exact muted chestnut brown Lacey repeatedly dyed black on her own head. Renee's head slumped forward like a rag doll with the deflated airbag in her lap. Blood coursed down her face and coated her chest. Lacey clawed at the door handle, panic building inside her as the bent metal refused to give way.

"Here, let me." Damien grasped Lacey's shoulders, forcing her to step aside despite her protests. He curled his fingers under the handle and braced a foot on the frame. He pulled hard, leveraging his body against the car. For a second, it seemed like it wouldn't move. Then it broke free in a sickening screech. Lacey rushed forward, brushing shards of green glass from her mom's shoulders.

"Mom? Mom, it's me." Lacey cupped her mom's chin, lifting her limp head. Bright red blood ran in a steady stream from Renee's nostrils, and a fresh wave of nausea threatened to make Lacey collapse.

"Mom? Please, wake up." Her voice wobbled as she brushed her mom's cheek, already darkening with ominous bruising.

"Stop!" an unfamiliar voice yelled.

Lacey looked up to see a paramedic rushing toward her.

"Don't move her head and don't touch her!" The woman carried a bag at her side and forced Lacey back and away.

Damien wrapped his arms protectively around her, his chest to her back. "It's going to be okay," he murmured into her hair. "She's going to be okay. They're going to help her."

Lacey's head spun as she looked at the blood on her hands. Her mother's blood.

This is all my fault. She came here because of me.

Another paramedic joined the first. Someone shouted to make way as a stretcher was pulled out of the emergency vehicle. Tears sprung to Lacey's eyes, and she spun around to bury her head in Damien's embrace.

Oh, Cupid, what have I done?

In her pocket, her phone buzzed again. Lacey ignored it, the sickening fear that her mother was about to die the only thing she could focus on. She grasped Damien's body tight to hers, the only center of gravity as her universe spiraled apart.

"It's okay, Lacey. I've got you. I won't leave your side."

"We need everyone to please step back." The orders rang out cold and hard. Lacey stumbled as Damien pulled her farther away.

"No," Lacey cried, twisting in his arms. "That's my mom." She pushed against Damien but he didn't let go. "Please!"

She watched as an EMT strapped a board to the back of her mom's head. Lacey's heart hammered as they pried open Renee's eyes and passed a mini flashlight over them.

Let her be okay. Please, Cupid, let her live and be okay.

CHAPTER III

It's really gone.

Sebastian stared at his bare forearm in disbelief. A moment ago, Cupid's magic was chanting that his soulmate was only steps away. At least, that's how it felt. Now, in the tattoo's absence, a hollowness filled Sebastian's heart—a distinct not-there-ness where his soulmate link had thrummed the past two weeks. Sebastian planted one hand firmly against the brick wall at his back as he scoured the unknown faces around him. Any one of them could have been his fated life partner. Now there was no way to know who Cupid had chosen for him.

Screams of sirens filled the streets. The sidewalks were packed with people. Employees rushed out of businesses to their cars, phones pressed to their ears, keys in hand. And the crying… It was as if a bomb of devastation had been dropped over the city.

Sebastian staggered as he tried to stay out of the way of the panicked swarm, but as he stepped back, his left ankle tipped, and he lost his balance. He barely caught himself against the brick wall as familiar searing pain lanced up his lower leg. In Sebastian's years of playing football, he'd had more than his fair share of ankle sprains. That was how he instantly knew this was a bad one. He hobbled a cautious step and winced as the nerves burned like white fire up his calf.

Stars, I want to go home.

The simple thought struck hard and true. Sebastian would rather be across the world with his self-absorbed sister and lovestruck parents than falling apart in the streets of a foreign country. But an ocean stood between him and England. Sebastian willed himself to pull it together. His hand trembled as he pulled up his Canadian exchange family's contact information. The married men had given Sebastian their number and wishes of good luck before he'd struck off to follow his compass. He never considered a scenario where he'd have to call them because he'd failed. The other end picked up instantly.

"Sebastian? Are you okay? Where are you?" The echo of both Philip's and Huan's voices rushed together through the phone speaker.

He wasn't all right, but he wasn't about to let them know that.

"Can you—" Sebastian coughed, a feeble attempt to hide the unexpected croak in his voice. "I need help."

"Send us your location, son. We'll be there as soon as we can."

The next forty minutes passed painfully slowly. Sebastian limped up the street to a nearby bus bench. The car horns nagged the sharp headache behind Sebastian's eyes as the streets slowed to a gridlock around him. Thankfully, no one stopped to talk with him, let alone sit beside him. Alone, he tried to make sense of what it all meant.

Sebastian had never wanted a compass tattoo, terrified of becoming like his parents, but what would his future be without a soulmate? Would he never get married or have kids? His throat bobbed. At sixteen he hadn't thought that far ahead, but having the possibility erased made him realize that a life with marriage and children was what he'd pictured all along.

A hand on his shoulder made Sebastian jump out of the miserable trance he'd settled into. He sat up tall, trying to mask the emotions that threatened to bury him. Behind him, Huan stood with a worried expression. His dark eyes searched Sebastian's.

"We're here, Seb. I'm so sorry it took so long." Huan was a short, athletic Chinese man, with a square jawline and a broad chest. Clearly he worked out a lot based on how his white T-shirt hugged his biceps.

Philip jogged up next, keeling over as he came to a stop. The tall man gasped as if he'd run blocks without taking a break.

"Yes, we're here. But Pluto have mercy, I think I need a minute."

The corner of Sebastian's mouth tucked in the tiniest of smiles as he met Huan's amused smirk. Philip sagged onto the bench beside Sebastian.

"And you say my morning jogs are a waste of time." Huan's eyes twinkled. Philip waved Huan off, focusing on long, deep breaths. He leaned against Sebastian ever so slightly as he caught his breath.

"If I'd known how far we'd have to go on foot, I would have worn better shoes."

Sebastian's gaze flicked to the brown dress shoes on Philip's feet.

"I don't think running shoes was the issue," Huan teased. He squeezed Sebastian's shoulder as he redirected his attention. "I know you've been here awhile, but would you mind sitting for a couple more minutes while my dear husband recovers?"

Sebastian nodded, not sure he had another choice—but he didn't really mind. He didn't have anywhere to go. Huan took a seat on Sebastian's other side, effectively sandwiching him in, and wrapped an arm around his shoulders.

"How are you?"

The weight of sadness swelled yet again. Sebastian tried to nod. He wanted to convince his exchange family everything was all right, but Huan's darkening expression suggested he wasn't falling for it. Instead, Sebastian rubbed his temple where his bright pink scars splashed toward his eye and down to his cheek.

"I am so sorry you missed finding your soulmate, Seb," Huan said, his voice filled with pity.

The tears started falling before Sebastian could stop them. He hated this—he didn't want to care. But now that it had started, any ability to restrain his anguish was well and gone. Philip's hand clasped Sebastian's knee, giving a gentle squeeze as Sebastian let his grief consume him.

Neither man spoke as Sebastian cried. They sat like patient bodyguards, shielding him from onlookers. When Sebastian was sure he had nothing left in him, he sat back and sniffled. He rubbed his eyes with the heels of his hands. Neither Philip nor Huan made a move to leave or speak.

"I…" Sebastian choked out between sniffles. "I don't think I'll be able to walk far. I hurt my ankle."

"Let me see." Philip rose instantly, kneeling in front of him. "Which one?"

Sebastian held out his left ankle, embarrassed. Philip's long, lean fingers raised Sebastian's foot gently as he took stock of the swelling. He *tsk*ed in disapproval.

"I'm sure it's just a sprain," Sebastian quickly added, not wanting to cause an even bigger fuss.

The soft worry lines between Philip's brows deepened. "Can you weight-bear? How bad is your pain?"

"It's nothing, really," Sebastian replied. "Just a bit sore." He tried to stand to prove his point, but whatever relief he'd gained from sitting was replaced with a burning fury. Sebastian swayed and each man grasped one of his elbows.

Philip's mouth pitched in a grim line. "Home and ice tonight. X-rays tomorrow depending on how the swelling and bruising is in the morning."

"Philip was a medic in the military," Huan explained. "He's seen his fair share of injuries. Listen to him, Seb."

Sebastian submitted as each man took an arm to support him. Huan was close to his own height, but Philip's tall frame made them a clumsy, unbalanced trio. Exhaustion pulled at Sebastian's limbs as they headed back to find where the Suns had abandoned their car. When they passed the spot where Sebastian's compass disappeared, a dull knife twisted in his heart.

As if realizing how heavy the mood was getting, Huan straightened and smiled. "Did you know the Endless War is actually how Philip and I met?"

"Really?" Sebastian's lips parted in surprise.

Philip smiled, the lines of his forehead creasing in soft waves. "It's quite a romantic story, really."

"I wouldn't call you taking a saw to my leg romantic," Huan retorted, a playful lilt in his grin.

Sebastian tilted his head. "Pardon?"

Huan paused to pull up the cuff of his track pants to display his prosthetic foot. Sebastian had been so consumed by his own anxieties he hadn't realized Huan was missing his lower leg. Sebastian's rolled ankle seemed ridiculous in comparison. Before

Sebastian could stammer an apology and shrug out of the men's supportive arms, Huan dropped the leg of his pants and pulled Sebastian close again.

"Well, the surgery wasn't romantic," Philip amended, his smile taking on a wistful gleam. "My compass was the last thing on my mind when Huan's battalion was dragged into my medical tent. It wasn't until I was assessing Huan's injuries and my tattoo flared that I realized my soulmate was bleeding out in front of me."

Huan scoffed. "I wasn't bleeding out."

Philip gave Sebastian a flat stare. "As I said, my soulmate was bleeding out in front of me. And I knew both of our futures rested in my hands."

Huan grinned. "I couldn't have asked for a better caretaker following that horrid day."

Philip's smile widened in agreement. "I boarded that flight thinking I was risking my life for a war I didn't believe in. Little did I know I would find the love of my life in that infirmary."

"And I left a foot on the front lines facing the Northern Alliance and came back with a dashing husband. I'd say the trade-off was worth it." Huan squeezed Philip's shoulder in agreement.

Sebastian didn't know a lot about the Northern Alliance—he'd never cared for history class—so his knowledge of the war could be summed up in a few facts. The Northern Alliance was made up of the brutal winter countries the Emperor hadn't been able to invade and claim. The centuries-long military standoff between the Roman Empire and the Northern Alliance stretched over miles, the current most active military point being Old Germania.

Philip's smile fell. "We were lucky to come home at all."

As the men dropped into a knowing silence, Sebastian realized they were likely mourning their friends who hadn't made it back. He swallowed as he took in all the information and realized how little he knew about his temporary family.

"So, are you both still in the military?"

Philip's laugh was a bright, wheezing cackle. "Jupiter Almighty, absolutely not. The minute we came back to Canada, we both washed our hands of that mess. I'm an anesthesiologist now at the university hospital." He gave Sebastian a knowing look. "It's less stressful than amputating limbs."

"And I went back to school and got my degree in psychology," Huan said. "I work as a veteran counsellor."

Sebastian smiled politely as he tried to match the men's easy chatter despite the noise and panic around them. He could tell they were doing it for his sake, to take his mind off what had just happened, but even their gentle tugs and soft smiles couldn't make Sebastian forget he'd lost his compass today, and with it, his chance of ever meeting his soulmate.

CHAPTER IV

"Nylah, we need to talk." The café manager's tone was somber, as if all the life had been sucked out of him along with Cupid's magic. They'd closed the coffee shop early, using the past hour to do the nightly closing chores. It felt strange to go through the motions when the sun was still high and the streets were blaring with traffic, but there was no point in staying open. No one was coming in, and Nylah had nothing left to give.

Has it really only been five hours since Jazz showed up covered in blood at my apartment? Only one hour since my soulmate link disappeared?

For a normal person, the quiet café might have been

therapeutic—a time to contemplate what losing Cupid's compass would mean for them and the world—but not for Nylah. Instead, they'd spent the whole time playing over a single minute in their mind.

Did I make it up? Was the dark-haired boy not my soulmate?

Already the memory was a sluggish fog. There was the light, woozy moment when the clock matched their compass time and the door swung open. Then the pain, the aching rip as magic was stripped away. And then a heartbeat, like the eye of a storm, where a boy walked in. Everything after felt dark, as if Nylah had been hit upside the head. The only clear piece was the girl. The girl who had maybe, possibly, stolen Nylah's soulmate. Her jet-black hair and wide hazel eyes had burned in Nylah's mind as the glass door closed between them.

She saw me. She saw me and she looked like she knew.

"Nylah, you're fired."

This yanked Nylah back to the present. "What?"

The manager massaged his forehead as if he was in pain. "You were three hours late for your shift this morning."

"I told you, I had an emergency to deal with." Nylah couldn't hide their shock as they tossed the dirty rag into a hamper and pushed up the brim of their glasses. The last thing they'd expected was to spend their morning hurrying Jazz to the hospital. The reminder of his stupid attempt at bleeding out to make his soulmate come faster made Nylah angry all over again. None of this was their fault.

"Today wasn't the first time you were significantly late. Last month you missed half a shift—"

"I had to take my cat to the vet!"

"You take excessive smoke breaks—"

"It's my right to take breaks," Nylah interjected, suddenly desperate to make a case. They couldn't lose their job on top of losing their compass today too.

The manager glared, effectively cutting off Nylah's outrage. "You're argumentative and refuse to take any accountability when you've made a mistake."

"I—"

He held a polished finger out. "You interrupt me all the time."

Nylah seriously considered reaching out and breaking the manager's accusatory finger, but even as outrage burned in Nylah's veins, his points hit with undeniable truth. He lowered his hand as Nylah deflated.

"Leave your apron and name tag. I'll have your vacation pay added to your last check."

I can't believe this is happening.

Nylah untied the black strings that secured their simple apron.

"Fine. I'll go." As much as Nylah yearned to make some kind of dramatic statement like *good luck without me*, there wasn't any point. The café was dead. Compasses were gone. And maybe the manager was taking his own loss out on Nylah, but what was said was done.

As the glass door swung shut behind them, Nylah was met with bittersweet freedom. They didn't love their job at the café, but they needed the income.

How am I going to pay for rent? Or Boots' food? Or my trip to the Roman Empire?

As each worry stacked up, Nylah's shoulders stiffened. This was bad.

What am I going to do?

There was only one logical place to go next. Instead of their usual route home to their beloved cat, Boots, Nylah walked back toward Toronto General Hospital. Nylah would check in on Jazz first, then figure things out from there.

The hospital was even more cluttered than earlier, with a blend of abandoned cars and wailing horns of people trying to get in or out of the vicinity. A quick text to Jazz confirmed he was still in a bed, and a few replies later Nylah had his location narrowed down to a wing on an upper floor. Nausea clawed their gut as they navigated inside around the frenzied crowd and tried to ignore the pungent scent of overused antiseptic laced with something more foul.

Nylah ultimately found their best friend in a cramped hallway. Jazz sat upright on a hospital gurney pushed tight against the ivory wall. His posture was casual, one leg extended out along the bed with the other pulled up and tucked close as a support for his chin. His face lit up as he saw Nylah, his perfect white teeth shining in a beacon of welcome. Nylah's heart surged as they clasped Jazz's shoulders.

"You look so much better!"

Jazz had undeniably improved since this morning. His skin had regained its rich russet color, and his left arm was now wrapped in a crisp bandage that covered his wrist and forearm. An IV pierced the back of his right hand, the tubing strung up to a post attached at the corner of his bed. Jazz didn't give Nylah a chance to say anything more—the unexpected death grip of his muscular shoulders and broad frame caused the air to rasp out of Nylah's lungs. They inhaled the cologne that still clung to Jazz's skin, a welcome reprieve from the stale hospital smell.

"You came back," Jazz murmured in disbelief.

"Where else would I go?"

"I know I pissed you off this morning."

Nylah leaned back and splayed a hand on his chest to put space between them. "Yeah, you did, but that's a conversation for later. Update me on what's going on. When can you get out of this zoo?"

A flash of periwinkle-blue scrubs caught Nylah's attention in the nick of time. They ducked as a nurse hustled by, waving her clipboard to clear a path. Jazz shifted back to the wall and over, making extra space on the gurney for Nylah to avoid the stampede. Nylah shimmied up beside him, tucking their knees up to avoid being clipped.

Jazz's voice was quiet as he explained he got his stitches before the hospital was completely overrun. He'd since been on an IV to replenish his fluids because of how much blood he'd lost, but he expected to be discharged soon.

"The hospital just can't support the number of patients. They're sending everyone they can home. I was in a room for all of five minutes before they moved me out here to the hall. The nurses can barely keep it together to treat the swarms of injuries and heart attacks."

"Heart attacks?" Nylah asked.

Jazz nodded. "At least, that's what it seems like most people are coming in for. I think it's because of the magic being ripped out. Some people's bodies can't handle the shock."

A cold fist wrapped around Nylah's spine. They understood perfectly why some people couldn't handle it. Nylah had a clean bill of health, and the pain of losing their compass had felt like a jackhammer carving out their heart. Unconsciously, Nylah's fingers shifted over their own chest.

The corner of Jazz's smile dropped. "Are you okay?"

Nylah leaned in, pressing their cheek to his shoulder. "I'll be okay."

It wasn't fully a lie. Other than a minor fainting spell and surviving the longest day on Terra Mater, Nylah had been spared any external injuries.

"Nylah, what happened?" Jazz gave them his nonnegotiable look, and Nylah sighed, tilting their head back to the block wall.

"I almost met my soulmate." Just admitting it felt like a rip in the fabric of the universe. A truth Nylah would do anything to deny but couldn't avoid.

"What do you mean?" The commotion around them buzzed as Jazz leaned closer.

"After I left you here, my compass started moving. Like a lot. Then I was at the café and everything got all light and woozy. I checked the time, and I knew it. I knew I was about to meet my person." Nylah met Jazz's fixed stare, the corners of their eyes already prickling with emotion. "And then… compasses disappeared."

"Oh, Nylah." Jazz squeezed their hand. "I'm sorry you didn't find your person in time."

Nylah swallowed. "That's the thing. I could have sworn I saw him, Jazz. There was this boy who walked in, right when everything fell apart. I was so sure he was my match." Nylah shook their head, the words sounding even less realistic as they tried to explain what happened.

"Did you talk to him?"

"I couldn't." Nylah's gaze fell on their wringing hands. "I think I must have been in shock, because I just froze. Then he was gone."

Jazz wrapped a protective arm over their shoulders. Nylah sniffled and bit their lip.

"I should have called out. I should have moved or done something, anything. Now I'm never going to know if it was actually him." Nylah took a shaky breath, their words quieting to a whisper. "Now I'll never meet my soulmate."

Jazz lifted a hand to brush back one of Nylah's curls. "I don't believe that. Compasses may be gone, but just because the map disappeared doesn't mean our fates have changed."

Nylah pressed their head into Jazz's chest. "How can you be sure?"

"You have to trust in the Fates."

The sound of someone clearing their throat made both Jazz and Nylah look up at the frazzled nurse.

"Are you Jazz Singh?" The man looked relieved when Jazz confirmed who he was. He handed him discharge papers and went to work removing the IV.

"Supply is already dwindling on basics, so if you don't have a stock of Tylenol or painkillers at home, I would recommend grabbing some immediately. Obviously, avoid any strenuous activity and change your bandages if they become soiled." The nurse paused as his attention flitted down the hall at a sharp scream. "That is, if you can find any. Keep the wound clean and dry, and don't pick at your stitches. They're dissolvable so you won't need to come back unless the wound gets infected. Do you have any questions?"

The nurse's attention was clearly elsewhere, and when Jazz released him, the man broke out in a swift power walk through the crowd. Nylah wrapped their arms behind Jazz's back.

"Let's get out of here."

Jazz clutched his bandaged arm close, and Nylah switched to his bad side to keep people from bumping it. As they wove their way back to the stairwell, a dark head of hair caught Nylah's eye. From behind, the girl should have been unrecognizable, but somehow her sleek jet-black hair had been burned into Nylah's memory. The girl who might have stolen their soulmate was only ten feet away. As the girl pivoted, her companion came into focus.

It's him.

Nylah couldn't move. It was as if every muscle in their body had instantly calcified.

"Nylah? What is it?" Jazz followed the line of Nylah's gaze.

The oblivious pair stood out in the frantic hospital. The girl nestled tight against Nylah's maybe-soulmate, her head buried in his chest as he murmured into her hair. The intimacy of it made Nylah's fingers curl.

"Come on, let's get out of here." Jazz nudged them toward the stairs, but everything inside Nylah screamed.

You stole my soulmate. Look at me.

The girl tipped her head up to the boy, her eyes glistening with unshed tears. She was clearly upset, but so was Nylah.

See me.

As the girl's chin turned, the exact moment she would have met Nylah's stare, Jazz stepped between them.

"Nylah?"

Nylah tried to hold in the flood of jealousy that threatened to collapse their sanity. "I—I know that girl."

Jazz peeked back. "The pretty one with headphones around her neck?"

Nylah leaned to glance over his shoulder. "Yeah. She was at the café when everything happened. And that's… that's him." *My maybe-soulmate.*

"What do you mean?" Jazz held his bandaged arm tight as he tried to get a better view. The pair had started walking again and pushed through a swinging door into the intensive care unit.

"I think that's my soulmate," Nylah whispered, the cloud of doubt resurfacing and doubling down.

Jazz cocked his head. "Nylah, if you truly think that's your soulmate, you should go after him."

But that was the problem. Nylah couldn't be sure. They might have felt woozy the moment he walked in, but what if their soulmate was someone driving by? What if those two were actually meant to be together and Nylah was just confused?

"I can't, Jazz." The truth ached in Nylah's chest. "I have no proof that he was meant to be mine."

Jazz challenged. "So, you're just going to let him go? Without even asking?"

The moment at the café played through Nylah's mind once more. The boy's eyes lighting up as they landed on the girl. Her undeniable delight as he gathered her in his arms. And the look she gave Nylah as they left. The fear. Maybe the girl knew, or maybe she just didn't want the happy moment to be spoiled by an envious bystander.

"I need proof." Nylah stumbled as an elderly woman ran by with a baby in her arms. "I couldn't do it without some kind of physical evidence. I'd look crazy."

Jazz paused, weighing what he said next. "You want compasses back."

Nylah finally tore their gaze from the swinging door. The look on Jazz's face was unreadable. "Of course I do."

Jazz was silent for a moment, his straight face unreadable.

"How far would you go to get them back?"

As far as it took. I would give up anything.

Jazz nodded at the unspoken answer. "I thought so. Let's get out of here so we can talk. My place or yours?"

Nylah scoffed. "Like I would ever choose your place. We both know my apartment will actually have food. Besides, Boots is probably eating plants to puke on my carpet out of spite because I had the audacity to go to work today. Jupiter knows she needs more attention than even you."

Jazz grinned. "After you."

CHAPTER V

NESSIE

Nessie jumped when the cabin door slammed open. Blake stalked in, looking ready to murder someone. Behind her, Jaylynn sagged like a wilted flower. Her steps were slow until she met Nessie's questioning gaze, then saw Psyche.

"Oh, for the love of Cupid. Psyche…" Jaylynn dropped down beside Nessie.

Nessie had curled up on the edge of Psyche's cot, dabbing at the woman's burning forehead with a cold, wet towel. The crisp water inadvertently also reduced the sting from Nessie's own injuries.

Jaylynn's hands shook as her dirt-covered knuckles caressed Psyche's face. "What happened to her?"

"What happened to you?" Nessie retorted, her eyebrows knit together. "You look like you crawled through a swamp and met Neptune's trident on the way." No one laughed at Nessie's joke about the sea god. She stared at the red streak across Jaylynn's face, then looked at Blake. "Did you do that?"

Blake gave a noncommittal shrug, refusing to meet Nessie's accusatory stare. "I found her like that."

Jaylynn glared at Blake's back but didn't deny it. Nessie gave Blake a doubtful look before turning back to her charge.

"Psyche's skin is on fire. It's like she has a fever or something. I checked her over for injuries, but she seems okay other than her hands. They're burned too."

Jaylynn held her hand out for the cloth, but Nessie clutched it tighter.

"Maybe you should clean up first. We don't want anyone's burns to get infected."

Jaylynn's expression shifted from hurt to submissive. As she crossed the cabin, she paused at Charity's back. Nessie's mom sat in the same position Nessie had left her: huddling in the quilt, staring into the coals of the afternoon fire.

"Charity, are you okay?" Jaylynn asked. She reached out a tentative hand to her friend's shoulder but seemed to think better of it. Charity didn't move. A familiar pang of fear twisted in Nessie's core.

It's happening all over again, just like when Dad died.

Nessie remembered the day of Luke's funeral when Charity's depression shifted from endless weeping to stillness. At eleven years old, Nessie had done everything she could to help her mom recover. She slept with her when the night terrors struck. She learned how to do the laundry and cook basic meals. Through her mom's haunted days and dark nights, Nessie did everything she could to hide Charity's fragility from the world as she grieved.

Then Jaylynn came into the picture. In the span of weeks, Charity started sleeping better and seemed more alive than Nessie could have dreamed, all because her tattoo changed. Nessie finally had someone else she could trust with her mother, and she felt like she could focus on her own problems—like her frozen compass tattoo. But now, since Venus appeared, Charity stared at the fire with a familiar bleakness that terrified Nessie.

"We need to come up with a plan," Blake said as she sifted through the exposed floating shelves holding dishes and dried flowers. "Do you know if Psyche kept a first aid kit?"

Nessie sighed and pointed at the foot of Psyche's cot. "She did, but I already went through it. There's not a lot." She held her palms up. "At least, not for these kinds of injuries. The bandages alone will probably only be enough to cover one person's hands."

"So, we need to get supplies, then. Bandages, burn ointment. What else?"

Nessie stood. "Probably more food? I mean, I don't know what the plan is, but—"

"You're right," Blake agreed. "We don't need to be foraging for stupid berries, and we can't live off tea and biscuits forever."

"You could take Jaylynn's truck and I can stay here to keep an eye on things?" Nessie suggested.

Blake hesitated. "I, uh, can't drive."

A surprised smile crept up the corner of Nessie's mouth. "Really?"

Blake shrugged. "Didn't really need to in New York. Just took the subway everywhere."

"Okay…" Nessie drummed her fingers on her knee. "It's just, I don't think my mom can drive right now, and Jaylynn doesn't seem like she's in the best shape either."

"Can't you drive?"

Nessie rinsed the cloth with cool water again. "I've practiced, but I don't take my learner's test until the fall."

"Sounds like you'll be better than me. Let's leave Jaylynn here with your mom and Psyche. You and I can be quick. With two sets of hands, we'll be more likely to get everything we might need."

"You realize it's illegal for me to drive?" Nessie tried to make it sound like a joke, but it was true, and she wasn't typically a rule breaker.

"I think we'll have bigger problems if we don't get a move on. We'll get what we need quickly, reconvene, and then figure out what to do next."

Twenty minutes later, Nessie reluctantly took Jaylynn's truck keys. "You're sure you don't want to go?"

Jaylynn shook her head. "I think I'm still in shock, so it's probably best if I'm not driving right now. The gas station isn't far down the main highway we took here. It's a five-minute drive at most. If you feel confident, I trust you."

Even in a fresh change of clothes, Jaylynn still looked like a shadow of her vibrant self. There was a smallness to her, the way her shoulders wrapped forward and her chin tucked low. The red mark was less obvious on Jaylynn's face, but her left cheek flushed a heavy crimson compared to the right. Nessie really wanted to know what had happened between her and Blake.

Nessie fiddled with the keys. While part of her thrummed at being entrusted with this responsibility, nerves at being caught without her license burned in equal measure. Nessie pressed the back of her hand to her mom's shoulder.

"Are you okay to stay here with Jaylynn and Psyche?"

Charity didn't even nod.

I need to fix this.

Blake was right. The first step was supplies.

"We'll be back as soon as we can."

With a brief wave, Nessie followed Blake out to the old truck. Nessie hopped into the front seat and let out a heavy sigh.

I can do this. It's just an enormous car. Just gas and brake and turn.

Blake didn't offer any comments as Nessie jarred Jaylynn's truck back and forth, turning it around to avoid having to back up the length of the gravel driveway. The truck accelerated slowly, the pedals sticky and heavy as Nessie coaxed the beast forward.

Oh, Minerva, please let there be no traffic, easy parking, and no cops. And don't let me crash. Please, great goddess, don't let me wreck Jaylynn's truck.

Nessie's prayers to her favorite goddess, the goddess of strategy and wisdom, repeated like a mantra in her head. Where the gravel road met the paved highway, Nessie stomped on the brakes, throwing both her and Blake forward.

"Sorry."

Blake smirked and sat back, tugging her seat belt on. "You do you." Blake relaxed into her seat, and Nessie forced her fingers into a softer grip, much to the relief of her stinging palms.

Stay calm. You've got this.

She signaled right, and the truck lugged onto the highway. It was painfully slow to accelerate, roaring in protest as Nessie gained speed. She held her breath as a car whizzed by, keeping her attention on staying between what felt like very narrow lines.

Relax, Ness.

Once the speedometer hit one hundred kilometers an hour, Nessie's shoulders dropped incrementally. She peeked over at Blake, grateful to see her companion seemed entirely unbothered. Blake sat on the other end of the bench seat with her elbow propped on the window frame. The light brown roots of her hair stood out against the rest, which was dyed blue. It parted around her pierced and stretched earlobes, then reached down in thin wisps over her black leather jacket.

Nessie decided to take a chance. "So, are you going to tell me what happened with Jaylynn?"

"There's nothing to tell." Blake traced her thumb over her bottom lip.

Nessie let out a sigh. "Blake?"

"Hmmm?"

"I'm glad you're here. Even if you did smack Jaylynn. I just hope she deserved it."

"Trust me. She did."

Nessie hummed, unsure. The highway straightened and stretched ahead, quiet and peaceful, much to her relief. The sun shone above, and as she relaxed into the truck's steady hum, Nessie's mind reorganized the events of the morning. One thing nagged at her.

"Why do you think we're less affected by our compasses disappearing than the others?"

Blake sighed. "I don't know. Maybe because we're the youngest of the group?"

Nessie's brow furrowed. "Jaylynn is barely older than you."

"Oh?" Blake picked at a piece of flaking leather on the seat.

"Isn't she only twenty-one? So that makes her, what? Two years older than you?"

Blake didn't answer.

"I just can't imagine the cusp of crippling damage is if you're over twenty. It's got to be something else." Nessie squinted as she watched for the turnoff she knew could come at any time.

"What, then?"

What makes us different? Neither Blake nor I wanted our compasses, but neither did Psyche, and she's the worst off in the group.

"Maybe it's because they each had more than one compass link?" Nessie spoke as she thought, each idea scrambling over the next. "Like, as far as you know, your compass only ever pointed to Psyche, right?"

Blake nodded.

"My mom had Luke, then Jaylynn. Jaylynn had her fiancé. What was his name again?"

"Elias."

Nessie nodded, slightly surprised Blake remembered that detail from their few days of getting to know one another. "Right. And then her compass changed to point to Psyche. And maybe Psyche's compass only ever pointed to Cupid, but you'd have to assume that with you and Jaylynn linked to her, when the compasses were torn away, those missing links could have affected her too. So, she would have lost three soulmates, Jaylynn and my mom lost two, then you and I only lost one."

If you even count a broken compass as one.

To Nessie's relief, in the distance, a tall blue gas station sign came into view on the left just as Jaylynn had promised. Nessie checked over her shoulder and changed lanes.

"Did it hurt?" Blake asked.

A car sped by in the right lane, and Nessie gave an apologetic wave.

"What?" Nessie asked, trying to calm her nerves, her attention split.

"Did you feel pain when you lost your compass?"

Nessie considered the moment when Venus had voiced her decree. "I don't know if I'd say it hurt. It just felt wrong. Like all my organs got jumbled up. I felt super nauseous, but it passed almost as soon as Venus disappeared."

Blake stared out her window.

"Why? Did it hurt for you?"

Blake sighed. "Yeah, it did." She loosely clasped a hand over where her compass tattoo had been, and Nessie wondered if it still hurt now.

Well, there's even further proof I've always been cursed. I never even had a soulmate to lose.

The truck groaned as Nessie safely crossed the other side of the highway and pulled into the parking lot. There were only a couple other vehicles in the lot, with plenty of pull-through parking available. Nessie took a deep breath in relief when she turned off the motor.

See? Easy-peasy.

Blake hopped out and Nessie followed, but they parted ways naturally when they entered the convenience store. Nessie went up the aisle of medicine and bandages, while Blake headed to the food. Within five minutes, they had a large enough pile of items stacked on the counter to make the other two customers stare. Nessie kept her aching hands in the pockets of her jean jacket as much as possible, her eyes cast down to her now-filthy white sneakers.

The man at the till was polite but grudgingly slow as he scanned each and every bottle of Tylenol and Polysporin. Behind him, a small cube TV flashed with bright red captions. The breaking news flitted between cities as footage displayed car wreckages and swamped hospitals, panicked crowds, and pale broadcasters with grim faces. Nessie's shoulders only grew more rigid with every new scene.

We did this.

Guilt burned in the back of Nessie's throat as a silver-haired reporter came into focus.

"It's the question everyone is asking. Where did compasses go? What made them disappear? And will they come back? Join us at six tonight

when we sit down with the prime minister to ask the questions everyone wants answers to."

Nessie almost scoffed. Unless the government had some secret phone line to the gods, it wasn't like they'd know anything. She jumped as Blake dumped more items on top of the pile—a few pairs of thin black cotton gloves.

The man behind the till frowned. "This is the apocalypse, I tell you," he muttered. "My whole store is going to be bought out by the end of the day. Just you wait."

Nessie pinched her lips together. They probably looked innocent enough, but she felt like she was walking with a sign on her back screaming *guilty as charged.* She wanted nothing more than to get back to the cabin and hide. Blake glanced over her shoulder, seeming equally unnerved.

"How will you be paying?"

Nessie held up her mom's credit card. All it took was a quick tap then they gathered their haul and left the store. Jaylynn's truck roared to life again under Nessie's command. The blinker light ticked with impatience as she waited for a big enough gap to merge back onto the highway. Nessie forced herself to take even breaths as her pulse thrummed. There was one other thing eating away at her.

"Blake?"

"Hmmmm?"

Nessie hesitated, but she knew Blake might be the only person who would understand. She dropped her voice before asking the one thing she probably shouldn't voice. "Do you think it's selfish if I feel relieved not to have a compass anymore?"

Blake's jaw visibly relaxed. "No, Ness. I don't think that's selfish."

Even with Blake's affirmation, the pool of guilt only grew, threatening to swallow Nessie whole.

CHAPTER VI

KADE

"Excuse me, I'm looking for my wife? Renee Baker? Brunette, thirty-six years old. She was in a car accident?"

Kade tried desperately to keep his voice steady even as his knees shook. It had taken him hours to get to Toronto General Hospital. He was sure if he'd stayed in his car, he'd be watching the sunset right now, still stuck in traffic miles away. He'd never seen the city in a gridlock so bad.

After the first two wasted hours sitting in traffic, Kade found the nearest transit station, parked his car illegally, and took the GO Train instead.

The Toronto hospital was in utter chaos. Around him, throngs of people scampered left and right. Kade pressed the palms of his hands against the administration desk as the nurse searched the server. The intercoms rang nonstop with alerts Kade couldn't understand, but he prayed they weren't related to his wife.

"I'm sorry, sir. We're having a hard time keeping everyone in the system organized. The rooms are overwhelmed, so we have lots of people in unmarked beds through the halls. We're doing the best we can. It's just that we've never had—"

A woman shoved her way up beside Kade in a bout of hysterics. "My son! Please, I'm looking for my son!"

Kade stepped back and pulled out his cell phone. Renee's last text was still on the screen.

RENEE: Can't talk, come to Toronto General Hospital. Mom was in an accident. Hurry.

Terror had grasped Kade's lungs. In an instant, he put Ladybug, their eleven-week-old rescue puppy, into her crate and raced out the door. His fingers flew over the keyboard as he grabbed his keys and ran to his car.

KADE: On my way.

Now in the hospital, he tried to call Renee's phone for the hundredth time that day. The call didn't go through the customary five rings as it had the other times he'd tried. Instead, the call dropped after the second ring, followed by a text.

RENEE: Bad service and it's too loud to talk.

Seeing his wife's name flash on the screen but knowing it was his daughter sent an added jolt of pain through his lungs. As Kade started to reply, another text came through with a room number.

Finally!

The trip deep into downtown Toronto had been agonizing. For hours Kade was stuck imagining every possible scenario where his wife had crashed and Lacey was left texting him from her phone. Did Renee rear-end someone? Did his wife and daughter get T-boned? How bad was the accident?

Mom was in an accident wasn't nearly enough information. Was Lacey not in the accident as well? Why wouldn't she have been in the car? And why, of all wretched days, was today the one time his daughter wasn't glued to her phone?

Kade wrestled through the crowd and fought his way to the stairwell. The ICU wing was swarmed with pastel scrubs. As the admin had suggested, the hallways were filled with impromptu beds and patients holding one another in various states of injury.

At least Renee got a room. Though the thought wasn't entirely welcome. How bad was she if she'd been given an actual room? And in the ICU no less? Did they just beat the crowds? The lack of information he'd gotten from Lacey terrified him.

At the end of the hall, Kade finally found the matching room number to the text. Before he could open the door, a nurse came out with a preemptive glare.

"Gown and gloves, please, sir."

Kade looked over at the sanitary boxes and folded blue sheets. He dressed in a hurry, the foreign material clinging to him as fresh sweat dripped down his spine. When he finally pushed the wide door open, the first thing he saw was Lacey's wide hazel eyes. She appeared unharmed—no scratches marred her face, only the signature red puffiness in her cheeks that meant she'd been crying. She held hands with a stranger in a matching ICU gown. Kade couldn't spare a moment to figure out what was going on with that. He turned with dread toward the bed. Two nurses blocked Kade's view as they chattered in hushed but intent voices. Kade's heart threatened to rip out of his chest as time slowed.

He had to know how bad it was, but Kade had never felt more fear in his entire life than he did in this moment.

Is she paralyzed? Did she lose any limbs? Is she brain-dead?

The only logical thought keeping him anchored was that his wife wasn't dead. She wouldn't be in her own room with nurses if she was dead. Kade took a steadying breath and reached for the closest nurse's shoulder. Before he could speak, Lacey surged up into his arms, crying anew. Kade staggered with the force of her hug, his heart torn between comforting her and freeing himself from the torture of not knowing how bad Renee was.

"Oh, Dad, I'm so glad you're here. They kept asking me questions and I didn't know what to say. They took her into surgery so fast and they needed to know if she had any allergies or medications, and I just blanked. Like, how am I supposed to know those things?" Lacey gasped for breath as the information came out in a flood. "I didn't know what to do, and then next thing I knew they put us in this room, and no one will answer my questions."

Kade stroked his daughter's hair and urged Lacey backward so he could see what was happening, her words swirling in his head along with all the loud beeping machines. *Surgery. They took her for surgery.* As he closed the space between him and his wife, his heart plummeted. Renee's face was obscured by tubes and bandages, the thickest white tube secured to her mouth with surgical tape. A bandage bridged her black-and-blue nose, and long clear IV lines dripped down to her arm. The monitors beeped steadily as a nurse hustled about, double-checking her charts.

An unexpected wave of dizziness made Kade stumble. Seeing Renee's sedated, limp body was so much worse than he'd imagined. Every fleck of her warm skin was a wash of unnatural yellow. Her chestnut-brown hair was slicked back and disheveled, with hints of what Kade prayed wasn't blood on the ends.

I should have gotten here sooner. I should have been here before they did the surgery.

But Kade had spent the last few hours frantically calling his wife with no answer. What should have been an hour-long drive to the hospital took him four. No matter how hard he'd tried to race here, it was as if every step of the way was blocked. His grip on his daughter tightened.

"Lacey, what happened?"

Lacey looked up at him, her tears staining the blue disposable medical mask covering her mouth. "I don't know. I wasn't there. I was—"

Before she could answer, a doctor rushed into the room. When she saw Kade, she paused only for a moment. "Are you kin?"

"Renee's my wife." Kade stepped back as two new nurses scurried in.

"As you can tell, the hospital is overloaded. Even if we had a full shift of staff, we're further beyond capacity than ever before. I'm sorry I can't debrief you now, but someone will fill you in as soon as possible." The doctor looked over the bags of fluids, then she lifted Renee's eyelids one at a time, shining a small flashlight into each eye, and jotted down some notes.

Kade wanted to scream. Was the beeping good or bad? Did Renee's pupils do what they were supposed to? What were they even checking for? But no words came out as Kade swallowed against the growing mass in his throat.

"Clear here. Notify me if she decompensates." The doctor nodded to the nurse and turned back toward the three of them.

Her face was strained with seriousness. "If anyone tries to move her from this room today, don't let them."

Kade's lips parted. "Why would they do that?"

The doctor stripped off her gloves, moving to the sink. "We're flooded with cases and every room counts right now. They'll move her as soon as they can, but it's still too soon." The doctor leaned into the door with her shoulder, shaking her clean hands dry.

"Stop! I—"

"Either stay in this room or leave the hospital. Do not invite guests or any extended family right now. We cannot bear the load." The doctor paused, taking pity on the undeniable fear that plastered Kade's face. "Your wife is going to be all right, sir. Sit tight. Someone will be with you soon."

The doctor and nurses filtered out into the chaos, the surge of noise quieting slightly as the wide door clicked back into place behind them. Lacey pulled free of Kade's arms and moved back to her previous spot. Kade's blurry vision tracked her steps and he stared in confusion.

"Who are you?"

Kade was sure he'd never seen this boy before, but the mask obscuring his features didn't help. Lacey took a protective stance in front of him.

"Dad, this is Damien. He's my soulmate."

Kade squinted, confused. *What?*

"Mom and I were on our way home, and then my compass started to move." Lacey pulled at the neckline of her gown. "I— I left Mom to find him and then—" She sniffled as she cut off, and the boy stood, wrapping his arm over her shoulder.

"So, you weren't in the car?" Kade asked, his mind scrambling to make sense of the information. He'd suspected it, but he hadn't been able to imagine a scenario where Lacey wasn't with Renee.

Lacey shook her head. Kade glanced back at his wife's battered face, his terror bleeding into something hotter.

"Why weren't you with her?"

Lacey frowned. "I told you, Dad; I was looking for my soulmate."

It didn't make sense. Kade should be glad his daughter hadn't been in the vehicle, but why did it have to be his wife? If it wasn't for Lacey's stupid adventure, Renee wouldn't have even been driving in Toronto when the chaos hit. She would have been at work, in her office, safe.

"You need to go." Kade turned on Damien, his tone flat and warning. This boy didn't belong by Renee's side while Kade had been stuck in traffic for hours trying to make it to the hospital.

"Dad!" Lacey grasped the boy's hand tightly. "He's not leaving me."

"You heard the doctor. No one that isn't kin. He goes."

Lacey's wide eyes flashed with a familiar fury, but before she could lash out, her soulmate pulled her toward him and murmured in her ear. Whatever the boy said to her seemed to calm her down. He rested his forehead against hers, squeezed her arms in one last reassurance, then made his way to the door. As he passed Kade, the boy offered a quick wave.

"I hope your wife is all right."

Kade didn't answer. He couldn't answer. His nails dug into his forearm where his compass had been as he stared at the swinging door. Then Kade turned back to his unconscious wife.

CHAPTER VII

"What is the veil?" Nessie asked, her thumb tracing over one of Psyche's books.

Jaylynn sat up straighter. She'd returned to Psyche's side after dinner, methodically removing each of the woman's glittering rings as gently as possible. She put them in a tray with her own engagement ring. Luckily, Psyche's elevated temperature leveled off, but she hadn't moved or made a sound all day—the only sign she was alive was the shallow rise and fall of her chest.

Blake was curled up on the couch, her knees pulled up to her chest and her arms crossed over them, and Charity had settled back into the rocking chair with a quilt.

The quilt of Apollo. Jaylynn had grown very familiar with the cabin's belongings and had often wondered how Psyche had handmade so many blankets. Now that she understood the woman had been alive for 3000 years, it made a lot more sense.

"A blanket for each of the gods to keep in their good faith," River had once told her.

Maybe you should have sewn extra for Venus…

Nessie had spent the last few hours pacing back and forth through the kitchen, desperate to find a solution that didn't exist. She scoured Psyche's little brown dropper bottles as if one might have a cure, then tackled the books. Reading didn't relieve her agitated state, though. Instead, the girl just continued her pacing back and forth with a book in her hand.

Jaylynn kneaded her temples, wishing she'd been able to braid her hair back after she'd showered, but her injured fingers couldn't bear it, so instead her curls dried naturally wild. She considered Nessie's question.

"The veil is the invisible barrier that separates gods and mortals."

By the look on Nessie's face, Jaylynn quickly realized she'd just opened a whole new can of worms for Nessie's endless inquisitions.

"When did it go up? Why did it go up? Who made it?"

Jaylynn sighed. Thanks to her father's research, Jaylynn had a fairly extensive understanding of religious history, but there were a lot of elements up for speculation.

"People have been looking for those answers for thousands of years. We barely know the cusp of *why* the veil was put up."

"What are the theories?" Nessie sat on the couch beside Blake, her attention trained on her newest source of information.

At least she's stopped pacing.

Jaylynn sank back into the hard chair she'd pulled up to Psyche's side. "My father believed the three Fates put the veil up. Whether it was to protect humanity from the gods and monsters, or for another reason, he never said. He wrote extensive theories on it."

The memory of her dad tucked in his study gave Jaylynn bittersweet feelings. What were her parents doing now, with compasses gone? Was Richard buried even deeper in his old leather-bound books looking for answers? And what of her mother? How was she coping without her compass link? Nylah wouldn't have their compass anymore either, and they hadn't met their soulmate yet.

And it's all our fault.

"What else did he say about the veil? Could people or gods cross it?" Nessie asked.

Jaylynn tipped her head back. "It's controversial. Some people think once the veil was installed there could be no communication between the gods and mortals whatsoever. Others clung to the belief the gods could still hear us and bless us—they just couldn't interfere with our fates anymore."

"So… the fact that Venus appeared to us is probably a bad sign, then," Nessie hedged.

Jaylynn let out a heavy sigh. "Probably."

Blake cleared her throat. "So, what, the veil is gone?" Her face paled at the idea of gods walking among mortals.

"No, I can't imagine the veil is gone," Jaylynn amended. "Sure, Venus communicated with us and withdrew Cupid's magic, but she didn't physically touch anyone. She never left the altar."

Nessie's gray eyes brightened as her mind worked. "You think the veil is just weakening?"

Jaylynn swallowed. "Maybe. And if we consider Psyche would have been alive before the veil was installed, it makes sense we found a loophole to contact the gods." That's what Jaylynn had been telling herself all day. They hadn't broken the veil; all they'd done was make a goddess mad. Not that Cupid's magic being ripped from Terra Mater was acceptable, but it was better than a world where gods roamed free again. The veil had to still be intact.

"I bet Psyche would know," Blake mused as she chewed on her nail. "When do you think she'll wake up?"

"I'm not sure it's a matter of when," Jaylynn murmured. It was a matter of *if* she woke up.

Could it be a good thing if Psyche never woke again, though? Wouldn't she be grateful to be free of her curse? Or is her mind still wandering, longing for closure in her comatose state?

Psyche's usually lustrous golden tan seemed even more pale than this morning. Jaylynn couldn't be rid of the fear that her closest friend and mentor was fading away. And if Psyche was gone, what did that mean for Jaylynn? Could she survive losing another soulmate? Who would she be without her spiritual mentor? Would she have to go home to her parents, tail between her legs, and submit once again to the quiet life she fought to escape?

"We have to do something," Jaylynn said, fear driving her reasoning. "For Psyche's sake, if not for the rest of the world. For every hour we sit here doing nothing, we are accountable for the pain being caused."

Maybe it was madness to hope they could fix things, but didn't they need to try? Nessie met Jaylynn's eyes with a knowing stare.

"You're thinking what I'm thinking," Jaylynn said, her heart sinking as Nessie's brilliant eyes reflected Jaylynn's guilt.

"We've tried everything to wake Psyche short of dumping a bucket of cold water over her head. She's not waking up and we all know it," Nessie reasoned.

"What are you suggesting?" Blake said, glancing between them.

Jaylynn braced, knowing full well what Nessie was about to say.

"We need to call Venus back." Nessie crossed her arms.

In the same instant Blake jumped up to disagree, a whimper came from Charity. They all turned to look at her.

"Mom?" Nessie's demeanor softened instantly into care-provider mode. As sweet as it was, it also worried Jaylynn. Nessie treated her mom like a fragile porcelain doll, as if Charity could break if Nessie made one wrong move.

"You want to call the goddess we insulted *back*?" Charity whispered in horror. They were her first words all day.

Jaylynn stood and ran her fingers over the folds of her freshly bandaged hands as she thought. "Nessie is right. My gut says Psyche won't just wake up. Besides, I think we owe it to the world to at least try to get compasses back."

Blake was the picture of utter dismay. "And are you two suggesting we try to *barter* with Venus? The very goddess who just about smote us with her godly being and destroyed her son's magic out of spite?"

"In the old days, gods and goddesses loved making bargains with mortals," Jaylynn replied, her own nerves conflicting with her internal obligation to mend what they broke. "Are you telling me you don't want compasses back?"

Blake glared. "I mean, if I'm being honest, not particularly?"

"I want compass magic back," Charity answered. Her voice was small, with a touch of uncertainty. "It brought me so much peace when I was connected to you, Jaylynn."

Like the last pieces of a puzzle, Jaylynn could see it coming together. Jaylynn and Nessie both turned to Blake expectantly.

Blake sank deeper into the couch cushions, her shoulders raised like a cornered animal. "Do I need to remind you that Venus thought sacrificing us was literally a reasonable payment for Psyche to have Cupid back?" Blake held her arms out in a plea. "It's a suicide mission to ask for compasses back! What else do we have to give the goddess other than our lives? I don't want to die."

Jaylynn tucked her hair behind her ears. "We're not going to die, but we can't know until we ask, Blake. And we can't leave things like this."

Nessie nodded. "We need to fix things, and fast. Before people look for someone to blame."

"There's no proof we did it!" Blake retorted, her teeth practically bared. Jaylynn knew the girl was on the brink of either walking away or giving in.

"Blake," Nessie murmured. She rested a hand on the girl's rigid shoulder. "It's the right thing to do. You saw the news reports. It's chaos out there and you know it's all our fault."

Blake's resentment was palpable, but she didn't get up to leave.

"It's settled, then? We call Venus and make a bargain to get compass magic back?" Jaylynn glanced between each person for confirmation.

"You're sure it has to be Venus?" Blake asked. "There's not another god we could call on?"

Jaylynn pursed her lips. Any god would probably be better than Venus, but if the goddess had already intervened in their attempt to summon Cupid, what would stop her a second time? "I'm not convinced any other god would answer. No, I'm sure calling on Venus is the only way."

Blake's misery was plastered on her face. "Great."

The embers in the fireplace sputtered, a small fray of sparks fading as quickly as they rose.

"Tomorrow, then? Sunrise?" Jaylynn asked.

Nessie nodded. "We call Venus back."

"As long as we specify we are not trading our lives. There must be something else she wants," Blake grumbled.

Jaylynn nodded. She couldn't explain it, but in her gut, she knew Venus could be bartered with. It was just a matter of what the price would be.

DAY 2

WITHOUT COMPASSES

In her bed of roses, this goddess's power lays waste,
Taunting human and celestial alike to take a taste.
Her intoxicating spells reap hearts both below and above:
Venus, the aphrodisiac; goddess of sex, fertility, and love.
The ultimate enchantress whose beauty defies law;
Gaze on her marbled face and you'll never find a flaw.
—The Seductress

CHAPTER VIII

Dusty violet clouds painted the horizon as the rising sun claimed a new day—a day that Nessie had no desire to attend despite being the one to suggest the idea. It felt wrong to be here, back where their original ritual to call on Cupid had failed and the bronze table sat abandoned. It felt wrong to be here without Psyche. But they didn't have a choice. Nessie might have been cursed to a lifetime of loneliness without a working soulmate link, but the rest of the world didn't deserve the same sentence.

"Are you finally realizing this plan is insane?" Blake came to stand beside Nessie. She'd pulled her hair up and back in a messy bun, highlighting her sharp cheekbones. Her hands sported the thin black gloves with the fingers cut off, hiding the bandages underneath.

Nessie wanted to shake her head but couldn't. She *was* terrified. What if Venus was even more insulted and did something worse than ripping away Cupid's magic? What if Blake was right and Venus used her divine form to smite them to cinders and ash?

"Do you think Jaylynn can do this?" Nessie asked instead of answering.

Blake glanced to the center of the clearing where Jaylynn fretted at the altar. "She spent the most time with Psyche. If anyone knows how to call on a god, it's Jaylynn."

You mean a goddess. Nessie shivered. She'd never really given much credit to the gods before yesterday. She'd assumed they'd existed at some point, but she hadn't considered them real or tangible, let alone actively able to affect the world. Nessie had thought of them more as legends who'd set Terra Mater on her spinning path, then left to watch it play out. But now she knew with horrifying certainty that the gods were closer than ever, and they were not to be messed with.

Jaylynn stretched her back as she assessed her work. The broken pieces of the heart-shaped rock sat realigned on the table, next to newly handpicked flowers and fragments of rose quartz. They had no salt left to line a new ritual border—Venus had scattered it all through the forest when she'd unleashed her magic on the world—but Nessie wasn't convinced it made a difference either way. Salt wasn't holding the gods back; the veil was. Or at least, it was supposed to.

Minerva, please let the veil hold.

Nessie sent the prayer to her favorite goddess, the ruler of wisdom and strategy, then refocused. She cupped her mom's elbow. "Mom, are you sure you want to be here for this? Maybe you could stay in the cabin with Psyche."

"We need her," Jaylynn interrupted, her nose scrunching. "I'm not even sure the four of us are strong enough, let alone three. Psyche said we all contributed different things that made the call possible. I'm sorry, Ness, but she has to stay if we want to fix things."

Jaylynn's soft blue eyes were weary, and the spring that once bounced in her every step had vanished.

Nessie sighed. "Okay. I'm right here with you, though, Mom, so you don't need to worry." Nessie held her mom's hand, the cotton bandages a soft buffer between their singed palms. Jaylynn took Charity's other hand.

"We're all in this together."

Blake let out a heavy sigh before taking Nessie's hand, then Jaylynn's. With four instead of five, their circle around the small altar table was much tighter, and Nessie could hear every jagged breath. Following Jaylynn's lead, they knelt and dipped their heads.

"Venus—" Jaylynn's voice hitched as she broke off and coughed.

Despite her bandaged palms, Nessie's hands went slick with sweat, burning her blisters anew. She tried not to flinch as her mom's grip tightened. Jaylynn cleared her throat.

"Goddess of love," Jaylynn started again. "Goddess of beauty, to you we pray."

Nessie could practically feel Blake roll her eyes at Jaylynn's praise.

Maybe it won't work. Maybe we can't do it without Psyche anyway.

The dash of hope in Nessie's heart died as the mild morning breeze in the clearing stilled and the rustling shrubs quieted. Jaylynn's voice rang in the canopy of trees as she gained confidence in her request.

"Venus," Jaylynn called. "Please hear us. Let us make a barter that gods and mortals alike will speak of for generations to come. Let us—"

A flash of white startled Nessie, and she fixed her eyes shut as Jaylynn was cut off.

Like the first time, tendrils of air ran through Nessie's long blond ponytail. The icy breeze investigated her, coiling around her limbs like snakes. The hairs on Nessie's arms stood up as the breeze wrapped around her throat, a gentle but insistent pressure, and tilted her chin up. The white light had faded, leaving a rainbow of spots behind in the darkness of her sealed eyes.

"Look. At. Me." The honeyed voice was closer than Nessie expected, thick in its assertion.

Naked fear pulsed through Nessie's nervous system. Mortals were obliterated if they dared to gaze upon a god in their true form. She wasn't ready to die, and her mind raced for any other solution. As she delayed, the tendrils of air under her chin continued to tighten around her throat until Nessie knew she had no choice but to open her eyes. As she did, the goddess's magic relented, the wisps of air returning to their master, and Nessie gasped. Blake's hand dropped, and Nessie followed her lead, creeping backward, away from the figure. Nessie couldn't believe what she was seeing. In front of her, standing on the bronze table altar, was a stunning young woman.

"Ahhh," the girl sighed in relief, rolling out her wrists experimentally. "The perks of the falling veil continue. I missed being able to take a mortal's shape."

The singsong voice had an eerie, otherworldly quality that did not match the body at all. The blond stood tall and proud, her glinting smile inhumanly white. Nessie's hand covered her gaping mouth because the girl in front of her was terrifyingly familiar. Nessie was staring at herself. At least, herself if she was on super-beauty steroids.

While the goddess mirrored Nessie's naturally curvy body, it was as if a filter had been slapped over it. Venus' long blond hair showered down and around her shoulders, bleached bright and straightened compared to the soft honey tones of Nessie's own waves. Where Nessie's cotton button-up hung loose and comfortable, Venus had hers tied at the waist, leaving the unbuttoned neckline plunging. Everything about Venus was manicured and perfected, and undeniably *wrong*. But what nauseated Nessie most was the warped reflection's eyes. Instead of Nessie's own stormy gray irises, Venus' eyes twinkled with molten gold.

A foreboding sense of danger rang through Nessie's body, begging her to run. She tore her gaze away from Venus and looked to Blake for support. Blake's face was so pale it was almost blue. She stared slack-jawed at the altar, her pupils black holes. Nessie wondered what Blake saw. Was it Venus' beautified version of Nessie? Or did the goddess reflect Blake's enhanced self back to her?

Unperturbed, Venus twisted on the altar, her clean white sneakers scraping against the bronze top. A wicked grin cast over her face as she came to a stop in front of Jaylynn. The goddess raised a single polished finger, testing the air in front of her for resistance. Her smile fell.

Relief soothed Nessie's erratic heart as Venus' nail scratched an invisible barrier.

She's still contained. She can't hurt us.

Jaylynn recovered her wits first and bowed her head. The only hint suggesting she was unnerved was the beet-red flush of her freckled cheeks. "Great goddess, we are honored you've answered our summons. We called on you today to both worship your undeniable power and beauty, and also in the hope that you have mercy to spare."

Nessie's stare returned to Venus. The pounding of her heart in her ears was deafening. Nessie couldn't say whether it would be better if time stopped or if it went faster. All she knew was that she did not want to be here anymore.

"Go on." The eternal being smiled, her dimples pitching up on her heart-shaped face.

Jaylynn took a deep breath. "You have proven you're formidable by stripping Cupid's magic. Compasses are gone, and people worldwide grieve. They turn to the stars for answers. We turn to you."

"Ah, so that's what this is about. You want me to bring compasses back? How lackluster." Venus' smile fell.

Jaylynn met Venus' imposition without blinking. "Venus, your power over beauty is unmatched, but you are also the goddess of *love*. The world is suffering without their soulmate links. You could reconnect them."

The answer barely sparked a response in Venus. Her focus shifted away from Jaylynn, her gaze slowly circling the women at her feet. Venus' eyes paused at Blake, whose typical scowl had deepened to a visible burning hatred. Nessie swallowed hard, mentally praying that Blake wouldn't provoke the goddess further.

"If you ask me, mortals have become too fixated on the idea of soulmates. They believe love will save the day and last forever, when, in reality, there is nothing more fickle." Venus crouched in front of Blake, one elbow perched on her knee. "You can't disagree."

Blake's scowl flattened into an even harder line. Venus' sly smile suggested she'd hit her mark.

"Love was never meant to be *gentle* or *sweet* as Cupid has painted it," the goddess continued, her voice rising as she stood. "Love is meant to burn and devour. It's meant to consume you and spit you out on the other side."

Jaylynn raised her voice to pull the deity's attention from Blake. "Venus, no matter what true love is or isn't, soulmate links are all our world has ever known. Please, let us earn the magic back, before any more damage is done."

To Nessie's disbelief, this captured Venus' attention. The goddess spun gracefully on her heel to face Jaylynn.

"Earn it back? That is interesting." Her lips curled around the last word with a faint smile. Venus steepled her fingers in thought. "It has been ages since mortals scrambled for my favor, and I *have* been bored to tears since the veil went up." The goddess's face split into a wide grin. That was when Nessie knew they were in real trouble.

CHAPTER IX

Every time Venus grinned, Jaylynn's spirits sank further, but she forced her spine to stay straight as she faced their reckoning. The vision the goddess presented outright shocked Jaylynn at first.

Venus had tamed Jaylynn's wild curls to soft Hollywood waves, and her usually sky-blue eyes sparkled gold—but the part Jaylynn couldn't help but stare at was Venus' dress. Seeing the lace sleeves and soft flowing skirts tore open old wounds that Jaylynn had been sure she'd worked through and healed in therapy. The goddess wore the exact wedding dress Jaylynn tried on the day Elias died. Jaylynn wanted to rip the eucalyptus crown right off the smug deity's head, but she forced herself to remain kneeling as the goddess tapped her chin thoughtfully.

"How about this," Venus purred, her freckled face brightening. "A task for each of you who tried to release my son. Should you complete my trials, I'll return compasses and the world will return as it was."

"And if we fail your trials?" Nessie asked. Jaylynn wanted to kick herself for not thinking of asking that herself.

But that was why we were chosen. We each contribute something different.

Nessie had risen to a standing position, placing herself between her mom and Venus, as if shielding Charity's already fragile state from the tormenting goddess. And while Charity's eyes were clear enough that Jaylynn knew she was present, they were wide with horror. Jaylynn wasn't sure she wanted to know what Venus reflected to Charity.

Venus' eyes sparkled at Nessie's question. "Simple. No one will get compasses back, ever."

The goddess watched each of them process the offer. Compasses were already gone, so even if they failed, no new harm would be done, but Jaylynn's mind spun as she tried to imagine what tasks the goddess would request. The glint in Venus' eye had a hint of malevolence that made Jaylynn's intuition tingle in warning.

"What if I sweetened the pot?" Venus offered. "A reward for each of you should you all succeed."

Jaylynn cocked her head. Venus really seemed to want this, which couldn't bode well for them.

Venus adjusted her flowing skirts as she turned. "Blake, when compasses return, you will be spared and can live your life without a soulmate link, as you've always wished. And you, Nessie, I promise to find you a love match where Cupid failed."

A small pit of worry curled in Jaylynn's stomach as she saw the promises fill each of her friends' eyes with surprise and wonder.

"Jaylynn," Venus sang as she turned to face her. "I will wake your beloved Psyche from her enchanted sleep. And, Charity, I will send word to the Underworld myself to have your husband's soul put to rest at long last."

Jaylynn took a sharp breath in. Venus' power stretched further than she would have guessed.

And if she can do all that with the veil weakened, what will happen if it falls altogether?

Jaylynn shook her head. They had no control over whether the veil remained or fell, but getting compasses back? That they could change. And didn't they owe it to the world to try?

"What are the tasks?" Charity asked.

Nessie's eyes widened as her mom took a similar bowed position of fealty beside Jaylynn. Sadness and understanding filled Jaylynn as she considered Venus' incentives. They were all too good to deny. Of course Charity would kneel to rest her husband's soul, just as Jaylynn would to bring Psyche back. A long moment passed before Nessie conceded, her brow folded in skepticism even as she knelt. Blake was slower to follow, reluctantly thumping her knee to the ground at Nessie's side, her face still a mask of disapproval.

Venus' delighted laugh echoed in the too-quiet clearing. "Oh! I forgot how daring and brave mortals can be. My tasks will be simple—each of you will prove how fickle and easily manipulated love can be."

Blake stiffened as Venus' gaze settled on her first target. The goddess clasped her hands under her chin, her smile wider than ever.

"Jordan Blake. Stubborn, angry, rebellious girl. Your honest hatred for soulmates bleeds from your very pores. Yes, I know exactly what task is best suited for your... *disposition.* Before you are free of Cupid's magic entirely, you are to fall in love. Not with just anyone—they will be of my choosing—but you will know exactly who they are when they come for you."

Blake visibly paled—whether from hearing her full name or the given task, Jaylynn couldn't guess as her own thoughts swirled. Venus flicked her wrist, and Blake braced as she was hit with an unseen force.

"Blake!" Nessie's hand struck out to support her friend as Blake hunched in pain, but Charity grabbed Nessie's arm, stilling her.

Jaylynn swallowed, worried more than ever that her intuition was wrong about calling the goddess in the first place.

Venus laughed, her musical voice clashing like cymbals. "Oh, what a spectacle that will be. And yet, a more dashing tale of love than Cupid ever had in store for you."

The goddess turned to Charity next, whose eyes were pits of open fear.

Cupid, help us. Let Charity be strong enough to bear whatever Venus deals.

"Charity McKenzie, the gentle soul. The compassionate one." Venus' eyes twinkled like sparks in a sea of flames. "Let us see that your heart can be vicious. You will steal someone's soulmate. Same rule as before: I will choose who." With another flick of the goddess's wrist, Charity also crumpled forward, grasping her left arm to her chest and letting out a stifled cry.

"Mom!" A fat tear tracked down Nessie's cheek, and Jaylynn's heart ached at her friends' pain.

Stars, am I still the fool who sat in River's psychic shop ten years ago?

"Nessie McKenzie. The girl so desperate to be loved." Venus grinned as she twisted the diamond on her ring finger. "For you, I offer a gift to lighten your solitude."

Jaylynn knew instantly that whatever the goddess was about to say would not be a present anyone wanted to receive.

"Make my chosen candidate's heart yours by the end of the trial. Charm him, bewitch him, and make him forget all about his soulmate link."

Nessie crumpled as Venus' hands wove in an intricate series of twists and turns. The cry that came out of Nessie's throat felt like an added lash to Jaylynn's back as the girl clutched her arm to her chest.

Oh, Psyche, what chaos have I unleashed by trying to bring you back? By trying to right what we wronged?

Sweat broke out down Jaylynn's back as Venus turned to her. "Last but not least, Jaylynn Clare."

Terror bled into Jaylynn's veins as she knelt in front of the manipulative goddess.

"Did you know I can taste it? How even now you remain a hopeless romantic, dreaming of the day you will join Elias in the Underworld?" Venus' eyes lit up with mischief. "You think you know what true love is. Guide your mark's heart to the *right* choice, and our deal will be sealed."

Jaylynn braced for whatever pain might come as her trial was voiced. Instead of something sharp and violent, Jaylynn felt the magic contract lock into place in her bones. So much like the soulmate link, the sensation of something foreign but uniquely hers wove itself into the fabric of Jaylynn's being. The feeling terrified her. Her mind raced over Venus' tasks, desperate to memorize them.

Blake has to fall in love, Charity has to steal a soulmate, Nessie has to make someone fall in love with her, and I have to help my mark choose the right soulmate?

Venus spun, her ivory skirts wrapping around her legs, arms wide to the blue sky. "These are your trials to earn my favor, to return compasses to the world, and to earn your personal rewards." Venus' gold eyes sparkled as they landed once more on Jaylynn. "You have until sunset of the next supermoon." Venus began to levitate, her wedding gown glowing brighter.

"Shut your eyes!" Jaylynn cried out, realizing that the goddess was about to take her divine form.

A bright flash rippled against Jaylynn's closed eyelids. She took slow, measured breaths as she registered the sound of birds returning. Jaylynn peeked an eye open, no longer afraid of the goddess but of what her friends would think of the mess she'd gotten them into.

Nessie sagged and crawled toward her mother. "Mom, are you okay?"

Charity nodded and looked up to Jaylynn, her eyes sharing Jaylynn's unspoken question.

Did we make a mistake?

"How long is it until the next supermoon?" Blake asked, her own eyes glassy with shock.

Jaylynn looked up at the sky, remembering the shape of the moon the night before. "Not long enough," she whispered.

Blake offered a hand to help Nessie up but froze as the girl reached out. "What is that?"

Blake grasped Nessie's wrist and twisted it face up. Jaylynn leaned forward, curious. On Nessie's left forearm, where Cupid's compass had once sat unmoving, a new mark glimmered. The same silver curls and stardust that had decorated Cupid's tattoo were remastered around a bordered circle. However, instead of a compass-clock and bow, a stunning hourglass spun, its stardust sand filling one end and a tiny stream trickling into the empty chamber below.

"What in Jupiter's name…" Charity murmured as she stared down at her own imprint.

The pieces clicked together in Jaylynn's mind. Venus had given each of them a task, and a new tattoo to guide them. As Blake's grip slackened, Nessie levered her arm side to side, watching the hourglass turn.

"It's like the compass," Nessie whispered. "But mine actually moves."

"Why don't I have one?" Blake asked.

Nessie looked up at Blake in surprise. "What do you mean you don't have one?"

Jaylynn shook her head. "Venus probably gave your tasked person a mark to find you. I don't have one either."

CHAPTER X

The blackout blinds hid Sebastian's temporary bedroom from the late-morning sun as he scrolled his phone. After Elise and Kenyon video-called to check on him, he hadn't been able to fall back asleep.

"Your parents seem to be taking the loss of compasses extra hard, so we offered to help out by keeping your exchange partner, Liam, with us, just until things settle."

Sebastian wanted to crush his phone, but he'd smiled gratefully at his best friend's parents. As much as he hated that the Williams family was making up for his parents' failures, he was also relieved. If Liam was anything like Sebastian, he would likely be happier with Gareth's family. Sebastian was sure Dakota, Gareth's exchange partner, would be equally happy with the arrangement, but were Elise and Kenyon really okay with an extra boy in their house? Or only saying they were?

A knock at the door made him jump. He dropped his phone as Huan's cheery face poked around the corner.

"Hey, Seb. We're just deciding what to have for breakfast. Would you come up and join us?"

"Oh, sure. I'll be right there."

Huan's warm brown eyes softened. He came into the room and sat at the foot of Sebastian's bed as he sat up. Sebastian gripped his sleeve, a habit he'd unconsciously started since his compass tattoo disappeared.

"Do you want to talk about it?" Huan prompted, his knowing eyes tracking Sebastian's movement.

No.

"I don't know," Sebastian mumbled instead.

Huan leaned back, concern etched in his eyes. "Liam gives me trouble anytime I prod, but sometimes it can better to face hard questions head-on. If you can, tell me how you're feeling after everything that happened yesterday."

The invisible knife that felt lodged in Sebastian's chest sank deeper. He couldn't help but agree with Liam's objections. *If I was home right now, no one would bother me, let alone be interrogating me like this.* But he wasn't home. He was in a stranger's house and had to make a good impression. Sebastian swallowed as he tried to summarize the swirl of emotions.

Betrayed. Strung along. Humiliated. Instead, Sebastian settled on something simpler but still true.

"Let down, I guess."

Huan's eyes shimmered in sorrow. "I'm sorry, my boy. I wish for your sake it hadn't happened like that. It was terribly unlucky."

New tears hung on the edge of Sebastian's dark eyelashes as he took a steadying breath.

"Do you think—" Sebastian paused, reconsidering his question. Why was he opening up to this man? But even as Sebastian thought it, the opposite thought rose. Would there be any harm in telling Huan the truth? A month from now, he would never see any of these people again. Sebastian forced out the question. "Do you think Cupid's magic will come back?"

Huan sighed as he clasped his palms together.

"I think it's too early to tell. Until they find out *why* compasses disappeared, who can say? What I can tell you is that everyone is grieving, and all we can do for now is support one another." Huan reached out and gave Sebastian's knee a reassuring squeeze. "You are welcome to take all the time you need to process this, but I hope you know that Philip and I are here. If you want to spend this time hanging out and keeping life simple, we can absolutely do that. If you want to see more of Canada, we'd be happy to show you. But for now, why don't we start with breakfast?"

Huan held out his arms as he stood.

"Are you a hug person? I won't be offended if you aren't."

Sebastian winced as he stood on his tender ankle, but he managed to step forward into the embrace. Though he'd originally felt it was just the polite thing to do, he was surprised by how much comfort it brought him. He hadn't hugged his own parents in years, though Gareth's mum, Elise, always went out of her way to give Sebastian a squeeze whenever they said goodbye. Sebastian buried his head into Huan's shoulder and let out a heavy sigh. Huan didn't let go until Sebastian stepped back.

"Come," Huan said.

Sebastian tried to play off his sore ankle as he took in his new temporary home with fresh eyes. The spare bedroom where he'd slept was in the huge basement. Glass doors led out to a lush backyard, a small bar rounded one corner, and a giant TV faced a deep, plush sectional couch. Sebastian itched to pick up one of the many controllers he saw on the coffee table. If he had to curl up somewhere for a month, this would be more than comfortable. It was a dream of space and privacy.

Upstairs was brighter than he remembered it being when they'd finally rolled in late last night. Vaulted ceilings and tall windows bathed the open concept kitchen and living area in morning sun. A black piano gleamed in one corner, and a bright blue sectional split the oversized room in half. Philip shuffled about the marble counters in the kitchen wearing a ridiculous apron with *kiss the chef* written in cursive across the front. When he caught sight of Sebastian, he brightened considerably.

"Well, we have half the food we need, and I for one am not getting groceries while these streets are paved with madmen. Seb, how do you feel about eggs and toast?"

Huan echoed, "Madmen?" as Sebastian shrugged.

"I'm not a picky eater."

Philip nodded. "Good to hear. And yes, madmen, Huan! Have you seen the news?"

On the far wall, the telly flickered quietly in the background. Sebastian's attention fixed on the screen.

"I've told you to stop watching the news, Phil," Huan reprimanded.

Sebastian wandered closer, dropping onto the soft couch. The screen flashed between videos of various department stores, all with ransacked shelves. A group of people clawed over the last rolls of toilet paper before the view shifted to a woman. On her hip, she bounced a crying infant while she was interviewed. Philip hovered closer and turned the sound up.

"This is the fourth place I've stopped today looking for baby formula. People are acting wild, wrestling over essentials like we're living in a war-torn country. This is Canada, for Jupiter's sake!"

Philip sank down beside Sebastian. His back curled in a dramatic hunch as he rested his elbows on his knees. When the channel transitioned to global news, both Sebastian and Philip sat up a little straighter. A new broadcaster clutched her microphone.

"I'm coming to you live from the streets of Brussels, where tensions are running higher than ever as the stalemate between the Northern Alliance and the Roman Empire has taken an unexpected turn."

A map of Europe took over the screen, with white lines tracing country borders and a red one highlighting the moving front line of the war. Sebastian's pulse skipped as he watched it shift closer to the UK. The grim news reporter returned.

"Today the Northern Alliance claimed the city of Cologne in blazing gunfire. Tomorrow, Brussels could meet the same fate. Citizens are barring their doors, and many are fleeing as the battlefront continues to shift closer."

The camera panned down a lane of shops. Wood planks of all shapes and sizes covered doors and windows.

"For centuries the civil tug-of-war between these two political forces has burned, but we haven't seen the Northern countries gain this much traction in generations. Has the disappearance of compasses changed the course of the war? How far will the Northern Alliance push back?

"Already the Roman Empire is pushing for allied countries like the UK, Canada, and the USA to increase their military recruitments to fight their cause, but will it be enough? Stay tuned for more live coverage of the Endless War."

Philip gripped the remote tighter. When he realized Sebastian was watching him, he softened into a slouch. "I'm sure everyone in the UK is fine. The war is still a good distance away, and they have the Channel as protection."

Sebastian pressed his feet firmly into the ground to keep his knees from shaking. "That lady comparing her grocery store to a war-torn country looks pretty dense now."

Philip nodded gravely.

Behind the couch, Huan crossed his arms. "I'll be curious to see which countries stay allied if the Roman Empire continues to lose ground. Some might see this as a chance to claim their own freedom."

Sebastian rubbed the back of his neck, a bitter tang burning in his throat as the muted telly panned over a burning city. Was that what his family would have to face if the Northern Alliance kept winning? Would his own home be the next war-torn country? Philip sank his head in his hands as if he couldn't bear to watch the television anymore.

"Don't do that," Huan warned, coming to sit beside his husband. "Liam is perfectly safe. You have to stop being such a worrywart."

"I'm not being a worrywart!" Philip groaned.

Huan gave his husband a disbelieving look before turning his attention back to Sebastian. "How are your parents faring with everything?"

"I don't really know," Sebastian answered honestly. "I assume not great seeing as Liam is staying with the Williams family."

Huan and Philip exchanged glances. "Liam mentioned the new arrangement. You haven't heard from your parents at all?"

Sebastian shook his head, a sudden uneasiness flushing his cheeks as both men pinned him with concerned stares. Sebastian hadn't considered it odd that his parents hadn't called yet. It hadn't even been a full day since he'd arrived.

"I talked to Elise and Kenyon this morning, though," Sebastian said, not sure why he felt a need to smooth things over. "And I'm sure my parents will call when they have time. They're probably just busy."

Philip pinched his lips together and toggled the broadcast off. "Well, I'll go start breakfast. I'm sure everyone is starving."

A ting from Sebastian's phone drew his attention.

GARETH: What are you doing today?

Sebastian typed his answer quickly, his mood lifting ever so slightly. He hadn't seen Gareth since he'd left to try to follow his compass.

SEBASTIAN: Nothing planned yet that I know of. You?

GARETH: You should come to the Harts' art gallery this afternoon with me.

While Sebastian had no idea what gallery Gareth was referencing, if there was anything that could improve Sebastian's bleak mood, it would be seeing his best friend.

"Gareth wants to know if I'd like to go to the Harts' gallery this afternoon?"

Huan steepled his fingers. "I don't see that being a problem."

"We've never been to Winona's art gallery," Philip mused as he cracked an egg into a sizzling pan. "I know she has poured a lot of time into it."

Huan nodded. "It's honestly a shame we haven't been. That will probably be one of the best perks of having you with us, Seb: it will challenge us to try new things right in our neighborhood."

Philip hummed in agreement. "We always said we should go, but it's crazy how time can just slip away."

On the marble countertop, a phone chimed.

"Oh, that must be work." Philip slumped. "I should have known with compasses disappearing it was only a matter of time until they called."

Huan took the spatula from Philip without question, taking over the role of cook.

"Hello?" Philip left the room, the worry lines from earlier plastered across his forehead again.

"Phil took this week off as vacation time to help with your transition, but I hate to say it, I wouldn't be surprised if he has to go in to the hospital to lend a hand."

"Are you using your vacation hours to be here too?" Sebastian asked, plagued with guilt that these men were wasting free time for his sake.

Huan nodded as he flipped the eggs one by one. "I have more vacation time than I know what to do with. I was happy to take some time off to help you settle in."

Sebastian rubbed at his temple, discomfited. These men had gone out of their way to coordinate his arrival, and his own parents had cast Liam off without a second thought. Maybe things were worse at home than he knew? Maybe he should be the one to initiate the call? The sudden thought that maybe there was a darker reason for his family's silence made Sebastian's heart pound. He resolved he'd call after breakfast.

CHAPTER XI

The urge to say *I told you so* echoed over and over in Blake's mind. Calling Venus back had been a huge mistake.

Fall in love with someone. Blake wanted to spit at the goddess's feet. Why was it she had to fall in love in order to be freed of her soulmate link? The irony of the task made Blake's blood boil. Venus clearly delighted in the twisted, likely impossible task.

Blake kept replaying the scene in her mind: the way Venus twirled on that stupid altar with her thick blue hair sculpted into a stylish faux-hawk and her sleeve of perfect black roses tattooed over healthy muscles. To see how much happier Blake could look without bags under her eyes and bruises on her legs was almost as hard to come to terms with as the fact that they'd made a deal with a goddess.

Anger twined with panic as Blake considered her absurd trial. Who would the vindictive goddess send for her to fall in love with? Would they have the hourglass marker as proof they were the right person? And did Blake have any chance of succeeding? Of course she would try—they all had to. Because if any one of them failed, no one would get their promise from the goddess.

The acid taste of fear coated Blake's tongue as the realization settled in. Whether they succeeded or not, Blake wouldn't have a compass anymore. But if she failed, Nessie would be alone forever. Psyche would never wake. Charity's husband's soul would never rest. They would all hate her if she failed, and somehow that consequence was worse.

The late-morning sun crept higher in the sky, time a strange blend of standing still and running too fast. In a desperate attempt to soothe her unsettled stomach, Blake rummaged through the granola bars on the shelf. She tore one open at random, promptly coughing against the dry, grainy texture.

"I know they aren't gourmet, but you're really not selling me on those bars," Jaylynn teased.

Blake's grip tightened on the package of her late breakfast. She wasn't sure what it was about Jaylynn that made her feel so edgy, but Blake couldn't wait to be rid of the redhead.

This will all be over soon. If we complete the trials, then I can leave this wretched cabin and never come back.

"We should have got coffee while we were at the store, Blake." Nessie moaned as she slumped at the table. "The Fates did not create me to live off tea."

Blake snorted and threw Nessie a granola bar. "And I could use a whiskey, but we can't all have what we want, can we?"

Jaylynn scoffed, but Nessie smirked as she picked up a chocolate-dipped oatmeal bar.

"I could go for tea," Charity chimed in, wandering into the cabin behind Nessie.

"Of course you could, Mom. You're convinced tea could save the world."

Jaylynn plopped the kettle onto the oven burner. "I'm with you, Charity. There's a tea for everything."

Blake kicked at a corner of the rug that was curling up. "Yeah? Can you make me a tea that will make me fall head over heels?"

Nessie tore open her granola bar. "Blake, I'm not convinced that even one of Psyche's potions could make you fall in love with someone."

It was a joke, but somehow Nessie's words carried a heavy weight of truth. How was Blake supposed to achieve her task when she was undeniably the most heartless in the room?

"Have you ever been in love before?" Charity asked. She sat beside Nessie, her shawl wrapped tight around her shoulders. The glaze over her eyes had lifted slightly, but Blake wasn't convinced Charity was fully here, even if she was speaking now.

Is this what I looked like all those days running from New York? Hardly conscious? A corpse pretending to be alive?

"I don't know." Blake shrugged. "Probably?" But even as she said it, she knew it was a lie. She had no childhood love for the father who'd abandoned them or her mother, who'd cared for nothing more than drugs and alcohol. And even though Blake had told Tatiana that she loved her, she wasn't convinced she'd meant it the same way her girlfriend had.

The squint of Charity's and Nessie's concerned eyes made Blake's cheeks tinge pink.

"I guess I'm going to figure it out, though."

Jaylynn fumbled as she put cups out along the counter, the clatter driving the group's attention away from Blake. "I wish my task was to fall in love with someone. That would be so much easier than getting other people to fall in love. Or stealing someone's love." She looked expectantly at Charity, but Charity said nothing.

Nessie stretched her arms above her head. "Blake could have probably nailed that one. I guess that's why we got specific tasks, though: to make it harder. Venus wants us to struggle."

Blake frowned even as she acknowledged they were probably right.

"I think you have the hardest one, Ness," Jaylynn mused. "Make someone fall in love with you? At least, it's just as hard as helping other people find love. Neither of those things are in our control."

Nessie gave a weak smile that didn't meet her eyes. "Yeah, I know."

Jaylynn leaned against the stove, the tips of her fingers playing with her loose hair. "Does anyone have any guesses how the new tattoos are even supposed to work?"

Nessie splayed her arm on the table. "I can't say for sure about yours and Blake's matches, but I already have a few guesses how the marker works. The whole hourglass spins, just like Cupid's compass did. But do you see here?"

Blake and Jaylynn stepped closer in unison. Their shoulders bumped as they both leaned in, eager to see the mark neither of them had. Blake glared at Jaylynn briefly and took a slight step sideways. Nessie pointed to the rim of the circle.

"There's the same diamond arrowhead as Cupid's compass on the rim. I'm guessing that's the heading to follow." Nessie traced the edge of the circle where elaborate cursive script split in two, framing the glittering heart. "But I have no clue what this says. Does anyone know Latin?"

Jaylynn reached for Nessie's wrist. "I took one class in university, but I can't say I'm very good." The redhead leaned close as she made out the tiny curving script of the border. "*Nunc scio quid sit amor. Ubi amor, ibi dolor.*"

Blake stepped back, conscious she had absolutely nothing to contribute.

"Amor means love, right?" Nessie asked.

Jaylynn nodded, the wrinkle of her forehead creasing in concentration. "I have no clue what dolor is, though. Maybe sadness?"

Nessie glanced up at Blake. "Can you grab my phone? It's plugged in on the counter."

Blake dutifully retrieved Nessie's device. They all waited patiently as she typed in the text.

"Here!" Nessie's face lit up. "It loosely translates to: Now I know what love is. Where there is love, there is pain."

Great. Blake groaned.

All four people sagged a bit at the translation.

"You should also double-check when the supermoon is, Ness," Jaylynn said.

Nessie sighed and picked up her phone again. Her fingers zipped across the screen. "Today is Wednesday, right? Man, this place is like a time vortex. So, it's July sixth right now and the next supermoon is… hmmm." She paused. "Oh, here it is. The thirteenth."

"Of July or August?" Blake choked on her granola bar.

Nessie's face was stricken as she answered. "July."

Jaylynn spun back, her lips parted in shock. "How is that supposed to be enough time?"

"We should get a move on. Now." The legs of Nessie's chair scraped across the wood planks as she stood. A blend of adrenaline and panic set in, and even Charity jumped up, alert.

Blake glanced back at the comatose woman on the cot, then did a double take. "Jaylynn, does Psyche seem... worse to you?"

"What do you—" Jaylynn froze as she came to Psyche's side, stifling a gasp. "Psyche."

Jaylynn fell to her knees, and Blake knew her observations were right. The changes were subtle. Psyche's cheekbones seemed a bit more prominent. There was a swollen darkness under her eyes, and new wrinkles touched the corners of her mouth.

"Is that... gray hair?" Nessie asked as she and Charity joined them at the head of the cot.

The dashes of white in Psyche's raven-black mane were undeniable once pointed out.

"She's aging," Blake whispered.

"I thought she couldn't age or die?" Charity said.

Jaylynn shifted from foot to foot. "And yet, she looks like she's aged five, maybe ten years."

No, no, no...

Panic bled into Blake's pulse, and she gently took Psyche's bandaged hand. "Did Venus do this?"

Jaylynn shrugged. "It could also be an effect from the veil weakening."

Nessie tilted her head back. "Why can't we catch a break?"

Blake huffed in frustration. There was no getting out of this now, and as much as Blake didn't want to fail, a new motivation pushed her into action. Blake wanted to beat Venus. She wanted to win these trials and shove it in the goddess's stupid face.

"Ness and Charity, you're the only ones with markers to follow, so you should leave and get bearings on your tasks," Blake suggested.

Nessie nodded. "Okay. And you two are, what? Just going to wait here until you hear back?"

"I'm not leaving Psyche like this," Jaylynn declared. "Not until I have to."

Blake scowled. The last thing she wanted was to be stuck in a one-bedroom cabin with Jaylynn. While Blake had started to realize Jaylynn wasn't always the cheery optimist she'd first taken her for, there was still something about her that made Blake crazy.

Fifteen minutes later, Charity's and Nessie's bags were repacked and loaded into Jaylynn's truck. The tea was abandoned, phone numbers were exchanged, and the medical supplies were divided. Jaylynn held Charity in a tight hug and murmured something soft in her ear. Nessie twirled Jaylynn's keys, her lips pursed as she stared down the driveway.

"You've got this," Blake said. "You did great driving yesterday." The decision that Charity wasn't ready to drive was mutual among the group.

Nessie nodded, though she was clearly unconvinced. "Thanks. You'll be okay here with Jaylynn?"

"Psyche's here too."

Nessie suppressed a smile. "You know what I mean."

Blake held her gloved hands up in surrender. "I'll behave."

Nessie pushed the sleeves of her jacket up, her eyebrow arched, both entertained and unconvinced.

The flicker of silver caught Blake's attention, and she reached out for Nessie's wrist. "You need to keep this hidden, okay?"

Nessie pursed her lips and pulled the sleeve of her coat down. They'd brushed off the dirt, but grass stains still streaked the back. "I'll do my best."

"Maybe when you're not actively following it, you could bandage it like your hands. People will just think it's part of your injury."

Nessie nodded. "Good idea. I think I'm going to take Mom home first before we try to follow the markers anyway. We both need to change and clean up."

"Don't take longer than you have to. You have no idea how far you'll have to travel to find your mark."

Blake considered how many days it took her to walk from New York all the way to River's cabin. Though much of it passed in a blur, walking all the way to Canada, past Toronto, had been enough of a trek that Blake's feet still ached.

Jaylynn came over, her arms open wide. Nessie leaned into the hug. "Drive safe. Text updates when you can."

"Will do," Nessie replied.

Both McKenzies waved as the truck pulled away. Jaylynn and Blake were left standing on the porch, relieved and tense at the same time.

"They'll be back before we know it," Jaylynn said. The hope in her voice made Blake's eye twitch. She turned and stalked back into the cabin.

CHAPTER XII

"This is... not what I was expecting," Sebastian said with an appreciative tone.

"Right?" Gareth agreed.

Gareth's fingers traced the edge of a drum as Sebastian sized up a giant wooden canoe. Gareth hadn't known what to expect when he'd found out his exchange family owned an Indigenous art gallery—maybe a bunch of paintings hanging in a row in a fluorescent white room.

Instead, sunshine filtered into the vast space from the big bay windows, and the heavy scent of sage and juniper lingered everywhere. Lights shone on bright paintings, but there were also wood carvings, drums, and beadwork. The space was dominated by striking primary colors.

Yet, as cool as the gallery was, Gareth couldn't shake off the eerie chill from their drive here. The number of abandoned cars in the streets made navigating the city slow, and while some businesses flashed with Open signs, it seemed like most people were tucking away to wait out a storm. Gareth wasn't sure if his own hollow sadness was from the abandoned city, jet lag, homesickness, or his body trying to adjust now that Cupid's magic wasn't beating alongside his heart anymore.

"How long did it take Winona to collect all of these?" Sebastian mused as they passed an exhibit of masks. From what Gareth had deduced since he'd arrived, the gallery was Winona's passion project. Her husband, Mikom, did everything he could to support her when he wasn't working as a full-time electrician. Their fourteen-year-old twins had both protested coming today, and Gareth guessed the pair spent a lot of time here.

Gareth shrugged as Huan came up beside them. "I have no idea."

"Absolutely wonderful," Huan said. "Don't you think, Seb?"

Dyani and Tokala, his new sisters for the month, stalked past. Gareth smiled, only to receive matching deadpan looks from the twins. He sighed. It was going to be a long month if he didn't find an in with those two. Idly, he wondered how his exchange partner, Dakota, was doing with Gareth's own little brothers.

Winona sidled up to Gareth. She had a long tawny face and soft eyes lit with eagerness. "So, what do you think? Any favorite pieces yet?" She wore a bright ribbon skirt layered with horizontal stripes of red, green, blue, and black. Intricate flower-shaped beadwork decorated her top.

"I'm not sure." Gareth glanced about, settling on the first thing he saw. "Probably the drums?"

Winona nodded, as if this was exactly what she'd expected him to say. Then the faint smile disappeared as she spied her daughters sulking at the front desk.

"Girls, please put your phones away," Winona begged. "Tokala, why don't you go help your father break down boxes in the back."

With a sigh, Tokala stuffed her phone into the pocket of her oversized hoodie.

"Fine. But I'm leaving in an hour for hockey practice."

Winona rubbed at her forehead with her finger and thumb. "Dyani, you should help too."

The second twin tipped her nose to the ceiling. "And get paper cuts for nothing?" Dyani's flamingo-pink nails glittered in the sunlight as she looked over her extended hand. "No, thank you."

Compared to Tokala, Dyani was clearly more of a diva. Gareth made a mental note about her nails, hopeful he might have figured out a way to tell the twins apart.

"Dyani." Winona's warning tone only made the twin's scowl deepen.

Dyani crossed her legs and pulled out a jingling pouch from her bag. "I still have a million sequins to add to my fancy shawl, which you promised I'd have time to work on before the next full moon ceremony. I agreed to come, not to be put to work."

Huan chuckled. "Sometimes I think boys are hard, but then I spend one day with you, Winona, and I remember how easy I have it with just one teenager."

"I wanted to ask…" Sebastian trailed off as everyone's eyes landed on him. He shuffled back and forth before continuing. "Is, uh, Liam adopted?"

Huan huffed a small laugh. It hadn't even occurred to Gareth to ask the pair of men how they'd ended up with a sixteen-year-old son.

"Liam was my sister's son," Huan answered, his smile falling. "Unfortunately, she passed away shortly after he was born."

"I'm so sorry," Sebastian muttered, clearly not expecting that answer.

Gareth swallowed, curious but unsure he wanted to know. "And his father?"

Huan shook his head, his eyes growing impossibly heavier. "He didn't make it a year without her before joining her in the Underworld. They say it was the loss of his link that caused the heart attack."

Winona took Huan's arm. "I am so sorry. It never occurred to me to ask."

Huan gave her an appreciative half smile. "We are blessed to call Liam our own after so much tragedy."

Winona and Huan settled into easy conversation, so Gareth and Sebastian went deeper into the gallery. There was something about being together that helped quiet the uneasiness Gareth couldn't seem to shake.

"I talked to Vee this morning," Sebastian mentioned casually. He ran a thumb over a glass case featuring decorated stone mallets.

"Vee—the queen narcissist herself—talked to you?" Gareth asked in disbelief. They'd long ago agreed that Sebastian's older sister was the absolute worst and worth avoiding at all costs.

Sebastian shrugged. "I tried calling Mum and Dad, but they didn't answer. So, I called Vee."

Something about Sebastian's nonchalance didn't sit right with Gareth. Before he could ask more, Sebastian continued.

"Apparently losing compasses really messed my parents up. Vee says they've barely left their bedroom and they've been fighting a lot."

It didn't surprise Gareth that the Evans family was taking compass loss hard. They'd always taken their magical soulmate link a little too seriously in his opinion. Gareth ran a hand over the back of his head where his hair was buzzed close to his scalp.

"I don't think losing compasses has been easy on anyone."

At this admission, Sebastian looked up. His sea-green eyes landed on Gareth's, open and honest. In silent agreement they both wandered farther away from the rest of the group.

"Are you okay?" Sebastian asked once they were out of earshot.

Some part of Gareth relaxed at the direct question, conscious he didn't have to fake things with Sebastian. "I don't know." Gareth considered the last twenty-four hours. "Everything here seems so strange. I'm starved but can't eat without feeling nauseous. I'm exhausted but can't sleep. Everything just feels... wrong."

"Are the Harts all right?"

Gareth considered Winona, Mikom, and the twins. He couldn't tell for sure whether it was losing compasses that had the family so solemn or if they were just a quiet household. Mikom had hardly spoken a word to Gareth since he arrived, and the twins gave him a wide berth. Only Winona seemed able to turn on any brightness, but it was clear it was an effort for her too. All Gareth knew for sure was the big, silent house made him miss his mum's singing, his raucous little brothers' wrestling, and his dad telling them to settle down.

"Yeah, the Harts are good. I'm just missing home is all."

He didn't mention his phone call with his parents that morning. Gareth could still see the disappointment in his parents' faces when he turned down their offer to fly him home. He was tempted to take them up on it, but he couldn't leave

Sebastian. Gareth wouldn't go home early unless Sebastian also wanted to.

There was an empathetic sadness in Sebastian's nod, as if he too kept thinking of home.

"I'm sorry you missed finding your soulmate," Gareth said.

"I'm sorry you didn't get a chance to figure out why your compass changed," Sebastian answered.

Gareth looked away, his stomach coiling again. Was it silly to grieve a compass that had never worked? It wasn't until it was gone that he realized how much hope he was holding out that a specialist could explain the problem—whether his soulmate link was broken or if there was something wrong with him.

The mood hung heavy between the boys, and Gareth let out a deep sigh. This trip was supposed to be a fun opportunity for them to hang out for a whole month in a new country. Gareth didn't want to waste whatever time they had here being blue. He bolstered whatever energy he could and wrapped an arm over Sebastian's shoulders, crushing him in a side hug.

"Who knows. Maybe we'll still find our soulmates without Cupid's magic."

Sebastian rubbed at his temple where pink scars flecked the side of his face. "There's no way to know who Cupid matched either of us with."

"But they're still out there," Gareth insisted, more for Sebastian's sake than his own. "Maybe when we find who we were meant to be matched to, we'll just know."

It was an optimistic take, Gareth knew that, but he could see how the dash of hope helped ground Sebastian. And while Gareth had no idea what his life would turn out like without his compass, part of him wondered if he might be happier without the twisting dial making him second-guess everything.

CHAPTER XIII

There are two types of numbness a person can experience in life. One is the tingling not-there-ness when the mind abandons the body. The other, the hollow void of emotions when a heart has nothing left to give. Charity McKenzie's numbness was twofold, encasing both her body and her spirit. She welcomed the trance that came with it. The gray world stretched on, everything a touch out of focus. The only thing disturbing Charity's peace was an unclear, continuous mumbling.

Charity squinted as she realized the ceaseless noise ruining her peace was Nessie, talking to herself. Her daughter sat tall in the driver's seat, muttering as she looked back and forth between her mirrors and the road. The urge to close her eyes and sink into the seat grew more enticing. If she could just sleep for a few hours, she could forget Venus wearing her face and a crisp military uniform, handing out orders to go out and needlessly ruin lives.

Seeing herself wearing the camouflage green reminded Charity of the last time she'd seen her husband, Luke—geared up with a bag over his shoulder, kissing her cheek goodbye. That memory was always quickly followed by the night her compass went dark.

"Come on, Mom."

Charity jolted awake. The truck wasn't moving anymore, and the passenger door was open. Nessie was staring at her with a pained expression. She held her hand out patiently. Charity's eyes settled on her daughter's frown, and the inkling that something was wrong nagged.

I'm disappearing all over again, aren't I?

The too-bright afternoon sunlight painted the outside of the house. Forgotten plants hung limp and faded on the porch. Guilt sat like a boulder on Charity's stomach. Suddenly, the freedom of her gray-dazed world shapeshifted into what it had been for years: a prison. One Charity swore she wouldn't return to.

Charity squeezed her daughter's hand but kindly dismissed being guided into the house. She was an adult. She was a mother. More than both those things, Charity didn't want to be lured into the easy darkness again. Even if she had to fight every atom in her body, she was going to stay present—as much for herself as for Nessie.

And Luke. Because I finally have a real chance to put his soul to rest.

Venus' offering only confirmed what Charity had always suspected. Something had gone wrong when Luke tried to pass into the Underworld. That was why she'd been able to hear his whispers after he died, and why his echoing cries had taunted her for the last five years. She *had* to complete this task.

"You okay?" Nessie asked as she dropped their bags in the front entry.

Charity gave herself a little shake and took a deep, resolved breath in. "Yes. I'm good."

The tiniest relief in Nessie's gray eyes was the exact reinforcement Charity needed.

"I'm in desperate need of a shower," Charity said as she slid her coat from her shoulders.

Nessie nodded. "Same. Meet you back down in twenty to figure out our plan?"

They parted, each lugging a bag up the stairs and splitting off to their separate bedrooms. Charity pushed her door open, pausing as she met the too-warm, stale room. She dropped her bag and rested her hand beside the framed memorial photo of Luke. He stood tall and proud in his army jacket, his freshly cropped hair tucked under a cap that hid his blond curls. Charity sighed as she picked up his photo and sank onto the bed.

I will save you, Luke. I promise.

Like she had endless times over the last five years, Charity clutched the frame to her chest, falling back onto the bedspread. The bone-deep ache to sleep crept back up. Sleeping would be easier than grieving. It would be easier than facing what she had to do.

Steal a love. What would Luke say to that? Would he be crushed to know her compass had changed and led her to Jaylynn? What would he think of their dealing with Venus? Would he scold her?

"I can see you will be the least of my concerns."

Charity lurched up, searching for the face behind the melodic voice. There was no one in the room. As she twisted, Charity caught her reflection in the large oval mirror that hung over her vanity.

Venus.

As it had in the clearing, Charity's reflection had golden eyes and wore the soft camouflage jacket with stripes on each shoulder. There was a confidence and strength to Venus that filled Charity with inexplicable yearning. No stress wrinkles marred her forehead and no laugh lines creased her cheeks. It was the healthiest, happiest, and most at peace Charity could ever have imagined herself. And gods, though she knew it was fake, she wanted it. Charity ached for that security, that stability.

"Be gone, Venus." Charity ground her teeth, absorbing any resilience she could from Luke's photograph. There was no one else here to say whether the reflection in the mirror was her imagination, but Charity suspected it was real.

"And miss watching you morally fall apart? Oh, I don't think so. This is the best entertainment I've had in millennia." Venus' smile stretched wider. "Tell me, now, do you have a plan for how you're going to ruin someone else's relationship? Or were you going to let your daughter solve that for you too?"

Frustrated, tired tears crested Charity's eyes for what felt like the millionth time. She wasn't strong enough to bear this load, not when Venus knew every sore spot to lean into. Charity knew she didn't have the heart to steal someone's love. She wasn't a master seductress. Giving up would be so much easier.

But all I have to do is interfere with one love match. Then Luke will be free and compasses will be back. Nessie will have a love match. I will know peace. We all will.

"Mom?"

Charity turned in a fright, surprised to find Nessie standing in the doorway. Venus' reflection had disappeared.

Or was it even there at all? The thought that her night terrors had elevated to full hallucinations gave Charity chills. Nessie's mouth pitched in a worried slant.

"Did you say something?"

"No," Charity replied, probably too quickly to sound convincing. She gave a forced smile. "Just talking to myself."

Charity got up, gently placing Luke's photo back on the dresser. She couldn't let Venus get to her.

The afternoon slipped away faster than Charity would have liked. It would be dinner before long, and they'd only just struck out to follow their marks.

At least we're moving. It was nice being back in her own car, leaving Jaylynn's truck parked in front of their house. Nessie also seemed relieved, likely because Charity had insisted on driving. The immediate task of following her hourglass had pushed back the heavy shroud rimming the edge of Charity's consciousness.

They'd only gone a couple of blocks before Charity stopped and did a double take as her attention caught on her hourglass mark. After looping around the subdivision, she couldn't deny they were in the right place. Charity pulled into the familiar visitor parking stall.

"Why would it bring us *here?*" Nessie asked, the worry in her tone undeniable.

Charity had rewrapped Nessie's hands in bandages earlier, and now she couldn't unsee just how much all of this was weighing on her daughter. Nessie's usually clear eyes were bloodshot and strained, and the skin on her forehead and chin had broken out in tiny rashes of acne—typical signs stress was getting to her. But it was the sense of duty that Charity caught in her daughter's eyes that made her feel the most guilty.

"Maybe it's someone else who lives in the building," Charity suggested. Nessie tilted her head, cracking her neck.

"Well, we're about to find out."

They walked into the apartment lobby arm in arm, both concealing their hands in the pockets of their coats. Luckily, they caught the elevator alone. Nessie gave Charity a questioning look.

"I guess we just try every floor until you feel something?"

Charity nodded. She needed to do this. She held her left wrist up and pulled at the edge of her bandages to watch the hourglass tattoo. "I'm ready."

Nessie hit the button for the second floor. Before the doors even opened, Charity could already feel the difference. Instead of the lightness that Cupid's magic brought, Venus' mark burned. An unpleasant warmth licked up Charity's spine as she stepped out and glanced down the hall to the left.

"You're sure it's this floor?" Nessie asked. "We could go up another and see if it pulls more."

Charity knew why Nessie wanted to get back on that elevator. Instead of answering, Charity walked forward, letting her mark guide her. When they stopped in front of the second to last door, Charity dropped her head.

"I'm so sorry, Ness."

Nessie's lips flattened into a hard line, but she squared her shoulders.

Oh, Luke. She is your daughter in so many ways.

Charity released the edge of her bandage to cover her hourglass tattoo, then took a deep breath and knocked. There was a scramble before the door opened. Charity plunged her hands into her pockets. She already knew what she'd see as the light poured into the hallway.

Kade stared at Charity in confusion. He looked, well, terrible. His eyes were even more strained than Nessie's, and he had the undeniable look of someone who'd been crying. Charity had been worried about Nessie facing Lacey after their fight, but now the realization of what this meant for Charity's task hit in full force.

Not Kade. Great gods, please don't make me steal Kade from Renee. I can't. I won't.

Charity gave a hesitant smile, remembering what Nessie had said on the drive. They weren't here to do the actual stealing, just to identify her task. Before Charity could break the awkward silence of their unexpected arrival, a familiar tuft of bright red hair crashed into her shins.

Ladybug.

The burning sensation from Venus' magic disappeared in an instant. It was like a trapdoor had opened at Charity's feet and the heat flooded from her head to the ground, leaving a cooling buzz in its absence.

"I'm so sorry." Kade went to scoop up the puppy, but Charity waved him away.

"Oh, it's nothing." Charity knelt down, stroking the dog's wavy ears. She didn't need to double-check her hourglass to know Venus' trial.

I have to steal Kade's love... as in Ladybug?

CHAPTER XIV

KADE

Kade sighed as Ladybug tried to bite at the chopsticks holding Charity's hair in place. *Why do puppies have to eat everything they see?*

The last twenty-four hours had physically drained Kade beyond measure. A sleepless night in the ICU hadn't helped. Then, despite returning to walk Ladybug at the crack of dawn, Kade had come back this afternoon to the puppy whimpering in her soiled crate.

There just wasn't enough time in the day to be at Renee's side, navigate the roads still packed with abandoned cars, and take care of a puppy.

When he'd tried to pick Ladybug up for a bath, she'd shot out of her crate like a rabbit, tracking filth through the apartment and right up onto the couch. The process of bathing and drying her was not something Kade was eager to relive. Luckily, Lacey only complained a bit when he asked her to strip the couch covers and throw them into the wash. Exhausted and smelling like wet dog, Kade had been sitting on the floor when the knock on the door came. He'd left Ladybug furiously rubbing her too-clean body against the rug.

"Is now an okay time?" Charity asked as she nudged the puppy away from the door so she wouldn't escape down the hall. Kade took a hesitant step back into the messy apartment as Nessie closed the door. He rubbed the back of his neck, unsure what to say. It was most definitely not an okay time.

"I— Sorry, you just caught me in the middle of tidying." Kade cocked his head and called across the room, "Lacey, Nessie is here to see you."

Nessie shrank back behind her mom with an undeniable look of panic. Kade frowned. Lacey must have had her headphones blaring, because her bedroom door didn't open. As he went to yell again, Charity reached out with a bandaged hand. Before he could ask how she got injured, Charity gave him a supplicating look.

"We're actually not here to see Lacey. I wanted to see how you were doing."

The sheer exhaustion must have been spelled out on his face. One glance out the window sent a shiver up Kade's spine as he counted how many hours he'd been away from the hospital already.

"You heard about the accident," Kade surmised, assuming Lacey had texted Nessie.

"What?" Charity and Nessie said in unison. Their faces were mirrors of confusion.

Kade paused, not quite understanding why they were here if they didn't already know. "Renee is in the hospital?" he said.

Charity's face tightened. "No!"

Kade took a shuddering breath as he tried to hold back the tidal wave of grief that roared to the surface. The reminder that his injured wife was alone in a room full of beeping machines pulled at his heart like his compass used to. "Renee was in a car accident yesterday when compasses vanished."

Nessie's face went paler than Kade had believed was possible.

"Jupiter Almighty, was she injured badly?" Charity asked.

Kade brushed the heel of his hand over his brow. "She had to have emergency surgery. A broken rib pierced her lung." Kade tried to take in a steadying breath, but ever since he'd seen Renee with her black-and-blue face, he couldn't catch his breath no matter how hard he tried.

"Oh, Kade, I am so sorry. What have the doctors said about her prognosis?"

The undivided attention of Charity's concern threatened to crumple his weak facade. "She should be okay. It's just… a lot. Renee wakes up for small bursts but she's still pretty incoherent." Kade willed his heart to slow so he didn't inadvertently give himself a heart attack.

"Kade, that is absolutely terrifying." Charity guided him to a kitchen chair. He took the seat gratefully. "What can we do to help?"

The offer was like a life jacket thrown to a drowning sailor.

"I mean…" Kade paused, weighing whether it was too much to ask. How else was he supposed to do this? He couldn't be home enough for Ladybug. He couldn't solo parent Lacey when she apparently had a boyfriend now. And more than anything, no amount of time by Renee's bedside would soothe the black hole in his heart he'd been feeling since his compass disappeared. "I just need to be with Renee right now."

Charity was nodding before he could finish his request. "I can take both Lacey and Ladybug. You should be with Renee. You don't even need to ask."

Relief and guilt twisted in his core. "Thank you, Charity. You don't know how much this means to me."

Charity spread her arms in a silent question. Kade nodded. A fresh sob caught in his throat as he clasped her tight.

"Renee is going to make it. She's the toughest woman I know." Charity's hug grew tighter.

"Thank you."

Kade couldn't help it as his eyes flicked back to the clock. The obligation to stay and get his family settled tore at him as he longed to speed away, back to Toronto General Hospital. Charity seemed to sense his conflict. At the front door, Nessie bounced on the balls of her feet, her eyes darting back to Lacey's closed bedroom door.

"Go. I've got this," Charity reassured him.

"I don't know how long I'll need help for."

"It doesn't matter. We'll figure it out. That's what friends do." The look Charity shot at Nessie was unreadable, but Kade didn't have time to figure it out. He had to get back to the hospital.

Kade knocked twice before cracking open Lacey's door. As expected, his daughter was curled up on her unmade bed, headphones snug around her ears. The steady rap beats were loud enough that Kade could hear them across the room. Lacey lurched up at the sight of him, pulling her headphones down around her neck.

"Is Mom okay?"

Kade understood too well the slight panic in her voice, the fear that things might have suddenly gone from bad to worse. "No news about Mom. I just wanted to tell you that Charity and Nessie are here."

Lacey sat up a little straighter, her expression split between surprise and worry. "Oh."

Stepping over bundles of clothes, Kade wove his way to Lacey's bed. "They're going to take you and Ladybug for a bit."

"Oh." Lacey's tone dropped, clearly disappointed.

"Just until Mom can come home." Kade interlaced his fingers, mentally sending a prayer that Lacey wouldn't choose this moment to pick a fight with him. "I don't know how long it'll be, but I can't keep running back and forth."

"I could stay here with Ladybug," Lacey offered.

Kade huffed out a small laugh. "Not a chance." Just because his daughter was fifteen years old didn't mean she was equipped to be home alone for an untold amount of time, let alone with a new puppy. And especially not when the world seemed to be coming apart at the seams.

Besides, Kade could tell Lacey was more affected by Renee's condition than she let on. She needed someone to lean on, and Kade knew he wasn't cutting it.

Lacey rolled back into the pile of pillows, not meeting his eyes.

"What's wrong? You usually jump at any opportunity to stay at Nessie's."

His daughter shrugged. "I don't know."

If Kade could banish those three words for the rest of time, he would. "Lacey, please. I love you, but I need to be at the hospital. And to do that, I need to know you're taken care of."

Lacey itched at her nose. "Okay, okay. Fine. I'll pack a bag."

Thank the gods.

Kade pulled Lacey into a bear hug. She didn't protest.

"I love you, Lace. Everything is going to be okay."

Kade pulled back the curtain that separated his wife from the others in recovery. As soon as Renee had woken and her condition was stabilized, the hospital staff had carted her to this new unit.

"Hey." Kade's heart lurched as he met Renee's half-lucid eyes. He rushed to her side, careful not to bump her bandaged torso. "Renee, can you hear me?"

She nodded, her eyes softly closing.

"I'm sorry I had to leave, but I'm back now and I'm not going anywhere." Kade brushed back her damp hair and placed the gentlest of kisses on her forehead.

"Lacey…" While it came out in a mangled murmur, the word was undeniable. Of course the first thing Renee would ask about was Lacey.

"Lacey is okay. She's safe. She's with the McKenzies."

Kade took Renee's hand in his, cautious of the IV needle taped there.

"The car?" The unusual depth and ragged sound of Renee's voice made Kade nauseous. He was sure when the nurses had removed the horrifying tube that went down her throat it was a sign of improvement, but the way Renee now winced as she tried to speak filled him with worry. As Kade sank back into his chair at her side, he noticed the bruising on her nose was even worse than yesterday.

Kade shook his head. "It's nothing to worry about right now." He hadn't seen the smashed-up SUV, but the way Lacey had described it, he didn't imagine they'd be getting the vehicle back. It was also the least of his concerns at the moment. "How are you feeling?"

Renee slowly shook her head from side to side. He noticed that every time she swallowed, she tilted her chin up slightly.

"Everything hurts." A tear streaked down her face, and Kade caught it with his finger, drying its path.

"I'll ask the nurse to give you more pain meds." Kade's heart thumped as he reached across her for the call button.

Renee's talking. That's an improvement. She's okay. We're going to be okay.

Kade repeated the mantra in his head as he held his wife's hand, his entire world shaken to the core.

CHAPTER XV

NESSIE

The minute she caught Lacey's eye, Nessie froze.

Not now. I don't have time for this. I can't—I'm not ready.

But despite Nessie mentally willing her mother to realize this was a terrible idea, Charity had prattled on and practically signed Nessie's arrest warrant.

How were they supposed to keep their tasks secret if Lacey was living with them? What if Lacey found out they were the reason compasses disappeared and turned them in to the police? Nessie's throat dried as all the secrets she would have to keep raced through her mind.

Lacey didn't look eager to come as she slunk her backpack over her shoulder like a reluctant hitchhiker. It was as though she could tell Nessie didn't want her there.

Good. At least she knows to feel bad.

They all filtered out of the apartment carrying Ladybug's endless things: a crate, food, leashes, toys. Nessie wondered exactly how long Kade thought Lacey and Ladybug would be staying. The car ride back was painfully quiet apart from Ladybug's objections to being in her crate. It wasn't until they shrugged off their coats that Charity tried to smooth the tension.

"Lacey, why don't you take your things up to Nessie's bedroom?"

Nessie gave her mom the best what-are-you-doing stare she could manage. Lacey sidestepped around Nessie with an apologetic touch of a smile. Nessie didn't return it. The minute Lacey hit the top of the stairs, Nessie turned on her mom.

"What were you thinking?" Nessie whispered furiously.

Charity shook her head, shushing Nessie with a finger over her lips. Charity started to unwind the bandage on her left hand.

"Stop! You're going to get us caught." Nessie grabbed her mom by the elbow hard and shifted to shield the secret.

Charity gave Nessie a stern look before unraveling the last of the bandage on her wrist. Nessie tightened her grip in fear. The bandage unfurled to reveal the spinning hourglass as Nessie expected, but the new erratic movement of the mark drew her curiosity. It was as if the tattoo couldn't decide where to point.

Charity gave Nessie a knowing look, then pointed to the scampering puppy with her eyes. The arrowhead followed Ladybug as she dashed left and right, investigating the front entry as far as her leash would allow.

"No." Nessie stared in horror.

Steal a love. Mom has to steal a love. But she has to steal Kade's love? Ladybug?

It didn't make any sense. Why would Venus want Charity to steal the Baker family's dog?

Charity reached out, and as her hand touched the puppy's head, the tattoo stilled.

"It's nothing like Cupid's compass, Ness," she whispered as she took Ladybug into her arms. The puppy licked Charity's chin repeatedly. "There's no floating euphoria or emotional high. It was like my body was burning the closer I got to her, and then as soon as she touched me, it cooled. Now I just feel—I don't know—drawn to her."

Nessie nodded as she tried to piece together the new information. "Okay, so Venus' imprint isn't the same kind of magic."

"And now we know my task," Charity murmured.

The lights flickered, and they both glanced up to the top of the stairs. Lacey startled as well, realizing she had leaned against the light switch accidentally.

"Sorry."

Nessie fought the urge to glare at Lacey, who had apparently dumped her bag at lightning speed and returned. Had she overheard what they were saying? Nothing on her face suggested she had, but Nessie still worried. Lacey couldn't know how much more difficult she made things. Consciously shielding her mom, Nessie crossed her arms and stared their houseguest down with inexplicable anger.

Maybe Lacey coming here inadvertently helped us complete a task, but it doesn't mean anything is better between us.

Charity set Ladybug down on the floor and unclasped the leash. Lacey came back downstairs, and Nessie bristled at her closeness, the memory of their last interaction flashing clear through her head.

"You're a loner, Ness, but I have a soulmate out there. If you were a real friend, you wouldn't be holding me back."

Their parting fight in the Montreal train station speared through Nessie.

But now, if Venus stuck to her word and they all succeeded, Nessie wouldn't be a loner anymore. She would have her own match and be like everyone else. There was the added incentive that her dad's soul would be put to rest, which would mean her mom might finally be herself again.

Lacey broke the silent tension by turning her attention back to the dog.

"Well, Ladybug, looks like we have a new home for now. No eating Charity's plants, okay?" Lacey glanced around the room.

"We should probably puppy-proof this place before she rips down your curtains too."

Charity's eyes widened and Nessie raised an eyebrow.

Now you're starting to see what you've agreed to.

Nessie shook off the smug feeling. She couldn't waste time being mad at her mom for not thinking things through. Charity had done the right thing, even if it was the most inconvenient choice on Terra Mater's green earth.

"Where do you suggest we start with puppy-proofing?" Charity asked Lacey.

For the next ten minutes, Ladybug scampered between their feet as the three girls rearranged the main floor. They put up a gate to block the stairs, and Nessie gathered all the ground-level plants and brought them up to the yoga room. At Lacey's advice, Charity folded her drapes up and over the rods out of the puppy's reach, then they started taping down all the stray lamp cords.

When Lacey brought Ladybug outside for a potty break, Charity pulled Nessie aside.

"You okay?"

"No, Mom. I'm not okay. You know exactly how I feel. Does she have to share my room?"

Charity wrapped her arm around Nessie's shoulder. "I know I put you in a tough situation, but I don't know what choice we have. If it becomes unbearable, you can always come sleep with me."

"I am *not* going to sleep with you."

Charity chuckled. "The offer is there if you change your mind. You get to choose how tough this is going to be, though. You could try to open your heart to Lacey again."

Nessie pursed her lips. "I'd rather not."

"I know. But choosing anger and bitterness is a path of self-harm. Choosing forgiveness is a real strength."

The clarity in her mom's eyes took another layer of stress off Nessie's mind. Even though they'd have to be extra cautious, at least the task had snapped Charity out of her depression—for now.

Nessie gave her mom a wan smile. "Did you read that advice in one of your self-help books?"

Charity grinned. "Actually, I made it up on the spot."

"Well, maybe you should start writing."

Charity ruffled Nessie's hair. "Maybe I will. Now, go." Charity gently nudged Nessie toward the back patio door.

Nessie stepped out into the small treed backyard. Ladybug bounded between pots of tomato plants and Lacey sat cross-legged on the grass, her rose-gold headphones wrapped around her neck. She wore a baggy black concert T-shirt and jeans, and her fingers methodically pulled pieces of grass out one by one.

"Hey." Nessie took a bracing breath and crossed her arms to ward off the cool evening breeze.

"Hey," Lacey's guarded tone echoed back.

Ladybug stopped at Nessie's feet and tried to scale her legs, her little paws scratching for purchase. A small smile tugged at

Nessie's lips as she pushed the puppy down, accidentally giving Ladybug a new target. Sharp teeth cut the edge of Nessie's palm, and she sucked in a breath as pain lanced up her arm. Ladybug gripped Nessie's bandaged hand, excited by the new opportunity to play tug-of-war.

"Ladybug—no." Lacey reached over to pull the dog away. The puppy's teeth clenched tight in resistance.

Nessie panicked as the bound injury unraveled.

"Ness, stop," Lacey commanded. "The more you pull, the more she'll think it's a game." She lifted Ladybug up, her voice stern. "Drop it."

Ladybug did not drop it. Instead, she thrashed her head side to side harder. Nessie winced as the bandages tightened in some places and loosened in others.

"LADYBUG! Drop it." Lacey forced a finger into the corner of Ladybug's mouth, prying her teeth open and finally freeing Nessie.

"I'm so sorry."

"It's fine." Nessie did not feel fine, though. She already knew what was coming next, and she was not prepared.

"What happened to your hands?"

"Hmmm?" Nessie asked, trying to delay as she attempted to wrangle her bandages back into place. It was hopeless. She would have to redo them.

"Did you get hurt? I noticed your mom had her hands wrapped too."

Nessie crossed her arms, giving up on the bandages for now. "Yeah, but we're both fine."

Lacey blinked. "What happened?"

Various lies raced through Nessie's mind, and she spat out the first thing that seemed rational.

"It was a cooking accident. Nothing, really."

"A cooking accident?"

"Yeah." Nessie scrambled to think of something. "I grabbed a pot out of the oven without thinking."

"And your mom did too?"

"She tried to catch it as I dropped it." Nessie's jaw ticked at the improbability of her lie. Ladybug let out a high-pitched bark, as if calling Nessie out.

"No. No barking." Lacey redirected her attention to the dog, which only made Ladybug bark more. Nessie could already feel a headache coming on.

"I should go back in and rewrap my bandages."

"Ness, wait." Lacey's hand caught her elbow. "Please."

Nessie let out a frustrated huff and sat down on the iron bistro chair. Ladybug turned her fury on a nearby bush, wrenching at a gangly branch.

"You're mad at me."

Nessie gave Lacey a flat stare. "You're surprised?"

"No." Lacey leaned back. "I just wanted a chance to apologize. I know ditching you in Montreal was wrong."

Nessie raised a doubtful eyebrow.

"I know I hurt you," Lacey added.

"You did more than just ditch me, Lacey." Nessie's voice dropped. There was no reason to hold this part back. "Not only did you abandon me alone in a foreign city, but you broke my heart. You decided that finding your soulmate was more important than our friendship. Do you have any idea how hard it was to be there with you that day knowing I'd never be able to follow my own compass?"

Lacey held eye contact but said nothing.

"I gave you everything to help your dream come true, Lacey. And you threw all my efforts back in my face when I asked you to wait."

"I'm sorry, Ness."

"No. No, you're not. And you know how I know that you're not?" Nessie's hands trembled as her anger burned hotter. "Because I know, whether or not you found your soulmate, you would do it again. Because that's the kind of person you are. You're impulsive and selfish. You always have been."

Tears pricked in Lacey's hazel eyes. "Ness—"

"No." Nessie cut her off. "You want my forgiveness and I'm saying no." She stood abruptly, nearly tripping over Ladybug as she rushed back into the house. "And you're not staying in my room. Sleep somewhere else."

CHAPTER XVI

Nylah's heels skittered across the cold stone floors of the Triad church's basement. The large dramatic space was exactly as they remembered it: windowless, candlelit, and muggy. A group of Fates' Followers watched apprehensively as Nylah passed. Jazz was going to kill Nylah for being so late. All day Nylah had fixated on Jazz's words: *Fates' Followers can bring compasses back.*

Could it be true? And if they succeeded, would the benefits only serve the faithful, or would the cult be able to return Cupid's blessing to the whole world? Just in case it was the former, Nylah wanted in. An even more worrisome question beat like a drum in Nylah's mind, though: *How far would a cult go to bring magic back?*

Nylah scoured the gathering for their tall, beautiful best friend, but the flood of matching clothes made it hard to distinguish anyone. Crimson robes dominated the group, but there were still a few people dressed in simple black—marking them as new to the cult. Nylah owned a total of one black outfit, which they'd dug up for tonight: a baggy suit jacket with sharp shoulder pads and high-waisted dress pants they'd worn to their grandmother's funeral. Overall, the style was more androgynous than they normally dressed, but Nylah liked the lethal edge it gave off.

A loud bong of a cymbal hummed through the room, and all murmuring hushed. Nylah's heart hammered as the group reoriented their focus to the front of the room. The pudgy head priest was exactly as Nylah remembered. His velvet maroon robes draped the cobblestone floors in heavy layers, and thick golden cuffs hung on his wrists.

Tenderness shot up Nylah's elbow as fingers pinched the sensitive spots of their arm. They shot an alarmed look over their shoulder.

"Jazz," Nylah whispered in relief. It was as if a cool breeze had swept through the room and Nylah could finally breathe.

Jazz did not look happy. In fact, Nylah would say their best friend looked livid.

"You're late." He tugged Nylah so they were both standing at the back of the pack.

"It took longer than expected to get here."

"You should have stayed home," Jazz murmured to himself. While he seemed physically healthy, his skin glowing and broad shoulders held back with confidence, his eyes darted around the room with an uncharacteristic edge.

Yesterday Jazz insisted I come to this meeting, but now he doesn't want me here? Just because I'm late?

The priest at the front cleared his throat. "It is time to decide where your fealty lies!" His voice boomed off the arched ceiling and candle chandeliers. His voice deepened in reverence, as if he was sharing a great secret. "Priests across the globe have confirmed the veil between gods and mortals is falling, which means our devotion is more critical than ever before."

Stars, these people are crazy.

Being among these fanatics who believed the veil was more than a myth rubbed a childhood sore that Nylah hadn't missed. Jazz subtly shook his head as if reading their mind, an unspoken plea for Nylah to keep their disbelief hidden.

The priest raised his arm, the gong mallet spearing the air.

"History reminds us that Cupid's compass was not created by the god of love alone. Alongside his bow and arrow, the Fates contributed their magical clock. Prayers to Cupid will be wasted if the Fates are forgotten. We will not let that happen. Tonight, we vote as a community to do whatever it takes to earn the favor of the Fates."

"Vote yes," Jazz whispered.

"What? Why does it matter?"

The pair of people directly in front of them shot withering glances back. Jazz gave them a tight-lipped smile, gripping Nylah's elbow harder.

"Do it."

Nylah leaned into Jazz, dropping their voice as low as possible. "Maybe I should just go."

"Unfortunately, now you have no choice but to stay. They'll track who votes no and anyone who leaves," he murmured, his attention fixed on the front of the room. Jazz released their elbow, and Nylah sagged in relief until he casually threaded his fingers between Nylah's. Nylah swallowed, a flurry of confused emotions clouding the moment.

Since when does he hold my hand like this? Not that they never held hands, but it was usually in a more casual, palm-to-palm kind of way. The intimacy of their fingers woven together made Nylah do a double take.

The head priest commanded quiet over the new hum, and they all went still.

"All those who vote yes, who will worship the Fates like never before, and who are ready to be the saviors of soulmate magic, raise your hands."

Jazz pulled Nylah's hand up with him, his grip tightening. So he wasn't holding their hand to be sweet. It was to force their vote. Nylah shot him an exasperated look, but he didn't meet their eyes. Around the room, dozens upon dozens of hands shot up. A few were slower to agree, but after glancing around, most joined the fray. Only four people did not vote yes. The head priest's eyes landed on each of them in turn before nodding to the door.

"May the Fates have mercy on your faithless souls."

The crowd echoed the final sentiment as the four people turned one by one, each picking their way through the crowd to the back stairway. Jazz murmured the prayer, which sounded more like a curse in Nylah's opinion. Nylah mumbled incoherent jargon, not willing to say the actual words and hoping no one would notice.

Two of the deserters were clearly husband and wife. They ducked their heads together as they left, hiding their faces. The third person, who passed closest to Nylah, had a birthmark on her right cheek and the unquestionable glint of resolution in her dark eyes. The last person, a young Korean man, shot anxious glances left and right as he followed. When the four people had each exited, the head priest lowered his arms and glowered over the group.

"Blessed are those who pray to the Fates."

The crowd replied with the answering chant: "And may the nonbelievers burn in Tartarus."

The mention of the realm of monsters seemed odd, if not extreme, to Nylah. Most of the time when people damned someone else it was to the Underworld. In Nylah's father's religious texts, Tartarus was always described like the

Underworld's basement, a place of torture and madness. It was where the creatures of nightmares were imprisoned. Supposedly. The way these priests talked about it almost reverently made Nylah's skin crawl.

"With the vote concluded, there will be little delay. Fates' Followers, please be sure your contact information is registered with the priests upon exit, and expect to hear more in the coming days. All elevated priests, please remain for an extended meeting."

As soon as they were outside, Nylah dug out their lighter and a cigarette. The lenses of their glasses fogged in the cool night, and Nylah tipped their head, patiently waiting for them to clear. Jazz said nothing as they walked away from the gothic spires and curling archways.

"Well," Nylah hedged. "That was only borderline psychotic." Nylah inhaled the swirling smoke, trying to play off how uneasy the cult meeting had made them feel.

Jazz's mouth pitched down. "I was wrong to drag you into this. It was probably a good thing you were late. If you'd been there for the whole meeting, I know you would have voted no."

"And I'd be damned by the cult that's clearly bananas? Who cares?" Nylah flicked the growing ashes from the end of their cigarette. "No one's actually going to Tartarus."

Nylah dropped the cigarette as Jazz spun and grabbed both their shoulders, pushing them to a stop against a cold brick wall.

The growing fear Nylah had been trying so hard to suppress crawled back up their spine.

"Damn it, Nylah! You don't understand." Jazz's eyes were pained, genuine concern flickering in them. He glanced over his shoulder before leaning close. "I was wrong. The price of getting compasses back, what Fates' Followers want to do—" Jazz cut off, clenching his teeth. "If I had known, I wouldn't have dragged you into this."

Nylah swallowed, feeling smaller than ever under Jazz's tall frame. There was one thing that came up time and again in their father's endless years of research papers—the thing that had solidified Nylah's belief that all religious zealots were mad. "They're going to start making sacrifices, aren't they?"

Jazz didn't reply. The chill from the night had nothing to do with how cold Nylah's limbs suddenly felt. They strongly suspected goats weren't going to satisfy the gleam they'd seen in the head priest's eyes. Nylah pushed their glasses back up, their hand trembling slightly.

"Jazz, that's literally insane." Momentary panic made all their earlier worries of the day fade to the background. This was so much more serious than Nylah had realized. "Let's leave. We don't have to go back."

Jazz sighed, his shoulders falling in defeat. "The risk of leaving them now is too great. They know my face. They know where I live." When they'd left the church, Jazz had marked Nylah down as their roommate on the signup sheet. It was a lie Nylah reaffirmed without thinking twice.

"They're clearly erratic!"

"Exactly. And if they can't find willing tributes?" Jazz's dark eyes glinted with what Nylah realized was true, bone-deep fear. "Those people who voted no today will regret it. Anyone who stands against them will."

The thought of the four people who voted against the church made Nylah sick. This was all wrong.

"Murderers don't go to Elysium, Jazz. They don't even make it into Asphodel. You will either be cast to roam Purgatory forever or cursed to Tartarus for supporting this."

Nylah may have given up most of their faith but in their heart they believed in the Underworld's realms. *Heroes go to the glorious fields of Elysium; lost souls roam Purgatory forever; the wicked are cursed to Tartarus; the rest of the dead live out their afterlife in the city of Asphodel.*

Jazz pressed his eyes shut, shaking his head slowly.

"Nylah, I don't see any other option."

"You can't seriously stand beside them through this. Please, Jazz, leave them. I'm begging you." Nylah softened their hands, brushing a thumb over Jazz's sharp cheekbone, his deeply masculine beauty even harsher with the sadness casting over his features.

"I can't leave yet." Jazz let out a shuddering breath as he leaned into Nylah's touch. "Once Fates' Followers have their way and get compasses back, everything will go back to normal, and I'll leave then, I promise."

Compasses back. Jazz leaving the cult. It was everything Nylah wanted.

"Do you believe they can really do it?" Nylah whispered.

Jazz paused before letting out a shaky breath. "I know it's crazy, but yeah. I do."

Nylah stomped on the smoking butt of their almost-forgotten cigarette.

"Well, if you're staying, then I am too. I won't let you damn your soul alone."

Jazz glared. "Listen to me. No matter how hot you look in this suit, you will not put it on again. Do you understand me? You are going to go back to your sweet and colorful life, because I will not drag you down with me."

Nylah's cheeks flushed at the unexpected compliment. "You think I look hot?"

Jazz kept his gaze locked with theirs, a slight smirk at the corner of his mouth. "I will rip this jacket into shreds if it means keeping you safe." His hands moved slowly and intentionally, curving up and over Nylah's shoulders.

"I would just buy a new one," Nylah whispered, slightly awestruck. "Jazz, I—"

He placed a finger over Nylah's lips. "Stop."

Nylah froze, acutely aware of his proximity. For some reason, the night they'd first met flashed by in their mind, gone before Nylah could fully grasp it. That memory was always fickle. Neon strobe lights, sweaty dancing, and the heavy bass of electronic dance music dominated what little Nylah could remember from the night before their compasses arrived. They'd celebrated horribly hungover the next morning, the shared experience of finally being blessed by Cupid the exact same morning setting their friendship in stone.

Ever since the night they met, Jazz and Nylah had always been flirty with one another, but now that compasses were gone… Nylah wasn't sure what to think as he cupped their chin.

"Promise me, Nylah, that you won't come back. I don't have a choice, but you still have a chance."

Nylah shook their head slightly, surprised by the growing need to stay. Even if it meant joining a cult, Nylah wasn't going to leave Jazz alone in this mess. They were going to save him from this.

Nylah stood their ground. "I go where you go."

"Nylah—" The muscles of his jaw ticked as he cut himself off.

The plea in his eyes almost had Nylah convinced—until an odd shadow bent across the street, catching their attention. Nylah followed the arc to see a priest in crimson robes. She wore her hood up, but her dark eyes stayed level on Nylah and Jazz.

"We should get out of here," Nylah whispered. Jazz followed Nylah's stare, stiffening as he noticed their audience. Jazz cursed.

He took the lead, pulling Nylah under his arm as they walked briskly away.

"Great," Jazz sighed, his tone more brusque than usual. "For Fates' sake, Nylah, you have no idea what you signed up for."

A natural spring came into Nylah's step as Jazz agreed to let them join the cult. Nylah knew they had to make the most of every day now that the countdown to the end of their life had started. Beyond the fanatic cult and the fear of what extent they might go to, the worst part of today had come earlier that afternoon.

Nylah wondered if they should tell Jazz about the strange hourglass tattoo that had appeared on their inner forearm. Nylah had scoured the internet, but as far as they could tell, no one else was talking about the phenomenon. Only when they'd translated the Latin text did Nylah realize they were in deep, deep trouble.

Where there is love, there is pain.

The sands were falling fast, and Nylah knew without a doubt what it meant. This mark wasn't Cupid's compass. And if it didn't point to love, there was only one certain thing it could point to.

Death.

Nylah was going to die. They weren't sure if they had days or weeks, but so much sand already pooled in the bottom.

No, they couldn't tell Jazz about the new tattoo. It would certainly make things worse than they already were. Instead, Nylah needed to make the best of their time left, and if that time was spent saving Jazz from a cult, it would be worth it.

6 DAYS

UNTIL THE SUPERMOON

Cunning, and clever, and crafty to a fault,
This traveler's deity fills worshippers' vaults.
Earning his favor can yield both wealth and fertility,
But the cost of his prosperity is a person's tranquility.
For with his winged sandals and herald's staff he flies,
And wherever Mercury goes, he weaves chaos and lies.
—The Trickster

CHAPTER XVII

Twenty-four hours after receiving her new hourglass marker, Nessie faced her computer. Her mom had sorted out her task, which meant today they had to follow Nessie's mark. But Nessie wasn't about to go out searching without some sort of plan.

How to make someone fall in love with you. Typing the words into the internet search engine felt embarrassing. The question should have been easy to answer, yet so far all Nessie had scribbled on her notepad was:

1. *Look pretty*
2. *Be nice*
3. *...*

It was at that point she decided to do research. Unfortunately, many of the websites she scrolled didn't offer anything helpful. *Have unique interests, be funny, smell nice.* All these things sounded good in theory, but other than buying a new perfume, how was she supposed to adopt an entirely new personality overnight?

Nessie opened her phone to the group text she'd created last night between herself, her mom, Jaylynn, and Blake. The last messages glowed.

NESS TO CABIN CREW: Figured out Mom's task, hard to explain over text, though. You're going to have to see this for yourselves. Going to do mine tomorrow, then maybe we can meet up?

JAYLYNN: You guys are amazing!

BLAKE: Bring whiskey when you come.

Smirking at Blake's last message, Nessie tapped the phone keyboard as she turned to her last source for advice.

NESS: Any final suggestions on making someone fall in love with me before I go humiliate myself?

Three small dots appeared.

BLAKE: Shower? Don't be rude?

Nessie's dimples deepened as she suppressed a laugh.

JAYLYNN: Just be yourself!

She slumped. Herself was not going to cut it. She had only a matter of days to make this happen. Nessie needed to be perfect from the very first moment.

MOM: I agree with Jaylynn. You are already a wonderful person.

NESSIE: Wow. Here I thought the internet wasn't being helpful, but you all are actually worse.

She added a winky face to the end of the message before setting her phone down. Nessie pressed her eyes shut and kneaded the soft point between her eyebrows.

Think, Ness. Another text lit up her screen.

BLAKE: Stop thinking and start hunting.

Nessie groaned. Blake was right. She couldn't put this off any longer. Nessie rolled her chair back and faced her walk-in closet once again.

I just need to find something cute.

"Would you like help?"

The hairs on Nessie's arms shot up. She turned slowly, her attention landing on the small round mirror on her desk. Nessie didn't need to look twice at the flawless skin reflected back at her to know it was Venus. Her mouth went dry. On instinct, Nessie rushed to close her bedroom door. The last thing she needed was Lacey walking in.

Nessie stalked back to her closet, trying to appear less flustered than she felt. "No, thank you. I can do this myself."

"You do know I am also the goddess of beauty, don't you?" Venus cooed.

Nessie clenched her teeth but didn't answer. The unexpected presence of the goddess in her room made her stomach twist. What did it mean if Venus was free of the altar? Was the veil falling further? Was it only a matter of time until the goddess could walk free?

"Here, what about this?" Venus said, her eyes glittering. Before Nessie could object, Venus' invisible touch swirled around her. Nessie froze, the fear from the clearing rising again, crisp and new. The warm winds grew in force as they twisted around her, pulling at her hair and clothes. Nessie shut her eyes as her pulse hammered. The miniature tornado rocked the pictures on her walls and scattered the neatly organized papers on her desk. When the wind dissipated, Nessie took a shaky breath as her heart climbed up her throat. She didn't want to know what Venus had done.

"Come, now," the goddess drawled. "You aren't really going to turn down a goddess-blessed makeover, are you?"

Nessie forced down the rising tide of panic and opened her eyes. The first thing she saw was black. Nessie took a hesitant step into her en suite bathroom and her jaw dropped at her reflection. Venus hadn't changed anything physical about

Nessie's body. While that should have been a relief, Nessie couldn't stop the mounting horror as she absorbed everything Venus *had* changed.

Gone were her baggy sweater and comfy pants. In their place, Nessie wore a scandalous black dress. The dark sequined material reached only the tops of her thighs, and the neckline plunged way past her sternum. Nessie had never felt more naked despite the mesh sleeves and nylons covering her bare skin.

"What did you do?" Nessie crossed her arms over her chest, horrified to realize her bra had disappeared with the enchantment. "Venus! I can't go out in the middle of the day looking like this."

Her reflection flickered, and in its place golden eyes stared back at her.

"I think you look ravishing."

Nessie's voice shook as she fought back panicked tears. "I look like I'm going to a club."

Venus frowned. "You don't like it?"

"No!" Nessie exclaimed. "Change me back."

Venus ran her tongue over her teeth. "Maybe you're right. This is more of an evening look."

Before Nessie could object, her hair lifted as Venus' winds swirled anew. She stood frozen in fear, an impossible weight flattening her lungs and stealing her breath as the goddess's magic ravished her.

"How's that?"

Nessie staggered as the winds released her, grasping the side of the door for balance. She took in her new outfit between gasps. The skintight summer dress was even worse than the last. Pastel pink cotton clung to her curves, the thick straps and scooped neckline exposing her breasts even further. The dress was short enough that if she walked, her underwear would surely show. Nessie couldn't bear it. She spun out of the bathroom and raced to her bed, crawling under the large gray duvet as the tears struck.

Stars, I can't do this. I will not leave the house in this.

Nessie burrowed deeper in the blankets, cursing the stupid dress as it rode up. Every gasping breath hurt as Nessie tried to ward off the panic that flooded her senses. She clawed for any logical solution.

I'll just wait. Venus can't watch me all day. As soon as she leaves, I'll change and go find my task alone.

Even at the small semblance of a plan, blood pounded in Nessie's ears. She could be in here for days. She might starve. And if Venus could change Nessie's clothes, what was stopping the malevolent goddess from stripping her naked when she was out in the streets?

It was madness—Nessie knew that. Her mind spun the nightmares, each worse than the last, and all Nessie could do was sob into her sheets, wishing she could shut her brain off but instead being held hostage by her anxiety and terror.

An hour passed before Nessie forced herself to creep out of bed. She tiptoed, her breathing as quiet as a mouse as she edged toward her closet, afraid any noise might draw the goddess's attention. Nessie peeled off the pink dress and threw it to the ground. She grabbed for the closest thing of her own: her favorite periwinkle summer dress. The familiar curls of flowers and flowy skirts were easily a thousand times better than Venus' offerings. Nessie stepped into the dress carefully.

No makeup, no hair. Avoid mirrors and reflections at any cost.

But as Nessie turned, the haunting feeling of Venus' magic swirled her skirts around her thighs.

"No, no, no, no, no…" Nessie grasped at the skirts of her dress as they shrank before her eyes, up and over her knees. The bodice tightened and the neckline opened up, displaying her heaving chest once again. She thought she'd run out of tears, but Nessie was wrong.

I'm never going to be able to leave this room. I am never going to complete my task, and we're all going to fail.

The small rational part of her brain whispered she needed to go, no matter how much she hated Venus' makeover, but the weight of it was suffocating. Nessie couldn't walk out into the world when she felt so vulnerable and exposed. Nessie crawled back into her bed, grieving her favorite dress. She cried for the baggy sweater and pants she'd been wearing this morning, and for her most comfortable bra, all gone like they never existed.

And when her breathing started to slow, Nessie wondered what she'd done to fall so far on the bad side of the gods.

CHAPTER XVIII

"Wait, do you hear that?" Blake stilled as the sound of crunching gravel caught her attention. Jaylynn looked up from her book. She'd been folded up beside the fireplace all morning. Now she left the book spread open on the couch and crept forward to the window.

Jaylynn's fingers wrapped around the soft white curtain. "Do you think it's the police or the military?"

Blake hit the side of Jaylynn's triceps with the back of her hand. "Even if it were, we did nothing. We can't be held accountable. If anyone asks, we lost our compasses the same as everyone else. They can't prove anything."

Jaylynn's lips puckered, but she nodded.

It's probably a good thing Nessie and Charity aren't here if it is the police. That would be even more stories to keep straight.

A truck came around the bend in the road. It was an old dusty blue Ford.

Not authorities, then.

Something about the truck seemed off to Blake, and she slipped her hand into her jacket pocket. Her fingers landed on cool wood and metal. Jaylynn wasn't a scrapper, and Psyche was still unconscious. Dealing with whoever these strangers were was up to her.

"Back away from the door," Blake murmured, her grip tightening on the folded knife. Blake took a breath, stepping back from the window as the truck engine halted. Jaylynn crossed over to the counter, her fingers wrapping around the handle of a frying pan before she retreated to Psyche's side.

Blake shot her a look. "What are you doing?"

Jaylynn shrugged but didn't let go of her grip on the pan.

Boots crushed up the gravel, heavy and slow. Blake's heart rate doubled. A large shadow fell across the window, and Jaylynn looked at Blake for guidance.

Bang, bang, bang.

The knock was loud and demanding. Blake swallowed before stepping closer.

"Can I help you?" she called out, hopeful she could get around opening the door.

There was a scuffle of feet, and then a tall man's face filled the window. A grim expression frowned from under a ball cap. Blake instantly knew that face and scampered back before she could be seen.

No.

Blake lost her grip on the switchblade.

There's no way. It's impossible.

Jaylynn stepped forward, taking Blake's place without asking. Blake scoured her mind for any rational way it could be possible.

How did he find me?

Jaylynn cracked the door open, and Blake's knees wobbled.

"Hello, can we help you?" Jaylynn's smile and singsong voice were excessively cheerful.

White crackling filled Blake's ears as the man's deep voice responded. The desperate urge to hide blazed through Blake's veins.

Jaylynn gave a serene smile, her hand fluttering in a dismissive wave. Blake couldn't hear what was said as her mind tried to make sense of the moment.

Jaylynn closed the door.

"… waiting." Jaylynn's nose scrunched as she realized Blake wasn't listening. "Blake? Are you okay?"

Blake stared at Jaylynn.

It's impossible.

Jaylynn stepped in front of Blake and clasped both her arms. "Blake?"

Blake shook Jaylynn off, the touch giving her the jitters.

Jaylynn gave her an appraising look, then nodded toward the door. "I told him to wait by the campfire. He said he was looking for someone."

Blake couldn't answer. Fear and guilt beat in equal melodies, the orchestra of her emotions drowning out her ability to think.

"I asked him to give us a minute." Jaylynn glanced out the window. "You recognized him, didn't you?"

All Blake could do was nod.

"Where from? He seems nice enough. Is he going to give us trouble?"

Blake shook her head. "I don't know where. I was in the middle of nowhere when I met him. Some tiny mountain town."

Jaylynn narrowed her eyes. "Friend or foe?"

Blake's heart sank. "I don't know. Probably foe? We had a fling of sorts."

"And then…?"

Blake stared at Jaylynn, willing her to understand without an explanation. The memory of the compass-less man from the bar surged forward: his young face, his gentle hands, his patient kisses, his hopeful face before Blake ran away.

Jaylynn's face darkened. "Oh, gods, do you think this is Venus' task for you? To fall in love with him?"

The black pit of despair in Blake's belly deepened. *No, no, no, no, no…*

Jaylynn crossed her arms. "Well, there's only one way to find out. Get out there and say hi."

Blake shrunk back. "What? We didn't exactly part on the best terms."

Jaylynn raised a suspicious eyebrow. "What did you do?"

Blake pulled the knife out of the pocket of her leather jacket. The smooth wood was soft under her thumb as she traced over the engraved name: *Brooks.*

"I might have ransacked his house before I snuck out."

Jaylynn's suspicious look turned to a disapproving glare.

Blake didn't know what to say. She didn't know what to do.

"Well, if this is your task, it sounds like Venus intentionally picked a challenging one. First, we need to go out there and figure out what he knows, if anything."

Blake attempted to stall by pulling her fingers through her limp, faded blue hair and dashing blush onto her pasty cheeks, but it bought her only minutes before Jaylynn prodded her out of the cabin. To her relief, Jaylynn took the lead outside. Blake wished she could mimic Jaylynn's easygoing smile.

How does she do that? How can she possibly look happy right now?

Blake was getting the impression that Jaylynn was pretty good at faking her own happiness.

"Sorry to keep you waiting," Jaylynn called out. "You just caught us at the end of lunch. I'm Jaylynn."

The man stood and tipped his chin in greeting. His boyish face flushed dark when his eyes landed on Blake.

Jaylynn raised an eyebrow, but Blake's mouth stopped working.

"This is Blake," Jaylynn added, taking over.

"It's, uh, nice to meet you," the man responded. "I'm Hunter. Hunter Brooks."

Hunter. How strange to have a name to place on her one-night stand mountain man.

"Well, Hunter…" Jaylynn smiled as she sat by the fire and offered him a seat. "What brings you to our neck of the woods?"

Hunter turned to stare at Blake. "I was hopin' you could tell me."

Blake's face burned. She'd forgotten the soft drawl of his accent and his serious eyes. In the pocket of her leather jacket, the blade with his last name carved into the wood hung heavy.

Jaylynn took a seat on a lone tree stump. Blake moved forward with robotic steps, settling on a horizontal log. Hunter hovered uncertainly before settling next to her on the farthest edge of the log. Blake withered under Jaylynn's insistent stare. Her leather jacket felt too hot, too tight, and she knew she had to say something—she had to do anything but sit here doe-eyed and terrified. Blake fished the knife out of her pocket and handed it over.

"This is yours," she murmured. She knew she should apologize or explain, but nothing else came out.

Hunter's lips parted in surprise at the admission. Blake averted her eyes as he reached for it. She flinched as his fingers grazed the tips of hers, and she dropped the knife. That was when Blake saw it. The dark sphere with a distinct hourglass on Hunter's arm was a perfect replica of Nessie's and Charity's.

"You got the new tattoo, then?" she ventured.

Hunter shot her a look she couldn't read and then started rolling the knife between his fingers.

"I don't know what it is. I just woke up with it and I thought— well, I don't know what I thought. The sands were falling, so I followed it."

"To Canada?" Blake scrunched her nose, a touch more mocking than she'd meant to come off. Even though the drive between his home in Pennsylvania and the southern edge of Ontario couldn't have been more than a couple hours, it had taken Blake days to walk.

"I didn't know it would bring me here." Hunter's honey-brown eyes softened as he looked down at his knife. "It's crazy, ain't it? One day I was the only one without a compass, and the next the world didn't have tattoos and I did."

Jaylynn nodded. "A few of our friends got them too."

Blake frowned, not convinced that was good information to share.

Hunter glanced across the ashes of the firepit, his face etched with curiosity.

Blake interjected before Jaylynn spilled too much. "We don't know why, but we figured we'd keep it a secret for now, at least until we know more."

If Jaylynn was annoyed by Blake's insistence on keeping this under wraps, she didn't show it. The redhead leaned forward, a thin and sweet smile wide on her freckled face. "Hunter, I have to ask. Do you feel like your arrow, well, hourglass, points to someone specific?"

Hunter's eyes flashed to Blake, but he said nothing.

"Well." Jaylynn stood on some unspoken cue. "Blake, are you good if I finish cleaning up from lunch? Or would you rather I stay?"

Blake wasn't sure Jaylynn's presence was helpful, but the thought of being alone with Hunter made her insides squirm.

"Yeah. Go ahead. I'll, uh—" She didn't finish the sentence. She caught Hunter's eyes and fell into an uncomfortable silence.

Hunter's attention dropped back to the knife in his hands once Jaylynn was out of earshot. "Why did you take this?"

Blake deflated. She rested her head in her gloved hands. The healing blisters ached at the weight, but she deserved the sting. "I thought it would keep me safe on the road."

Hunter didn't respond, so Blake rambled on. "Listen, I'm sorry I didn't stay. I couldn't. And I shouldn't have stolen from you. I know that. It's just—" She waved her hands in the air as if the sky could explain her behavior and absence.

"This used to be my grandad's," Hunter murmured.

Blake swallowed, unsure why he'd changed the topic. Was that his way of forgiving her? She cleared her throat.

"I was never close with my family," she said. "Sometimes I forget other people are."

Hunter nodded. He flipped the blade out, rolling it in the light as if assessing it for damage, pausing as his hourglass tattoo glimmered in the sunshine. "I still don't understand why this thing brought me here."

"You mean to me."

His face was a mask of seriousness. "Yeah."

Blake tried to swallow the jab. "Maybe the stars don't have it out for you after all?"

He scoffed. "Or this is their way of continuing to punish me."

Blake wilted. This wasn't going the way she needed it to.

"I—I'm sorry." The apology felt insincere even though she meant it. She reached out to him and clasped his hand in hers.

Tatiana, her old girlfriend, had always responded better to apologies with Blake's touch. She could only hope Hunter would be the same. But if he was affected by her reaching out, he didn't show it. Instead, his face got impossibly harder. He pulled away.

"Brooks, I don't know what to say."

He looked up at her, his once-soft eyes now glowering. "It's fine. I know talkin' isn't your strong suit."

Blake felt a flare of resistance burn up her chest. As much as she wanted to lash back at him, she also knew she couldn't.

Everything depends on me falling in love with this man.

Nessie, Jaylynn, Charity. The whole world's compasses. If they were going to win, Blake needed to convince Hunter to stick around. Blake forced herself to lower her shoulders.

"You're right. I am far from perfect. You know that better than anyone. And as much as I want to be mad that you're here, honestly, I'm not." She dropped her voice to a whisper. "Maybe we were meant to come back together. Maybe our story wasn't done yet."

Hunter didn't smile. There was not an inch of forgiveness in his face as he got up, wordless.

Blake stood, a touch of panic catching her in its claws.

"Brooks?"

Hunter stopped at the sound of his last name, his fists clenched at his sides. Blake willed herself to be softer. To be sweeter. To be anything remotely like Jaylynn. "Would you stay? Here, I mean, at the cabin, until we can figure this out?"

His teeth grazed his bottom lip, frustration set in his jaw. Instead of returning to his truck, he turned to the cover of trees.

"I need to take a leak."

Blake sighed and leaned back as he walked away. This was the man Venus had chosen for her. The person she was supposed to fall in love with. And he hated her.

But at least we know what my task is now.

CHAPTER XIX

If yesterday's drive through the city had felt like the calm before the storm, today it was as if the fury of the gods had been unleashed. Gareth swallowed as they passed yet another abandoned car with smashed windows and keyed doors. His knee bounced with nerves in the back seat as they drove on.

"The gallery was hit." Those were the only words Winona had been able to whisper when she'd gotten off the phone this morning. Mikom had shifted out of his naturally stoic quietness as his wife wavered on her feet and fell apart. On his orders, the whole Hart family had dressed and loaded into the van in less than five minutes, all of them imagining the worst.

Now, as Mikom coasted up the gallery street, everyone held their breath. Then Winona let out a pained cry that tore Gareth's heart in half. She was tumbling out of the van even before Mikom had parked, and they all rushed in behind her, ducking under the yellow caution tape that crisscrossed the front.

The state of the gallery was worse than Gareth had expected. While every store down the lane had varying levels of damage to their front, Winona's wide front windows had given the rioters an easy entry point. Shattered glass projected across the wood floors. Gareth gasped as he stepped inside after the twins. Neon spray paint covered everything in hostile slashes, ruining masks and paintings alike. The side of the canoe was destroyed by bright pink jagged lines. Canvases split open by knives hung limp on the walls. All the stands that held hand-carved masks had been knocked over, the ceramic ones smashed to pieces.

Dyani clutched her bag to her chest, tears dripping down her cheeks. Always her opposite, Tokala's eyes were hard and glazed with anger as she took in the vandalism. Mikom held Winona tight as she fell apart in his arms, fighting his own impending tears.

A short police officer was already on scene waiting for them, a notepad in her hand. Gareth and the twins lingered a few steps back as Winona made her statement between sobs.

"We're going to get them. It's only a matter of time." The officer gave Winona a compassionate squeeze. "Any camera recordings you can supply will help."

Gareth followed the group to the back room in a trance. The storage space had been spared from the graffiti because it was locked, and all five people stood in shocked silence as they watched the video playback on a small telly. The camera was tucked in the front corner, so the assailants all had their backs to it when they entered. Their bats and crowbars pounded the open air in celebration, and though there was no sound to the video, Gareth could imagine their delighted hollering. They smashed art pieces at random, covering the ground in beadwork and feathers. Then the spray paint came out. The vandals were quick and dirty about it, racing around wall to wall, leaving their mark everywhere.

Winona's wails deepened as the rioters turned toward the front and one figure pointed to the camera. They wore strange metal masks, almost gladiator shaped, obscuring any details of their gender or race. One vandal climbed up on the front desk and spray-painted the camera until the video was a white blur.

"Why would they do this?" Dyani's voice caught. Her long nails clawed into her sister's arm.

The police officer shook her head. "Who can say. All I know is crime has been getting worse every day since compasses disappeared." As the uniformed woman went over the next steps of their investigation, Gareth left the back room. The footage replayed in his mind as he looked over the disaster. Winona had done nothing to deserve this kind of hostility. None of the Harts had.

"They all deserve to rot in Tartarus for this." Tokala appeared on his left, startling Gareth out of his own brooding. She picked a carved wooden mask off the floor, turning it over to assess the damage.

Gareth nodded and picked up a face-down canvas. The picture of the brightly painted turtle was torn through the middle. He grimaced and ran his finger over the slashed artwork. They both turned as a growing chatter came from around the corner. Sebastian and Huan froze in the frame of the shattered window, their jaws hanging in disbelief.

"No—" Huan's shoulders fell as he took in the scene.

Sebastian stepped carefully over the glass, scanning the room in horror.

"You guys came." Gareth's cheeks burned. He'd texted Sebastian when the call first came, but once he laid eyes on the gallery he'd completely forgotten. Now Gareth wasn't sure Winona needed more people here to witness the massacre.

"Of course we did, mate." The pity in Sebastian's voice only made Gareth feel worse. Why did it seem like ever since he'd arrived in Canada things just kept getting worse?

Huan shook his head as he looked around. "Pain and fear make people act in horrifying ways." He went to Winona's side as the officer lifted the tape to leave. "Come, sit." Huan guided Winona to the stool at the front. "Mikom, are there any blankets here?"

Mikom nodded, soothing his own fury to focus on his wife. Gareth massaged his scalp, overwhelmed at everything ahead of them. Who would do something like this? What benefit did all this destruction bring? And how could they possibly fix everything that was ruined?

"How can we help?" Sebastian asked.

Dyani sniffed and brushed away a tear. "We should probably start by clearing whatever glass we can. There's brooms in the back."

Twenty minutes later, everyone had a job. Winona had wrapped herself in a thick woven blanket at the front desk and oversaw the work, deciding which pieces could be salvaged. Her sobs never stopped for more than a few minutes at a time. Mikom and Huan took turns at her side, holding her through the worst of her grief. Gareth carried a large black garbage bag while Sebastian and Tokala found brooms and swept up the glass. Dyani gathered all the dresses, ponchos, and any other fabric splattered with paint, adamant she would be able to fix them.

Even in the early-afternoon sun, the studio felt like a graveyard. Gareth's heart sank heavier in his chest. He didn't have the energy to make jokes or try to make the others smile. Instead, he focused on the job at hand, deep in thought—if things were this bad here, how bad must they be back home?

CHAPTER XX

One day. That was how long it took for Charity to admit she knew nothing about raising a puppy. She'd given her bedroom up to Lacey and slept on the couch last night beside Ladybug's crate. And while the constant threat of tiny teeth was doing untold damage to Charity's hands and arms, there were benefits to housing the mini velociraptor. Having to keep a constant watch kept Charity's mind busy.

Charity rested her head on the cupboard as the water for her morning tea boiled. Ladybug—apparently not at all tired after crying all night—raced by, her body hardly keeping up with her tiny feet. She jumped up Charity's leg, and when Charity didn't give her the reaction she wanted, Ladybug bit the dish towel down from the stove handle, then pranced away. Charity couldn't help but smile as the puppy stumbled away with her prize.

Who would have thought the best dog toy in the house would be a dish towel?

Lacey came downstairs in her pj's: an oversized band T-shirt and plaid shorts. Ladybug dropped the towel, barking in excitement as Lacey stepped over the gate.

"Good morning, Ladybug." Lacey scratched the dog's ear. "I see you're still being a brat."

The kettle flicked off and Charity poured herself a cup of chamomile tea. "Would you like tea, Lacey?"

"No, thank you."

Charity joined Lacey at the kitchen table, and Ladybug curled up in the corner with a huff. Hardly a minute passed before the puppy's eyes were drifting closed. Charity was strongly considering joining Ladybug's impromptu nap when Lacey spoke again, her voice hushed and concerned.

"I don't know how to fix things with Ness."

Realigning her place mat, Charity thought of her daughter shut in her room upstairs. She knew how deeply Lacey had hurt Nessie. She wasn't even sure she herself had forgiven Lacey for the girl's stunt yet.

"You've tried apologizing?" Charity asked.

"Yeah, but she won't hear me out. She's still so mad."

"Well, Lacey, she's allowed to be angry." Charity dipped her tea bag a few times. "An apology doesn't erase the other person's feelings. Give her time. I'm sure she'll come around."

There was a doubtful look in Lacey's wide hazel eyes. "And if she doesn't?"

At this, Charity could only sigh. "Nessie can be firm when she sets her mind to something, but she's also compassionate. You're just going to have to be patient as she processes her grief and decides what she wants moving forward."

"I didn't mean to hurt her," Lacey whispered.

Charity gave Lacey a knowing look. "The way you treated her is not how friends treat one another. Your actions speak louder than your words. If you want to win Ness back, you're going to have to prove it with more than an apology."

Lacey swallowed hard, her eyes cast down. As the words landed between them, Charity worried if this was the right advice to give. The last thing Nessie needed right now was Lacey badgering her for attention. Charity wasn't even sure she wanted Lacey and Nessie to make up.

Either way, it isn't my choice.

Ultimately, it fell to Nessie to decide whether she would let Lacey back in. Charity could only pray her daughter would make the right call. As Charity scoured for solutions, she realized just how much was on her plate. She needed support.

"You know, I bet Ladybug would love River's cabin." Charity sipped her tea. "We could go tomorrow for the afternoon."

"Who's River?" Lacey asked.

"Oh, one of our new friends. She has a beautiful cabin out of town. Ness and I were talking about going back for a day trip."

"What friends are these?"

Charity slowed herself as she spoke, trying to sort out what truths she could share. "Well, Lacey, since we last saw you, we've had some interesting new developments in the family. Before compasses disappeared, I actually was blessed with a new soulmate link. After you and Renee left us on the weekend, Nessie and I followed my mark."

"What?" Lacey's voice peaked in pitch, a blend of shock and excitement.

"I'm not really sure why," Charity mused, "but it brought me to Jaylynn. Not in a romantic way, mind you. But I think we were meant to help one another move on after both losing our soulmates."

Lacey leaned back in her chair. "Huh, I guess we were both lucky to meet our matches before compasses disappeared, then."

Charity coughed at the subtle mention of Lacey's news. "Oh, congrats, Lacey. It's great to hear you found your soulmate. When do we get to meet them?"

"Damien has a soccer game tomorrow night—well, he calls it football—and I was hoping to go."

Charity's shoulders sank as yet another responsibility fell into her overflowing lap.

Venus' tasks. Nessie's heartbreak. The hyper puppy. And now Lacey's social calendar.

"Where is the game, and at what time?"

"It's at eight, so kind of late, and in Toronto somewhere. I can get him to text me the details."

The weight of another task threatened to collapse Charity's resolve.

But Renee isn't here.

"We will do our best to make it."

Lacey smiled gratefully. "I was thinking, maybe today I could go back to the hospital and spend time with my mom… if it's not too much trouble."

"You don't need to ask to go see your mom, Lacey. I will happily take you." Charity sighed and dropped her voice. "How are you doing with all of that?"

"I… I don't know. Dad says Mom's improving. She's still sleeping most of the time, and I think he's barely keeping it together."

Charity leaned closer, the soft wrinkle of her brow deepening as Lacey's eyes went glossy.

"If she's improving, why the tears?"

Lacey took a couple of rapid breaths. "I just—It's all my fault." The confession spilled out and Charity froze.

"What is?"

Lacey burrowed her head in her arms. "The fact she was in an accident. If I would have waited… if I hadn't gone looking for

Damien… we would have never been in Toronto— What if she died?" Lacey cut off as a deeper sob caught in her throat.

Charity stood and went to Lacey's side. "She's going to be okay, Lacey. The doctors are doing all they can. We can leave within the hour if seeing her will help reassure you."

"Thank you." Lacey sniffled and rubbed at her face. Charity's heart panged in guilt, because it wasn't only the girl's fault that everything went haywire that day.

"Come on, Ness. It's time to go." Charity knocked on her daughter's door for what felt like the fifteenth time that morning.

"Just go without me," Nessie murmured through the door.

"You are not spending any more time holed up in this room. Once we drop Lacey off at the hospital, we can run a few errands and get lunch." By errands, Charity meant following Nessie's tattoo, but she wasn't about to call that out when Lacey was just down the hall.

A disgruntled moan came through the door.

"You have ten seconds to open this door, Ness. That is my hard limit."

There was a series of shuffling before the door unlocked.

Nessie peeked through the crack. "Where's Lacey?"

Charity rolled her eyes and pushed her daughter's door open. Nessie had her duvet blanket wrapped around her shoulders. She tripped as she stepped out of Charity's way and dove to close the door behind her. A patch of powder blue popped out from under the gray blanket.

Charity frowned, taking in the black circles under her daughter's eyes. "What is going on with you, Ness? Out with it."

Nessie's lip trembled, then she dropped the blanket. Charity barely recognized the dress she'd bought her daughter last summer. "Is that…?"

"Yes." Nessie's lip wobbled as she flopped down on her bed. "Venus ruined it."

"Venus did this?" Charity glanced around the room, noting the missing mirror from Nessie's desk and the closed bathroom door. She also considered what it meant if the goddess was starting to affect things in the physical world like Nessie's clothes.

Nothing good.

"She tried to sabotage me with my task by giving me a makeover. One I can't seem to undo." Nessie dropped her eyes as if ashamed.

"Honey, why didn't you tell me? Is this why you've been hiding up here?"

Not hiding. Stuck. She's been stuck up here and I thought she just needed space from Lacey.

Nessie batted a tangle of hair away from her face. "I couldn't bring myself to leave."

"It's not so bad. You've always looked great in this color." Charity's attempt at comfort was met with an unrelenting glare. Nessie pointed at her chest.

"And you're fine with me going out like this?"

Charity swallowed. "Well, it is a little… revealing." She stood and went to her daughter's closet.

"Please don't, Mom. I don't want Venus to ruin any more of my stuff." The plea in Nessie's eyes was desperate, and Charity's heart fractured at the sight of her daughter's torment. She pulled the cream-colored cardigan off her own shoulders and handed it over.

Nessie shot a nervous glance at the bathroom, then pulled each sleeve on. They both held their breath waiting for a chiming laugh, but nothing came. Nessie looked so relieved she could have melted into the bed.

"Come to Toronto with me," Charity urged, anxious to get away from Venus' haunting presence.

"I can't." The way Nessie's vocal cords wavered plucked at Charity's heart. "Please. Take Lacey and just leave me here today. My head is killing me, and I feel sick to my stomach."

There was a long pause before Charity spoke again. "Okay, well… promise me you'll eat while we're out and call me if you need anything."

Charity gave her daughter a hard hug, wondering if they could afford to waste a day of Nessie hunting for her mark, but she couldn't force Nessie to do anything.

CHAPTER XXI

"So, Hunter. Tell me a bit about where you're from." Jaylynn did her best to keep the peace as the two storm clouds of tension swirled in the cabin while she diced potatoes for her soup. In typical Blake fashion, the grumpy tattooed girl stalked around the room like a caged tiger.

Hunter shrugged. He'd taken off his tan leather jacket and now sat at the kitchen table. His hands were knit together, and he had a glower that could almost match Blake's. *Almost.*

"Small town in Pennsylvania. Nothin' special. Spent the last couple years working at the lumberyard in the mountains."

Jaylynn smiled. "Did you like it there?"

Blake finally stopped her pacing to sit on the edge of Psyche's cot. Hunter didn't ask many questions after Jaylynn explained their friend was sick, but she had no clue how long they could pass Psyche's magical coma off as a simple illness. Especially if Hunter planned to stay here.

"Meh." Hunter shrugged.

Jaylynn forced her smile to stay in place as she stirred the boiling vegetables. "I was just telling Blake we'd need to cut more firewood soon. We're lucky you turned up." Across the room, Blake crossed her arms. They had not, in fact, had that conversation, but Jaylynn knew she would roll with it. Blake was a born liar.

"My last job was at an animal shelter," Jaylynn offered, desperate to find something Blake and Hunter might be able to talk about.

"Does that pay well?" Hunter asked.

Jaylynn chuckled. "Well, I guess it wasn't really a job. I volunteered there."

Hunter seemed perplexed by this information. "How did you afford to live?"

"Her parents were obviously rich," Blake interjected.

Jaylynn's smile slipped slightly. "My family isn't *rich*. But yes, they were supporting me before I came out here to be with Psyche full-time."

Hunter and Blake both stared at her.

Shoot, I should have said River...

But there was no way Hunter would think their friend was the famous Psyche. At least, that's what Jaylynn tried to tell herself. Jaylynn floundered, desperate to shift the spotlight from herself and recover from the mistake.

"What about you, Blake? Were you working before…" She trailed off, not sure how to finish that sentence.

Blake shrugged. She picked at the edges of her fingerless gloves. "I've done lots of jobs over the years. Waiter. Tattoo apprentice. Whatever I could do to keep a roof over my head. Not all of us have mommies and daddies paying our bills."

The jab stung a little, but Jaylynn willed herself to stay composed. Of course Blake would resent how easy Jaylynn seemed to have it, but she had no idea what it was like living under her parents' thumbs. Jaylynn sorted through Psyche's glass jars of herbs for the thyme, trying to think of something they could talk about that wouldn't inspire Blake's barbs.

"So, how did you two meet?" Jaylynn ventured. "Before, I mean."

Hunter cast a glance over to Blake, then stood. "Do you have any beer?"

Jaylynn sputtered to a halt. "I— No, I'm sorry. Psyche never drank."

Hunter let out a sigh and sat back down.

"I could get you some kombucha?"

"The last thing anyone wants is kombucha," Blake groaned.

Jaylynn crossed her arms, affronted. "Psyche's is homemade and fantastic."

Hunter shot Jaylynn a wary glance. "What is… kamboochaa?"

The way he drew out the word experimentally brought a spring back to Jaylynn's step as she went to pour him a glass. "It's a fermented black tea!"

She turned back, jug in hand, to see Hunter's stricken face.

"Really, you have to try it before you judge. Don't listen to Blake. She hates everything."

Jaylynn winced, realizing her comment probably wasn't helpful when they were actively trying to create feelings of romance and love. The tall glass jug swirled with a cranberry hue as Jaylynn poured three short glasses. She slid one across the kitchen table to Hunter, then handed the other to Blake.

"Cheers!" Jaylynn held her glass out toward Hunter in a toast. "To trying new things."

Blake saluted her glass, squinted at the cup for a heartbeat, then slugged the whole thing back. Her face contorted as she smacked her lips.

"I think it's time we stock the liquor cabinet." Blake coughed.

Hunter sipped from his cup as if it was poisoned. When he noticed Jaylynn was watching him, he took a deep breath, then chugged it back. The scrunch of his button nose suggested he shared Blake's sentiment.

Well, at least I've given them some common ground to bond over.

As she had dozens of times in the last couple hours, Jaylynn peeked out the window to the darkening sky, curious if anyone else would wander up the road. She was torn between morbid curiosity and desperation for her task to reveal itself. Then there was the question of how everything worked. Would her tasked person and their partner both have hourglasses, or would only one of them? And how was she supposed to start her task of reconnecting lovers if she didn't have a clue who they were? What role exactly was she meant to play if Venus' goal was to prove how frail love was?

Jaylynn checked her soup, then excused herself to the bathroom. She already knew what she would find there. Since this morning, she couldn't stop coming back. In the mirror, her reflection twinkled a golden hue of glory. Jaylynn rested her wrists on the sink edge as she stared starry-eyed.

Mirror Jaylynn appeared exactly as Venus had in the clearing but without the golden eyes. She wore her lace-sleeved wedding dress with a circlet of eucalyptus and baby's breath crowning her hair. There was a healthy pink glow to her freckled cheeks. Jaylynn smiled wide, dazed with genuine happiness. But it wasn't the dress that drew her back to the bathroom every couple of hours. It was the reflection of the man standing behind her.

"Elias," Jaylynn whispered. She reached for the mirror, her hand meeting cool glass where her dead fiancé's face reflected back to her. Elias glowed with joy, his round cheeks and red-tinged beard exactly as she remembered them. Jaylynn's heart could have burst as she swept over his features, soaking up this impossibility. She knew Venus was playing mind games with her, showing her the beauty and happiness she could never have, but Jaylynn couldn't help herself from stealing this bit of fantasy and wishing in some other world it might be reality.

"You know, you could join him." Venus' voice broke Jaylynn's reverie. It was the first time Jaylynn's reflection had spoken. Elias kissed the side of Venus' head and hugged her close, as if she'd just said the sweetest thing.

Jaylynn didn't know what to say. Her previous joy morphed into something thick and taut.

"Come, now." Venus smiled. "Don't you want to join your lover in the Underworld? To have and to hold?"

The sound of the fire grate drew Jaylynn's focus away from the mirror. When she looked back, Elias was gone. Only Venus remained. Jaylynn's fingers curled, her heart crashing with disappointment. She pursed her lips and dropped her voice.

"Elias is in Elysium. Only heroes go there. I wouldn't get to join him if I killed myself." It was a dark truth, but one that had stayed Jaylynn's hand in the darkest months after her almost-husband's passing.

Venus' eyes twinkled. "So sure of yourself. Why exactly do you think Elias earned Elysium? What did he do to roam the fields of paradise?"

Jaylynn froze. "He… he deserved Elysium." But even as she thought back, Jaylynn questioned it. Did dying in a fire make his soul special enough to go where heroes went? Or would he end up in Asphodel, Pluto's great city where most souls went to rest? Elias was the best human she knew, but how did the god of the Underworld sort souls?

"Well, if you're so sure your fiancé was made of all things pure, then maybe you're right." Venus massaged the palm of her hand.

Jaylynn leveled her shoulders and gave one last wistful glance at her wedding dress.

"Well, as wonderful as this is, I have a couple to help fall in love."

At least, that was Jaylynn's plan. She might not know who her mark was yet, but she could help Blake with her task every minute until she did. Jaylynn left the mirror of madness to return to her two storm clouds, her intention set.

CHAPTER XXII

The sour smell of the cult chamber had an extra acidic tang to it tonight as Nylah and Jazz entered the vast space. Candle chandeliers cast shadows left and right. There must have been fifty people assembled today, half in black, half in crimson. The head priest greeted the lineup of guests, and Nylah's nose scrunched as he kissed their foreheads one by one.

"Give him the customary greeting," Jazz mumbled.

Nylah rolled their eyes. That was the easiest part to guess and fake. Jazz went first, grasping the pudgy priest's hand with vigor.

"Father."

The priest tilted his head in acknowledgment. "Child of the Fates."

"May the Fates be with you."

"And with you."

Then it was Nylah's turn to stare into the heavy-lidded eyes of the priest. As they shook hands, Nylah tried not to look disgusted as his clammy hand grasped theirs.

The priest paused as he scanned Nylah's face. "Have we met before?"

Nylah cleared their throat. "No, Father. I recently moved from Montreal." Their tongue felt like it weighed a dozen pounds at the rehearsed lie. "But I was grateful to know your city also hosts meetings."

The bridge of Nylah's glasses slid down their freckled nose as they tilted their chin in deference, but Nylah suppressed the urge to push them back up. Whatever the priest saw seemed to suit him as he squeezed their hand once more.

"Welcome, child of the Fates."

Nylah grimaced as his lips fell on their brow. They bowed before fleeing back to Jazz's side. He had come up with one rule if Nylah wanted to tag along for these meetings: they had to be forgettable, nothing more than a shadow in a crowd.

It will all be worth it if we can bring compasses back. At least Nylah hoped it would. Nylah personally wouldn't benefit if compasses came back. It would be too late if their fated hourglass death came as expected. There was no world where Nylah would find out if the boy at the coffee shop was their soulmate anymore, and they had come to terms with that. But if the cult succeeded in getting magic back? Jazz would get his tattoo back, and he'd be able to find his soulmate. And maybe, just maybe, he'd be okay once Nylah was gone. At least, that's what Nylah was now telling themself.

"That was different," Jazz murmured as they exited the greeting line. "And did you notice the new camera installed in the entry?"

Nylah nodded, only half paying attention as they walked arm in arm deeper into the chamber. Around them, people murmured in private hushed tones, a nervous energy crackling among the crowd. Jazz continued across the room, passing the statue of the three Fates, to the farthest wall, which featured an enormous fireplace. It hadn't been lit during Nylah's previous two visits, so they'd never noticed how giant it was. A mediocre fire burned that barely filled half of the grate.

"How nice of them to make it even stuffier in here tonight," Nylah commented, picking at a piece of lint on their black dress pants. Jazz gave Nylah a pointed stare suggesting he didn't appreciate the sarcasm, then cocked his head.

A new sound rose above the murmurs: a quiet clattering, like metal on metal. Nylah sagged into Jazz's side as two figures were led into the room from the stairway. They were both worse for wear, their black clothes covered in mud as if they'd put up a fight, their faces freshly bruised black and blue.

"Let me guess," Nylah said, sucking in a breath. "This is new too?"

Jazz grabbed Nylah's hand, anchoring them both in place as he nodded. The prisoners were led behind the head priest, their wrists chained and linked together, but instead of walking to the front of the room, his billowing robes stopped at the foot of the Fates statue in the center. Everyone reoriented themselves. Nylah and Jazz hovered at the back of the circle. The church was so quiet that Nylah could hear every labored breath the woman prisoner took.

I know her.

The chained woman had dirt on her cheeks, streaked from tears, but Nylah could still see the birthmark on her face. The prisoner was one of the four people who had voted no at the previous meeting. Nylah glanced at the man in tattered clothes to confirm their suspicion. Though less recognizable than the dark-eyed woman, the combination of circumstance and his shorter disposition suggested he was the solo male who'd left that night. Bruises scattered his face, and the swelling made his eyes mere slits.

"Welcome. Welcome. Welcome." The priest took an extended breath between each word, seeming to savor the fearful anticipation humming in the sticky air. "For the purpose of creating a perfect, safe place of worship, you may have noticed we have increased our security measures."

Yes, such a safe place, Nylah thought coolly. *One where if you leave, you get chased down and beaten.*

"As you all know," the priest continued, "the world as we know it is changing. The veil between gods and man continues to weaken. As such, the devoted must take advantage of this time and pay our utmost respect to the Fates while we are most likely to be heard."

Nylah clawed the edges of their nails into Jazz's hand, a silent request to lighten up on his death grip, which was making their hand go numb. His hold softened incrementally.

"Gone are the days where mortals can get away with half-hearted prayers and inadequate offerings. The Fates do not want the last piece of your meal. They demand the first bite. They do not want your oath to remember them. They demand your undying piety."

The chained man and woman were ushered forward until they stood on the long flat plaques that circled the statue, each depicting a different Roman god. Nylah cringed at the memory of the cult's burning salvia being poured over the gods' faces, its flames licking at the three headless Fates' feet as the priest forswore the other deities.

"Jazz?" Nylah whispered.

He shook his head, silencing them.

Don't draw attention to yourself. Be forgettable.

Was this why Jazz didn't want Nylah noticed? Were less pious followers often punished? Based on the unanimous concern etched on the faces of the crowd, Nylah guessed most of Fates' Followers also didn't know what was going on. The head priest turned, pointing to one of the men along the back wall.

"The lever, please."

Crimson robes swished as the ordered priest hurried toward the fireplace. He rested his hands on a long wooden bar and waited.

"And as with all rituals, the oldest always holds the most power." The head priest nodded, and the man beside the fireplace wrapped his hands around the bar, prying it from the wall. It must have been both heavy and rusted over, because it groaned, refusing to be pulled all the way down. After an awkward moment, another priest joined the first, the two leaning their bodies against the lever until it finally gave in, snapping into a downward position.

The sound of whirring machinery and grinding gears filled the room, and people gasped, many stumbling backward. Slowly, the statue of the three Fates rose, then glided in the direction of the fireplace. The chained woman let out a sob, and the hunched man at her side panicked, fighting to be released. Another priest stepped in to hold them in place.

In the middle of the floor, a giant black hole appeared. The god portraits that once circled the feet of the Fates now framed a pit into the earth, easily six feet in diameter. Nylah crushed Jazz's hand as every nerve in their body screamed at them to leave.

"BEHOLD!" The head priest held out his arms as the statue of the three Fates locked into a new position. His gold-cuffed sleeves swung dramatically. "The greatest sacrifice to the darkest place beyond Terra Mater." The priest turned, his gaze narrowing on the two shaking in chains. "May the Fates feast on your Tartarus-cursed souls."

Nothing could have stopped the momentum of the two people as they were shoved into the pit, but Nylah cried out anyway. Jazz's hand clamped over Nylah's mouth and pinned their body to his chest. It was a mistake to scream, but luckily there were many other gasps and cries, and everyone's eyes were on the pit. The initial uproar quickly silenced, and the screeching horror of the unwilling sacrifices got quieter and quieter as they fell. Nylah waited for a thud, for any kind of end to their haunting cries to indicate they'd hit the bottom, but it never came. The screaming just kept getting softer.

How far does that pit go?

Tears sprang to the corners of Nylah's eyes and they shoved an elbow into Jazz's ribs, wanting to be released.

"Don't do anything to get noticed," Jazz hissed.

Nylah did not need to be told twice. What they needed was to be able to breathe and to look less suspicious. Jazz released their mouth but kept a firm grip on Nylah's waist. Around them, people turned away, many faces cast in pale shock.

None of them knew…

The head priest pivoted, taking in their reactions. Nylah swallowed as their survival instinct kicked in. They lifted their chin, doing their best to look unaffected.

"May the Fates see our offerings as but the beginning of our devotion to the return of compass tattoos."

Nylah sank a bit into Jazz's side as the unspoken threat landed. They were in danger. Real, physically threatening danger. A new realization crept in behind the first. Nylah's hourglass tattoo had appeared the day they'd come back to the cult. The blackness of the pit seemed to curl up and out as Nylah tried to take a steadying breath.

Was being sacrificed by the cult how they were going to die?

CHAPTER XXIII

BLAKE

Blake yawned, the warm fire coaxing the long day to a close. She'd spent so much of it high-strung, second-guessing everything she said and did. Now she was hitting a wall. Blake curled up in the rocking chair by the fire as Hunter paced, both unsure what to do or where to go.

"Ugh!" Jaylynn stumbled back from the stovetop as her metal whisk clattered to the ground. Blake sat up straighter. Jaylynn had changed into forest-green satin pj's after dinner. The copper tones of her hair were brighter than ever against the button-up, and the tiniest pinch of angry heat flared in Blake's sternum when she'd seen Jaylynn's bare legs.

You couldn't have worn something else in front of Hunter? Seriously?

Jaylynn was clearly clueless how good she looked in satin shorts, though, her attention set instead on whatever mess she was making in the kitchen.

"You okay over there?" Blake asked. After cleaning up their soup—which Blake refused to admit was delicious—Jaylynn had returned to the stovetop with a large leather-bound book in tow. It'd been over an hour of the girl fussing over ingredients and murmuring to herself.

"No, I am not *okay,*" Jaylynn whined. All day Jaylynn had been the epitome of kind and cheerful in Hunter's presence. The hint that her facade might be coming to an end gave Blake mixed feelings.

"Do you need help?" Hunter stopped to pick up the dropped whisk.

Jaylynn bookmarked her page as he came close. "You wouldn't mind? I swear this steam is seeping through my bandages and making my hands worse."

Blake stood and glanced at the oversized pot on the stovetop. The contents were a thick, bubbling pale pink mixture. Her hope that Jaylynn was cooking up something yummy disappeared at the sight of the liquid. It looked nothing like the kombucha from earlier but left Blake just as wary.

"What can I do?" Hunter asked.

"Can you keep stirring this?" Jaylynn brushed her hair over a shoulder. Blake would have given anything to have such rich, thick curls instead of her own too-thin bleached hair.

"Sure." Hunter took Jaylynn's spot as she worked around him, grabbing various dried flower bunches from Psyche's collection. Blake tried not to outright glower as the two settled into companionable silence.

Three things were irking Blake. First was Jaylynn's never-ending attempt at acting like everything was completely fine when she was clearly faking it, though there were hints she might be reaching her breaking point.

Second was Hunter's silence. He never asked any questions. He didn't ask about Psyche or their matching burns. He just wandered around helplessly until Jaylynn gave him a task—which brought her to the third item of frustration: Hunter did everything Jaylynn asked.

"You know, you can say no to her," Blake jeered.

"But he won't," Jaylynn sang as she held up a jar of rose petals, "because he's a gentleman."

Psyche's quiet presence drew Blake away from the dynamic kitchen duo. The comatose woman haunted the main room of the cabin, tucked under blankets on the cot under the window. It was the cot Blake had been sleeping on prior to the apocalypse (as Blake now considered recent events, thanks to the convenience store clerk), before she'd taken over the couch. Blake fussed with the tips of Psyche's cool fingers, uncovered by the bandages. She gently kneaded warmth into them.

If we fail, she won't ever wake up. The truth sat heavy in Blake's lap. She'd spent so much of this day angry with Venus and Jaylynn that she'd barely worked toward completing her task. But here Psyche was, withering away, incapable of saving herself.

"Ow," Jaylynn cursed under her breath. Blake looked back to see her trying to open a jar.

"Here." Hunter held out a patient hand, and Jaylynn gave him a huge smile as he opened it for her.

Blake was officially over it. She couldn't sit here for another minute watching Jaylynn and Hunter play house. She stalked over before she could change her mind.

"What can I do to help?"

The way Jaylynn's face lit up, Blake would have guessed she'd won the lottery.

"You can help me count petals? The recipe calls for two hundred and twenty-two."

Blake's jaw dropped. "Is that a joke?"

Jaylynn shook her head. "Nope." She opened her recipe book to the marked page. "It says right here, two hundred and twenty-two rose petals crushed and sprinkled in once the contents start to foam."

"Give that thing to me," Blake demanded. Before Jaylynn could protest, Blake ripped the book out of her hands. Jaylynn's mouth pinched as Blake looked at the recipe Jaylynn was working on.

Re-Sparking Love Potion: once brewed, cool and serve to both partners once a day until effects take.

Blake threw the book onto the counter. "I am not helping you make that."

Jaylynn raced to catch the recipe book as it slid across the counter. It bumped the open jar of tiny dried rose petals. Blake watched as it tipped and the contents spilled across the stove and floor.

"Jordan Blake!" Jaylynn screeched as she leapt back. "How could you?" Jaylynn bumped into Hunter as she spun on an angry heel. Hunter lifted the whisk so quickly, pink liquid shot up and splattered the wall and roof.

Crackling blackness clouded Blake's vision. The sharpness in Jaylynn's accusatory eyes fled as Blake swooped. She stomped over the petals and grabbed Jaylynn's chin between her finger and thumb. Pale aquamarine eyes met Blake's, bursting with instant guilt; Jaylynn knew exactly what she'd done wrong.

"Never call me that again. Do you understand? That name is dead to me."

Jaylynn's lips parted. "I'm sorry—"

Blake squeezed harder before flicking her wrist, releasing Jaylynn's chin with a snap. "You were the one who asked me what name I preferred when I first got here."

Hunter glanced at the open recipe book, then gave Jaylynn a hard look.

"It's not what you think—"

Hunter didn't wait for Jaylynn to finish. He strode to the front door and grabbed his coat from the hanger. Blake's anger cooled for a heartbeat, suddenly overtaken by worry.

"Where are you going?" Blake voice cracked.

With one hand on the collar of his coat, Hunter stopped. "I don't know what's goin' on here, but you two clearly have things to sort out."

"I thought you might stay the night?" Jaylynn clasped her hands, the shame on her freckled face clear as day.

Hunter shook his head. "I'm sure there's a motel or something—"

"Please stay," Blake added, conscious of how important this was. If Hunter got a room elsewhere, Blake would have no way to find him, and no way to complete her task if he decided not to come back.

Hunter squinted in disbelief. "*You* want me to stay?"

Blake nodded, her foot crushing rose petals as she stepped closer to him.

Be open. Be kind. Be like Jaylynn.

"I do. Please stay."

The air was thick between the trio as Hunter glanced around the cabin.

"I'll make you a bed here on the sofa," Jaylynn offered. "Blake and I can share the bedroom."

That was not Blake's first choice, but was she ready to suggest Hunter share the bedroom with her? Absolutely not. Hunter seemed torn as he glanced between the front door and the couch.

"Just for now, until we can figure this all out," Blake added.

She loosened a breath as he dropped his coat back on the hook. Jaylynn turned to the mess in the kitchen. Blake didn't bother following her to help. Whether Jaylynn had meant the potion for Blake and Hunter or for her own matchmaking task, she had crossed a line. Then calling her Jordan… The rage was still so close to the surface. Blake slammed it down, desperate not to drive Hunter away. She gave him the softest smile she could manage even though her veins were burning with frustration.

"Thank you."

Blake escaped to the bedroom to soak up what little alone time she could to rally her emotions. She flopped down on the tall queen mattress, breathing in Psyche's musky scent of incense and cloves. Blake clenched the blanket in her fists at the sound of Jaylynn's murmurs to Hunter. The wave of anger Blake had been moderating all day reached the cusp of intolerable.

I should have left that night Nessie found me in the woods.

The pair's muttering crept through the thin walls, and Blake pulled a pillow on top of her head. Something deep cracked in her chest. Blake took long, measured breaths, willing herself to get it together as furious tears threatened to burst forth.

"Jordan Blake! How could you?"

The memory of her mother's shrill voice drove a spike down her spine.

"Do you have any idea what you've done?"

Tara Blake clawed at the pills sinking to the bottom of the toilet. Jordan stared at her mom without flinching. She knew exactly what she'd done.

"These were hundreds of dollars! How am I going to— I swear, you are a child of Tartarus." Tara's thin, gnarled fingers shook as she frantically scooped the toilet bowl water. Jordan said nothing, braced with her back flat to the wall. Tara tossed the dissolving little white pills on the counter, water splattering the rusty mirror.

"You should have gone with your father when he left. You're cut from the same wretched cloth. I swear you were only put in my womb to spite me."

Still, Jordan stared on, the melting pills a tiny victory between her and her mother's vices.

A knock at the door brought the room back into sharp clarity. Blake wasn't sure how much time had passed, but the cabin was dark and quiet. She pushed the pillow off her face and glanced up to see Jaylynn leaning on the door frame. Jaylynn pulled at the strings of her shorts. Blake intentionally didn't look at her bare legs.

"You can come in."

Jaylynn sighed and came into the bedroom, leaving the door open so they could both easily see Psyche's silhouette under the window. Blake clamped her arms around her claimed pillow as Jaylynn folded back the sheets. Her nose wrinkled.

"Are you really going to sleep in that?" Jaylynn asked.

Blake glanced down. She had washed her gray shirt and jeans a couple days ago well enough that you could barely see the bloodstains anymore. Though the recent adventures with Venus had added a new mixture of dried mud, Blake had done a fine job brushing them off.

"I don't have anything else to wear."

Jaylynn turned to the dresser and started searching through the drawers. "I'm sure Psyche has something."

"I am not wearing Psyche's clothes."

"And I'm not sleeping with you in the same clothes you've worn for Minerva knows how long."

The light in the main room flickered off, and they heard Hunter fall onto the couch. The only light left came from a small stained-glass lamp on the bedside table. Jaylynn rummaged through a drawer and held up a silky floral slip. Blake dropped her voice quieter. "I am not wearing lingerie to bed with you."

"I wasn't going to say you should." Jaylynn's cheeks flushed scarlet as she stashed the satin deep in the drawer.

"Is that what Psyche wore all those weekends you used to sleep over here?" The thought of Psyche and Jaylynn's time together before her own arrival still inexplicably irked Blake more than she wanted to admit.

Jaylynn coughed in surprise. "No! Of course not." She rummaged through a few more drawers, finally finding a black nightshirt. It had long sleeves, a collar, and buttons from top to bottom.

"You want me to sleep without pants?"

"Blake, for the love of Cupid, can you stop being so difficult? It's black. It's basically the color of your soul." Jaylynn chucked the soft cotton at Blake's face.

"Fine," Blake said through clenched teeth. "Turn around."

Jaylynn rolled her eyes but did as she was told.

Blake turned to the opposite wall and pulled her shirt over her head. She unclasped her bra, letting it fall to the ground, and pulled the long shirt over her head.

"If you try to get into bed with those wretched jeans still on…"

Blake grumbled, shooting back a look to make sure Jaylynn wasn't peeking. The redhead still faced the opposite wall, her arms crossed. Blake shuffled out of her pants, instantly hating that the nightshirt fell just above her knobby, bruised knees. She forced herself to shake off the feeling of being too exposed and stripped off her socks, sure Jaylynn would complain about those too. Her toes were no longer swollen like they'd been when she'd first arrived, but the bruising had turned darker and spread up the tops of her feet.

Stars, I hate this.

Blake crawled into the bed, quickly covering her bare flesh in Psyche's cotton sheets and heavy quilt.

Jaylynn continued to stand facing the wall. Blake sighed.

"Okay. I'm done."

Jaylynn turned and crawled under the sheets, facing Blake. "You better not snore," she whispered.

"If you so much as touch me," Blake whispered back, positive Jaylynn would be the type to want to cuddle, "I will shave your head in the middle of the night."

Despite the shadows cast by the lamp at Jaylynn's back, Blake saw her lips part in shock, then press together in a scowl. "What is wrong with you, Blake?"

5 DAYS

UNTIL THE SUPERMOON

Between three regal brothers, the mortal realms were split:

Jupiter the skies, Neptune the ocean, and Pluto the crypt.

The buried brother lined his realm with rivers that burn,

His sprawling Underworld a beacon for all souls to return.

Pluto rules from his black throne, his ghastly castle of death,

Elysium, Asphodel, Tartarus; his cities all void of breath.

—The Reaper

CHAPTER XXIV

Lacey pulled her headphones down around her neck as they came up to River's cabin. Nessie coasted her mom's car up a gravel road with impressive ease considering she didn't have her license. Lacey had been shocked when she found out Nessie would be driving them.

They'd split up, Charity and Ladybug together to return Jaylynn's borrowed truck, and Lacey and Nessie in Charity's car. Lacey was pretty sure Charity had insisted on this arrangement so the girls would have a chance to talk, yet they hadn't spoken a single word to each other on the drive.

Nessie sighed as she turned the ignition off, clearly relieved they'd made it. A tall, muscular man with curly brown hair and a ball cap rounded the corner. Nessie waved with a bright smile as she opened her door.

"Hey, you must be Hunter!" Nessie practically leapt out of the car.

Lacey begrudgingly followed. She'd dressed cute today, conscious she'd see Damien later, pairing a black cropped tank top and baggy high-waisted jeans with a cute cardigan. At least, she'd felt cute until Nessie came downstairs. Nessie wore a pretty yellow sundress Lacey had never seen before paired with her favorite jean jacket. Maybe it was seeing her friend wear her hair down in heavy waves instead of her usual high ponytail, but something about Nessie seemed different.

Hunter gave the girls a polite nod and carried on his way, hauling what looked like a huge jug of water. Nessie didn't wait for Lacey as she strutted up to the cabin like this was her own house. Charity brought Ladybug out of the truck, and Lacey hurried to her side.

"I can take her," Lacey offered.

Charity handed the leash off gratefully as the cabin door swung open. A short redhead came out with a broad smile. She wore denim overalls and had a dishtowel slung over one shoulder.

"You guys are back so soon!" She crushed Nessie in a hug before rushing to Charity's side. "I missed you." Lacey guessed this must be Jaylynn based on the extended hug she and Charity shared. On the porch, Nessie grinned as a girl with tattoos, black cutout gloves, and faded blue hair joined her. They bumped shoulders, equally bright smiles on their faces.

Ladybug tugged the leash, so Lacey obeyed, walking closer to Nessie.

"Did you dress yourself in that?" Nessie asked, an eyebrow perched in curiosity.

The girl scoffed. "As if I'd ever wear something floral by choice. Jaylynn dumped my clothes in the tub and forced me into this."

Nessie barked out a laugh in surprise. "Okay, that explains a lot. I'm pretty sure we can find something that suits you better, though."

Lacey kicked at the dirt and waited to see if Nessie would introduce them, but she never looked her way. Instead, the two girls disappeared into the cabin, and Lacey was left wondering whether she should follow them.

"And who is this?" Jaylynn's cheery voice pitched high as she knelt to greet Ladybug.

Lacey cleared her throat, turning her attention back to Jaylynn and Charity. "This is Ladybug."

Jaylynn froze as she knelt, looking up to Lacey. "What did you say?"

"Ladybug. Because she's red with white spots on her nose?"

"I… I must be mistaken. I literally rehomed a pup… No. This has to be her. Do you know Kade?"

Lacey lit up. "That's my dad!"

Jaylynn sagged in relief. "Oh, that's amazing." She picked Ladybug up. "Who would have ever guessed we'd be reunited so soon, hey?"

Jaylynn shook Lacey's hand. "I'm Jaylynn, by the way."

"Lacey."

"It's nice to meet you."

Charity cleared her throat. "These two girls will be our special guests for a bit. I was hoping you might be able to give me some advice on raising puppies while we're here. I imagine you know some tricks to make a dog love you."

Jaylynn squinted as if confused for a minute. "Oh. Ohhhhh. Yeah, of course. I've got lots of tips."

Lacey glanced at the cabin door as Charity and Jaylynn chattered on, not particularly interested. There were still several hours before Damien's match, but she'd hoped she would get some time with him before the game too. She willed herself to be patient as she shuffled from foot to foot.

"Oh, I also grabbed burgers for everyone! I almost forgot," Charity said, twining her arm with Jaylynn's. "Why don't we go in and we can chat while we eat?"

"Is it okay for Ladybug to come into the cabin?" Lacey asked.

Jaylynn shrugged. "I'm sure Psych—I mean, River—would probably be fine with that." She paused, her forehead creasing. "Sorry, our friend recently changed her name and I'm still getting used to it."

Charity nodded. "Lacey, I should have mentioned more about River. She's not doing very well right now, so if we bring Ladybug into the cabin, we'll just have to be careful that she stays out of trouble."

Jaylynn smiled. "I'm sure it won't be a problem."

Lacey's feet dragged as she followed everyone inside.

The cabin was warm, and Lacey eyed each of the new people suspiciously. The girl with tattoos had changed into a black tank top and leggings. She and Nessie both sat on the edge of a cot where a tanned woman with onyx-black hair slept. Lacey assumed that must be River. Her hands were folded neatly over her ribs, each wrapped in bandages similar to Nessie's. The sight of the sleeping woman brought back the sharp reminder of her own mom. Lacey suppressed the twinge of shame that she wasn't at the hospital with her dad today.

"What happened to her?" Lacey asked, her voice wavering slightly as she stepped closer.

Nessie's face drained of all its color. She looked at her tattooed friend to answer.

"What was that?" The girl had naturally defiant eyes.

"River's hands." For a second, Lacey questioned whether she'd gotten the name right.

Nessie's friend stood. Despite her sharp collarbones and taut cheeks, the girl was menacing. "You know, I don't think we properly met. I'm Blake."

Blake walked toward Lacey, effectively blocking her view of River.

"Lacey," she replied, stepping back as Blake got closer.

"Mmmm."

Jaylynn cut in, brushing Blake back. "Blake, please remember your manners."

"Is River okay?" Lacey asked Jaylynn instead.

For whatever reason, Jaylynn also looked to Blake for an answer—just as Nessie had.

"There was a fire a few days ago that got out of hand," Blake responded, moving back to River's side. "She'll be fine. She just needs to rest."

Lacey realized Jaylynn was wearing bandages too, though hers didn't reach up her forearm like Nessie's and Charity's.

Vulcan's hearth, that must have been some fire.

Out of the corner of her eye, Nessie fretted with the hem of her dress. Lacey frowned.

Wait, was she lying to me about the cooking accident? Was she here for that same fire? Why would she lie about her burns? And since when can Nessie lie at all?

Nessie wouldn't meet her eyes. Hunter handed Lacey a cheeseburger without asking whether she wanted one.

And who is this grumpy quiet guy? How do any of these people even know each other?

Frustrated and feeling lonely, Lacey stalked over to the couch, hauling Ladybug on her leash to sit with her. As the group settled into eating, Charity caught Jaylynn up on Lacey's family situation. Nessie and Blake whispered over boxes of fries, still tucked beside River. Then Lacey's bad afternoon got even worse as Ladybug decided it would be the opportune time to squat and poop.

"Ugh, Ladybug, no!" Lacey jumped up, knowing it was already too late.

Charity looked stricken, but Jaylynn waved it off. "She's probably just nervous. New house, new smells, lots of people. Why don't you take her back outside for a walk, Lacey, and I'll clean that up."

Hunter rose from his seat. "I can clean it."

Jaylynn smiled appreciatively. "Thank you, Hunter."

Lacey crumpled the garbage from her burger, thanked Charity for the food, and scampered toward the door.

Less than eight hours and I'll be back with Damien. I just have to survive the afternoon.

She glanced down at her phone—well, her mom's phone, which she'd officially commandeered—and brightened to see a new message from Damien. Loneliness quickly forgotten, she skipped outside.

CHAPTER XXV

BLAKE

"**What do I** do?" Nessie groaned.

Blake shrugged. "I guess keep up your story. It would look worse if you changed it now."

Across the cabin, Hunter was gathering everyone's garbage, actively avoiding eye contact with Blake, as he had been all day. He had stayed when she'd asked him to, and now everything was weird because Blake had no idea what to do next. The unresolved tension between them was painful, to the point even Jaylynn had noticed.

"Maybe you two just need to have it out in the bedroom."

Blake hadn't been sure whether to snort or snap at her for being the opposite of helpful. No, Blake wasn't going to take Hunter to bed. She knew what her next step had to be. He needed to forgive her.

"Hunter," Jaylynn said. "Would you mind taking that and the rest of the garbage out to the bin? You're a doll."

Blake dug her nails into her palms but quickly released them. She'd abandoned her bandages this morning and opted for gloves. When Jaylynn had asked, Blake said she didn't need them. She hoped if the burns dried out, they would heal faster. She didn't mention how the dwindling bandage supply made her wary there wouldn't be enough to go around.

Hunter seemed happy to comply and turned his attention to the garbage. Blake grumbled incoherently as he left.

"Are things not going well? Also, you never told me how cute Hunter is," Nessie added, a sparkle of amusement in her eye.

Hunter's brooding and Jaylynn's endless advice were only some of the new problems Blake was juggling. She leaned closer to Nessie, dropping her voice. "I need to tell you something."

Before Blake could explain any more, Jaylynn cut in. "Okay, group huddle. We need a plan."

Charity and Jaylynn moved over to the cot. As soon as Charity stood beside Psyche, she repeated what Nessie had said when she'd first walked in.

"Oh, for the love of Cupid. She looks so much worse! What happened?" Charity looked to Blake and Jaylynn for answers.

Blake shrugged and tried to play it off like she hadn't been freaking out about the exact same thing. "We don't know."

It seemed like the stunning woman had aged twenty years in the span of a couple days. Blake swore the soft brown spots on Psyche's sunken cheeks weren't there before, and the gray hair at her temples grew more prominent daily.

"Should we take her to a doctor?" Nessie asked, her hands flattening the hem of her dress.

"No," Jaylynn and Blake said in unison. They met one another's eyes with a quick knowing and appreciative look. At least they were in agreement about one thing.

"Right now we need to trust Psyche will hold on while we focus on our tasks." Jaylynn rolled her neck as she refocused the group. "We have Blake's match here, and Charity's too, now that Ladybug is at the cabin."

Blake was still confused how Charity's tattoo was connected to a dog, and she wished someone had warned her they were bringing a stranger.

If I knew, I would have put Psyche back in her bedroom.

"I guess the only sensible thing would be to follow my mark next," Nessie said. "Jaylynn, still nothing on your end?"

Jaylynn shook her head. "Nope."

Charity sighed. "Jay, maybe you could come back to the house with us and give me a hand with the puppy. You love animals and I really could use a hand."

Blake brightened at the prospect of being free of Jaylynn.

Jaylynn shot the offer down promptly. "Trust me, Blake needs me more."

Blake snorted and crossed her arms. "I do not."

Jaylynn pretended not to notice. "I'll stay for a couple more days. If my match doesn't show up this weekend, then I'll come into the city and try something different."

"Maybe we could leave Lacey here," Nessie said under her breath.

"Absolutely not." Blake crossed her arms. She'd needed all of two seconds to decide Lacey was not her kind of person. She was prissy, her jet-black hair was too shiny, and her makeup paired with her baby face made her look like a dolled-up toddler.

Jaylynn rubbed Nessie's back. "Don't stress, Ness. We've got this. We have five more days until the full moon, and we already know what two out of four tasks are."

Blake wished she could take Jaylynn's romantic optimism and drown the girl in it.

Nessie's face blanched. "That leaves me five days to both find and make someone fall in love with me. Oh, Minerva, help me. I don't know how I'm going to do this."

Charity stroked Nessie's head. "Don't get ahead of yourself."

Blake couldn't blame Nessie for freaking out. Blake had been the first to identify her task, and even with her head start, she wasn't convinced she could fall in love with Hunter in such a short time span.

"We have to try," Jaylynn urged.

Charity nodded. "I'll do everything I can to help you, Ness." She wrapped her daughter in a hug as she turned to Jaylynn. "As for my task, I can't imagine my just stealing Ladybug is all Venus wants. What do I have to do to make this dog choose me over Kade?"

Jaylynn winced a bit. "Well, animals usually bond to their primary care provider. If you take over all her feeding, walking, and grooming, she'll trust you a lot faster."

Charity seemed much better than when Blake last saw her. Now if only someone could actually help Blake with her task, because whatever Jaylynn thought she was doing was the opposite of helpful.

Blake scowled when Lacey returned from walking Ladybug. She took her post at Psyche's side and crossed her arms.

"Lacey, you're back." Jaylynn's singsong, people-pleasing voice had returned. For some reason, every time Jaylynn plastered another fake smile on, Blake felt like punching something. She liked it better when Jaylynn was glowering at Blake's crude jokes or pinching her nose in frustration because Psyche hadn't labeled anything in the pantry.

Lacey went to Charity's side. "Will we be staying much longer?"

"No," Charity reassured her. "We'll be off really soon."

Blake excused herself, but as she stepped into the bathroom, she remembered why she'd been avoiding this room and exactly what she'd wanted to tell Nessie earlier.

The cabin bathroom smelled of Psyche's homemade lavender soap and was the only room in the house with a mirror. To most people it would probably seem cozy. Blake considered it a tomb. She intentionally stared at the wooden wall as she sat on the toilet, next to the basin filled with her soaking clothes. A murky gray film coated the top of the water already.

"Jordan…"

Blake strained to pee faster. She did not look up, and she most definitely did not look at the mirror.

I am not crazy. Everything is fine.

Then there was the issue of washing her hands. In her haste to pee, Blake hadn't taken off her gloves, so now she somehow had to wash her fingertips without getting everything else wet. For good measure, Blake kept her eyes cast down and tried to clean up as quickly as possible. She didn't need to look to know that piercing gold eyes were staring at her.

"How does it feel to know you'll be the reason everyone fails?"

Blake didn't bother drying her fingers. She rushed out and closed the door more forcefully than she'd meant to. Everyone in the room went still. Hunter had come back, his muscular arms full of small logs for the indoor fireplace. His face shifted from curious to hard when she met his gaze.

"Everything okay?" Nessie asked, rising from her spot at Psyche's cot.

Blake dropped her eyes and went to the kitchen counter, sorting through Psyche's tea tins without thinking. Hunter was careful to give Blake a wide berth before stacking the fresh logs beside the fire.

Nessie leaned on the counter beside Blake. "Listen, I think we're leaving. Sorry we can't stay longer." With a dramatized eye roll, Nessie dropped her voice. "Apparently we have to go meet Lacey's soulmate."

Blake snorted. "That should be delightful."

"Right?" Nessie sighed. "I wish I could stay here."

"You know you can't." Blake opened and closed jars, smelling the contents. She came to one with a particularly stubborn lid and ground her teeth as it bit into her palm.

"Is there anything you need from me before I go?" Nessie asked. "You said you needed to tell me something?"

Blake peeked over her shoulder at Hunter, distraught to catch him looking at her. She turned back quickly. "It's nothing. Just get your task over with as quickly as you can and come back."

"I will. Try to stop looking so grumpy?" Nessie bumped Blake's elbow.

Blake couldn't help the small smile that perked. "Grumpy is who I am."

"Well," Nessie mused, "I don't mind your grumpiness, but I'm sure Hunter would appreciate some warmth."

"Ugh. Not you too."

Jaylynn's impromptu lecture this morning had already set Blake on edge.

"Try to be more feminine. Relax a little. Maybe spend more time talking with him."

"Oh, and, Blake?" Nessie buried her hands in the pockets of her jean jacket. "Please don't murder Jaylynn while we're gone. We kind of need her."

"No promises."

CHAPTER XXVI

"What do you *think of the government's new recruitment campaigns?"* the radio show host asked. Nylah toggled the volume up as they drove back to their apartment, their curiosity piqued.

"They're ridiculous, that's what they are, Gary. Every single Canadian can name someone they loved who has died in the Endless War. It's no wonder recruitment numbers keep dropping as the Northern Alliance claims new ground, despite the incentives to enlist."

Nylah glanced in the rearview mirror at the meager groceries they had grabbed and the multiple bottles of wine. The outing had its fair share of unrest—they'd encountered military protestors handing out fliers and another group asking for signatures on a petition for the prime minister to bring compasses back. Nylah had dodged the former and doubtfully signed the latter, though they were pretty positive the government had no control over bringing magic back. The subtle indicators that the city was struggling was growing more apparent every day between the thinning shelves, business closures, and manic citizens.

"*I'm just saying,*" the second host continued, "*people are demanding change, and maybe it's time Canada extracted our troops from the war instead of doubling down to protect the Roman Empire.*"

"Oh, politics," Nylah murmured. They turned their turn signal on at the last stoplight before home and cracked open a new pack of cigarettes. In the small side mirror, a dark red fabric caught the corner of Nylah's eye.

Fates' Followers.

On the bench in front of their apartment complex, a priest sat with folded hands as if waiting for someone. Were they following Nylah specifically or just in the area by chance? The light changed to green, and Nylah slowly turned, keeping one eye on the road and the other on the priest. They passed their apartment and resolved to do another lap around the block for good measure. A small green car stayed close behind, and Nylah's paranoia grew as they realized the driver wore a dark red scarf over her head.

Nylah made a split-second decision. The priests thought Nylah lived with Jazz, so that's where Nylah would go. Their apartments were only a few blocks apart, and while their random detour was likely highly suspicious, Nylah was not about to get out of their vehicle if they were being tailed.

"Hello?" Jazz's muffled voice came through the car's Bluetooth. The one good thing about all the businesses shutting down was it meant Jazz was home in the middle of the day during the week for a change.

"Hey," Nylah said, drawing out the last syllable of the greeting and trying to sound more relaxed than they felt. "So, no big deal, but I think I'm being followed, and I'm on my way to your place so the cult doesn't find out where I live and kidnap me."

"What do you mean? Are you sure?" Jazz's voice sharpened.

Nylah made another turn, watching the small green car follow them. "Yep, I'm sure. Please meet me outside so I don't have to walk in alone."

As Nylah half expected, once they parked, the green car slowed and then parked on the other side of the lot. Maybe the stalker was just keeping tabs, but Nylah couldn't shake the fear of being dragged back to that church basement hole.

The screams of the two people shoved into the pit left Nylah tossing and turning all night, guilt burrowing deeper every time they played the scenario back. Did the hole really go to Tartarus? Did those people die when they hit the bottom, or did they live long enough to witness the horrors of the monster-cursed realm?

The bravado of protecting Jazz by joining the cult felt incredibly stupid now.

A rap on Nylah's window made their heart lurch. Jazz stood there in a sleek peacoat. He cast his eyes around, searching for the threat. Nylah forced a big smile and unlocked the door.

"Hey! Thanks for coming down to help me carry our groceries." Nylah wrapped their arms over Jazz's tall shoulders, drawing him close, and dropped their voice to a whisper. "Green car across the lot. Try not to be obvious."

Nylah released him and opened the back door.

"That's a lot of wine," Jazz teased, but Nylah could tell he was just making conversation.

"I have a lot of things I want to forget," Nylah retorted, probably too honestly.

It wasn't until they'd passed the front door security and were standing in the elevator that Jazz's cool front broke.

"What did you do?" His tone was accusatory, and Nylah brushed him off.

"I went shopping. Is that a crime?"

Jazz's earrings sparkled in the fluorescent lights as he shook his head. The elevator stopped at the twentieth floor, and they stepped off in tandem. In Jazz's apartment, the stainless-steel appliances glowed against the tall cabinets and black counters, the epitome of masculine grace and entirely Jazz. Nylah dropped their bags on the floor of their home away from home. Jazz scooped up the jackets that were lying over a chair and started hanging them one by one in the large mirror closet.

"Sweet Venus," Nylah teased. "I swear you own more jackets and shoes than I own clothes."

Jazz smirked. He'd been the best dressed in their high school, and he'd known it. It was probably his fashionable precision that made so many people assume he was gay. Over the seven years of their friendship, Nylah had witnessed many rants from Jazz demanding more normalcy around pansexual men. Jazz's ability to love someone regardless of how a person presented only made Nylah love him more.

Nylah walked over to the front entry table, which was covered in framed photos. Some showed Jazz with his family and one was of their high school friends' reunion. Nylah's personal favorite was a photo of the two of them with Boots when she was a kitten, squished between their faces. A dark thought crossed Nylah's mind.

Will Jazz take Boots when I'm gone? Or will Jaylynn? Would they fight over her? Or would she end up back at a shelter?

"You okay?" Jazz asked.

Nylah's hands shook slightly as they backed away from the happy photos. "Any idea what the cult wants with me?"

Jazz scrubbed a hand across his face. "I don't know. Probably to make sure you're not going to the cops." He gave Nylah a brief accusatory look. "Someone was bound to notice your reaction last night. They probably watched the footage and pinned us down as possible trouble."

Nylah crossed their arms. "Screaming in alarm was a perfectly reasonable reaction to witnessing murder. Because that's what that was, Jazz. Cold-blooded murder."

"I know that," he said quietly. "I'm just as scared as you, Nylah."

The fiery frustration at the wild situation they were stuck in simmered. Nylah's heart ached as they sat down beside Jazz on his black leather couch. When he met their eyes, there was so much vulnerability in them that Nylah's chest could have split in two.

"I'm afraid you're going to be next," Jazz whispered. "Every time I close my eyes, it's you going down into that pit, and it's all my fault for getting you involved."

Nylah grabbed Jazz's hand, desperate to ease his undeniable guilt even as he echoed their own greatest nightmare. "Jazz, no. Don't think like that."

His thumb ran over Nylah's, and they suppressed a shiver. In the past days, it seemed they spent more and more time touching. A brush here, a casual hold there. Was it the fact Nylah had lost their soulmate link that made every point of physical contact feel more intimate than before? Or was it Nylah's imminent death and never having felt real love that made them second-guess the meaning behind every one of Jazz's touches?

"What are we going to do?" he half whispered, half croaked.

Nylah looked around his apartment. This morning the sand in their hourglass was already almost half empty, which Nylah had deduced meant they had days, not weeks, before life as they knew it would end. Whether they were going to be thrown in the black pit or they were fated to be taken out by a bus, Nylah had only so much time left, and they had to make the most of it.

Once again, Nylah wondered if they should warn Jazz what was coming, but they shut the idea down. Nylah couldn't do it. It would break his heart. One thing was clear, though. Nylah promised themself that when the sands were about to run out, they'd make sure they were far, far away from Jazz. They would not let their best friend witness their death. Not like they'd watched the two people die last night.

Jazz gestured to Nylah's grocery bags. "Maybe you should stay at my place for the time being."

"I can't," Nylah sighed. "I have to get home to Boots. We can put the fridge stuff away so it'll stay cool, but I'll go as soon as the tail disappears."

Nylah didn't want to stay here, not if that was where the cult expected them to be, but they weren't about to lead their enemies to their own front door.

CHAPTER XXVII

"Look at that boy go!" Coach Trevor grinned wildly, displaying his mouth of crowded yellow-tinted teeth as he dug his fingers into Sebastian's shoulder. Sebastian followed the coach's bright gaze to the field, where Gareth was weaving effortlessly through the pack with the ball. Sebastian tried to act impressed or even remotely happy.

Only a couple more hours and Gareth and I can game the night away.

Huan had suggested Gareth stay with them for the weekend to help the Harts out and they'd happily agreed.

"Wow. I knew you boys would be an asset but— YES!!!" Coach Trevor slammed his fist in the air as Gareth jogged back from the net, his wide grin sharp and white. Sebastian leaned back to avoid the touch of spittle that flew. The celebration was undoubtedly overdone. Sure, it was a great goal, Gareth always played with style, but this wasn't even a real game. When the other team canceled, Coach Trevor insisted they have a mandatory practice and team meeting in place of the scheduled game. Huan and Philip were hesitant, but they resolved that because it was in a residential park, it would probably be safe and a good excuse to get out of the house.

"That's what I'm talking about! Whew!" Coach Trevor was like an amped-up Energizer Bunny on the sidelines. "Sebastian, you're sure you can't play today?"

Sebastian tried not to look as miserable as he felt. He buried his fists in his track-jacket pockets and shook his head. While his rolled ankle had improved a lot the last couple days, Philip had insisted Sebastian sit out this team scrimmage.

"Sorry, sir. I can't," Sebastian said, though it killed him to admit. Seeing Gareth and Damien running circles around the Canadian players made Sebastian ache with desire to play. Even the other two boys from back home, Edward and Freddie, were tearing it up. The UK boys were like football royalty out here and all Sebastian could do was sit and watch.

Coach Trevor started screaming at a defenseman, and Sebastian stepped out of his way as he raced up the line. Sebastian glanced back at Huan and Philip sitting in the stands. The aluminum seating was set back ten feet from the sideline, and encouraging smiles stretched both their faces. Philip had gotten off another long shift at the hospital but was adamant he would be here, regardless of whether Sebastian played or not, which seemed silly when it wasn't even a game.

Then Sebastian noticed a few latecomers. The girls were close to his age and heading his way. The first slung her long jet-black hair over her shoulder, a dazzling smile on her face as she neared the pitch. Sebastian couldn't help but stare as she grinned seemingly right at him. The second girl followed on her friend's heels. She was tall and curvy, her long blond hair falling over her shoulders. Her intent eyes traced the field, her mood deeply serious compared to the other's. Sebastian couldn't help but wonder who she was looking for as his attention snagged back to the first girl.

Coach Trevor blew his whistle to pause the play. Sebastian did a double take as Damien jogged toward the sideline.

"Tired already?" Sebastian quipped. Damien was famous for never taking substitutions and hogging play time.

Damien didn't seem to care, though. "Be right back."

Sebastian turned and watched as his rival jogged past, straight to the girl with the stunning smile. She skipped to close the distance between them. Damien threw his arms open and she leapt into them, her black hair glistening in the sunshine.

"You made it!" Damien sang. He spun her around and she laughed.

"I said I would! I'm so sorry we're late."

Damien set the girl down and crushed her in a hug. "You're forgiven."

Sudden anger simmered in Sebastian's core. *Of course Damien already has girls hanging off of him here too. What an attention-seeking twat.*

A sharp whistle right behind Sebastian made him jump. He looked back at the field and saw Gareth standing with his arms crossed as Coach Trevor waved his arms in the air, clearly demonstrating something that Gareth did not agree with.

"Seb!"

Sebastian turned, alarmed to find Damien by his side. "I want you to meet my soulmate. This is Lacey."

Lacey.

The girl tucked under Damien's shoulder glowed, her one hand splayed across his chest as she stared up at him. A fruity smell—maybe cherry?—filled the breeze, and Sebastian's lips parted in confusion as he tried to process what Damien had said.

"Your… soulmate?" he asked.

"Yeah. We found each other right as compasses disappeared." Damien grinned down at Lacey. Sebastian fought the urge to punch him in his perfect teeth.

Lacey's smile grew impossibly brighter. "Cupid was watching over us."

Of all the reasons Sebastian had ever hated Damien, this one took the cake. Damien's happiness radiated brighter than Apollo's sun.

How could Damien have found his soulmate, and I didn't? How is that fair?

The girl with the blond hair crept up, a curious but tentative look in her eye.

"Oh, Damien!" Lacey squeaked. "This is my best friend, Nessie."

Nessie gave Lacey a skeptical sidelong glance that made Sebastian wonder if they were actually best friends.

Damien stood taller and gave an appreciative nod toward Nessie. "Damn, Lace. You have hot friends."

A look of surprise flushed Lacey's face. Her lips parted at a loss of words. Nessie, however, stepped closer, steel flashing in her eyes.

"Call me that again and I'll kick you in the balls."

Sebastian couldn't help it as a sharp laugh escaped. Lacey stared at her friend in horror, but Damien just grinned at the threat.

"Huh, from Hot-Nessie to Loch-Nessie in an instant." Damien held his hands up in mock surrender, his eyes twinkling. "I'll steer clear."

Nessie's dark stare was anything but playful. She turned to Sebastian, a clear attempt at smoothing over the moment. "And you are?"

He held out his hand to shake hers as he said, "Seb," but was surprised when Nessie turned her palms up in apology. Both hands were wrapped in bandages that crept up her wrists and under the cuffs of her jean jacket.

"Sorry." Nessie blushed. She offered her exposed fingers and Sebastian shook them gently. "It's nice to meet you, Seb."

Seb nodded, unsure what to do. Damien was right, Nessie was also quite pretty, but in a different way than Lacey. There was a bright intelligence to her eyes, and sharp dimples accompanied her smile. He flushed, unsure what to say, and turned back to the field to check how Gareth was making out. As it was, his best friend was stomping toward them, his long arms swinging with each pace.

"It's not my fault he tried to go through me instead of around me!" Gareth yelled over his shoulder as he got to the sideline. He grabbed his water bottle. "Did you see that bollocks?" Gareth came to a sharp stop as he realized the company Sebastian shared.

"Sorry, mate. I missed it," Sebastian replied.

Nessie brightened as Gareth walked up, her eyes flicking between the boys. "Wait, are you all from England?"

Damien nodded. "We're here for a football exchange."

"You mean soccer," Lacey teased.

Gareth snorted. "No, we meant football. Have you heard of FIFA? The world's professional *football* league? It's in the name."

Nessie smiled, her dimples deepening. "Can't argue with that logic."

Gareth bumped Sebastian's shoulder. "Changed your mind about skipping today's practice yet? Those boys are sitting ducks. You're going to love it."

"Why aren't you playing today, Seb?" Lacey asked, twirling a piece of her hair around her finger.

"Sprained ankle," he mumbled with a wince.

Gareth jostled his shoulder. "I'll forgive you today. But if you think that's going to get you out of helping board up the gallery tomorrow, you're out of luck."

Sebastian scoffed and pushed Gareth away. "You know I'd help even if I had crutches."

Huan and Philip had originally planned on taking Sebastian to see Niagara Falls this weekend, but with the general civil unrest, they'd decided against it.

"What gallery?" Nessie glanced between the boys.

Gareth sighed. "My exchange family runs an art gallery and it was hit by rioters this week. Because so many people are boarding up shops, wood has been hard to come by, so they haven't been able to seal it properly. They've had the broken glass tarped off, but this weekend we're going to take apart pallets and board it up properly."

"Maybe we could help." Lacey looked up at Damien, clearly not realizing *he* was not invited.

"I would love to help too," Nessie quickly agreed.

Gareth gave Sebastian a knowing look. There was no getting out of this now. In Sebastian's peripheral vision, he saw Lacey nuzzle closer to Damien as they whispered their own private conversation.

Classic unnecessary PDA from Damien—check.

Standing with Lacey and Nessie through the rest of practice was a bit awkward. For best friends, they didn't acknowledge one another much. Nessie filled the silence with questions about London. Sebastian was grateful for her constant stream of inquiries to pass the time, but by the end of the match, Sebastian's spirits had sunk pretty low again. He ambled over to the audience seating.

"You guys didn't have to stay," Sebastian said as Huan wrapped an arm over his shoulders. "I don't think my own parents have watched a practice since I was ten." They were more of the drop-off and pick-up type.

"Of course we did!" Philip declared as he patted the bench to encourage Sebastian to sit beside him. The rest of the parents and players gathered around as Coach Trevor signaled for everyone to quiet down for the formal team meeting.

"As you all know, most teams are canceling or delaying their seasons." He ran his tongue over his teeth as if he wasn't impressed by this news. "I was told by the organizers I could only continue to run practices if everyone on the team agreed. So, we're going to put it down to a vote. Everyone who wants to continue with a weekly practice, raise your hands."

Almost all of the players' hands rose to vote to keep playing. But only one of the parents voted to keep practices running. Coach Trevor crossed his arms.

"Now, folks, I understand your concerns, but as you saw today, this was perfectly safe."

The prospect of not having any games this summer sucked. They'd literally flown across the ocean for this. Sebastian and Gareth shared a doubtful stare.

Huan cleared his throat. "What about running optional practices? Then families can decide for themselves what they're comfortable with as the summer goes."

The rest of the parents murmured in agreement. Though the coach didn't seem delighted, he eventually nodded and sent everyone on their way.

"Hey, Seb!"

Sebastian looked up from gathering his things to see Nessie jogging up to him.

"Why don't you take my number and text me the name of the gallery and when you'll be there?" she said. "We'd really love to help."

Sebastian glanced at Huan and Philip to gauge their reactions to the unexpected company.

Philip shrugged at Huan. "I'm sure Winona will appreciate more helping hands."

"Cool." Nessie broke into a wide grin. They swapped contact information, and Nessie gave a quick wave as she hurried back to her mom's car.

"I see you made some new friends." Huan nudged Sebastian's shoulder.

"I guess so."

Across the street, Lacey unrolled her window and waved. Sebastian flicked his wrist up in response, only to be bumped by Damien as he raced by, waving to Lacey. Sebastian scowled. He already regretted the extended invites to help tomorrow.

"Are things okay between you and that Damien boy?" Huan asked, seeming to pick up on Sebastian's annoyance. "It feels… tense between you two."

"He's just a dickhead from school." As soon as the words came out of Sebastian's mouth, he wanted to take them back. He hadn't meant to be so blunt.

Philip glanced back at Sebastian. "Back home? Or here too?"

Sebastian shrugged. "Both, I guess. Though he does seem a bit better here." Other than being obnoxiously over-affectionate, all of Damien's usual antics had faded away after Lacey showed up. He hadn't slide-tackled Gareth unnecessarily or called Sebastian any names. It might have been a new record of Damien being *almost* tolerable.

Huan gave Sebastian a sympathetic look. "I'm sure this trip is an opportunity for all you boys to break out of the patterns of who you used to be and try on new hats as to who you might like to become."

Sebastian wasn't convinced Damien could ever be anyone but a dickhead. But then he considered himself. Without a compass, without any arrow guiding his future, did he have any idea who he wanted to be?

CHAPTER XXVIII

The struggle of waiting for her task to appear was eating away at Jaylynn's sanity. The day had stretched painfully, and now that dinner was finished, Jaylynn didn't have any cooking or cleaning she could preoccupy herself with.

Jaylynn passed a worried glance over Psyche, a bad habit she was starting to do all too often. Hunter sat at the kitchen table with a book open in his lap. The lines on his forehead creased in a frown that Jaylynn had coined his thinking face. He hardly spoke, especially to Blake, but he had kind, intelligent eyes when he wasn't hiding them under a ball cap. Jaylynn appreciated his sturdy demeanor—even if it came off broody.

A horrifying crack and the sound of shattering glass brought them both to attention.

"Blake?" Jaylynn called, her attention zeroed in on the bathroom door. "Is everything all right?"

The sound of Blake crying out made Jaylynn's stomach plunge. Both she and Hunter rushed to the door.

"Blake, what happened?" Jaylynn opened the bathroom door without thinking twice.

Inside, the sink and ground sparkled in glass. The shattered mirror had a black jagged hole in the middle, with only fragments of glass left hanging in the top corners. Blake sat curled up with her back to the tub. Tears streamed down her face as she clutched her wrists to her chest and rocked back and forth. Hunter stepped forward, gently directing Jaylynn aside. He ignored the broken glass and rested his hands on Blake's shoulders.

Jaylynn stood frozen. She'd never seen Blake cry before. Blake couldn't cry. She couldn't break. She was the strong one.

If Blake is falling apart, what chance do any of us have?

"What happened?" Hunter's voice was gentle as he knelt in front of her in the tiny space.

Blake shook her head.

"Blake, I need you to stand up, okay?" Hunter pulled at her arms, and Blake submitted, her head bowed as she tried to slow her sobs.

The glass crunched and crackled as Blake staggered forward, and Jaylynn winced. Hunter didn't flinch as he guided her through the doorway. He led her to the couch, pausing only once to brush off his own feet.

"Jaylynn, we need the first aid kit."

Right. Of course.

Jaylynn forced herself to move. They'd taken to leaving the kit open on the counter because they redressed their hands so often. She gathered what she could and put it on the ground by Hunter's side. It would have been nice if Psyche's bronze table was here, but no one had had the heart to bring it back from the clearing yet.

"We need tweezers to pick out any glass, then probably some antiseptic," Hunter instructed.

Blake wasn't actively crying anymore, but her face was still damp and bright red; her arms clasped tight to her chest. She looked like she'd seen a ghost.

"Blake, show me your hands." Hunter coaxed one hand free, but Blake stared past him and kept the other tight to her body.

Jaylynn found the tweezers tucked in a side pocket of the red bag.

"I have them."

"Good. Check her feet." Hunter released Blake's hand. "Give me the other one, Blake."

He pulled her right hand away from her body, and Jaylynn's knees buckled as blood gushed over Blake's knuckles. Shards stuck up and out of the broken skin.

She punched the mirror?

"Tweezers."

Jaylynn handed them over, her stiff fingers trembling. Hunter didn't hesitate. He went for the largest shard stuck in Blake's skin, pried it out, and dropped the piece on the couch cushion. Hunter methodically continued as Jaylynn tried to piece together what had happened. Blake must have taken off her gloves to shower. Between the healing burns and fresh cuts, Jaylynn could only imagine how much her hand hurt, and she winced as Hunter dug out another glinting triangle.

Come on, Jay. Be helpful.

Jaylynn knelt down to assess Blake's socked feet.

"Blake?" she asked. "Is it okay if I take your socks off?"

Blake didn't respond. Her pupils were wide like an owl's, staring at the window with a blend of terror and shock.

"Just do it," Hunter muttered, his focus on the small tool and Blake's hand.

"She hates it when I touch her."

"I'm sure she hates having glass in her feet more."

Jaylynn shrunk and turned her attention to Blake's feet.

"Blake," Hunter murmured as the girl flinched, "I need you to stay still."

Jaylynn held her breath. She checked the soles of Blake's socked feet. A shimmer of powder coated the black soles, but gratefully no giant shards pierced out. Jaylynn held Blake's ankle as gently as possible, then pulled off each sock, turning them inside out. Blake's feet had older yellow-brown bruises around the toes. Jaylynn raised each heel, relieved to see the cotton socks had spared her from anything like her knuckles.

"She's good. Nothing major down here," Jaylynn reported.

"Get a warm cloth and wipe them down to be sure."

Jaylynn brushed the bit of glass dust off her lap, discarding Blake's socks onto the floor. As she stood, Blake's haunted face made her pause.

"Blake?" Jaylynn whispered, afraid to ask but desperate to know. "What happened?"

Blake's eyes met hers. Jaylynn held her breath.

"I just couldn't do it anymore." Blake's post-crying voice pierced Jaylynn's heart. It was too frail, with none of Blake's typical edginess. Jaylynn hadn't thought it was possible she could miss Mean Blake.

"Couldn't do what?" Even as she asked, Jaylynn guessed she wasn't the only one Venus was taunting.

Blake dropped her eyes and shook her head.

"Blake, what do you see when you look in the mirror?"

"Not with him," Blake mumbled.

Jaylynn fought the urge to roll her eyes. "Blake, we can't hide everything from Hunter forever. Tell me what you saw."

Blake shook her head again. Hunter tightened his hold on her wrist when she tried to pull away.

"I'm not done yet."

Jaylynn stood up and made her way to the sink. She soaked a cloth and returned to Blake's feet. She knelt and took a deep breath.

"Do you want to know what I see when I look in that mirror?" Jaylynn asked, keeping her eyes fixed on her task.

"Don't, Jay—"

"I see myself." Already her voice wavered, but she willed herself to go on. "I see myself in my wedding dress. The one I would have worn for mine and Elias' wedding. I see myself smiling without dark circles under my eyes, without burns on my hands. And I look genuinely happy."

Blake swallowed. Hunter continued to pick glass out of Blake's knuckles.

"And you know what the worst part of the torture is?" Jaylynn went on, a single tear trekking down her cheek. "At first, she showed me him: Elias alive and standing by my side. Now I keep staring at that mirror, wondering if she might put Elias in the frame again just so I can see him one more time, even if it isn't real."

When Blake finally spoke, it was hesitant and weary, and phlegm from crying lingered in the back of her throat. "She... she shows me... *me.*"

Jaylynn didn't look up. Instead, she picked up Blake's other bruised foot and gently wiped it down. There was a long silence before Blake spoke again.

"I see myself the same way I did in the clearing. I'm younger, stronger. There's actual muscle on my arms and legs. I stand straighter, but I have these horrid golden eyes. *Her* eyes."

Jaylynn nodded. "Me too."

Hunter squinted but kept working, the pile of glass growing at his side.

"But it's not seeing myself healthy that gets me, because I know she's just messing with my head, but then she talks to me. She keeps goading me, telling me I'll be the reason we fail." Blake took a shuddering breath. "Then today—"

Jaylynn held her breath as Blake fought to compose herself.

"Today, she showed me him."

Jaylynn looked up to Hunter, but Blake shook her head. "No, not him. *Him.*"

"I'm sorry, Blake, but I'm not following."

Hunter released her and Blake pulled back, drawing her foot away from Jaylynn at the same time.

"The man who drove me out of New York."

Jaylynn felt like she was seeing an entirely different Blake than she'd ever met before. Hunter sat back, his face set in a frown.

"The man who—who attacked me."

Jaylynn swore she could hear Hunter's teeth grinding. Blake's attention stayed fixed on the distance, her pupils pits of black.

"I was getting better at not looking in the mirror, but today, before I could remember not to look, he was there, standing behind me. I—I couldn't even scream. I spun around and as soon as I realized it was another one of her games, I didn't think. I just…" Blake raised her fists and stared at them.

"Blake, I'm so sorry." Jaylynn leaned back, kneading the towel in her hand. The news of the attack took her by surprise, and yet, somehow it didn't. She'd known Blake was running from something—Jaylynn just hadn't realized it was a specific someone.

Hunter cleared his throat. "Listen. I've tried not to pry, but would someone please tell me what is going on here?"

Jaylynn's and Blake's eyes met.

"He has a right to know, Blake."

CHAPTER XXIX

The sharp burn of pain lanced across Blake's knuckles. Adrenaline pumped fresh through her veins as she stared at Jaylynn's soft blue eyes. In them, Blake could see the desperate plea.

"Tell him."

What am I supposed to tell him? A goddess told me the world could have compasses back if I do the impossible and fall in love with you?

Blake retreated farther into the couch cushions. Hunter stared at her from the opposite side, his arms crossed tight. The red plaid shirt clung to his broad chest and shoulders, and his ball cap shaded his eyes. Blake could see she wasn't getting out of this.

"I'd need a drink to tell this story."

Jaylynn sighed but rose and made her way to the open kitchen. She opened a low cupboard and Blake raised an eyebrow. She'd scoured Psyche's kitchen in the past for something to take the edge off, but the dangling vines had obscured that particular cabinet.

Jaylynn pulled out a bottle of vodka. "Psyche never cared much for alcohol, but you'd be surprised how often vodka is called for in her recipes."

Blake and Hunter both held out a hand for the bottle. Jaylynn paused, looking between them.

"I have a feeling I'm about to need that," Hunter said. There was something about the way he spoke, with a touch of an accent, that made everything he said lower and gruff.

Jaylynn pressed her lips in apology to Blake, then handed it neck-first to Hunter.

He spun the top off and tipped it back, drinking directly from the bottle. He winced slightly and shook his head. Blake waited to see if he would hand her the bottle like he had all those nights ago at his trailer. He didn't. Hunter looked pointedly at her and took another large swallow. Then he rested the vodka in his lap and gestured for her to start talking.

Blake leaned back. "I don't know where to start." She held her hand out for the bottle, but Hunter pulled it farther away.

"Hunter," Jaylynn started. "Do you believe in the gods?"

Hunter didn't respond. Instead, he stared at Blake. She stared back, defiant. He took another swig of the vodka. Blake considered clawing across the cushions to snatch it but held back.

"You know the story of Cupid and Psyche?" Jaylynn continued.

Hunter nodded once.

"Well, this is Psyche. Like, *the* Psyche from the stories." Jaylynn gestured across the room.

She's going to tell him the whole damn truth, isn't she?

Blake cut in. "I know it sounds crazy. But if you want the full story, I'm really going to need that drink."

She shot Jaylynn a quick be-quiet glance, then held her hand back out to Hunter. Luckily, he relented. He leaned back in his corner of the couch, his face furrowing as he waited. Blake slugged the bottle back, her wrist weak at its weight and her injured hands aching. The immediate icy burn carved a trench straight to her stomach. She sighed, the pain bringing the room into even sharper focus. Blake held the bottle out to Jaylynn.

The redhead scrunched her freckled nose, then tentatively took it and drank the smallest sip. Her immediate look of disgust brought an inkling of a smile to Blake's lips. "Yeah, that's not the drink for me," Jaylynn said, passing the bottle over to Hunter. "Thanks, though."

Hunter stared at Blake expectantly, tapping his finger on the bottle. "Talk."

Blake let out a frustrated sigh. "Fine. The gods are real, and I mean, like, physically-can-appear-in-front-of-you real. Psyche is Cupid's soulmate. Venus cursed her to never see Cupid again."

She held out her hand for the bottle. Hunter stared at her as if she'd grown horns. He did not hand over the vodka.

Blake glared but pressed on. "Psyche was who my compass pointed to."

At that Hunter deflated a little. He took another large drink, then to Blake's relief, handed the bottle over.

"My compass also brought me to Psyche," Jaylynn added.

Blake swallowed quickly. She couldn't afford for Jaylynn to take over the storytelling. She would end up telling Hunter too much. Blake coughed into her fist against the burn.

"Psyche wanted to be freed from her curse. We tried to summon Cupid, but Venus showed up instead. Turns out the gods are psychos—who would have guessed—and Venus ripped compasses from the face of Terra Mater."

Hunter's face paled slightly and he held his hand out for the bottle. Venus' mark sparkled bright on his wrist. Blake wasn't sure how she was supposed to spin that part of the truth, but she knew she had to figure it out. She handed the bottle back. Jaylynn leaned forward to speak, but Blake interrupted her.

"Then Venus created that." Blake pointed to the hourglass tattoo as she grasped at straws, searching for any explanation that would make them seem innocent. "Only a few people got them."

Hunter's shoulders tensed as he spun the bottle in his hands. "Venus blessed me?"

"I wouldn't call it a blessing," Jaylynn mumbled.

Blake glared at her.

Let me handle this.

"Sure," Blake conceded. "And she put Psyche in a coma as punishment for trying to reach Cupid." *A coma that might actually kill her.*

Unfortunately, Jaylynn was not telepathic and kept talking despite Blake's clear insistence otherwise.

"Hunter, we were given a chance to get compasses back. Venus gave specific people these markings as tasks."

"What do you mean?"

Blake shoved the bottle at Jaylynn's face. She leaned back with a disapproving glare.

"The insane goddess wants to play games with people's hearts," Blake spat. "If we play along with her matchmaking, she will bring compasses back for everyone else."

Yes, that is simple. Clean. He doesn't need details.

Hunter rested his curled fingers over his mouth, the distrust on his face plain. Jaylynn offered him the bottle. He took it and rolled it between his hands for a long moment before he spoke. "And Venus paired you and me to be a love match?"

Blake wasn't ready for the vulnerability in his eyes when he looked up to her. All she could do was nod.

"I—I guess so."

The look that passed over his face was close to pain, and Blake couldn't help but flinch.

Of course he wishes it was someone else.

"And what am I supposed to do exactly?"

Jaylynn met Blake's eyes and shrugged. Blake kneaded her forehead with her index finger and thumb. She needed to spin this in such a way that Hunter would get on board. She willed herself to make eye contact with him again. "You and I are supposed to fall in love. And we need to do it before the full moon."

Hunter's eyes widened slightly. "Why then?"

Blake sighed, because she couldn't agree more that the deadline made this improbable. "That's when Venus said she'd be back."

Jaylynn reached out and rested a hand on Hunter's knee. "We have a chance to get compasses back for everyone if we play along. The least we can do is try."

Hunter got up abruptly. Jaylynn leaned back to get out of his way as he walked toward the door.

"Brooks, wait!" Blake stood as she called out his last name. He didn't respond. "Hunter, please don't go. We need you."

Hunter grabbed his coat off the hook and went outside without another word, taking the bottle of vodka with him.

He can't leave.

Jaylynn's chilly hands wrapped around Blake's biceps, holding her back.

"Let him go. He needs time to process this."

Blake shook her off, annoyed at her proximity. "Great. That went great. Brilliant idea, Jay. Tell the man everything and scare him off."

Jaylynn crossed her arms. "I'm not the one who lost their mind and punched the mirror. And why did you lie to him? Hunter deserves to know the truth."

"I did what I had to do. It will make my task easier if he thinks he needs to love me too."

"You don't even think twice before lying, do you?" Jaylynn scoffed. She strode to the bedroom but stopped at the threshold. "Oh, and Blake?"

"What?" Blake growled, her defensive walls surging up around her.

"If you want to get on Hunter's good side, lying isn't the place to start. And don't leave that mess for him to clean up."

Jaylynn closed the bedroom door, and Blake glowered at it, but her frustration wilted as she was left in silence.

CHAPTER XXX

Lacey's phone hummed in her hands, the yellow notification winking in the dark bedroom. She opened the photo-texting app instantly, greedy for another picture of her soulmate's beautiful face. She didn't want to spend any more time today worrying about her mom's health or Nessie's anger. Damien's texts were the only thing that made this endless week of stress bearable.

The one thing that drove Lacey crazy was that Damien had his app settings set so his photos disappeared in three seconds. Lacey would barely have a chance to soak in his dreamy eyes and read whatever he'd typed across the screen before the message and photo would be gone. And, of course, she couldn't replay or screenshot them without him being notified, so she'd quickly adjusted to consuming all she could in the limited time he gave her.

Lacey opened the newest message, her pulse buzzing with anticipation. In the photo, Damien's hand pushed back his dark waves and his perfect smile glowed at her. He rested on a red pillow, only a trace of fatigue in his eyes. Across the middle, the message read, "Is it too soon to say I miss you? xxx"

Lacey's heart soared at all the kisses marking the end of the message. He'd explained it was a thing British people tagged their messages with, the more kisses meaning the more romantic. She gave her widest, most genuine smile despite the dark lighting, and quickly typed a message back.

LACEY: I know exactly what you mean.

Though his messages disappeared too quickly, Damien made up for it by replying instantly. In his follow-up picture, his lips were tucked into a pout.

DAMIEN: I can hardly see you xx

Lacey sat up. She didn't want to turn on the lights in case Charity came to check on her. While the household phone curfew seemed forgotten, Lacey didn't want to risk losing her only connection to Damien. Instead, Lacey gathered her spilling bag of clothes and crept into the en suite bathroom. She'd planned on showering in the morning, but she felt too restless to sleep now anyway.

Charity's bathroom was simple. White walls hugged the small room, and a generic green shower curtain made for a perfect backdrop. The only decor was a couple of succulents clustered on the ledge of the frosted window.

Lacey adjusted her baggy crewneck T-shirt. When she'd packed for Nessie's, she hadn't considered packing cute pj's, so her usual black band shirt and cotton shorts were all she had. Lacey took picture after picture in the mirror, trying to catch her best angle in the light until she felt satisfied. She typed the new message.

LACEY: Is this better?

Damien replied instantly, his lopsided smile pulled into a smirk.

DAMIEN: Yes, but this also makes me miss you even more xxxx

Thank you, Venus, for blessing my man with such a gorgeous sleepy face.

Lacey sent another quick picture back, one that showed her sticking her tongue out to the side.

The hum of incoming messages was quickly becoming her favorite new sound. Damien's next picture was angled to capture more than just his face and Lacey drank in the three seconds of seeing his bare chest, the sweetest shade of golden brown.

She tore her eyes away to read the short text before it disappeared.

The way the kisses kept getting longer made her heart soar. Lacey put her phone down and took a steadying breath. She dug through her bag, looking for anything prettier than what she was already wearing. Unfortunately, she was sorely lacking glamorous options. Her pink bra spilled out on the floor, and a daring smile crept across her lips. It was the one thing her internet safety classes said never to do, but this was her soulmate. She pulled off her oversized T-shirt.

Four embarrassing minutes passed as she tried to capture something that didn't show too much of her soft belly while also making her breasts look as good as possible. When she finally took one she didn't instantly hate, she sent it before her courage left her. She almost always left her photos without a time limit, but this one she reduced to three seconds.

If Damien can tease me with fleeting pics, then I can do it right back.

The next notification turned her already tinted cheeks the deepest shade of red they could go.

Damien had taken a screenshot of her picture! The one time she wanted to tease him and take advantage of the disappearing content, Damien had the audacity to save the freaking photo. An unexpected blend of horror and discomfort burned in her gut. While she felt honored he wanted to keep a photo of her, she also felt inexplicably betrayed.

Damien replied quickly with no caption, his face dramatically melting in awe. As soon as it disappeared, a second picture came. The phone was closer to his face this time, his lopsided grin undeniably mischievous.

DAMIEN: I didn't have a shirt on in mine. Show me more? xxxxxxx

Lacey sat down on the bath mat, a mess of emotion. She took a picture of the wall instead of her face.

LACEY: I didn't screenshot yours.

DAMIEN: I would have been a fool not to xx

Lacey rested her chin on her knees. She couldn't explain what felt off, but she hadn't missed that the number of kisses had lessened. Instead of sending a picture, she sent Damien a simple chat.

LACEY: I don't know how I feel about you having that picture saved. What if someone accidentally sees it?

DAMIEN: No one will, I promise xxx

LACEY: Damien, I'm serious.

DAMIEN: You're really going to ask me to delete the sexiest photo I have of you? x

LACEY: Would you... please?

Lacey waited anxiously for his reply. Was she making things awkward? What if she'd upset him by asking him to delete it? Lacey held her breath as the next message came through.

DAMIEN: Okay, done. I promise not to screenshot sexy photos anymore, as long as you promise to keep sending them xx

Lacey wanted to believe he'd deleted it—she really did—but what if he hadn't? He wouldn't lie to her, would he?

LACEY: We'll see if you earn any more. Brb, I just have to shower.

DAMIEN: Send pics??? xxxx

Lacey scoffed.

LACEY: You wish.

She turned the shower on and undressed. Her phone buzzed on the counter. It was another photo. Damien mocked a crying face.

DAMIEN: I would do anything for a shower pic. Please, have mercy on my greedy soul xxxxxxx

Lacey sighed with a slight smile. She stepped into the shower and pulled the green curtain across her body, leaving only her face and the arm holding her phone exposed. She took a photo in the mirror's reflection and sent it.

LACEY: Missing you.

Damien didn't screenshot that one. Instead, he sent a new photo. His dark eyelashes hovered low, and Lacey melted a little.

DAMIEN: I would give anything to be getting in that shower with you right now xxxxxxx

Lacey set her phone on the bathtub ledge and stepped back, letting the hot water warm her skin and soak her hair, flushed by the whole experience. All the while, she wondered if Damien actually deleted the photo, or if he only said he did.

4 DAYS

UNTIL THE SUPERMOON

In his vast coral castle, ruling deep within the seas,
The bearded ocean god attends to his realm's pleas.
He judges from his throne, his lethal trident in hand,
Creatures kneel for mercy, sailors pray to see land.
And while the Underworld claims souls when they die,
Neptune's domain is where their sunken ships lie.

—The Marine

CHAPTER XXXI

"Elias!"

Blake woke to Jaylynn's strangled cry. Even in the cabin's darkness, Blake could see the physical pain streaked across Jaylynn's face as she thrashed from side to side, her arms tangling in the sheets.

"Jaylynn, wake up." Blake reached out and shook the girl's shoulder, but Jaylynn only turned her head away.

"Let me go to him, please!" Jaylynn pleaded.

"Jaylynn!" Blake spoke louder, crawling out from under the sheets. Jaylynn's arms flailed left and right. Blake clenched her teeth.

Enough of this.

Blake caught one wrist and then the other and pinned Jaylynn to the bed. Her pale blue eyes burst open and she shot up. Their heads collided with a crack, and Blake launched herself back, grasping at her forehead. She cursed as pain lanced behind her eyes.

"Blake?" Sweat beaded down Jaylynn's temples as she winced, gently cradling her own skull. Her cheeks were stained with tears that tugged at something deep in Blake's chest. Jaylynn clenched the sheets to her chest, her voice hushed. "Elias isn't here."

Blake wasn't sure if Jaylynn knew she was talking out loud. She glanced out the open door, but neither Psyche nor Hunter had stirred, so she slumped back on her side of the bed.

This is my punishment for agreeing to share a bed.

"I—I'm sorry," Jaylynn whispered.

"It's fine," Blake mumbled. "I probably deserved it after slapping you beside the creek."

Blake didn't know why she was trying to make Jaylynn smile. Unfortunately, the joke didn't land, and Jaylynn's bottom lip wobbled as she lay back down.

Pluto, take me now.

Blake knew she'd never be able to sleep to the sound of Jaylynn's muffled cries, so she did the one thing she figured would shut the redhead up. Jaylynn froze when she felt the weight of Blake's arm wrap around her.

"What are you doing?" she whispered.

"Shut up and go back to sleep," Blake growled. The smell of Psyche's lavender shampoo in Jaylynn's poofy curls filled Blake's nostrils, and she took long, measured breaths of it. Jaylynn's body gradually relaxed. Part of Blake's brain screamed it was a mistake being gentle with Jaylynn like this—the girl might misinterpret things—but if Jaylynn objected to Blake's attempts to soothe her, she said nothing. It wasn't until Blake was sure Jaylynn had finally fallen asleep that she let herself relax and focused on quieting her own hummingbird heart.

When the sun became too insistent, Blake peeked open an eye. Psyche's bedroom was bright, the heart-shaped suncatcher gems shooting little rainbows across the bed, yet it wasn't the sunshine that woke her. Jaylynn's incoherent mumble under the blankets made Blake freeze. The memory of the night rushed back to her, as did the accurate awareness of their bare feet touching under the sheets. Blake scampered back from Jaylynn's warm body.

Jaylynn turned onto her right side, still fast asleep. She was the picture of peace compared to her devastation in the middle of the night. The protective side of Blake wanted to stay here, to preserve this moment where Jaylynn wasn't crying or fretting over Psyche. Then, as quickly as she'd thought it, Blake shoved the sentiment away. She couldn't be worrying about Jaylynn's happiness. Her only responsibility right now was her task. After that, she could leave this cursed cabin and move on with her life.

Blake threw the blankets on top of Jaylynn and resolved not to talk about what had happened last night—whatever *that* was. Her gray shirt and black jeans hung neatly cleaned and dried thanks to Jaylynn. Blake ripped them down and stalked to the bathroom, inexplicably frustrated by the small kindness. As she walked by the couch topped with neatly folded blankets, Blake realized something was wrong—something other than her complicated feelings about Jaylynn.

Where is Brooks?

The windows were still damp with morning dew, obscuring her view of outside. Blake dropped her clothes and stumbled to the door, throwing it wide open.

Did he leave in the middle of the night? Did he realize he doesn't want to be involved with Venus' mind games after all? Or was the effort of trying to love me too much to ask?

The cool air wrapped around her bare legs, but Blake didn't care; she could have sunk to her knees in relief. Hunter's truck was still there. Its windows were foggy, suggesting he was sleeping inside. Blake sighed and left him to whatever comfort he might have found there.

After a scalding-hot shower, Blake applied a couple small bandages over the newest injuries to her knuckles before sliding her fingerless gloves back on. Her burns were starting to take a turn for the better, but it seemed Blake's body was determined to always bear some type of injury. Without the mirror, Blake didn't have any way to confirm how sickly her complexion was, but it was safe to assume it hadn't improved.

It's time I try to make real progress with Brooks.

Blake couldn't waste any more time being mad at the circumstances. The goddess set the terms and Hunter was here, so Blake went to work on making herself presentable. She combed and dried her hair, something she hadn't done in weeks. After some digging, she found her makeup compact in the bottom of her backpack and did her best to bring life to her face with the tiny mirror. Thankfully, either the compact reflection was too tiny for the goddess, or Venus knew she'd done enough damage last night, because no golden eyes stared back at her. It wasn't until Blake heard the whistle of the teakettle that she knew what she had to do next.

"Hunter slept in his truck all night?" Jaylynn stood at the window, still wearing her satin green pj's. The copper tones of her hair sparkled in the daylight. Blake closed the bathroom door behind her with a bit too much force.

"I need you to leave," Blake stated bluntly, pulling up every internal defensive wall she could.

"Excuse me?" Jaylynn choked out. She dropped the edge of the curtain, her freckled face pinched tight.

"I can't do this with you here anymore," Blake said. "You have to go."

"Go where?" Jaylynn glanced between Psyche and the front door.

"Go to Charity's place. Go see your family. You can go anywhere but you can't stay here." The relief of drawing the boundary made Blake stand taller. "You're making things complicated. Besides, it's Saturday. You said you would go if your match hadn't shown up by now."

Jaylynn stuttered as she tried to grasp what had set Blake off on this trajectory. "I was going to leave tomorrow…"

"Well, I'm saying you're going now." Blake moved the kettle off the burner so it would quiet. "The full moon is on Wednesday, and you need all the time you can get for your task."

"What about Psyche?"

A truck door slammed outside. Blake glanced at the front door, then back to Jaylynn. Blake ground her teeth. "Listen, Jaylynn. I can't compete with you. I'm not pretty or sweet or kind. You're making me look bad. I can't have you distracting him."

Jaylynn's nose crinkled in confusion. "What are you talking about?"

Blake abruptly stopped as the front door opened. Hunter paused on the threshold.

"Mornin'," Hunter said, glancing between them.

"Jaylynn is leaving after breakfast," Blake replied, her decision final.

CHAPTER XXXII

Nessie adjusted the bulky yellow construction gloves over her bandages. She really wanted to help board up Winona's gallery, but now that they were prying pallets apart, Nessie realized her healing burns made her practically useless.

Gareth grunted as he pulled out another nail.

"Here, Ness," he said as he handed her the small piece of metal. Sweat slicked his shirt tight to the lean muscles of his back, and she couldn't help but be both impressed and feel guilty she wasn't more helpful. She glanced away as their hands brushed.

Focus. I'm here for a reason.

Nessie added the nail to the coffee tin that she'd repurposed as a pail. "Where did Winona and Mikom go?" She hadn't seen Gareth's exchange parents for a while.

"They ran to the store for supplies," Huan answered. Sebastian and his exchange partner's dad were folding up the tarp that temporarily covered the entry. Huan's prosthetic foot glinted in the sunshine as he crouched. "They should be back in an hour or two."

Nessie couldn't help but glance over the damaged property again.

This is all our fault. If compasses hadn't disappeared, no one would be rioting or looting.

The truth struck like a blade in her side. Based on the shattered storefronts and graffiti-slandered doors all down the street, the Harts weren't the only family to suffer an attack, but somehow seeing this sacred space ruined up close was worse.

The twins were working on taking down the hanging canvases; Tokala did the heavy lifting while Dyani documented the damage on each piece before they tucked it in the back room for safekeeping. Not all the pieces could be tucked away easily, though. Namely, the giant carved canoe streaked in neon-pink spray paint.

Nessie readjusted the tin in her aching hands, careful not to look into the metallic surface just in case something gold lingered there.

At least there's no mirrors here.

In an attempt to appease Venus—and not lose any more of her favorite outfits to magical makeovers—Nessie had dressed in a tight white tank top and denim shorts. It wasn't the most logical outfit to do renovations in, but the goddess must have approved, because Nessie had managed to get ready without any divine interference. She'd even wrestled her hair back up into its signature high ponytail, though she'd almost cried fighting through the pain of her burns.

"Damien, should we grab more pallets from the back?" Lacey nodded to the storage room. Nessie rolled her eyes.

Sure, go make out in the back while the rest of us work.

Nessie gave herself a shake. She wasn't here to watch Lacey's budding romance story. She had Venus' task to work on.

Make my mark fall in love with me. Ensnare him. Bewitch him. Make him forget about his soulmate link.

Venus' hourglass burned under Nessie's bandages, and she cringed at the thought of how sweaty her palms would be by the end of the day.

Nessie tossed her ponytail over her shoulder. "Hey, Seb, can you lend a hand? Gareth is being defeated by a tiny nail."

Her teasing remark drew Sebastian's attention from the swinging door where Lacey and Damien had just disappeared together.

"I don't need help," Gareth gasped as he levered the hammer, freeing another nail.

Nessie took the bent piece of metal and added it to the collection. Sebastian came over, his mouth tugged down in a frown. She gave him a sideways glance.

"I take it you two aren't actually close with Damien?" Nessie hedged. It had been fairly obvious at the match that they weren't thrilled Damien was joining, but Nessie hadn't objected. Having him and Lacey here gave her an excuse to be here too, and she needed every minute possible if she was going to complete Venus' trial.

Before Sebastian could deny Nessie's guess, Gareth snorted. "Absolutely not. He's a complete wanker."

Sebastian's mouth twitched in amusement before meeting Nessie's curious eyes. "He's not our first choice to spend time with, let alone a monthlong trip."

Nessie glanced at the closed back door, unable to conceal the touch of concern on her face. Was Lacey's soulmate a bad guy?

Sebastian must have caught the worry in her face, because he quickly amended, "I'm sure he'll be great to Lacey. He's just a dickhead to us."

"Why?"

Gareth's long arms flexed as a board bowed under his grip. "Probably because he's full of himself and thinks we're beneath him."

Nessie nodded. She knew what that was like. Maybe Lacey and Damien were a good match for each other. Seeing as they only had one hammer, Sebastian started to gather the freed boards in his arms.

"Here, Seb. Let me help." Nessie put down her tin can and grabbed her own mini stack of boards, following him to the open entry. She adjusted her grip so the wood rested mostly on her forearms as she stepped out into the afternoon sun. It wasn't until she set them down that she noticed the graffiti across the street. Her feet froze as she read the giant, sloppy neon-orange script.

Cupid is dead.

The gods are gone.

This is our reckoning.

Sebastian and Huan stopped beside her to stare at the vandalism too. The eerie message sent a chill down Nessie's spine. The gods were in fact very alive, but no one else knew that. Everywhere she went, the pain from Cupid's missing magic rippled, and she could hardly bear the weight of the secrets she kept.

But I can fix this. I have to fix this.

Nessie reoriented herself to walk on Sebastian's other side as they went back for more boards. The world needed Cupid's magic—she could see that more clearly than ever—which meant Nessie had a matter of days to convince Sebastian to fall in love with her. Why it had to be this boy, she had no idea, but at the match last night, Venus' mark had been clear. The boy with the sea-green eyes, sandy-blond hair, and scarred temple was her task—and Nessie needed to make his heart hers.

Never mind if it was even possible to fall in love that fast; she had to try. She would do it to be freed from her cursed compass and to put her dad's soul to rest; for Winona and everyone else hurting from their mistake; and so maybe one day she could forgive herself for how much damage they'd caused trying to reunite Psyche and Cupid.

CHAPTER XXXIII

Lacey stumbled to a stop as she entered the back room. It was crowded with framed artwork, and there was barely anywhere left to walk. It was the exact opposite of the private romantic space Lacey had been hoping for.

"Here." Damien pointed to another door, which led outside. Lacey momentarily brightened, only to discover the second door opened to a tight alleyway that shaded stacks of dirty pallets.

Ick.

Damien started sorting through the pallets, discarding any with excessively broken boards. Lacey, not eager to get her hands dirty, threaded her fingers together, bolstering her confidence.

"So… you know, I've been meaning to ask…" Lacey trailed off, momentarily distracted as Damien ran his hand through his hair and looked up to her. Every time she thought she'd seen him at his most beautiful, he'd do something simple that dazzled her all over again. Damien stared at her expectantly. Lacey quickly stopped staring. "What was getting your compass like for you?"

It seemed a safe place to start, the one thing they had in common, but for some reason Damien's shoulders slumped at the mention of compasses. He turned back to the pile.

"Waking up to be blessed by the gods was all I ever wanted. To know I was chosen by Cupid and the Fates to have a happily ever after—" Damien sighed as he let a broken pallet fall back against the wall. "I couldn't bring myself to show my parents or anyone else. The magic just felt so personal, you know?"

Lacey nodded even though she couldn't relate. The minute she'd received her tattoo, she'd wanted to show every person she knew. Damien lifted a plank and twisted it side to side to check for cracks.

"I hadn't even had my compass for a day when Gareth saw it in the locker room." Damien's brow tightened. "And then everyone knew and everyone wanted to see it. But I didn't want everyone looking at my compass, not when—"

Damien cut off, but Lacey understood and finished the thought.

"Not when it was so special."

He nodded, but there was something in his look that made Lacey wonder if she'd said the wrong thing.

"Yeah."

Lacey longed to reach out and take his hand but resisted. Instead, she nudged a pallet with her shoe. "Well, at least you don't have to worry about that anymore, and we still found each other in time."

Damien sighed. "Yeah, I know that, but… don't you miss it? You know—the magic of being touched by the Fates and Cupid? Of knowing that the gods are real and watching over us?"

The statement surprised Lacey. She hadn't really considered her soulmate link that way. Having a compass was magical and romantic. Well, other than when Cupid had given Lacey's mom a compass tattoo that pointed to Lacey. The reminder of her mom chasing her across Ontario with her link brought up a swell of grief. Lacey shifted from foot to foot, anxious to keep the conversation flowing. She scoured for any other topic that would keep her mind from wandering back to the hospital room where her mom slept.

"You're still friends with Gareth even though he told everyone you got your compass?"

Damien's mouth tightened as he dropped his voice. "We're not actually friends."

Lacey's brow rose in surprise as she scrambled. "Oh. I'm so sorry… If I'd known—"

Damien shook his head as he set a plank down. "Don't worry about it. The excuse to do this as a group is what made my exchange family okay with me coming today. I'll take any time I can get with you, even if I have to spend it with Gareth and Sebastian."

Lacey melted a little as he took her hand and gave it a reassuring squeeze.

"Let's bring this pallet in. It's in the best shape of them all." Damien grabbed the boards and Lacey held the door open, then followed him back inside. As they entered the gallery, Nessie's laughter rang beside Gareth's. They held opposite ends of a plank while Sebastian swung a hammer, trying but failing every other stoke to hit the placed nail. Lacey couldn't help the touch of jealousy that surged as Nessie grinned with the other British boys. She wished it was that easy between her and Damien.

"Whew," Huan panted as he took the pallets from Damien. "I am definitely going to need time in the hot tub tonight."

Lacey brightened. "You have a hot tub? That's sweet!"

Huan grinned. "You are all welcome to come over and enjoy it too."

"That would be amazing!" Nessie gushed. "I'll have my mom drop us off after dinner?"

Huan stretched his arms over his head. "Your parents are welcome to join."

Nessie's face fell and Lacey instantly knew why. She glanced between Nessie and Huan before clearing her throat.

"Nessie's dad died in the war." She delivered the fact simply, knowing it would stun everyone in the room, but also conscious Nessie wouldn't want to be the one to say it. Lacey could see the way the truth sat heavy on her friend. The least she could do was spare Nessie the need to explain.

Huan's cheery demeanor instantly softened. "Oh. I am so sorry for your loss, Ness." Everyone else went quiet as he stepped closer to her. He gave her arm a comforting squeeze as she tried to look anywhere else. "Sometimes it seems like all the Roman war does is take the best souls and send them to Elysium too soon."

"It's fine," Nessie muttered, but Lacey could tell by the blotches on her forehead that she was fighting the urge to tear up.

"When did he pass?" Gareth asked, his voice low and concerned.

Nessie blinked back tears. "Five years ago."

If there was anything Lacey knew about Nessie, it was that she hated talking about her dad. Nessie also hated crying in public. Before anyone could ask more questions, Lacey coughed.

"So, hot tub tonight, then?" Everyone looked at her with a range of surprise. She didn't mind if she seemed rude steering the conversation off course, because the drop in Nessie's shoulders told Lacey it was the right thing to do.

"Would your mom like to join us?" Huan amended.

"Tonight?" Nessie's voice was hoarse, but she tried to smile. "I can ask, but between the puppy and our friend Jaylynn visiting, she may be too busy to do much more than drop us off."

Lacey gave Damien a worried look as she realized this would mean even more time with Sebastian and Gareth.

"Would you come?" she asked. Lacey wanted him there but wouldn't force him.

Damien gave Lacey a suggestive look and muttered under his breath, "And see you in a swimming costume? I wouldn't miss it for the world."

Lacey burst out laughing. "A swimming costume? Excuse me?"

Damien wrapped an arm over her shoulder, pulling her close. The warmth of his physical attention made her nerves buzz.

"What do you call it?" Damien asked.

Lacey grinned. "A bathing suit? Swimwear? A bikini? I don't know. Anything but whatever you said."

Across the room, Nessie flashed Lacey a small, grateful smile, and for a moment Lacey relaxed. She couldn't help her mom recover faster, but maybe she had a chance of making things right with Nessie. Then she'd have only one big question left to settle.

Since that first day, Damien had not once made a move to kiss her—clearly waiting for Lacey to make the move after she denied him not once, but twice. She'd hoped this afternoon would have given her an opportunity and some privacy, but every time she considered leaning in, a deep shyness held her back. Lacey wanted their first kiss to feel easy and natural, but she also didn't want to wait forever.

Damien gave her shoulders one last squeeze before going back to help mount boards. His crooked smile made her heart stutter.

For every day I stall, this will only get harder. Lacey resolved she would make the kiss happen today, no matter what.

CHAPTER XXXIV

Watching Jaylynn leave the cabin was bittersweet. On one hand, they'd just lost their primary cook. On the other, Blake no longer had to worry about fielding her own emotions around Jaylynn on top of Hunter's stiff presence.

Blake had known for days that Jaylynn had to go, but last night changed things.

Jaylynn's puppy dog eyes as she packed a bag was exactly why the girl needed to leave. The truth was, it wasn't Hunter getting distracted—it was Blake.

But what was I supposed to do when she woke up crying? It's not like I could have ignored her.

A week ago, Blake would have left and curled up beside Psyche before ever trying to soothe Jaylynn, but something had shifted since Venus' tasks were revealed. Whether it was because Psyche was out for the count, or because Blake was finally seeing Jaylynn's true colors, the girl had started to grow on Blake. Perhaps a bit too much. And if Blake was noticing Jaylynn's charms, surely Hunter was too.

Not that Jaylynn would have a clue.

Jaylynn seemed completely oblivious to Blake's attraction. She wore those satin shorts all morning while she packed, her bare feet dancing over the hardwood to music only she could hear. No, there was no way Jaylynn had any idea that by simply existing, she was effortlessly beautiful.

"Do you need help?"

Blake started. She'd zoned out staring at Psyche's pantry, scratching her head. Despite his hulking size, Hunter had quiet steps.

He's like a Pluto-damned ghost.

"Hmm?" she replied, casting away thoughts of both the god of death and Jaylynn.

"With lunch?"

Today, Hunter wore a fitted white shirt and blue jeans. His soft brown curls seemed flatter than usual, and faint lines on his brow made Blake wonder if he'd had a hard night sleeping too.

Well, that's what happens when you sleep in a truck.

"Oh, I mean… maybe." Blake looked over the pots hanging in neat rows. Psyche and Jaylynn had always been the ones to organize the meals. "I honestly don't even know where to start."

Hunter shot her a curious sideways glance. "What would you normally cook?"

Blake shrugged. "I don't know. I could make boxed macaroni and cheese if there were any." Unfortunately, Psyche's open concept pantry was packed with dozens of bins and glass jars, but nothing Blake's microscopic cooking skills could utilize.

Hunter rustled through the shelves, then turned his search to the fridge.

"You fine with eggs and toast?"

Blake shrugged. She had no complaints if someone else was cooking. She made herself busy tidying the cabin while he cooked, folding blankets and gathering garbage. Soon the food was steaming on the stovetop, and Blake's belly ached all the more. Praying for patience, Blake went and sat by Psyche's side while she waited.

Psyche looked worse today than ever. The gray hairs were really gaining traction now, growing out in heavy chunks and spurts. Her golden tanned skin was starting to slacken, and age spots had appeared across her chest. Blake rested the backs of her cool fingers against Psyche's forehead. Thankfully, the woman had showed no sign of a fever since that first day.

Oh, Psyche. What are we going to do?

Hunter's lunch setup was very simple compared to Jaylynn's, but Blake wasn't about to complain. They sat at the round kitchen table in silence, both digging in, until Hunter finally broke the silence.

"I need to go to town."

Blake looked up in surprise. "What for?" She desperately wished she could smother the fear that he was about to leave her.

"I need some supplies. And we should probably get more food."

The mention of food implied he planned on staying. Blake pushed the scrambled eggs onto her fork with her fingers. Hunter raised a judgmental eyebrow as she ignored the clean knife he'd set beside her plate.

"What?" she said through a mouthful.

He shook his head and went back to his own food.

Blake shoveled in another bite. "I also need stuff from town."

"I could grab it for you."

"Mmmm, I don't think so."

Hunter rubbed between his eyebrows as if he had a headache coming on. "What do you need?"

"Girl stuff."

Blake tried not to smirk as Hunter faltered. Despite Blake's best scavenger skills, she had yet to find a single pad or tampon in Psyche's cabin. She couldn't fathom what the woman did when she got her period, but based on the low-grade cramping that had started about an hour ago, Blake was going to need a solution, and fast.

"What about Psyche?" Hunter tilted his head toward to the cot.

"She hasn't moved in days. We'll be quick."

Hunter sighed but nodded. "Fine."

Half an hour later, they both grabbed their coats from the rack. Blake took stock of the footwear at the door. Her combat boots' soles were peeled back, and the thought of forcing her feet into them had little appeal. Sighing, Blake weighed her options between Psyche's flip-flops, which would expose her bruised toes, or the rubber boots.

"Only Psyche would own sunflower rubber boots," Blake mumbled.

Hunter pulled his coat on and glanced over. "I bet Jaylynn would too."

He was right, of course, and that made Blake hate the bright yellow flower boots even more. But she slid them on anyway.

Hunter's truck was a pleasant surprise. The scent of sawdust clung to the old bench seat, and Blake took a deep breath as she settled into the passenger side. The soft sound of country music filled the silence between them as they drove past the gas station and continued on to a tiny excuse of a town. Hunter pulled into a parking lot with a pharmacy and a Tim Hortons coffee shop.

"I'll meet you back here when I'm done."

Blake hopped out of the truck. Again, the threat of Hunter abandoning her swelled up as he pulled away.

Stop being so paranoid.

She took a steadying breath and turned to face the small strip of businesses. Half of them had signs saying they were closed despite it being the middle of the afternoon.

Blake readjusted her backpack and walked to the pharmacy, which luckily was open. The bright white lights and sterile smell made Blake's nose itch as she scoured the aisles to find feminine hygiene products. Seeing so many empty shelves reminded Blake that outside the cabin, the world was struggling. It took her a minute to realize that losing compasses was also likely the reason so many stores were closed.

She balked when she found the tampon section and read the price tags. Blake shot a glance back at the register and front door, wondering if she could get away with stealing a pack.

But what if the teller stops me? And I have nowhere to go until Hunter gets back.

She ground her teeth at the inevitable. Her trove of stolen wallets from unlucky tourists in Niagara paid for her purchase. With no other option, Blake entered the coffee shop. Other than the person working the register, one cook, and an old granny sitting alone, the place was deserted. Blake sat far away from the withering old lady, idly kicking the center support beam of the table. The gentle pain that flared with each kick helped manage her growing anxiety.

He left me here.

Kick.

He's not coming back.

Kick.

I'm not sure I blame him.

When Hunter finally returned, Blake forced herself to look disinterested even as cool relief flooded her veins. She picked at the crumbs from her donut as he came and sat.

"You took your sweet time," Blake commented, not hiding her displeasure.

"That's how long it takes to do a grocery shop and liquor stop. I also had to get some tools."

"For what?"

Hunter planted his hands on his hips. "There's some things that need to be fixed in the cabin."

Blake didn't know what that meant, but she wasn't about to ask questions. Though she'd said Psyche would be fine if they left, the guilt of leaving the unconscious woman unattended was starting to set in. "Well, should we head back?"

Hunter held up a finger and went to the counter. She waited impatiently while he ordered himself a coffee to go, then they strode out together to the truck.

"You want to drive?"

Blake looked at Hunter in shock, bordering on horror. "Your truck? Absolutely not."

"You don't know how?"

Blake shook her head. "Never needed to in New York."

Hunter tossed the keys at her. She flinched, letting them fall to the ground.

"I'm not driving that thing." Blake stabbed a threatening finger at the light blue truck. "I will crash it and we will both die." Maybe dying in an accident would be better than being toyed with by a goddess, but Blake wasn't in a rush to find out.

Hunter shrugged. He hopped into the passenger seat and closed the door with a heavy metal clank. Blake fumed as she crossed her arms.

"I'm not doing this!" she called out.

Hunter just settled back, his phone in one hand and his coffee in the other.

Blake stood with her arms crossed for a solid two minutes. Through the coffee shop window, the old granny watched.

This is probably the most interesting thing that's happened in this tiny town all week. Well, other than compasses disappearing, I guess.

She let out a frustrated growl and picked up the keys. Blake hopped into the driver's seat and slammed the door with way more force than necessary.

"I take no responsibility if we die."

Hunter smirked and Blake couldn't help it as the corner of her own lips twitched.

What a pain in the butt.

He pointed to the ignition. "You know the basics?"

Blake understood the essential mechanics of a car. She'd seen enough movies. Turn the key. Step the right pedal to go and the left pedal to stop. Blake suppressed the urge to snap a reply back.

Be nice. You want to warm up to this boy, remember? Just embody your best impression of Jaylynn.

The truck rumbled to life, and the steering wheel vibrated under Blake's fingertips.

"All right, toss it in Reverse." Hunter leaned over, pointing out the silver handle that stuck out at an angle. "Sometimes it can be a bit sticky, so give it a good pull."

Blake blew a stray hair out of her face as she pulled the lever.

"Good. Now give it a bit of gas."

The truck whirred and puffed.

"Take your foot off the brake. Never push both pedals at the same time."

Hunter's patience did not help as Blake's shoulders crept up. She let off the brake and the truck jolted back.

"BRAKES!"

Blake slammed her left foot back down as they came inches from a small white car.

Hunter grinned. "Okay, rodeo star. Easy, now. Shift it back into Drive."

"You still want me to drive even though I almost took out that granny's car?"

"How else are you going to learn? Take it around the parking lot a few times to get the hang of it before we go back on the highway."

As Blake hit the gas, Hunter launched forward, nearly spilling his coffee. The slight twinkle in his eye was the only thing that kept Blake from boiling over in frustration as she fought with the truck to find a smooth rhythm.

He's actually enjoying this.

Blake set her shoulders in fresh determination, surrendering to the moment.

If Nessie can do this, so can I.

After coasting around the parking lot a couple times, Hunter gave Blake the go-ahead to get back on the highway. She almost smirked when she stopped a little too hard at the stop sign and he grabbed for his seat belt.

Her heart thundered like Jupiter's storms as she coaxed the truck to highway speed. One car zipped by, laying on their horn, and Blake shot them a middle finger.

Hunter laughed.

He actually laughed.

Blake couldn't help her smug smile.

"Keep going. You're fine."

There was something oddly satisfying about driving the giant truck. Blake felt safe, even powerful, like she could plough through anyone or anything.

"You're a natural," Hunter commented as he rested an elbow on the window frame. Blake grinned back, sure she looked a tad maniacal. She didn't care. Hunter's smile gave her an unexpected flicker of hope that maybe—just maybe—she might be able to meet Venus' challenge after all.

CHAPTER XXXV

It took all of two seconds for Nessie to figure out Sebastian's exchange family was rich. She should have guessed it based on the upscale neighborhood when she typed it into her phone map. Now, standing in the pillared entry, Nessie looked at the rock garden fountain feature and knew her mom would regret passing up the Suns' invite. Instead, Charity had dropped the girls off with the promise to return whenever they texted.

It was an unspoken agreement that Nessie's usually strict curfew was dropped. If she was going to get Sebastian to fall in love with her in a matter of days, she needed to spend as much time with him as possible. The sands of her hourglass had already been half empty when she'd rewrapped her bandages that afternoon. Nessie was running out of time, and it was eating away at her sanity.

If I do this, everything will be fixed.

Lacey rang the doorbell a second time, rocking back and forth impatiently as if she too felt the urgency pumping in Nessie's veins. The silence between the two girls was deafening as they waited before the oversized door swung open.

"Hello!"

Nessie grinned at Philip. He was wearing a cooking apron that was ridiculously short for his tall frame, and a touch of white powder painted the cuff of his sleeve and the side of his cheek. Despite his smile, Nessie could see the fatigue behind his eyes. Considering Philip hadn't been able to come to the gallery because of an added shift at the hospital, Nessie was surprised he was happily hosting.

"Come in, come in. The boys are already out back." Philip ushered them inside, and the scent of warm vanilla and cinnamon made Nessie's mouth water.

"What is that smell?" she asked.

Philip beamed. "A family favorite. They won't be ready for a while yet, but I promise you'll go to Elysium when you taste them."

Nessie grinned as she slid out of her shoes. Huan met them in the entryway, his genuine smile wide.

"Girls! So happy you made it. Can I give you a house tour?"

Nessie nodded eagerly, curious to see the rest of the space. Philip and Huan led them inside, each taking turns to show off their favorite features. The clean, chic style was a perfect balance of masculine with pops of color sprinkled throughout the house.

"Your piano is gorgeous." Nessie traced a hand over the glossy black surface. "Do you both play?"

Huan let out a raucous laugh. "I couldn't play if Apollo himself tried to teach me. No, Philip is the musically gifted one in our family."

Lacey stared up at the roof, politely trailing behind but clearly less interested. A petty part of Nessie resolved the boys could wait even longer. While she appreciated Lacey's intervention when her dad came up, every time Lacey's eyelashes beat in Damien's direction, Nessie was reminded why they were fighting in the first place.

Nessie took her time, complimenting each accent piece as they moved room to room. Downstairs, the lighting was warmer and darker.

"Help yourself to anything in the fridge." Huan gestured as they passed a bar that ran the length of a brick wall. A glass fridge glowed, packed full of pop cans and a few energy drinks. Both girls politely declined. Gareth's booming laughter echoed from outside. The slightest ache of nerves toiled like snakes in the pit of Nessie's stomach.

This is going to be fun. Relax and play it cool.

Lacey skipped ahead, swinging open the double glass doors. Nessie fell in love with the property all over again as she stepped out onto the walkout patio. Tall old trees created a buffer of privacy, their long limbs swaying in the evening breeze. The hot tub, easily big enough to fit eight people, glowed with alternating neon lights. All in all, the Sun family's backyard was the perfect private retreat, and Nessie could already tell it would only become more lovely as the darkening orange sky gave way to stars.

Damien stood with his arms wide. "Finally!" His swim shorts were hot pink, and his eyes glittered as they landed on Lacey. She brightened considerably, waving like she hadn't seen him just hours before.

Sebastian and Gareth nodded in greeting, both seated with the bubbling water up to their chests. Sebastian's hair was wet and slicked back, and for the first time Nessie saw his scars in their entirety. The jagged pink lines framed his left eye and trailed down his cheekbone. She was surprised to see they stopped at his neck but then started again over his left shoulder.

She waved back, faking a confidence that was quickly fleeing.

"Have you been waiting long?" Lacey asked.

"Ages," Damien replied.

Gareth sloshed some water toward Damien. "He's been here for maybe ten minutes."

Lacey shrieked as Damien reached out and tousled her hair with a damp hand. "Go change!"

Huan and Philip led the girls back inside. Lacey pranced into the bathroom, slinging her backpack over her shoulder as she shut the door.

"Ness, you can change in Seb's room if you'd like?" Philip gestured to the next door.

She smiled gratefully. Though she wasn't as eager as Lacey to join the boys, she was curious what Sebastian's room looked like. Maybe it would help her figure out how to win him over. The spare bedroom was decorated with warm browns and creams. Beside the bed, a suitcase was propped open, all the clothes inside folded neatly. Nessie wandered around, a bit disappointed there wasn't more to show about who Sebastian was—though the lack of decor made sense, as it was only his temporary room.

Finally, when she was sure she couldn't stall much more, Nessie sat on the edge of the bed. She wished she could take her bandages off, but she had to keep Venus' mark concealed.

Come on, Ness. You know what you have to do. Everything depends on that boy falling for you.

Nessie changed quickly, pulling her blue one-piece suit over her curves and wincing as the spandex straps cut into her healing fingers. Out of habit, she approached the large mirror to adjust her ponytail and froze. In the reflection, Venus grinned. Her long blond hair cascaded freely over her shoulders, and her eyes glittered a malicious gold. Instead of a blue one-piece, the goddess wore a risqué red bikini. The scarlet triangles barely covered her breasts, and unnecessary decorative straps crisscrossed over her ribs. The bottoms were high-waisted, but the sides arched high and showed a lot of leg, and even more butt. Venus twirled a not-so-innocent finger around a lock of curls.

"Like what you see?"

Panic pounded in Nessie's chest.

Not here. Not now. Please, no.

Venus wagged a finger as Nessie went to step away. "Ah, ah, ah. You and I need to have a little chat."

"No, thanks." Nessie spun on her heel, the too-familiar fear of doom making the hairs on the back of her neck rise. She scrambled to pick her clothes up off the floor and shove them into her bag.

"I can help you," Venus said, her tone dark and sultry. "You really think you can charm that boy in a twenty-dollar bathing suit?" Venus' ethereal chuckle sent a chill up Nessie's spine.

Nessie hoisted her bag onto her shoulder and raced toward the door, but before she could open it, the unnatural wind that had become her living nightmare wrapped around her, forcing her back. It wrapped like a funnel cloud, whipping her ponytail across her face as it spun faster. Dread and terror clawed at Nessie's lungs.

Please, Jupiter, Juno, Minerva… Someone spare me this torture.

If the king, queen, or wisest of gods heard her plea, they didn't answer. Gasping for breath, Nessie dropped her bag and held an arm out to protect her face. When the winds finally settled,

Nessie's hands shook. She took in the unchanged room, her hair now falling over her shoulders.

"You're welcome," Venus hummed.

Nessie glanced back to the mirror and blanched. The reflection had changed. Venus was gone, and Nessie's usual silver-gray eyes stared back at her in shock, but all Nessie saw was red. Horrified, she ran her hands over her body, looking down to take in the skimpy, strappy red bathing suit.

"No, no, no, no…" Panicked, Nessie dug through her bag, desperate to find where her blue one-piece had disappeared to.

Venus' cackle hummed in the air, her voice a whispered echo.

"Good luck, Nessie."

CHAPTER XXXVI

The hot tub bubbled over her ankles as Lacey stepped inside, and her cheeks flushed a deep shade of garnet. Damien drank in the sight of her in a black bikini, his lopsided grin tucking up and into a perfect dimple.

She slid into the bucket seat next to him, her teeth nibbling at her lip in a blend of delight and nerves. He reached through the water and stroked her bare knee with his thumb. Lacey practically vibrated at the intimacy. Across from her, Sebastian's attention was fixed on Gareth as he spoke.

"My mum says everything is fine, but with the war getting closer by the day, I'm not sure I believe her." Gareth waved his hands back and forth through the water as if he couldn't keep still.

Sebastian hummed in agreement, his mouth twisted in a worried frown.

"I mean, with the number of people fleeing across the Channel, it's only a matter of time until…" Gareth trailed off, his attention snagged by something else. Lacey turned to see why he'd stopped and also froze. Nessie put her towel on the bench and wrapped her arms around her stomach as she came up the steps. She kept her eyes cast down at the water as she lowered herself in. Lacey's eyes almost popped out of their sockets.

When did she buy that? And since when does Nessie dress so racy?

Nessie cut between the four of them, sloshing forward to sit between Lacey and Sebastian, keeping her bandaged hands above the water. Lacey didn't miss Damien's quick glance over Nessie's brazen display of cleavage, and a new fire burned in her chest.

"Loch-Nessie returns to her natural habitat," Damien teased. His perfect smile was suddenly less lovable to Lacey.

She pulled her knee out of Damien's grasp, turning to give Nessie a pointed look. "That's new."

Nessie shot her an unreadable look back as she sank in the water. She looked even more annoyed than she had over the past couple days. Though Nessie's lips were pressed into a thin smile, her eyes burned with anger—or maybe even hatred.

What is her problem?

Damien stood. "Does anyone else want something from the fridge?"

They all shook their heads, the tense silence growing as Damien retreated. Sebastian's eyes stayed glued to the water, and Gareth kicked his feet in the middle of the pool. Lacey chewed at her lip, unable to explain why Nessie's bathing suit made her so… mad? Jealous? Uncomfortable?

And why does Nessie have to dress like that in front of Damien? What is she trying to prove?

"So, what did you guys get up to after the gallery?" Nessie asked.

Gareth shrugged, laying his arms out around the edges of the pool. "Not much. We video-called my mum and had dinner."

"Yeah, nothing, really." Sebastian's sea-green eyes, sharp and brilliant, met Lacey's. "What about you?"

Lacey glanced down at her hands as the underwater light display shifted from ruby red to deep blue. "I talked to my dad for a bit." When she glanced up, she was surprised to see the murderous look on Nessie's face soften.

"I should have asked, how is your mom doing today?"

Lacey shrugged, trying to act indifferent. "The same as before. She sleeps a lot and has a hard time talking. My dad says she's getting better, but they've got her on a lot of meds, so she's pretty out of it."

"What happened?" Sebastian leaned forward, planting his knees on his elbows.

"She was in a car accident." Lacey swallowed against the lump in her throat. "At first they thought it was just a concussion and a broken nose, but a broken rib pierced her lung so they had to do emergency surgery."

Her tongue felt swollen in her mouth.

"Is she going to be okay?" Gareth asked.

Wasn't that the million-dollar question?

"They say she's looking good. My dad won't leave her side. I think on top of losing his compass, my mom's accident is really wearing on him."

Lacey sniffed, fighting the sudden urge to cry. *Now is not the time to act like a sensitive baby.* She tilted her chin back, blinking the tears away.

"She's going to be okay, Lace." Nessie's calm tone caught her off guard. Lacey looked over at her best friend, and the slight glimmer of old Nessie helped push the heaviness back.

Maybe I haven't entirely destroyed this friendship.

The patio door opened, and Damien slunk out with one of Lacey's favorite grins plastered on his face. She smiled, hoping he wouldn't notice how close she was to crying.

"Guess what I found?"

Damien held a six-pack of cans decorated with a floral design. Lacey recognized them immediately as fruit coolers. She sat up, the opportunity to have alcohol brightening her mood. Her mother was adamant Lacey could have supervised drinks once she was sixteen despite the legal drinking age being nineteen, but Lacey and Nessie had experimented a bit in secret.

"Where did you find those?" Sebastian sat up taller too, a skeptical look on his face.

Damien shrugged as he stepped into the water. "In the fridge."

"Really? I don't remember seeing those." Sebastian frowned as Damien pulled the cans apart, handing one to each person. Then he settled back beside Lacey, his pale eyes twinkling at her as he handed her a can. "For you, love."

Lacey grinned, taking the grapefruit-flavored drink. The group lapsed back into easy chatter over the next hour as the sky darkened. Nessie asked the boys about their families, and Lacey tried to relax as they got to know one another better. The water danced as the lights flickered between jewel-toned colors, and Damien's steady hand found its way back to Lacey's knee. His thumb did slow circles, and every once in a while he would give her a reassuring squeeze. She smiled and laughed when everyone else did, but she couldn't help it as her mind plotted.

Hot tubs under the stars are romantic, right?

She traced his hand with her fingers underwater, acutely aware of how much higher up her thigh he'd casually crept.

"What if we played a game?" Lacey cut in, stealing a moment of bravery.

"I'm in," Gareth proclaimed, leaning back and stretching his arms along the walls of the hot tub.

Nessie laughed. "Without even knowing what it is?"

"Absolutely. And I'll beat you at it." Gareth and Nessie grinned at one another and a fresh pang of jealousy plucked at Lacey's nerves. She wanted to share the same playful banter with Damien.

Is it because we don't have compasses anymore? Is that making this harder?

Lacey shook the thought off.

"You boys have spin the bottle back home?"

CHAPTER XXXVII

Gareth had most definitely played spin the bottle before, but it was more common back in middle school before people started getting matched to their soulmates. In his limited experience, Gareth had never found the same enjoyment his friends did in the kissing game.

"Are you having a laugh?" he asked.

A mischievous grin split Lacey's face as she got up. Her wet hair clung to her shoulders as she looked over the group, daring them to join. Gareth couldn't understand why she would suggest it. She and Damien could kiss anytime they wanted. Why would she want to make it awkward in front of the group?

"I'm in," Nessie said. She was careful to keep her hands out of the water as she leaned back into her corner, her face calm.

That gave Gareth another bout of confusion. Nessie seemed different tonight. Her sarcasm and wit were still sharp, but her smile would fall when she thought others weren't looking. He wasn't sure what was going on with her, let alone what she would get out of playing spin the bottle.

"Sure. I'm in too," Sebastian added.

Now, that really baffled Gareth. He looked around the group. "Are you all mad?"

Nessie smirked. "What happened to beating me at any game we play?"

Gareth crossed his arms, his competitive side instantly recoiling. "What are the stakes?"

Lacey sat up on the edge of the hot tub, kicking her feet slowly. "If you won't kiss the person you land on, you have to run around the backyard naked."

Despite it being July, the evening breeze had already chilled Gareth enough that he'd been wary of leaving the warm water.

Canadian girls are absolutely mad.

Damien laughed outright. "Deal. Where's the bottle?"

Lacey lowered herself back into the water. "We'll play without one. Close your eyes, spin around while you count to five, and whoever you land on, you have to kiss."

Gareth looked at Sebastian, sure he'd back out, but his best friend just leaned back agreeably.

"You don't have to play if you don't want to, Gareth." Lacey's hazel eyes danced with the dare.

"I'll play," he said. "But you have to go first."

Lacey split into a grin as if that was exactly what she'd hoped for. She splashed into the middle. Lacey closed her eyes and slowly spun, counting out to what she believed to be five spins. When she stopped, Gareth was the one who split into a grin. Lacey was facing him, square on.

He gestured to the grass. "Fancy a gander in the nude?"

Lacey rolled her eyes. She stalked over to him, her back to Damien. Gareth shot a look over her shoulder, but Damien just shrugged.

What is wrong with these people?

Before Gareth could decide how he felt about kissing Lacey, she was leaning over, her wet hands clasping his cheeks in place. Her glossy lips pressed hard against his, and he sat stock-still through the entirely awkward and lackluster moment. He didn't dare move or take a breath until she pulled away with a dramatic flip of her hair.

I can't believe Lacey just kissed me.

Lacey strutted back to her seat between Damien and Nessie. A quiet and serious mood fell, despite Huan and Philip's upbeat music filtering out through the upstairs window.

I just kissed Damien's soulmate.

Gareth sat dumbfounded and confused.

"Your turn." Lacey stared pointedly at him.

He didn't bother to ask her to explain the rules. He stood, perplexed, and went to the middle. Gareth closed his eyes. As he spun and slowly counted to five, he considered who he would like to kiss, if anyone in the circle.

Fortuna, please, just don't let it be Damien.

He let his prayer to the goddess of luck and chance settle. When he opened his eyes, he swayed a little. Cool gray eyes stared back at him.

Nessie smirked and gestured to the grass. "Fancy a gander?" she offered, mimicking his earlier comment.

Gareth broke into a smile. This was probably the best possible outcome.

Nessie's grin softened into an amused smile as he approached. She sat up taller to rest her elbows on the edge of the tub, raising her bandaged hands up higher to avoid the sloshing water. Gareth sat down in the adjacent empty seat, angling his body to face hers. Their eyes locked in a playful stare down.

"I'm good. Unless you'd like to?" He flicked his gaze to the grass and back, giving her the option to opt out. Nessie stared back at him, a defiant twinkle in her eye.

She has eyes like a goddess. All mystery and mischief.

For a heartbeat Gareth faltered, unsure where to put his hands. With a bit of trepidation, he rested one on her shoulder, the playful atmosphere dissipating in an instant. His nostrils flared in surprise when she leaned in to meet him halfway. Nessie's kiss was nothing like Lacey's. It wasn't hard and fast or sticky with lip gloss. Her lips lingered for a beat longer, the perfect balance between soft and firm.

Gareth broke the connection as Damien's laughter rang out, and he leaned back a little breathless. Kissing Nessie was strange. He still wasn't sure if it qualified as a good kiss, but the way her serious eyes stayed trained on him, he wondered if maybe he'd just been kissing all the wrong people before.

He dropped back into his spot between Damien and Sebastian, a touch dizzy. Nessie stood, the tight red straps of her bathing suit biting into her curves. Everyone's eyes seemed to trace the zigzag pattern of straps across her middle.

Nessie spun slowly, her arms crossed over her chest, and counted out loud. When she stopped, Gareth's heart sank, and Nessie's dimples disappeared.

Damien grinned at her. He pointed to the backyard. "I won't complain if you'd rather strip."

Damien's jabs at Nessie were really grating on Gareth's nerves. He looked over to see Lacey also scowling.

This game isn't going as you expected, is it?

Nessie stalked over to Damien, stirring up the water in needless splashes. She kept her arms crossed, a firm boundary between them, and planted her lips hard and fast—much like Lacey had kissed Gareth, Nessie pulled away quickly and moved back to her spot. This seemed to placate Lacey, but only confused Gareth more as he compared their kisses. It couldn't be more clear that Nessie didn't want to kiss Damien, but did that mean she had wanted to kiss *him?* Gareth shook his head, trying to settle his rising heart rate.

Lacey rolled her shoulders back, putting on a patient smile as Damien sauntered to the middle of the circle and closed his eyes.

Mad. The whole lot of them are mad.

Damien spun slowly, counting under his breath. Gareth found himself praying again.

Please, Fortuna, bless me now. Don't make me kiss this dickhead.

Gareth resolved he would streak if Damien stopped on him. It was dark enough no one would see much, and the yard was plenty private. Instead, Damien stopped slightly to Gareth's left. He opened his eyes and Gareth looked back and forth between the two, curious which one would bail first.

CHAPTER XXXVIII

Sebastian stared at Damien, his eyes flat. While kissing Damien would probably land on his list of things he'd rather never do, he wasn't about to be a coward. Lacey, Gareth, and Nessie all watched intently, their eyes flicking back and forth. Sebastian tilted his neck and it cracked.

Damien sloshed over to Sebastian, his previous grin settling into something darker. Sebastian leaned back, his hands resting in his lap, not doing anything to stop the approaching moment. He wasn't about to ruin the game—not when his turn was next. Damien's dark curls fell forward as his fingers curled under Sebastian's chin to pull him closer.

Sebastian's shoulders tensed, but he didn't pull back as their lips crashed together. Gareth howled, either in shock or entertainment, Sebastian couldn't say. A mix of uneasiness and heat flushed through Sebastian's chest as Damien lingered one second... two seconds... three seconds more than necessary.

In those heartbeats, two things became clear to Sebastian. First, Damien was a practiced kisser. His fingers held Sebastian's chin until he pulled away with a wicked grin. The second was that Damien seemed to have no problem kissing another boy. All the years Damien had spent making gay jokes suddenly took on a new lens. Why would he spend so much time nagging Sebastian and Gareth about their bromance? Was there a chance Damien was so vocal about it because he was gay himself?

But he has Lacey?

The reminder that Damien had found his soulmate hurt all over again, and Sebastian lightly shoved Damien back. That kiss was not what he'd signed up for, but it was better than getting naked. And maybe, just maybe, he would land exactly where he hoped on his turn.

Sebastian slicked his hair back, his confidence growing with every step as he went to the middle of the hot tub. Was it losing his soulmate that was making him so reckless? Or was it jealousy eating away at him? Sebastian spun, counting his four turns quickly, then slowing for his fifth. He turned until the night breeze hit him square in the face, faintly smelling of cherry. All night Lacey had been tucking her hair back behind her ears as the wind blew it forward into her face. While it was probably a nuisance to her, it gave Sebastian a certain amount of confidence his spin would land exactly where he intended. He looked up to see Lacey's wide hazel eyes staring at him.

"Ohhhh!" The echo of Gareth's entertained surprise boomed in the night sky, and Damien narrowed his eyes. He waved his hand for Sebastian to get on with it. Lacey sat up a little taller, her eyes going impossibly wide as Sebastian walked toward her. Damien's arm draped protectively over Lacey's shoulders. A small joy tugged inside Sebastian at Damien's attempt to hide his displeasure.

Make it count.

Did it make Sebastian a horrible person to want to terrorize Damien this way? Maybe. And was Lacey caught in the crossfire of their feud? Yes. But if Sebastian had to kiss anyone to piss Damien off, he would happily choose Lacey every time. That cockiness, knowing they were stuck in the rules of the game, was what made Sebastian reach his hands out and pull Lacey up to a stand, out of Damien's protective grasp.

Uncertainty glinted in Lacey's wary eyes. She clasped hands loosely on his shoulders to balance herself. Sebastian nodded to the grass in an unspoken question as his hands settled on her hips. At this, the playful and daring girl from before returned. Lacey smirked and shook her head.

With the smallest tug, he pulled Lacey flush to him. She stumbled and he braced as their chests collided. Then Sebastian kissed her without wasting another moment. She huffed out a surprised breath as their lips met, the sweetness of her lip gloss daring Sebastian to take a deeper taste. Her rigid posture softened, and she tilted her head as he did.

Then Sebastian's vengeful kiss turned to something else. Desire. This was what he was missing out on not having a soulmate. This was what he'd lost.

Gareth hooted louder as Sebastian wrapped his arms around her lower back. He knew he'd already pushed things too far, but the way Lacey matched his kiss only made Sebastian crazier.

"Okay, okay. That's enough," Damien called out, shoveling a tide of water at them. Sebastian broke off as Lacey did, breathless. Everyone stared at Sebastian. Gareth's mouth hung wide open in shock. Nessie had slunk back in her seat, her inquisitive eyes darker than before. But they were nothing compared to Damien's icy black glare.

Then there was Lacey. She stared at him as she took a step back, her fingers over her parted lips. It was as if, for the first time since they met, she really *saw* him. Sebastian wasn't sure if the look that accompanied her shock was good or bad.

Damien stood up, pushing between them to leave the hot tub. The moment of triumph soared in Sebastian's heart until he heard Lacey's worried tone.

"Damien—"

Gareth leaned back as Lacey splashed after him. She grabbed a towel from the bench, wrapping it around her body. "Damien, wait!"

Sebastian sank into Lacey's old spot, facing Gareth. Gareth gave him a questioning look similar to Nessie's, but Sebastian just shrugged.

"It's just a game, mate."

Gareth frowned as if he didn't quite believe him. The glass doors crashed shut as the couple disappeared.

"Well." Nessie coughed. She'd nestled back into her seat, her arms still raised to keep her hands dry. "That was delightful. Now we get to listen to the lovebirds squabble the rest of the night."

She seemed a bit resentful, but Sebastian wasn't too worried. He'd accomplished his goal, and he wouldn't take it back for anything. Nessie stretched her legs and kicked her feet in the water.

"So, what do you guys have going on tomorrow?"

"I don't know," Gareth answered. "Seb?"

"It'll probably be a quiet Sunday," Sebastian said. He felt so light, the summer breeze a perfect complement to the steamy water. "Huan has some physio exercises he wants to show me for my ankle. I figured we could have a gaming day in the afternoon."

"You guys game? What do you like to play?" Nessie asked.

Sebastian stretched out his shoulders. "Mostly first-person shooter games like *Call of Duty*. Sometimes *FIFA*."

Gareth snickered. "Seb doesn't like *FIFA* because I destroy him."

"Whatever," Sebastian snorted, though it was true. Gareth was wickedly good at gaming as well as sports. Sometimes he was envious of how easily Gareth excelled at things, but it was also one of his favorite things about his best friend. He was always a great teammate.

"You guys play *COD*?" Nessie sat up taller. She seemed more relaxed now that Lacey and Damien were gone.

Gareth glanced back with a grin. "You play?"

"A little. I'm not very good. It's more Lacey's kind of game, but I do love to play."

Huh. It surprised Sebastian that Lacey and Nessie gamed. The bubbles of the water quieted as the automatic timer flipped off. Gareth leaned forward to turn them back on.

"Why don't you come and show us what you've got?"

Nessie smiled at Gareth's offering. "I'd honestly love to, if it's not too intrusive. But can we find a way not to have the tagalongs this time?"

Gareth laughed in agreement. "Deal."

Part of Sebastian's adrenaline high faltered. He didn't want Damien there either, but Lacey? Sebastian shook his head. No. Just because he didn't have a soulmate did not mean he could get hung up on her—no matter how pretty her smile was or how nice she smelled.

Nessie's eyes sparkled at something Gareth said, and Sebastian paused, considering her in a new light. Nessie had an easy way of settling in with them, always quick with her quips and ready to laugh. Gareth clearly liked having her around too. She just fit. At that moment, Sebastian made a choice.

He hadn't come to Canada to find his soulmate, and he wasn't about to waste a month mourning over that anymore. Maybe it was from kissing Lacey, but there was a new clarity in Sebastian's mind. Cupid's magic was gone, but here they were playing kissing games under the stars. The chance for love hadn't disappeared, and Sebastian wouldn't have to spend the rest of his life alone if he didn't want to. And while Sebastian was in no rush to find someone to share forever with, potential lifelong friends he could do.

CHAPTER XXXIX

LACEY

"Damien, please wait!" Lacey clenched the top of her towel tight to her chest as she skidded over the hardwood floors with damp feet.

Damien didn't so much as flinch as he entered the bathroom then closed the door in her face. Lacey leaned up against it, her palm spread against the wooden barricade.

"Damien! Open the door."

She rested her forehead on the cool surface. Her heart battered hard—a storm of confusion, stress, and fear. Her splayed fingers curled into a fist as tears gathered in the corners of her eyes.

"Damien, I'm sorry."

A faint rustle was the only notice she got before the door swung open and she stumbled forward. Damien's eyes were a flat fog that Lacey ached to see through.

This isn't fair. How can he be mad at me after he kissed Nessie?

Water trickled over his shoulders, and his pink shorts clung to his legs as they dripped all over the floor. He reached for her arm at the same time she stepped forward.

"Damien—"

He pulled her inside with a surprising amount of force, closing the bathroom door again.

Lacey chewed her bottom lip. She knew she'd gone too far, but in the same breath she also felt justified. Though the game had been her idea, Damien should have known Nessie was off-limits. He should have taken his clothes off and streaked across the backyard like a good, faithful soulmate would have. And how was she supposed to know Sebastian was going to kiss her like that?

Damien leaned his back to the door and let out a frustrated huff. Lacey sat back against the counter with her arms crossed. She held her breath, waiting for Damien to say something, but he stayed quiet. The longer she waited, the less guilty she felt. She had every right to be frustrated too.

"You're angry," Lacey said, blunt and to the point.

Damien took a deep breath through his teeth. His fists clenched and unclenched before he opened his eyes and met her stare, but he still didn't speak. Instead, he closed the distance between them. Lacey shrank back but had nowhere to go. He framed her body with his arms, clasping the counter on either side.

"You think I shouldn't be?" His eyebrows lowered and pinched together.

Guilt joined the flurry of emotions in her stomach. Lacey didn't know what to say, so she shrugged, feigning toughness.

Damien towered over her. "You think I like watching you get hot and heavy with another guy when I haven't even kissed you yet myself?" He leaned closer, then tilted his head to the side so his breath curled down her neck. It gave her instant goose bumps and she held her towel tighter. "Do you think that was fun for me?"

Lacey swallowed hard. There was no more anger or fire. Shame swelled in their place.

"Damien, I'm sorry. That's not what I intended."

"Oh, I think we both know what you intended," he scoffed.

"What do you mean?"

"Do you think jealousy is hot? Some kind of foreplay?"

"No?" she answered weakly, her bottom lip wobbling. Damien leaned back, and Lacey's shoulders sank in relief as he gave her space. "Damien, I said I was sorry."

He looked at her through his perfect dark lashes, and her heart pinched at the pain she saw there.

"And that's supposed to make me feel better?"

Lacey uncrossed her arms. "I don't know what else you want me to say."

Damien's anger deflated. He closed his eyes, moving closer to rest his forehead against hers.

"Tell me you regret it," he whispered.

"I do," Lacey whispered. "I regret it. The game was a stupid idea."

"Tell me you're done torturing me."

Damien leaned back, but his chest stayed flush to hers as their eyes met. He took his right hand off the counter and wrapped it around the back of her neck. "Tell me you're going to kiss me now or so help me, Lacey, I don't know how—"

She launched forward, kissing him hard and cutting him off. A tear streaked down her face as his left hand wrapped around her torso, pulling her tight against him. His fingers dug into her side, and she knotted her fingers in his dark curls like she'd wanted to for days.

His tongue pushed for more, and she opened to him instantly, desperate to make things better. This was what she'd wanted: Damien, and his lips on hers. She wanted to be consumed by him and forget every uneasy moment since they'd met. She wanted to start over.

Their kiss was nothing like the one she'd shared with Sebastian. It was clumsy—a hungry, starved meeting of sharp intakes of breath and tongue. Damien nipped at Lacey's lip and she flinched at the pain, but didn't pull away.

When they parted for air, they both sucked in ragged breaths. Lacey ran her fingers over Damien's shoulders as his hands grazed up her thighs. He tugged the back of her towel, and she obliged, letting it slip to the floor. He closed the space between them again, pushing her against the cold counter edge.

"Lacey," Damien groaned.

"Damien," she whispered back as his mouth moved up her neck. With only their bathing suits between them, Damien's desire was impossible to ignore. She gripped his shoulders, steadying them both, as his lips found hers once again.

"Don't ever do that to me again," he begged between kisses.

Lacey whimpered a soft agreement, the desperate urge to soothe the pain she'd caused. Then Damien stepped back, leaving her with a sudden chill. Lacey clasped her arms around her bare stomach. Damien's gray-green eyes were a mist of emotions she couldn't begin to guess.

"Lacey, I don't want to start a relationship built on jealousy."

Lacey shook her head, her mouth swollen and tender from their kiss. "I don't either."

"It's not fun or sexy." Damien crossed his arms, and Lacey could feel the invisible boundary he was drawing. Her guilt was back, pinned in place by his stare.

"I agree."

He watched her as she stood, shivering and waiting. Eventually, he reached up and stroked her cheek. Lacey's hammering heart slowed a fraction.

We're going to be okay.

"I know this is all new, and we're figuring each other out, but there's something I need you to understand." Damien brushed a thumb under the curve of her chin as he paused. She stared up at him, waiting for him to finish. He sighed. "My parents don't have a very good relationship. They fight, a lot."

Lacey dropped her gaze to the growing puddle of water on the floor. "Mine do too."

"It's just—I don't know. I want to prove to them I can be better. That love doesn't have to be toxic."

Lacey nodded, completely understanding.

Damien's hooded eyes met hers. "I want the world for us. Everything. The ultimate happily ever after."

Tears pricked the corners of her eyes, and Lacey smiled.

"I do too."

Damien held out his arms and she closed the distance. He crushed her in a hard hug. All she wanted was to shut out the rest of the world, for it to be her and him and for no one else to matter. Lacey pressed her heart against his chest, praying he'd feel how sorry she was. She turned her head and his lips met hers again, softer this time. There was no punishment or lust behind the movement this time. It was a lover's kiss—a tender submission to one another. Lacey shivered.

This is what love is supposed to feel like.

CHAPTER XL

The taste of the last sealed envelope was bitter. Nylah washed it away with another glass of white wine. The stack of letters Nylah had spent all day working on were finally done. One to Jaylynn, one to their parents, and one to Jazz. Nylah's heart ached. Etching their last words, their gratitudes and apologies, brought up so many things.

Maybe I should go by Mom and Dad's before the sand runs out. But it'd been years since Nylah went there without an invite. They would suspect something instantly. They'd assume the worst, that Nylah had cancer or something. But they couldn't know. And if the cult followed them there? Richard and Natalie Clare were purists. They prayed to the Capitoline Triad of Jupiter, Juno, and Minerva above all else. They would be religious enemies with Fates' Followers. No, Nylah couldn't go to their parents. The handwritten apologies would have to do.

Jaylynn's letter had been the easiest to write, but she remained the person Nylah wanted to see most. The fact that their sister was out at a cabin with River and had left Nylah no way to contact her was painful. But maybe it was for the best. Nylah would never get away with lying to Jaylynn, and Jaylynn would insist on being with Nylah to the bitter end once she found out about the hourglass tattoo.

Then there was Jazz. Five drafts in, Nylah finally sealed the last envelope. It had been by far the hardest to write, probably because Nylah couldn't sort their emotions out for themself. In the end, they'd written what was true. An apology for not warning Jazz about the hourglass tattoo, then a quick sign-off:

I love you more than you know.

It didn't cut it, Nylah knew that, but in a matter of days everything had changed. They'd lost their compass, lost their soulmate, lost their job, and now they were bracing to lose their life. And with all those foundations stripped away, what glimmer of happiness did it leave? The easy answer was their charming, dashing best friend. Nylah couldn't be sure how Jazz would interpret their last words. Would he read the "I love you" platonically? Or did he also feel the curiosity of them becoming more than friends?

No, he wouldn't. Jazz was a flirt, but he was always clear he wanted to meet his soulmate. He'd literally bled himself out to try to meet his divinely intended partner. Even with compasses gone, it was unlikely he'd changed his mind about that. So Nylah's letter remained a weak memorabilia of their best memories instead of the confession spilling from their heart. There was no point in admitting on their deathbed that Nylah wanted more from their relationship. Jazz didn't need extra baggage. Nylah dashed away a tear as Boots jumped up on the desk.

"Oh, Boots. What am I going to do?" Nylah scratched the cat's head. A knock at the door made both of their heads turn. Nylah stood hesitantly, tucking the three letters in a drawer, then snuck up to the peephole. They let out a breath of relief at Jazz's face and opened the door.

"What are you doing here? You just about gave me a heart attack."

Jazz's mood was somber as he slid out of his coat. "Relax. You're fine."

"Were you followed?" Nylah demanded.

"I think I might have been at first," Jazz replied, leaning down to scoop Boots up. "But I took an elaborate route and shook them."

This did not make Nylah feel better. If the priests thought Nylah and Jazz were intentionally avoiding their tails, they might get even more suspicious.

"Have they called for any more meetings?" Nylah tentatively asked.

Jazz picked up Nylah's glass of wine, then sank onto the couch. "Nothing formal. There's a big protest coming up that they want us to attend, but for now things are quiet." Jazz took a long drink before speaking again. "I think they're still hunting that couple who escaped."

Nylah's mouth dried. They went and poured themself a new glass of wine, adjusting the record player to restart the deep, rhythmic hum of blues music. Nylah sank on the couch beside Jazz.

"How did everything get so messed up?" Nylah mused, flicking away one of the stray red curls tickling their nose.

Jazz rolled up the sleeves of his dress shirt and unbuttoned the top few buttons. He sighed heavily, as if he was the one with a death sentence hanging over his head.

"I don't know."

Nylah tilted their head to rest on Jazz's shoulder, breathing in his cardamom cologne. He tipped the wineglass back, draining it, and coughed.

"While I can pretend this cheap wine is delicious, which we both know it's really not, what if I told you I brought something better?" The mischievous glint in his eye suggested Jazz was certainly up to no good. He reached into his inside pocket and brought out a small baggie that held little white tablets. Nylah shot up from their slumped composure.

"Where did you get those?"

Jazz smirked. "Not telling, but I promise they're reputable." He shook out two pills, holding them in his palm.

Nylah wavered for a heartbeat. They'd tried a couple of different hallucinogens before. The first time had been the night they'd met Jazz. Though they had the vague memory of it being fun, the fact Nylah had never fully gained back their memories from the party still worried them. But after two sleepless nights and days of pacing, wouldn't it be easier to spend an evening high than worrying over things they couldn't control? Nylah picked up the tiny pill, not entirely eager but also not opposed.

Jazz pinched his thumb and pointer finger, holding the pill out like a toast. "To our damned mortal souls, may we end up punished to roam Purgatory together forever instead of tortured in Tartarus."

That Nylah could cheers to. They tapped their fingers together, and Nylah followed Jazz's lead, swallowing the pill.

The high took a bit to set in, but once it did, it was different from what Nylah remembered: somewhere between their limbs melting and being on fire. Nylah's skin felt softer than velvet and a thousand times more sensitive. And Jazz… Jazz looked like he'd swallowed ambrosia and joined the ranks of gods. His skin glowed golden, his smile impossibly bright.

"You're so beautiful." The words pooled in Nylah's mouth, and they weren't even sure they'd said them out loud.

Jazz laughed, his voice sweeter than music. "I love you. You know that, right? You're my best friend in the entire world and I love you."

I love you too. Nylah thought the words back, aching to say them but unable to. The words wouldn't mean the same thing. Nylah pulled back, but it was like a magnet kept them locked together, and Jazz leaned closer. The way he was looking at them, the ravenous craving in his hooded eyes, it didn't take a genius to guess what he was thinking.

"Jazz—" Nylah whispered. What could they say? *Stop looking at me like you're going to kiss me? Don't do this, we're friends? You're high, you don't actually want this? You'll regret it tomorrow?* But even as every excuse crossed Nylah's swirling mind, they couldn't speak as Jazz reached for their face. He traced a thumb over Nylah's bottom lip and they shuddered at the gentle touch.

"Do you ever wonder why Cupid didn't match us?"

Cold electricity fired through Nylah's veins. They leaned back, worried the drugs had taken Jazz to an unreachable level. Or maybe he hadn't said anything at all and it was Nylah lost in the high. Were they imagining all of this? Nylah sucked in a breath, aching for some confirmation this was real.

"You think Cupid got it wrong?"

Jazz looked at Nylah like they were the rising sun, his pupils giant and reverent. "Whenever we're together I second-guess everything. I feel like I'm my best self when I'm with you, and all I can think is if I can feel this alive by your side, how could my soulmate ever top that?"

Nylah simply stared at their best friend, free-falling in their own surprise and disbelief. Jazz kept speaking, the hopeful yearning shifting to sadness as his gaze dropped.

"I just kept thinking if I could just find out who Cupid originally paired me with, then I would know for sure I'm not mad. That what we have is real. And that maybe, just maybe, Cupid would forgive me if I chose you instead."

"Jazz," Nylah gasped. This couldn't be real. It had to be a mistake. The high… They were too high. "Your soulmate…"

The pain in Jazz's eyes was undeniable.

He thinks I'm rejecting him. Before Nylah could reassure him, he grasped their hands tight between his own.

"Nylah, I know in the deepest part of my heart I want you. To be with you, in every way. I'm sorry I had to get high to admit it, and I'm even more sorry if you don't feel the same way, but this is killing me. Now that compasses are gone it feels like our chance, you know, to try things without the interference of the gods or the Fates."

"But what if compasses come back?" they whispered.

Jazz sat back. He gently pulled Nylah's glasses off and set them on the coffee table. Then he rested his forehead against theirs. Nylah took a deep, unsteady breath. A part of their intoxicated brain fantasized how nice it would be to fill a pool with Jazz's cologne and bathe in it. His voice sounded like honey and fire when he finally answered.

"But what if they don't?"

Nylah could hardly grasp the idea. If compasses never came back, if Jazz could be theirs forever, Nylah would never be happier. Then Jazz's lips were on theirs, and Nylah's high peaked. True euphoria as every nerve in their body exploded in sensation. A twisted déjà vu blurred Nylah's reality as two scenes played out in real time. Present Jazz, with his perfectly groomed beard and glinting earrings, and younger Jazz with the same beautiful face and pink rave glitter highlighting his cheeks. Was he wearing pink glitter the night they'd met? Nylah couldn't remember.

The kiss deepened, and Nylah's mind emptied, their arms pulling Jazz closer, desperate to press their hearts together. Even if Jazz didn't mean it; even if he was only saying this because he was high; even if this was all a dream and Jazz wasn't actually here—Nylah was glowing. Whether they were in the fields of Elysium or if this was what being placed in the stars felt like, Nylah could see only Jazz.

Jazz. Their best friend. The person willing to fight the world by their side no matter what. Nylah had never felt so hungry and so satiated at the same time. Thirst dried their throat while passion fueled their blood. Everything felt so wrong and so right at the same time. Every kiss felt like an unspoken *I love you.*

"Jazz." The word slipped out between breaths, their clothes dissolving with all their cares. Nylah tipped their chin back as their neck tingled wherever Jazz's lips touched. If this was the last of their days, Nylah wanted to stay in this high forever. Nylah closed their eyes, surrendering to what was likely their last happy moment in this lifetime.

3 DAYS

UNTIL THE SUPERMOON

A famed musician raised as an archer like his deadly twin,
The immortal oracle Apollo delights in judging human sin.
Distributor of sunshine, plague, and health in equal measure,
Apollo guides mortal virtue when he isn't seeking his own pleasure.
The sun god's golden chariot sails Jupiter's skies all day long,
His evenings spent with the muses, in poetry, prophecy, and song.
—The Oracle

CHAPTER XLI

"With that, our Sunday service comes to a close. May the sun god rest on this gloomy day only to ride his chariot across our skies all summer. Our talented harpist will see us out with a tribute to Apollo."

The priestess bowed her head and gestured to the woman sitting beside the giant string instrument. Charity sighed in relief. While the highly detailed ceiling murals were a beautiful distraction, they'd lost their appeal as the monotone priestess had droned on into her third hour.

"I think my stomach is growling loud enough it could compete with the thunder," Lacey murmured.

The reminder of the howling rainstorm outside made Charity less eager to leave. "We'll grab a bite to eat on our way home."

"Could we stay just a little longer?" Damien asked. He ran a hand through his tousled hair as he squeezed Lacey's hand apologetically. "I really want to connect with a priest before we go."

Charity sighed but nodded. Lacey mirrored her fatigue. They stood, letting Damien and the rest of the people in their pew file out, then Lacey and Charity both slumped back onto the warm wood benches.

Damien approached a priestess in scarlet robes and gave the woman a curt bow. The priestess returned the gesture before guiding him to a nearby confessional. While Charity couldn't understand the boy's desire to attend today's service, she'd agreed to chaperone. The city was too manic to let Lacey and Damien bus around on their own.

"You know, I was hoping to have lunch at the hospital today to spend some time with my mom," Lacey said.

The reminder of Renee's comatose state hung heavy on Charity's heart. "Oh, of course. I will have to run home and let Ladybug out, but I can come back for you before supper."

Lacey nodded, her eyes distant. "I feel like I've barely seen my mom these last few days. Thanks, Charity."

Nessie and Jaylynn were both off working on their tasks today. If Lacey and Damien were also leaving, Charity could finally focus on bonding with Ladybug—which, if she was being honest, was going only moderately well. The puppy would do almost anything if treats were involved, but Ladybug was undeniably a free spirit and still regularly nipped at Charity's heels and fingers any chance she got.

There's still time.

Charity let her eyelids fall closed, the ache in her temples insistent. The sound of the murmuring crowd blended into white noise around her. Charity kneaded her forehead. She had to succeed at her task of making Ladybug trust and love her. Luke's soul depended on it. Nessie's happiness did too.

"Mortal daughter."

Charity's eyes snapped open at the rich, melodious voice.

"Lacey?" Charity called out, her heart rate quickening as she took in the empty pews around her.

Did I fall asleep? Lacey wouldn't have left me behind, would she?

It didn't make sense. Despite the pouring rain, sunlight seemed to stream into the church from every doorway, bathing the temple in light that made Charity squint.

"You and your friends have become quite the gossip among the gods."

The voice echoed off the painted dome ceiling, and Charity stood, trying to place it.

"Hello?" Cold fear chilled her to the bone as she searched for a face to put to the ethereal voice. It was somehow similar yet entirely different from Venus' musical tone.

"Sit," the voice demanded.

Charity froze as a man appeared on her left, seated in the pew beside her.

"How did you—"

The apparition's golden eyes stayed fixed ahead as he waited for her to join him. Charity swallowed, letting her weakened knees fold to a polite sit.

"Do you know who I am?" the man asked.

"Yes," she squeaked.

Metallic gold leaves circled his shaved scalp, stark against his midnight-black skin. The simple white toga exposed his strong but slim arms as he leaned forward, planting his elbows on his knees and clasping his hands together.

"It has been millennia since I was last able to take a corporeal form. The experience is much less charming than I remembered." Apollo scrunched his nose.

Charity didn't know what to say, but she forced herself to speak.

"How did you… Why are you here?"

Apollo shook his head. "The right question, but the wrong time. Tell me, Charity McKenzie, do you regret your bargain with Venus yet?"

She shook her head, unable to answer. If Charity was honest, while she regretted getting into this mess, the possibility of putting her husband's soul to rest justified the means. With that said, if Charity had learned anything this week, it was not to engage with gods.

"Are you afraid of me?" Apollo turned his attention on her, and Charity could have melted in terror. His unnatural golden eyes burned so hot that she had no choice but to drop her gaze in submission.

"Yes," she whispered.

"As you should be." The god leaned back, turning to face the front of the church. "There is a reason mortals and gods were separated by the veil. The fact that it's falling is not good news for those who die so easily."

"Why is it falling?" Charity stuttered, trying to quiet the urgent patter of her heart.

"Again, right question, wrong time."

Apollo seemed to be waiting, but Charity couldn't figure out what for.

Nessie would know the right questions to ask. But her daughter wasn't here. Charity was going to have to figure this out on her own.

"What do you want?"

The simple question made Apollo's brow furrow. "Yes. That is the question, isn't it? What do *I* want?"

The heat in the church climbed as the god of the sun took in the temple's murals. Charity waited patiently, keeping her own gaze downcast.

"I suppose I want what every deity wants. To be worshipped. To be remembered." He turned his molten gaze toward her, and

Charity shrank in deference. "But what to be remembered for? How to choose a side of this war? That is what plagues me."

Apollo rose, the soft white folds of his toga brushing Charity's shoes.

"The gods are divided as the opportunity of a new era transcends. Venus and Mars have their claws so deep in mortal affairs, of course they urge for the veil to fall. But Minerva holds firm, my twin sister, Diana, at her side. They fight for what I imagine you want—for everything to go back as it was."

Apollo's voice carried as he strode up the aisle.

"And you? Does the veil falling serve you?" Charity found her voice, cautious but curious.

The god paused. "I have not yet decided." He turned, reaching a hand out.

Charity forced herself to stand and walk to his side. His hand burned cold and hot at the same time as he led her down the center aisle. When they reached the front where the priestess of the service had stood, Apollo turned to face her.

"Kneel," he commanded.

Charity didn't think twice, dropping so hard and fast to her knees that she was sure they'd instantly bruised black.

"Tell me, mortal daughter, of all my gifts, which do you think has the most value?"

Healing. Plague. Sunshine. Music.

But none of those answers were right.

"Prophecy," Charity replied, her tongue heavy like lead.

"Hmmm." Apollo circled her, the trails of white fabric wrapping around Charity's knees. "Is that what you came here for today? An answer to whether you will succeed or fail Venus' tasks? A prediction of whether the veil will fall?"

"I am here to receive whatever you choose to bestow." Charity willed her frayed nerves to steady as he circled back around.

"And you believe you're strong enough? That you have enough heart and fortitude to bear the knowledge of a god?"

I am going to die here, aren't I?

There was no right answer, and Charity knew that as well as she knew when her plants needed water. "I can only do my best."

"Hmmmm." Whether it was a sound of approval or concern, Charity couldn't decipher. She pressed her eyes closed as his cool shadow fell over her kneeling form.

"I suppose we shall see."

The impossibly soft touch of Apollo's fingers grazed her temple, and Charity's eyes rolled back. Apollo's voice bled into her mind like a haunting melody.

"Rise, oracle of mine."

Charity's whole body shook as her thoughts blended with Apollo's. The bones of her skull flexed as if there wasn't enough room for everything inside her head, the divine pressure clawing for purchase. Images with no context flashed behind her eyes. Landscapes, elements, and familiar faces spun in rapid succession, each bleaker than the last. Charity reached forward to steady herself, her fingers wrapping around cool wood.

"The goddess's tasks are but the beginning... all must repent for the hope of winning... do not discard the vengeance she swore... her bitterness fuels the Endless War."

Apollo's haunting voice made Charity's skin crawl.

"Charity?"

She snapped back to attention, the tug on her sleeve making her look down. Charity stood at her previous spot in the pews, with Lacey looking up at her with wide eyes.

"Are you okay?"

No.

Charity looked up to the dais and scoured the meager crowd for a glint of a god with skin of obsidian. Apollo was gone, but the pressure behind Charity's eyes wasn't.

CHAPTER XLII

NESSIE

The front pieces of Nessie's hair curled damp against her forehead as she pulled down the hood of her raincoat and stepped into the Suns' house.

"Quite the afternoon storm we're having today. Was your commute okay?" Huan held out an arm for her coat.

"Not too bad." Nessie handed her jacket over gratefully. "My mom dropped me off before going to church with Lacey and Damien." The relief of not having to watch the couple coo over each other for another hour was immeasurable, but it still felt strange coming here alone.

"I'm glad you came. I'm sure Sebastian will be grateful for the distraction from everything going on in the world. He seems happier with friends around."

"Thanks for having me," Nessie said with a forced smile. If Huan knew her true motives, she doubted he'd be so willing to host her.

"The boys are downstairs gaming already. Call up if you need anything?"

"Will do."

Nessie trotted down the carpet steps, intentionally pulling her shoulders back. Apparently Venus' stunt with her bathing suit yesterday had sated the goddess, because she'd left Nessie in peace today while she got ready. The basement echoed with surround sound theatrics as Gareth and Sebastian both called out in delight.

"Did you see that?!" Sebastian leaned forward over his controller, his eyes glued on the screen.

The two boys were seated side by side, and it was clear Gareth was much taller, his face plastered with a grin as he flicked buttons back and forth. Nessie walked up, watching the screen as one of their characters got shot by a rocket launcher.

"Who's winning?" she asked.

Gareth glanced back with a grin. "Me, obviously."

Nessie huffed out a laugh and walked around the giant sectional to sit beside Sebastian.

Another explosion covered the left screen in white. "Bloody frags." Sebastian shook off the blast but quickly died again. She waited patiently while the boys finished their game, grinning as Gareth landed jab after jab at Sebastian's expense.

"You guys play a lot?"

"Oh, yeah," Gareth replied, tossing his controller on the chaise as the end-of-match rankings filled the screen.

"You wouldn't know it based on how bad I just played." Sebastian leaned back in defeat. "Do you want to play?" Sebastian's easy smile caught Nessie's as he handed the controller over.

Nessie chuckled. "Sure, but I can't guarantee I'll be much better than you."

As the next match started, Nessie and Gareth teamed up in a small bedroom, guarding opposite doors. An explosion painted the room white, and they both made their characters lie flat on the ground.

"It's crazy to think this could really happen back home soon."

Nessie did a double take at Sebastian, her character promptly dying in the assault. She hadn't considered how much the war game might remind the boys of the battlefront getting closer than ever to the UK.

"If it's bothering you, we can change games?" she asked tentatively. "I'm honestly way better at *Mario Kart.*"

Sebastian shook his head, as if suddenly realizing he'd spoken out loud. "No, it's fine."

Nessie pressed her lips together, unsure.

"C'mon, Ness, at least finish this game first." Gareth elbowed her. She obliged, but the ever-present guilt loomed over her. How was she supposed to face the fact that thousands more people were dying because compasses were gone and the Endless War border was shifting?

When the match ended, she offered to change games again, but whatever melancholy had hit Sebastian earlier seemed to have passed.

The hour went quickly as the three alternated turns between the two controllers. Nessie's palms ached under the bandages, but she managed her turns with minimal embarrassment. Hearing Sebastian's building laughter at her continuous virtual deaths helped.

"Thought you kids might be getting hungry."

They all grinned appreciatively as Huan came down with a plate of sandwiches, simple Black Forest ham and mustard. Nessie consciously took only one, not wanting to have more than her fair share, but when Gareth went in for a third, she couldn't help but laugh.

"Does your exchange family not feed you?" she joked.

Gareth shrugged. "They do—just not food I'm used to. Lots of vegetables and healthy stuff. Not enough carbs."

Sebastian gave Gareth a questioning look, but Gareth waved it off.

"It's fine. They're not starving me."

Sebastian ran his fingers through his hair. "I have to say, it's really nice not to have Damien around."

Nessie nodded in agreement. "I was desperate for a break from Lacey."

"Where are they today?" Gareth asked.

"Apparently church," Nessie said with a laugh.

Sebastian cocked his head. "What's funny about that?"

Nessie crossed her legs. "I don't know if Lacey's gone to church a single day in her life." She paused, realizing how she must sound. "Not that church is a bad thing. It's just... We don't..."

Gareth waved her worries away. "Neither of us are super religious either."

Sebastian snorted and gave Gareth an expectant look. "Other than your shrine to Fortuna."

"It is not a shrine." Gareth sat up taller. "And it's not a bad thing to keep the goddess of luck in your heart. You never know when you'll need her."

Nessie nodded. Maybe if she'd been more religious growing up, she wouldn't be scrambling for Venus' favor now.

"Damien must be religious, then, I take it."

Sebastian shot Gareth a questioning glance. "His dad is the head priest at the Halls of Mars, isn't he?"

"The god of war?" Nessie choked out.

Gareth nodded. "Yeah, and agriculture. I think his mum was a priestess of Venus before too."

Nessie couldn't help it as her eyebrows rose in surprise. "So let me get this straight. Damien's parents married despite worshipping completely opposite entities?"

"Love and war." Sebastian nodded. "But that's Cupid's matchmaking for you."

"If only his magic always worked," Gareth said, kicking his feet up onto the footrest.

Nessie froze at the unexpected statement. "What do you mean?"

Sebastian picked up his controller to work on a new gun customization.

Gareth rubbed the nape of his neck as he leaned back. "Let's just say my compass didn't work exactly as it was meant to."

Nessie's lips parted. "No way. You too? I thought I was the only one!"

Gareth's eyes lit up as he leaned closer. "Yours changed directions too?"

"No..." Nessie paused, taking in the information, her mind reeling. "Mine was frozen. It never moved at all."

This made both boys stop and look at her. Heat flooded her cheeks as she dropped her eyes. "I was just in the middle of getting it assessed by a specialist. Not that they could have fixed it, but I was hoping they could explain why it never moved. They didn't seem to have any clue, though."

Talking about compasses was dangerous. One wrong question could put her in a position where she'd have to start lying. But the topic had caught the boys' attention, and maybe showing Sebastian that she had no soulmate would help her task.

Gareth stretched an arm across the back of the couch. "Strange. No, mine would be steady most of the time, but every once in a while it would shift off course and point to the people I was closest to."

Sebastian scoffed, his attention fixed to the screen. "It never changed anything between us."

This piece of information really intrigued Nessie. The boys were undeniably close, but she had a hard time imagining them as intimate partners. Maybe their link was like her mom and Jaylynn's. "Wild."

Gareth nodded, his voice dropping an octave. "You know, it's almost been a relief not having to stress over my compass going rogue. Not to say losing the magic was a good thing. I just feel— I don't know—lighter somehow. Like there's a freedom not worrying over my compass all the time."

The parallel to her own experience made her heart hum. Nessie looked at Sebastian expectantly to see if he would offer any information about his own tattoo. Then a new realization struck her. Venus had told her to make the boy fall in love, but Nessie knew nothing of his history.

What if he already has a match back home? When he didn't offer any more information on the topic, Nessie pushed herself to ask. She had to know.

"Are you glad compasses are gone, Seb?"

At this, Gareth and Sebastian both exchanged a look.

"I don't know," he murmured.

Gareth patted Sebastian's back. "It's okay, mate. Everything will work out."

Nessie glanced between the boys. "What do you mean?"

Gareth leaned over. "Seb was about to find his soulmate when compasses disappeared. He missed them by minutes."

If Sebastian was mad that Gareth had shared that nugget of information, he didn't show it. Instead, he kept his eyes glued to the TV, scrolling through gun camouflages.

"I'm so sorry, Seb," Nessie offered.

He shrugged, acting indifferent, but the hurt was clear by the tick in his jaw. The guilt swirled like a whirlpool in Nessie's heart, threatening to drown her as she ticked off yet another beautiful thing she'd inadvertently ruined. The room felt too hot, her skin too tight. Nessie stood.

"I need to use the washroom."

The sound of a new game starting echoed as she closed the door.

"There you are."

Nessie froze, her pounding heart threatening to burst.

"Go away," she whispered. Nessie couldn't handle any more taunting from Venus right now. Wasn't everything bad enough?

In the mirror, Perfect Nessie's golden eyes glinted. "And miss all the fun? I don't think so. It's a pity your match hardly seems to notice you. Maybe you're not trying hard enough."

"I'm doing everything I can," Nessie said, hating how her voice wavered. "And don't you dare give me another garbage makeover. Your way clearly isn't working so why don't you go harass someone else? I've got this under control."

It was awful to suggest Venus target another one of her friends working on their tasks, but Nessie couldn't bear the sociopath today. Her nerves felt frayed and her pulse leapt at her wrist and throat.

"Of course you do." Venus grinned maliciously. "I'll see you in three days, Nessie."

As her reflection flickered back to reality, Nessie couldn't help the sob that tore up her throat. *Three days.* She clamped her hands over her mouth, desperate to hold back the flood of stress and fear that erupted, but it was too late. Nessie staggered to sit on the edge of the bathtub, her palms smarting against the cool porcelain edge. Invisible metal claws wrapped around her chest, compressing her rib cage and stealing her breath. She gasped as the uncontrollable tears started to fall.

Nessie hated how much Venus scared her. She hated how guilty she felt. She didn't want to fail and lose the one chance at saving her father's soul and her mother's peace of mind. She didn't even want her own love match anymore. She just wanted this torture to end. More than anything. Nessie hated what she was going to have to do to set things right.

Breathe. Come on, get a hold of yourself.

But no amount of logic lessened her body's now-surging anxiety attack. All she could do was lean over and gasp, waiting for her nervous system to realize the threat had passed.

"Nessie?"

In the same instant she glanced up, the door opened an inch. "Is everything okay?"

She held out a hand to tell Gareth to leave, but the minute he saw her tearstained face, his shoulders slumped. He stepped inside, closing the door behind him.

"Nessie, what's wrong?"

She shook her head, humiliated. She desperately tried to regain control of her emotions, but they were like a herd of runaway stallions. Her heart crept up her throat, and she wanted nothing more than to vomit. Gareth came to sit by her side, scooping her body against his in a sideways hug. The insistent force of his arm relieved the pressure in her head incrementally, and all she could do was give in. Nessie curled into Gareth's chest, mercilessly drenching his shirt.

"I'm so sorry," she blubbered. "I'm not usually like this."

He rested his chin on the top of her head, squeezing her tighter. "It's cool. Let it out."

When Nessie was finally able to take a deep breath, she leaned away, and Gareth relinquished his grip. She reached for the tissue box, and blew her clogged and runny nose.

"I didn't mean to ruin game day."

Gareth shrugged. "You didn't ruin anything. I'm sure Seb hasn't even noticed."

Nessie stared at him with glossy eyes. "Thank you."

He tugged her ponytail, a wide smile on his face. "Anytime you need a shoulder to cry on, or snot on, I'm here."

Nessie choked out a laugh, and Gareth grinned. They both fell quiet, listening to the hum of the video game in the other room.

"Was it talking about the compasses?" Gareth finally asked.

Nessie nodded. She couldn't bring herself to lie, but it was as close to the truth as she could get.

"We don't ever have to talk about them again if it bothers you."

"No, it's fine. I'm fine." Nessie grasped Gareth's hands, giving them a gentle appreciative squeeze.

For a beat, it was as if his dark eyes were looking straight into her soul. "Can I tell you something?"

Nessie nodded, a wad of tension growing in her throat.

"My compass always flickered to people I felt safe with. Friends I could be entirely myself around without worrying what they'd say behind my back." Gareth ran his thumb over hers. "And I think, if I still had my compass, it would probably point to you too."

Nessie's heart cracked as the warmth of his words washed over her. She hadn't forgotten their kiss in the hot tub last night— sweet and gentle and not pressuring her at all. The way he looked at her now, it was like Gareth could see through all the masks she'd worn since they met, and Nessie wanted to stay here. But Venus' hourglass had been clear: she needed Sebastian to want her.

Oh, Venus, why couldn't my task have been Gareth?

A pang of sadness struck as Nessie realized what she would have to do next. Gareth and Sebastian were best friends. What if Sebastian was keeping his distance because he could see her and Gareth's natural chemistry? Nessie pulled her hands away and rubbed the tears from her cheeks.

"Gareth, can I ask you something?"

He looked at her with such vulnerable conviction, Nessie wanted to puke.

"Of course."

"Do you think Seb might ever move on from his soulmate? Would he ever date someone that wasn't matched to him by Cupid?"

A shadow crossed Gareth's face before he answered.

"I... I don't know."

Nessie knew she needed to put the nail in the coffin, even though it made her hate herself.

"Do you think—" She took a steadying breath as her heart wilted. "Do you think he would ever consider dating me?"

The blow landed as she knew it would. Gareth's expression shifted from surprise to what she guessed was disappointment. He schooled his face quickly, sitting up taller.

"I can't say for sure." He glanced at the door, his knee rising and falling in a steady rhythm. "He never wanted a soulmate before, but since compasses disappeared, he's been…"

"He's been what?" Nessie urged Gareth to continue.

Gareth pressed his lips together. "He's been different. I thought he was mourning, but then that kiss with Lacey…" He stretched his arms over his head as he stood. "He's just seemed different is all. Maybe he's changed his mind about wanting a soulmate after all."

Nessie wasn't sure if *different* would work in her favor, but she'd take whatever information she could get.

"Thanks, Gareth."

He squeezed her shoulder and smiled, but it wasn't the bright grin she'd grown used to.

"Come on. I'm ready to whip your butt at *Mario Kart*."

CHAPTER XLIII

JAZZ

Waking up with Nylah in his arms was Jazz's idea of living in the fields of Elysium. The warmth of their bodies pressed together under the sheets while rain fogged and streaked the window was paradise. It was everything Jazz needed after this Tartarus-cursed week. At least, it was until Nylah stiffened underneath him.

Oh, for Fates' sake… Please don't regret this.

Jazz drew out each of his breaths, waiting to see what Nylah would do. Sleeping together hadn't been his plan when he'd shown up last night, but now that it had happened, all he could do was pray that his best friend would be as happy as he was.

Nylah kissed me.

Well, *kissed* was the understatement of the millennium. In all his years of worship and prayer, he'd never known reverence so intimately. Seeing Nylah so undone, wanting him like *that*, it was the answer to the question he'd fought for years. But now Nylah was definitely faking still being asleep, which meant there was a chance they regretted all of it. Jazz decided he couldn't spend another minute not knowing.

"Are you going to keep lying there spiraling, or are you going to say good morning to me?"

Nylah's breath hitched at Jazz's muffled voice. They turned, pulling the loose end of the blanket with them to create the thinnest of barriers between their bodies.

"Hey," Nylah whispered. The red bursts of Nylah's freckles had never looked so bright. Jazz reached out and stroked their cheek, aching to lean in and kiss that button nose he admired so often.

"Hey to you too."

Terror was plastered on Nylah's face. They'd never been good at hiding their emotions, but now, seeing their fear made a stone drop in Jazz's gut.

"I can't tell what's going on in your head, but from over here, it's looking a lot like regret." Jazz's mouth quirked in a nervous smile that didn't reflect how lightly he spoke.

"No!" Nylah replied quickly. Too quickly. Jazz swore he could feel Nylah's heart battering like a ram to escape. He gave them a doubtful look.

"Okay," Nylah amended. "No regrets, but maybe some worries."

Jazz's thumb dropped from their cheek. He folded his hands together under his chin. "What are you worried about?"

Nylah brushed back a stray curl. "That you'll regret this. That we just ruined our friendship."

Jazz shook his head. "Not happening."

"What if compasses come back?" Nylah asked, borderline pleading.

Was this their way of confessing their fears? Or were these excuses because they didn't want the same thing as they had last night? It was objectively a good question, though Jazz had never felt more certain that he no longer wanted his compass. Not if it meant he could have Nylah, and not if the Fates required death as their payment to return the magical blessing.

"There's no guarantee they ever will come back," Jazz replied, desperate to win this game and to convince Nylah that this was what they should be fighting for. "Any other questions?"

Nylah curled their fists to their chest tighter, clenching the sheet.

"Nylah," Jazz murmured. He squeezed their exposed shoulder, pushing away the memory of kissing it only hours ago. "The world is changing. Compasses are gone. People are going crazy.

And though I have no idea where I'm supposed to stand among all of this, I swear I want to spend every chaotic day of it with you. You refused to leave my side at the church; now I'm refusing to leave your bed." Jazz paused, rethinking the last statement. "Unless you truly want me to go. But in case you're unsure, I don't want to take back last night. And I hope you don't want to either."

Breathing had never felt so hard. Jazz tried to pry Nylah's hands from their chest, but they shook him off.

They're actually going to make me leave.

A new kind of desperation filled Jazz's chest.

"Please, Nylah. I know we shouldn't have started this while we were high, but it doesn't mean last night wasn't real." He gave Nylah a weak smile, his own confidence faltering. He just needed to say the right thing to make them understand this wasn't a mistake. So, Jazz opted for another truth. "You know, even before compasses disappeared, I think I knew I wanted this. It's why I let you talk me into a trip across the ocean neither of us could afford."

At that, Nylah laughed. Jazz shuffled closer, and Nylah buried their head in his chest. They lay like that for what felt like ages but was probably only a minute.

"Nylah?" Jazz asked.

"Hmmm?" they murmured back.

"If you want this too, please say so. Because I feel like I just threw myself over a cliff and I don't want to keep free-falling."

Nylah glanced up, eyes wide. They opened their mouth, then closed it again. Any hope Jazz had been holding evaporated. He'd ruined it all. Their friendship, their opportunity to be anything more. He'd gone too fast, read the mood wrong. He'd given Nylah everything, and now they were trying to find the most polite way to say no.

Jazz's world crumbled anew as he tried to read Nylah's face. It shifted so fast between emotions, but then it settled on one Jazz knew very well. Resolve. Then Nylah kissed him. Jazz took a deep, shaky breath through his nose as he kissed them back. It was like a floodgate of emotions had opened, warmth and desire flowing freely, and Jazz fought to stay on the surface, to stay present for this in a way he hadn't been last night. He pried at Nylah's arms once again gently, pleading for them to drop their walls and worries. Nylah pressed a hand to his bare chest.

"Jazz, I—"

"Hello?" a voice echoed down the hall. The distinctive sound of the front door closing made Nylah sit up lightning fast. The feminine voice called out again. "Nylah?"

Jazz clenched his fists. Nylah raced to the door, sheet in tow, and Jazz grappled for the duvet to cover himself. Nylah rested a hand on the doorknob, then seemed to think twice.

"Just a minute!" Nylah yelled. They turned and pointed once to Jazz, then to his jeans on the floor. He obliged, leaving the warmth of the bed.

Nylah scampered around the room, clearly trying to get dressed while exposing the least amount of skin possible. Jazz smirked but turned his back to give them their privacy. Nylah had kissed him. Whatever they'd started, this wasn't over. He grabbed his belt from the nightstand, then went on a hunt for his shirt.

"Nylah," he whispered. "I can't find my shirt."

Nylah was jumping up and down, pulling on a pair of jeans. They glanced around the messy room, then blanched.

"I think I took it off in the living room," Nylah said, horror-struck. The scarlet that flared in Nylah's cheeks was one of the sweetest things Jazz had ever seen. So, he'd have to go shirtless. He was confident it was just Jaylynn out there. Nylah pushed up the sleeves of the oversized sweater they'd chosen and faced the mirror, brushing away any hints of smeared mascara from the night before. And that's when Jazz saw it.

"Nylah… What is that?" He stepped closer, the glimmer of a tattoo on Nylah's wrist leaving him in disbelief. Compasses were gone. The unfamiliar mark twisted as Nylah spun on their heel, quickly pulling their sleeve down. Jazz frowned and grabbed their wrist.

"Jazz, don't—"

The sound of blood pounded in his ears as he ignored Nylah's plea. He took their arm and pushed the soft fabric back up, even as Nylah tried to pull away. There, where Cupid's compass had once been, a new mark glittered in silver.

"Nylah, what is this?"

"It's nothing." They tried to pull away, but it was too late. Jazz stared at the mark, so similar to Cupid's. But it hadn't been only Cupid's magic that flowed in those tattoos—it was the Fates'. Jazz's mind whirled.

CHAPTER XLIV

There were only two places on Terra Mater where Jaylynn felt like she could be 100 percent herself: Psyche's cabin and Nylah's apartment. Today seemed to be the exception to the rule, though.

"Nylah?" Jaylynn tiptoed into the living room. She hadn't thought twice about letting herself into Nylah's place; she had texted an hour ago that she was on her way. When Charity had left for church and Nessie had gone to work on her task, Jaylynn knew where she had to go next.

Empty bottles of wine cluttered the counter and two glasses sat dirty on the coffee table. Her sibling's collection of plants hung limp, and the rain hammered on the balcony windows, casting a heavy mood into the room. Even Boots was acting reclusive, curled up on her cat tree with her tail idly flicking back and forth in greeting instead of the ankle-brushing she normally offered.

"Just a minute!" The frantic sound of her sibling's voice made Jaylynn hesitate. Sure, it was before lunch, but it seemed a bit late to still be in bed. Had losing their compass affected Nylah this badly? The gruff sound of whispering made Jaylynn's eyebrow pitch up.

Ohhhh...

This was more than just sleeping in. The black shirt cast over the couch cushions confirmed Jaylynn's suspicion.

"I can, uh, come back later?" Jaylynn called out, already picking her bag back up. Nylah's bedroom door swung open. It bounced back with a loud clatter as it hit the wall, only to have its momentum stopped as both Nylah and Jazz stepped out. Jaylynn couldn't help the small gasp of surprise that escaped her.

Jazz gave a too-casual wave considering he was shirtless. His usually perfectly styled hair was in disarray as he walked across the living room and picked up the black shirt.

"Hey, Jay. How's it going?"

Jaylynn stood stock-still, unsure how to act. "Good. I, uh... I texted. Sorry, I didn't mean to interrupt—"

Jazz gave her one of his best smiles. "It's all good." He strode across the kitchen like this was a perfectly normal day, then poured himself a glass of water.

Nylah came to stand beside Jaylynn, still adjusting their clothes in their haste. If Jazz's hair was disheveled, Nylah's was a disaster. Red curls twisted this way and that, framing their scarlet and guilty face.

"So…" Nylah had on the fakest smile Jaylynn had ever seen. "What are you doing here?"

Jaylynn had most definitely made a mistake coming here today.

"I texted." Jaylynn offered her flat excuse, shrugging a shoulder in apology. "I'm sorry. I shouldn't have come—"

Nylah's mask fell, their eyes darting back to Jazz before their shoulders dropped. "No, I'm sorry. I told you to come by whenever. I'm sorry I didn't see your text." Nylah brushed their bangs into place. "I actually really wanted to see you. I didn't know you were back in the city."

"Is everything okay?" Jaylynn asked.

"Yes! Of course. Why wouldn't it be?" Nylah's tone was not convincing. "Here. Let me take your coat."

The energy definitely didn't scream "come in," but Jaylynn slid off her jacket. Nylah rubbed at their arms even though the apartment was hotter than an oven and they were wearing a giant knit sweater.

"Can I get you something? Tea? Have you eaten lunch?" Nylah eyed the bag at Jaylynn's feet. "And are you… planning to stay?"

Why is this so awkward!? Jaylynn wanted to claw at her hair and shake answers out of Nylah and Jazz, but she also wasn't sure she wanted to know what was going on.

"I don't have to stay," Jaylynn offered. "I just thought it might be nice to catch up after everything. If it's a problem, I can go back to Charity's."

"No." Nylah waved a dismissive hand. "Of course you can stay."

"Nylah," Jazz murmured in warning. Jaylynn shot a curious glance between the pair as they had an unspoken conversation.

Nylah crossed their arms at Jazz. "She's my sister. She is always welcome here."

Jazz leaned back against the counter. "If you say so."

"Nylah," Jaylynn murmured. "I'm sorry. I didn't know you were in the middle of something."

"I can go," Jazz offered.

Nylah pivoted and held their hands up to stop him. "No." There was an urgency there that Jaylynn couldn't understand. "Stay. There's, uh, some things I need to talk about, and it might be easier if you're both here."

Now it was Jaylynn and Jazz swapping stares.

"Nylah, what is going on?" Jaylynn asked.

Nylah wove their fingers together, a nervous habit from their childhood.

Jaylynn grabbed the kettle off the stove. "All right. Here's what's going to happen. I'm going to make us all tea, then you two can tell me what on Terra Mater's green earth is going on here."

Nylah hung their head like they'd lost a fight. They crossed to Boots' perch and gathered the cat in their arms before settling into the corner of the couch. Jazz sat too, staring at Nylah like they were a wild animal about to bolt. Jaylynn moved around her sibling's kitchen with easy familiarity, though the empty fridge and pile of dishes only added to Jaylynn's worry about her sibling's mental health.

Five minutes later, soft pink tea swirled in three classic teacups, steaming with notes of roses and berries. Jaylynn grabbed an oversized cushion and settled on the floor. She crossed her legs, placing her body in attentive listening mode fully facing her sibling.

"Tell me what's happened since I last saw you." It was a question River had graced Jaylynn with every time she'd come out to the cabin. Things were so easy back then. Jaylynn dismissed the thought, forcing herself to stay in the present.

Nylah's lip wobbled anew. "I'm not sure I can..."

"Yes, you can. You just don't want to." Jaylynn couldn't guess for the life of her why Nylah would even try to keep a secret at this point. Obviously, they'd slept with Jazz. It wasn't a big deal. In fact, Jaylynn had always been suspicious of their friendship. But Nylah clearly hadn't wanted Jaylynn to know about this, and the fact her sibling was keeping things from her hurt.

Not that I'm any better.

The memory of Venus speared in Jaylynn's chest.

"I don't want to endanger you too," Nylah murmured. Clearly Boots objected to Nylah's mood, because she leapt down and walked up to Jaylynn.

That's more like it.

Jaylynn welcomed the cat into her lap. "Nylah, you have two seconds to tell me what's going on with you, or so help me, I will—" Jaylynn glanced around the room for any kind of leverage they might have. "I will take Boots with me back to the cabin and you'll never see her again."

It was a lie, and they both knew it. Nylah slumped farther into the corner of the vintage green couch.

"You have to promise not to be mad."

For the next ten minutes, Jaylynn's jaw slowly grew heavier and heavier as it fell to the floor. Their teacups sat forgotten as Nylah recounted the past week's events—Jazz almost bleeding out on their floor, then Nylah nearly meeting their soulmate. Jaylynn's guilt sharpened with the consciousness that it was entirely her fault Nylah hadn't found their perfect match. But Nylah's stories weren't close to over. They rambled on, tears falling as they recounted getting fired from their job, then inadvertently joining the cult. Jazz looked stricken as Nylah explained that Fates' Followers had promised to return compasses.

"How could they do such a thing?" Jaylynn asked. She'd been so convinced another god wouldn't be able to right their wrong.

But the Fates had created compasses with Cupid, so maybe they were the exception? Jaylynn kicked herself for not considering them before calling Venus back.

Jazz cleared his throat. "We were sworn to secrecy, and the cult takes the vows very seriously, so we can't say, but you have to trust me, Jay—I will keep Nylah safe. No matter what. And as soon as the unrest settles, I will get us both out."

He reached out and Nylah took his hand. They were both dancing around something darker, but Jaylynn wasn't sure she wanted to know what it was. Nylah rubbed at their eyes with their sweater's sleeves.

"I probably sound so crazy right now. I'm so sorry to just dump all of this on you."

This made Jaylynn frown. "Stop it. For the love of Cupid, Nylah. You shouldn't have gone through all of that alone. I'm sorry I wasn't here for you." Jaylynn fought her own desire to cry as she took a steadying breath. She clutched her fingers together, knowing what had to happen next.

"In the name of sibling honesty…" Jaylynn cleared her throat. "I have things I need to tell you too. But I'm not sure you're going to believe them."

This caught Nylah's attention. "Things? What things?"

It wasn't ideal that Jazz was here, and while Nylah's story hadn't elaborated on whatever was happening between them, Jaylynn made a split-second decision to trust them both.

Jaylynn coughed. "Well, to start, I think I need to tell you the truth about River."

It was inevitable. Jaylynn knew it now that she was here. There was no world she could ever keep this from her sibling. Unlike Nylah's summary of the week, Jaylynn's story was interrupted dozens of times as Nylah demanded answers and Jaylynn did her best to explain things—from how her compass had led her to the cursed mortal, Psyche; the story of how Blake, Nessie, and Charity came into the fold; then everything with Venus.

At the mention of their barter with the goddess, Jazz swore and got up, pacing around the apartment. Nylah's eyes got particularly wide when Jaylynn started explaining the tasks they'd been presented with as an opportunity to bring back compasses.

"I know it all sounds insane, but I swear I'm not making it up. I just have to help someone choose the right love match." Jaylynn pleaded her case, sure she seemed insane. But Nylah had seen Jaylynn at rock bottom before, and Jaylynn trusted her sibling more than anyone.

"I believe you." Nylah's whole body seemed to deflate with the admission.

"You do?" Jaylynn asked. She should have known that of everyone in the world, it would be Nylah who'd understand, but she was still shocked.

"There is one more thing I haven't told you." Nylah pulled up the sleeve of their sweater. "I believe your story because I think I'm your missing clue."

Venus' hourglass glittered, its sands twirling down the center spire in an elegant swirl. Jaylynn's heart soared.

"Nylah, this is amazing news! All we have to do is follow it and find your match, then we'll get compasses back and Psyche will be okay. Everything will go back to normal."

Jazz had stopped pacing, the rich tones of his face washing out. He stared at Nylah like Jaylynn had just delivered their death sentence. Suddenly, the news didn't seem as good.

Nylah shook their head, tears cusping anew. "Jay… I spent the last few days thinking that when the sand ran out of this hourglass I was going to die."

The pain behind Nylah's confession made Jaylynn's heart split in two. She took Jazz's abandoned spot, wrapping a protective arm over Nylah's back.

"Oh, Nylah. That's horrible. I am so sorry I didn't come sooner. I didn't know…"

"So, I'm not going to die?"

"You're not going to die," Jaylynn affirmed, pulling Nylah's keening body closer. Nylah sobbed, and Jaylynn's heart shattered as her sibling processed the news.

By the time Nylah finally pulled it together, their voice was hoarse. "Jay, I hate to say it, but I think Venus is intentionally setting you up to fail. Did you miss the part where I told you I think my soulmate was stolen?"

Jazz had crossed the room to the tall windows and was staring out, his back to them both. It pained Jaylynn to have this conversation, but she had to convince Nylah to follow their mark, even with the complications of their relationship with Jazz. Maybe he was exactly *why* Venus had said to guide her mark's heart to the right choice. Jaylynn would have to convince Nylah to give Jazz up and find their original mark.

"We'll just show your soulmate the hourglass."

Nylah sat forward, shrugging Jaylynn's arm off. "And you think a perfect stranger will believe everything you just told me? No one else knows what these markings mean, and if we start telling the truth and people realize who is to blame…" Nylah's eyes darkened with horrified understanding. "If anyone knows why compasses really disappeared, all of you would be hunted."

Goose bumps prickled Jaylynn's arms. "Hunted? Why would you say that? Besides, they don't have to know that we were the reason."

"How do you plan on explaining Venus' mark, Jay? How do you plan on convincing my soulmate they have the wrong match?" Nylah bumped the table as they got up, making the delicate teacups clatter against their saucers.

"We'll find a way—"

"No. I already have the cult to worry about. I don't want to worry about your safety too. This is all too dangerous."

Boots skittered out of the room as Jaylynn stood with her fists clenched. "But can't you see? If we can just find your soulmate and get compasses back, you won't have to worry about the cult anymore!" Jaylynn grabbed Nylah's wrist and softened her voice. "Nylah, you have a chance to fix not only your fate, but everyone else's."

As Jaylynn said it, she could see the responsibility settle on her sibling's shoulders. Instantly, Jaylynn wished she could take it back.

Nylah shook their head. The bright red veins of their bloodshot eyes stared back at Jaylynn.

"I can't do this, Jay."

"Yes, you can. And I will help you. That's the entire point of my task."

"And if we fail? If my soulmate rejects me? What if we get thrown in jail?" Nylah pulled free of Jaylynn's grasp. Jazz tensed as Nylah moved to his side.

"What if I don't want to find my soulmate anymore?" Nylah whispered.

The grief in Jazz's eyes filled Jaylyn with remorse. She took a step closer, the desperation leaking into her voice. She didn't want to pull Nylah and Jazz apart, but everything was at stake.

"We have to at least try."

The muscle in Nylah's jaw ticked.

"Please, Nylah," Jaylynn whispered. "I know it's too much to ask, but please, I need you to try. For me. For Psyche. For compasses. This could literally stop the war."

Jazz turned, wrapping Nylah into his arms like a cocoon of safety.

"Nylah," he murmured.

Nylah shook their head, their nails clawing into the front of his shirt. Jaylynn hated herself. She wished it could have been any other way. Jazz tilted Nylah's chin up in an affectionate gesture that seemed practiced.

"If you do this, the cult will stop," Jazz said quietly.

Nylah sniffled and suppressed another sob. Jaylynn's own tears ran down her cheeks. Finally, Nylah answered.

"Not tonight."

Jaylynn swallowed, the weight of all the pain she caused threatening to bury her. "Nylah, we only have days left—"

"I said not tonight!" Nylah's eyes burned as they whipped around. Jaylynn shrank back. "I just need a night, Jay," Nylah whispered as their shoulders fell. "Let me process everything."

Jaylynn bit her lip. "Okay. Tomorrow morning, then. First thing."

"Tomorrow."

A tingle of warning hovered in Jaylynn's nerves, but she ignored it. If this was what Nylah needed to agree, Jaylynn would make it work. They were going to find Nylah's soulmate. They were going to make everything right. They had to.

CHAPTER XLV

The eerie thrill of deceit crept up Lacey's spine as she turned the key to the apartment.

"Dad?"

There was no answer, as she'd hoped. Lacey flashed a daring smile behind her.

"Welcome to my home."

Lacey hadn't been to the apartment in days, and it looked like her father hadn't either. Take-out containers burst from the trash, dog toys were scattered across the living room rug, and unopened mail sat in a pile on the kitchen counter.

Damien wrapped his arms around her waist from behind, and Lacey laughed, glee swirling anew. It was ironic that she was sneaking into the apartment instead of out of it for a change. Outside, the storm escalated, thunder rumbling in the distance. Lacey pivoted, wrapping her arms around Damien's neck.

"I told you no one would be here."

"And you're positive your dad won't be back?"

Lacey shook her head. "No. He'll be at the hospital all day. I'm not convinced he ever leaves."

Lacey bubbled with pride that she had pulled this off. The white lie to Charity had gone so smoothly, and after they'd walked in one wing of the hospital, they went right out the other side. Lacey would have loved to stop in and actually see her mom, but that would have meant seeing her dad. No, it was easier to avoid that heavy room with endless beeping and frantic nurses. Today Lacey just wanted to be happy and in love.

"Well, how would you like to spend our rainy afternoon?" Damien asked, pulling her closer with a suggestive grin.

Lacey pressed her palms into his chest. "I was thinking we could watch a movie."

"I love movies," Damien murmured, lowering his lips to hers.

Lacey kicked off her shoes as she leaned into the kiss, instantly starving for more. Damien followed suit, and she pulled him backward to the couch. The backs of her knees hit the cushions, and Lacey's breath caught as he gently pushed her down. She grinned.

"What kind of movies do you like?" she asked.

Damien slid out of his coat. "You could put on anything right now and it would probably be my favorite movie." His eyes raked over her, and Lacey flushed in delight. She pushed herself up and grabbed the remote.

The TV turned on to a news broadcast of a man in military uniform standing behind a podium. The caption scrolling across the bottom in red text read, *Commander in chief warns Canadians if recruitment numbers continue to drop, stronger action will be taken.*

Lacey quickly flipped to the first streaming service she could find. Damien sunk onto the couch beside her, his arm draped over her shoulders.

The first movie that came up was an old Marvel movie. Lacey figured her dad must have put it on to fall asleep. She hit Play and tossed the remote onto the table, turning her full attention back to her actual priority.

"For the love of Cupid, Venus, Juno, and whoever else I have to thank," Damien murmured as Lacey turned to straddle his lap. "How did I get so lucky?"

Lacey's chest ached and she grinned, leaning forward and taking his lip between her teeth.

You aren't the only one who got lucky.

She had prayed her soulmate would be gorgeous and smart and charming. The fact he came with a beautiful English accent and a sensitive heart was beyond her wildest dreams. The opening music of the movie was too loud, but she couldn't be bothered to retrieve the remote.

"Lacey. Gods, you're so gorgeous." Damien's hands slid under her oversized hoodie, gripping her waist and pulling her down harder against him.

Adrenaline coursed red-hot through Lacey's veins as she kissed him into silence. Damien's greedy hands moved up under her sweater to cup her breasts, and her breath caught in surprise.

"Too fast?" he asked as she broke off the kiss, his hands freezing against her skin.

Lacey shook her head, though internally she battled between surprise and exhilaration.

Damien pulled back and lowered his hands to her ribs.

"Tell me what you're thinking," he said.

Lacey shook her head again and leaned forward to close the gap. "Nothing."

Damien frowned. "Lace, I'm not going to rush you if you're nervous."

"I'm not nervous." She knew she'd said it too fast to sound convincing.

With slow, calculated swirls, Damien ran his thumbs over her bare skin. "Let's play a game. For every step we take, I'm going to ask if you want it hotter or colder." He leaned closer, his lips brushing her jawbone. Lacey tilted her head, revealing the length of her neck to his gentle kisses. "If you like what I'm doing, say hotter. If what I'm doing is giving you any kind of conflicting feelings and you want to go back a step, say colder."

Exactly how far is he thinking of going? And why does he seem so practiced at all of this?

Her nerves felt frayed and extra sensitive as Damien's hands moved back up to cup her breasts.

"Hotter or colder?" he murmured against her neck.

How was she supposed to answer that? Couldn't he just read her mind and know that it was both? Damien squeezed gently.

"Lacey, answer the question."

She swallowed, fire licking in her veins.

Be brave. Be cool. This is your soulmate. Everything is fine.

"Hotter," she whispered.

Damien grinned, releasing her, only so he could pull her in for a kiss. Lacey relaxed into his mouth, these motions familiar and easy. His hands grasped the back of her sweater and he pulled it halfway up her back.

"Hotter or colder?" he taunted into her mouth.

"Hotter?" Lacey answered, though doubt swirled anew. The daring rush made her skin feel like it was on fire as he leaned back and pulled the sweater over her head. Immediately she felt entirely too exposed. She wrapped her arms around her soft stomach, trying to hide every flaw on display.

"Lacey, Lacey, Lacey… Let me see you." Damien pried her arms away from her body, and it took everything in her power not to put them back. His eyes drank her in, and his body tightened like a cobra ready to strike. "You are so beautiful."

Lacey ached to cover her body. Her simple white lace bra was terribly bland, and she felt entirely too naked. Desperate to escape his inspection, Lacey pulled at the hem of his shirt. Damien raised his arms willingly and she clumsily pulled it off. Their cooling bodies crashed together, and Lacey tried to drown her rising worries in his kisses.

The movie behind them was entirely forgotten, the action music only adding to the fervor.

Damien's fingers prodded the bottom edge of her bra. "Hotter or colder?"

Lacey squirmed.

Not yet.

She wished she could say the words he wanted to hear, but this was all too fast. But at the same time, this was her soulmate. Didn't she want to give him everything?

"Lacey. Hotter or colder?"

"Colder," she whispered.

Damien pulled back, his questioning eyes finding hers. She regretted saying it instantly.

I'm letting him down. She felt like a failure.

"I take it back. Hotter," Lacey said in a rush, leaning into his chest to hide herself.

"Shhh." Damien pet her hair, pulling her close. "Don't do that, Lace. That's the point of the game. I can't know where your head's at if you don't tell me."

He lifted her chin, and Lacey wanted to curl up and die because she knew what he saw: the cusp of tears; her ugly lack of confidence when it mattered most. Why couldn't she be more confident like him? The whole scene made her feel prudish and immature in comparison.

"This is okay. We are okay. Come." Damien pulled her down so they could lie side by side, chests still flush together. "Let's watch the movie and make out. This is supposed to be fun, not stressful."

Lacey couldn't fathom how he was so cool and collected.

"Relax, Lace."

She let her eyes close as she tried to steady her heart, which raced like a rabbit. Damien's lips found hers, and he coaxed her back to him with gentle, reassuring kisses. Between them, his phone vibrated in his front pocket. He pulled it out, pausing for only a minute to glance at the text on the screen.

ALVA: I miss you too xxxxx

Lacey's heart plunged in momentary shock. That was a lot of kisses to sign a message with. "Who is Alva?"

Damien leaned over to put his phone on the coffee table face down. "Just a friend back home."

"Do friends normally sign messages with five kisses?" Lacey curled her arms protectively over her chest as he settled back to face her.

"She's like a sister to me. It's nothing to worry about." Damien pressed his lips to her forehead, but Lacey's mind scrambled to make sense of that information.

The message said "too," like he said it first. Idly, Lacey wondered how many kisses he'd sent.

"Lace. Remember what we said. No jealousy, no fighting. We're together now exactly as we were meant to be," Damien implored.

But Lacey's mind spun as the music of the movie got louder. Then an unexpected sound of metal on glass caught her attention. Lacey jolted up in horror. Standing in the entrance to the room, Kade stood with his mouth hanging open in disbelief. But what scared her even more was the murderous look on her mother's face as she gripped the handles of her wheelchair.

CHAPTER XLVI

***Fury* didn't begin** to capture Renee's impending explosion.

"Put your shirts back on right now." Deep and throaty, Renee's voice hardly sounded like her own, and the strain instantly burned like a torch had been plunged down her throat.

Both Lacey's and the boy's faces drew tight as they scrambled. Of all the things Renee didn't have the strength or energy for, this took the cake.

"Kitchen. Now," Renee rasped, stabbing her finger toward the table.

Kade wheeled her chair back, careful not to bump the wall as he brought her over.

Renee had the worst headache of her life. It was as if someone had taken an axe and cleaved her skull in two. Everything felt too bright and too loud. The doctor's diagnosis echoed in her mind.

Concussion, whiplash, broken nose, broken ribs, pierced lung…

"Kade, please turn the TV off."

She rubbed her temple. Paired with the pain that tore down her throat, Renee wasn't sure she'd ever felt worse in her life. No matter how many times she swallowed or how much water she drank, her throat felt flayed open. The incision in her chest also ached, but checking her pain medication schedule was the least of her worries now.

As everyone sat, Renee tightened her fists, her blood boiling.

"Mom." Lacey's voice came out as a whimper. "I—"

"Not a word." Renee leveled each of them with a glare as she whispered as loud as her voice allowed. She swallowed hard and pinned her stare on the boy. "Who are you?"

The boy sat up taller, his muted brown skin paling. "Damien, ma'am. I'm Lacey's soulmate. I'm so sorry—"

Renee held up a finger. "Enough," she rasped. Renee turned to her husband. Kade's eyes burned with a white-hot anger, but it couldn't compare to Renee's.

"How did this happen?" she seethed.

Kade squinted. "I didn't let this happen. I left Lacey with Charity."

Renee's fingers clawed at the table. "Lacey is your daughter. She is always your responsibility."

"Renee. I—" Kade scrambled. "It was the only way I could stay with you in the hospital." Pain etched Kade's brow.

"You should have known the best way to take care of me was to take care of our daughter."

"I did my best—"

"Well, obviously your best wasn't good enough!" Renee croaked, wincing at the pain that lanced up her throat.

"Mom, I'm sorry."

Renee turned to see Lacey's eyes flooded with tears.

Oh, I am not falling for that today.

"You are grounded until further notice." Renee's voice wobbled. "You will not leave this house. You will not visit your friends—" she shot a meaningful look at Damien "—and you most definitely will not be spending time with your soulmate until you learn to act your age."

"Mom!" Lacey slammed her palms on the table in outrage.

"No. This is nonnegotiable." Renee pointed at Damien. "You are going to leave this house, and you will not come back until I personally invite you. Understood?"

Damien swallowed. "Yes, ma'am." He stood with shaky legs, giving Lacey a quick guilty look. He tilted his head at Renee. "I am so sorry this is how we met."

"Get. Out."

Lacey's tears melted to rage, but Renee couldn't care less. She'd just walked in on her fifteen-year-old daughter topless.

"Call Charity, now." Renee didn't have to look at her husband as she choked out the command. He pulled out his phone and dialed. "You stay seated, young lady."

Lacey dropped like a stone into her chair, leveling a glare back at Renee.

"Charity?" Kade's voice was strained, his own anger barely contained. "Do you want to tell me why I just came home to my daughter unattended, naked with a boy?"

"Sweet Venus, Dad, I wasn't naked!" Lacey shouted.

Renee grabbed her daughter's wrist. "Silence." Her hand shook with the effort, and the incision in her ribs pinched as she leaned forward.

The murmuring on the other end of the phone was too quiet for Renee to make out, but she could see her husband's cool slipping.

"That doesn't change the fact that I trusted you!" Kade yelled into the phone.

It was less likely Charity was to blame as was Lacey, but Kade clearly didn't want to see that truth. Renee itched to take the phone from him. Instead, she tried to gesture for him to put it on speaker mode.

Kade didn't notice, though. He stood, shoving his free hand through his hair. "I never should have asked you to take them—

I know that now and I'm sorry. Bring Ladybug over now and we can talk face-to-face."

Renee's last concern was the dog at this moment. She held out her hand expectantly, but Kade ignored her, turning on his heel.

"WHAT DO YOU MEAN YOU CAN'T?"

Lacey shrank in her seat, but defiance still lit her eyes.

"Charity, you are going to bring her back right now."

Then, before Renee could intervene, Kade chucked his phone across the room. It cracked into the drywall, leaving a long splinter in the pale gray paint.

"Kade Baker! Get yourself together," Renee demanded, her throat screaming for reprieve. She wished she could stand. She wished she could meet her husband's blatant rage. But as she pushed up on the armrests of her wheelchair, pain ripped through her ribs, and she sank with a gasp.

"Mom, are you okay?" Lacey leaned across the table, the anger in her eyes quickly cooling with concern.

"No, I am not okay." The foggy depths of exhaustion clawed at her. "I am going to go take my meds and lie down. When I get up, the three of us are going to have a *very* serious conversation." She pointed a finger at Lacey. "If you leave before I wake up, I will take your phone away for the rest of summer."

Lacey swallowed. "I, uh, lost my phone. Remember?"

Suddenly, the days before the accident rushed back. Lacey hunting for her soulmate. Her fight with Nessie.

And Kade sent Lacey to stay with her, clueless of their friendship implosion.

There was still no memory of the accident itself, despite Kade describing it to the best of his ability. All she understood was that she'd hit a light post and totaled their SUV.

"Give me my phone back." Renee held her hand out.

Lacey pushed the legs of her chair back. "Mom—"

"Now, Lacey. You will stay in the apartment. You will not leave. We will talk about your phone later."

A threatening storm played out across Lacey's face, but she slid the phone over before stalking to her room.

"Don't slam the door!" Renee rasped.

CRACK.

This family is going to be the death of me.

A violent wave of nausea ripped through her stomach, and Renee pitched forward, which only made the burning pain in her ribs worse. She sucked in a gasp.

"Renee." Kade was at her side in an instant. "What do you need?"

"Water," she whispered, clutching the arms of her wheelchair. Hot tears fell as she tried to take level breaths.

Why did breathing have to be so damn hard?

Kade placed a glass of water in front of her, then grabbed the bag of prescriptions. He rolled each orange bottle in his hand, weighing the time passed against her last dose. Renee closed her eyes, wishing the thunder outside would quiet.

"Kade," she gasped. "I'm going to puke."

Bottles clattered to the counter, and he lunged toward her with the white pharmacy bag.

Renee heaved. As she doubled over, her stitches burned as if doused with liquid fire. Renee cried out.

"What can I do?" Kade's cold hands rested on her upper back, and Renee tried to focus on them instead of the rolling wave of blackness that threatened to overcome her.

"Gravol." Renee begged for the antinauseant. She shifted in her chair, trying to lessen the sharp pain. The paper bag shook in her hands.

"Here. I'm here, Renee. Focus on me." Kade's worried forest-green eyes swam in Renee's vision.

At least if I black out, the pain would stop for a bit.

"Stay with me, Renee, please."

Renee nodded, her limbs weighing her down like blocks. Kade brushed her hair behind her ear.

"Breathe slowly. You've got this."

Renee took the first pill from her husband, her hands shaking.

CHAPTER XLVII

Blake stabbed a fork into a boiling potato, a small joy swelling as it broke apart in the water.

"That should be good." Hunter leaned over Blake's shoulder. After learning that Blake's cooking skills consisted exclusively of noodles, Hunter had insisted on teaching her the basics, and tonight was apparently steak, vegetables, and mashed potatoes. Luckily, he had taken over the barbecue portion and she was just in charge of the side dishes. Blake turned off the element, proud that the other skillet of fried vegetables was only slightly burnt.

Hunter guided Blake through the last steps of mashing the potatoes. They each dished their own plates, and as Blake brought the food to the table, she glanced over at Psyche. She now had more gray in her hair than black, and her muscles continued to waste away. It was as if her soul was draining out of her.

Hunter followed her gaze. "How long can someone go without eating?"

Or peeing?

"I don't know." Blake shrugged, trying to act like it was perfectly normal to have a comatose woman aging decades in a matter of days. "But I imagine if Psyche couldn't die before, she's not going to die now."

At least that's what I'm choosing to believe.

The rainy day had only darkened further as the downpour persisted into the night.

Hunter poured measured amber liquid into two glasses and retrieved a can of cola from the fridge.

This is so much better than tea, biscuits, and fruit.

Though Jaylynn had masterfully crafted a few veggie-forward bowls Blake would never admit were delicious, the simplicity of steak and whiskey smelled like Elysium's finest.

"What're we gonna do tonight?" Hunter asked, taking his seat across from her.

Blake shrugged. "I have no clue."

Passing time was already proving to be an ongoing issue. Now, with a full night of rain in store, Blake was more stumped than usual.

"It's too bad Psyche doesn't have a TV."

Blake sipped at her whiskey, melting into the familiar aroma. "I'm not surprised. Psyche's more of the outdoorsy type. I bet if she was awake today, she'd be out there barefoot in the mud." A small smile tugged at the corner of Blake's mouth before it fell as she remembered why their hostess wasn't pushing them out to embrace the rain.

Hunter's forehead furrowed as he swallowed a bite. "Really? She seems so… fragile?"

"Psyche?" Blake barked out a laugh. "I've never met anyone more ruthless. Honestly. Imagine a wood witch bent on you exploring your deepest secrets. That's Psyche."

Hunter took a bite of crisped broccoli, mulling over his thoughts. "And this woodland witch is your soulmate?"

"No. Well, sure, my compass led me here, but we could never—Psyche doesn't feel that way about me." Heat bloomed up Blake's chest.

Hunter kept his eyes on his own plate. "So, is she a potions witch? Does she have a cupboard of voodoo pincushion dolls?"

Blake appreciated that he spoke about Psyche in the present tense, as if she wasn't lost forever. "Well, her teas are basically potions the way she talks about them. And no, not voodoo that I've seen. Just tarot cards and energy reading. All that stuff was fine, though. I don't know what to call her soul-digging interrogations, but those were the worst."

"What d'you mean?"

Blake talked as she chewed. "She'd make us do these practices where she'd ask all these heavy-hitting questions and you had to be honest."

"What kind of questions?"

"Mmmm, I don't know. The first few days, it was a lot of stuff about our compasses and how we felt about love. The worst one was where we all had to tell a secret we'd never told anyone else."

Hunter gave her an incredulous look. "Why would she ask that?"

"I'm not sure," Blake answered. "Maybe to get to know us better. To help us bond? Either way, it sucked."

"It's kinda interesting." Hunter kept his eyes on his plate.

Blake laughed, shoving the last bite of steak into her mouth. "If you were there, you wouldn't use the word *interesting*. Vulnerable, awkward, intense. But not interesting."

"What was the secret you shared?" Hunter's eyes were looking anywhere but at Blake.

"You want to know my deepest secrets?" Blake leaned forward, a hint of a smirk on her lips.

Hunter shrugged. "Why not? It's not like we're going anywhere."

"Well, if we're going to do it Psyche-style, you should know that it's not just one secret. She does this really annoying thing where you take turns going back and forth."

"Until?" Hunter's eyes met hers, and the softness in their deep brown depths already felt too intimate.

"I don't know. Sometimes until someone cried. Most of the time until Psyche randomly decided it was enough."

"How does it start?"

Blake pushed her plate away. "Well, we would sit facing each other. Then I look at you and say: tell me a secret." She parroted the question she'd been forced to face days ago.

How was that only days ago?

It felt like a lifetime had passed.

Hunter leaned back in his chair, his usual serious, borderline grumpy look cast over his eyebrows. The silence stretched for a minute before Blake realized he was actually trying to come up with a secret.

"When I was a kid, I wanted to be a banker because I thought that meant I'd be rich."

Blake choked back a laugh. Based on Psyche's rules, she was absolutely not supposed to be laughing, but Hunter's secret seemed so ridiculous she couldn't help herself. He took a drink, then placed his cup down.

"Your turn," he said when she regained her composure.

Blake settled back, a twinkle in her eye. "You have to deliver the request in full if we're doing it Psyche's way."

"Tell me a secret."

Suddenly, the fun of the moment started to slip. She was going to have to come up with a secret to share.

What can I tell him that won't scare him away?

She considered the secrets the other girls had shared: Jaylynn's story about being on antidepressants after Elias' death; Nessie's honesty about hating the fake grave they'd placed for her father's missing body; Charity's blunt truth about her night terrors.

There wasn't even one that Blake could use and play off as her own. Thinking back to that day, it struck her now that Psyche hadn't even revealed her biggest secret of all. Psyche had simply said, "I am terrified of the gods." At the time, Blake had scoffed and barely considered it a secret. Now it seemed like a significant understatement.

Could I tell Brooks the same secret I told the group?

It technically wouldn't count as a secret anymore, but Psyche wasn't here to monitor her cheating. And wouldn't telling the truth count for something?

"I used to play the guitar. You know, one of the big acoustic ones? I dreamed I'd be a singer one day."

Hunter tilted his head. "What happened?"

"I sold my guitar to the pawnshop when I was sixteen and never looked back." Blake wasn't about to tell him why she'd had to sell her cherished instrument. He didn't need to know the depths of poverty she'd sunk to or how much she cried walking away with only forty more dollars to her name. Her secret, though meant to be relatively lighthearted, clearly dampened the mood. Blake cleared her throat. "Anyway. Your turn again. Tell me a secret."

Hunter crossed his arms. For a minute, Blake thought their moment of storytelling had come to its natural end, but then he sighed and answered.

"I hospitalized two people once."

Blake arched an eyebrow. Hunter had more than enough muscle and height that she didn't doubt he could hold his own in a fight, but in the days she'd been essentially living with him, he'd never shown even a hint of aggressive behavior.

"Go on." She waved, her curiosity getting the best of her.

He cleared his throat. "My sister came home one night all roughed up. She had this long yellow dress on with tiny white flowers. One of the sleeves was torn, and the back was all covered in mud. I'll never forget the look on Kennedy's face." Hunter swallowed. "I didn't ask questions—Kennedy wasn't the type to go askin' for trouble—I just put her in my truck. She didn't want to go, but I wasn't takin' no for an answer. When she finally led me to a house on the far side of town, I didn't think twice. I've never been so angry in my life.

"I went into that house, and before I could ask who'd attacked my sister, I just started throwin' punches. There were two guys there, both close to my age. And I just blacked out. It wasn't until the next day, when Kennedy told me the guys were both hospitalized, that I knew I'd gone too far. I just—" Hunter flexed his hand. "She was my sister. No one touches my sister."

Blake's brow creased. "You were protecting her."

Hunter shook his head. "I could have killed them both. And the way Kennedy looked at me after that? I think keepin' my secret is what made her move away. She left for Berkeley that fall and never came back."

"Hunter—"

"She never was able to press charges because she didn't want me to get caught."

The way his throat hitched made Blake's stomach feel hollow.

"You acted on instinct."

Hunter's eyes darkened. "I split up our family because I couldn't think straight."

Blake leaned across the table and took Hunter's wrist. "Nobody died."

Hunter held her gaze, his face unconvinced.

Blake picked up her whiskey, slightly annoyed but also impressed. "Well, if you think that makes you a bad person, then I am terrible. I once stabbed a complete stranger just because they bumped my arm." The memory of the poor soul on the other side of Blake's blade back in Niagara was hazy, but she still held no guilt for her knee-jerk reaction.

The secret had the desired effect on Hunter, snapping his attention to her. "And… did they die?"

Blake shrugged. "I don't think so. They had a pretty big coat on. But I didn't hang around to find out."

Hunter shook his head.

"What?" Blake asked.

"It's just—I don't even know you and I'm staying here in this cabin." He adjusted his ball cap, tilting it down to cover his eyes.

"Then get to know me," Blake replied, a knot of uncertainty twisting in her gut.

Hunter stood up and cleared their plates. "With Psyche's interrogation questions?"

Blake shrugged. "If that's easier. Or you can just ask me what you want to know."

Hunter rested his hands on the sink, bending his head down.

"Tell me something you want to know about me," Blake offered.

Hunter turned back to face her and leaned against the sink edge. "Do you have a family?"

"None that matter."

He gave an exasperated sigh as he turned back to the sink and started filling the basin to do the dishes.

"What?"

"You act like you're so forthcoming and willing to answer questions, but you never share anything real about yourself." Hunter's tone held an edge of frustration.

"It's true! My family is essentially dead to me."

Hunter spun around, the potato pot clasped in his fist. "That's exactly what I mean. I don't know if you have brothers or sisters, what your family did to lose you, or why you act indifferent about things that are obviously a big deal."

Blake glared. If Hunter wanted honesty, she could give him that.

"No, I don't have any siblings." She stood and marched up to his chest, a small satisfaction building as he dropped the pot into the soapy water. "My dad left my mom years ago because he was a coward and couldn't face her addiction problems. He decided he'd rather go find his happily ever after without his designated soulmate, and left me to care for her when I was only thirteen." Blake shoved her pointer finger against his chest. "And I'm not indifferent. I'm an emotional mess that apparently has PTSD, and now I have to save the entire freaking world from a wrathful deity when I don't even believe in the magic and love everyone so desperately wants!"

The tightness in Hunter's face shifted to something different. Blake crossed her arms. She didn't want his pity.

"Is that what you wanted to know?" Blake bit out. "That I'm a mess and I'm just faking being tough? Do you want to know what it's like finally giving in to following your compass, only to find out it points to someone who will never love you back?"

When the first tear fell, Hunter didn't flinch. Her anger at all the injustices she'd been forced to face burned hotter.

"SAY SOMETHING!"

Hunter lifted his thumb to wipe away a touch of spit that had landed on his cheek. When he finally spoke, his voice was quiet but he held her eye contact. "What do you want me to say, Blake? That I like when you scream at me?"

"I do not—"

"You asked me to speak, so don't cut me off." Hunter stepped forward, whatever pity had once been in his face now gone. Instead, Blake could have sworn there was a flicker of hurt in his brown eyes. "You're one of the most violent and bitter women I've ever met. And I don't know what I did to get tangled up in this mess, but I'm really startin' to think Venus was wrong thinkin' you and I could ever be a match."

Blake was speechless as his words sank in. An age-old hurt lanced up her spine. Not even someone as gentle and patient as Hunter could see something worth trying to love in her. Blake spun on her heel and raced to Psyche's bedroom, slamming the door behind her.

2 DAYS

UNTIL THE SUPERMOON

Reigning over wheat and his plains of destruction,
Mars kneels to none but the goddess of seduction.
March through October the god of war roams,
Through acres of bodies, his bloodied spear combs.
Beware his savage brutality and his deadly blades,
Mars may seek peace, but it's mortal soldiers he trades.
—The Warmonger

CHAPTER XLVIII

KADE

"We are coming to you live from Ottawa, where the prime minister has made a new official military statement following the escalating Endless War." The TV screen cut from the reporter to the man behind a podium. Despite standing tall, the weariness in the Canadian prime minister's eyes showed. His voice carried through the microphone, loud and clear. "In accordance with our allegiance to the Roman Empire, we are now changing our national military requirements. Any able-bodied citizens over eighteen who have not already served will now be mandated to join the Canadian army for a minimum of two years, effective immediately. Previous recruits are strongly encouraged to reenroll."

The objection of the crowd thundered over the prime minister as he strove to take reporters' questions. Kade toggled the volume down with a shaky hand. He was thirty-seven years old. He was too old to join the army, wasn't he? And they couldn't possibly expect him to leave Renee as she was… would they? The door of Lacey's bedroom creaked open. From his armchair, Kade saw her pale face instantly.

"Dad?" Lacey's lip trembled. "You're not going to go, are you?"

Gone was the coldness and fury she'd worn like a uniform since Damien left. Now, Kade's daughter stared at him like she was a child.

"I—I don't know, honey." Kade grasped for his phone as his heart rate elevated. There had to be an age cutoff or some kind of exception. He couldn't go to war. Lacey sat on the sofa closest to him.

"You can't go. Mom needs you."

Kade swallowed. As much as he knew that, he was also sure that in the eyes of the government, Lacey's grandmother could act as Renee's caretaker if necessary.

"I know. I just don't know what the laws are exactly." Kade pulled up the search engine on his phone.

Lacey's eyes cast over the room. "Can I use your laptop? Let me help."

Kade nodded, his fingers flying over the keys as he tried to find verified information instead of the dozens of reports that were sharing the exact news he had already heard. Lacey pulled out Kade's work computer and settled on the sofa beside him. For the first time all week, Kade's mind wasn't on a running loop of worry about Renee's health. Now his worry rounded back in frightening high definition for his own life.

I'm not going to war. I am not going to have to fight. I am not going to die.

He repeated the mental affirmations as he and Lacey scoured the internet for more information.

"Forty." Lacey flopped back in shock. "The age maximum to enter the military is sixty, but the new laws apply to anyone between eighteen and forty."

I am not going to war. Kade repeated, desperate to make it true.

"We need to find a list of exemptions." Kade cleared his throat. "Find out who they want and who they don't."

Dread clawed down Kade's back as he scoured for anything that could solidify his case. Lacey's fingers hammered away at the keyboard with lightning efficiency.

"Here." She pushed the laptop back and Kade leaned over. Lacey moved so he could sit right beside her. The words on the screen blurred as Kade fought to read the tiny script.

Lacey murmured under her breath as she scrolled down the page. "Jupiter Almighty, I don't even know how to pronounce half of these words."

The list of medical jargon continued down the screen as they scoured for anything Kade might have.

"You have kind of bad eyesight?" Lacey said in a hopeful tone.

"Lacey, I don't even wear my glasses to drive. I don't think that qualifies." Kade leaned back, giving up reading as Lacey scrolled on.

"Concussions, head wounds, mental impairment," Lacey read out. "At least we finally have a reason to be thankful for Mom's accident."

Any able-bodied citizens.

The horrifying thought of Renee going to war pushed Kade over the edge. His fingers raked over his scalp at the mental image of her in uniform with a gun slung over her shoulder.

Lacey's clammy hand gripped Kade's forearm, bringing him back to the moment.

"Dad, we're going to find a way out."

But it wasn't going to be okay. He was an able-bodied man. He was perfectly healthy other than the occasional flare-up of gout in his big toe. There was no getting out of this. Kade was joining the military. He stood, his knees wobbly.

"I'm going to go check on your mother."

Lacey leaned forward, planting her elbows on her knees. "I'll keep looking."

In their bedroom, Kade barely made it to the edge of the bed before he tripped. He grasped the headboard for stability. Renee's chestnut hair splayed over her pillow like a crown, and Kade crawled into bed beside her. He tucked close without bumping her bandaged ribs.

What he wouldn't give to have his compass back now, to feel the relief of being close to his soulmate. Then he remembered his compass last pointed to Ladybug, the other piece of his life spiraling out of his control.

"I'm sorry, Kade, I can't bring her back right now." What reason could Charity possibly have for withholding his dog? Ladybug should have been here. Even if things were hard, their family needed to be together. Kade stared at his wife as the world around him went blurry.

How long would he have at Renee's side? Should he call his mother-in-law now? When would the military come to collect him—or was he expected to voluntarily show up? What if he just didn't go? Was there a punishment for avoiding duty?

"What's wrong?"

Kade glanced up as a tear cast down his cheek to see Renee's eyes open. Her forehead wrinkled with concern as she brushed his stray tear away with the backs of her trembling fingers.

"Kade, what happened?"

He knew he couldn't afford to look weak, but Kade spent the last week trying to hold it together and now he felt like a ripped-up flag in the wind. Renee shifted, wincing slightly as she shuffled closer to hold him. But Kade couldn't say the words out loud. He wouldn't be the one to deliver the news to his wife. He couldn't. Instead, Kade let himself truly cry.

CHAPTER XLIX

"Morning, Seb." Philip strode into the kitchen wearing a pair of reading glasses, with a newspaper tucked under his elbow. Dark circles still hung heavy under his eyes. Sebastian suspected the lack of sleep and extra stress were causing him more trouble than he was letting on.

"Hey." Sebastian picked up his piece of toast and went back to scrolling his phone. Tomorrow would be a week since he'd arrived in Canada and Sebastian finally felt like he was settling in. Maybe it was Huan's constantly chipper mood or Philip's careful accommodations to make sure Sebastian was cared for, but things were easy here compared to back home. There was no walking in on passionate embraces or siblings looking to barrage him at every turn.

"Seb…" Philip's eyes softened with a concerned crinkle as he sat across the table. "Can I ask you a personal question?"

Sebastian glanced up and set his phone down. "Sure."

"I was curious about your burns."

"Oh." Sebastian traced a hand over his temple. "They're nothing. I've had them since I was three."

The natural wrinkles of Philip's forehead folded deeper. "Jupiter Almighty, so young? What happened?"

"I don't really remember it." Sebastian leaned back into his chair. "My mum says I grabbed the tablecloth and accidentally dumped a mug of tea over my head." Sebastian waved off the concern in Philip's face. "It was a long time ago. The doctors said I was lucky it missed my eye."

"I'm so sorry that happened." Something in Philip's gaze darkened.

"It's really nothing," Sebastian reassured him. "It was an accident."

Philip had probably seen significantly worse burns in his time as an army medic. Sebastian's old injury was nothing in comparison. Philip's face grew more strained as he took a good look at the front page of his newspaper.

"Oh, Vesta, save us."

Sebastian perked up. He rarely heard people pray to the goddess of the hearth and home.

"What is it?"

"They changed the army's enlistment rules." Philip wiped a hand over his face. "I'm guessing the Roman Emperor is tired of losing ground."

Sebastian's stomach roiled as a new unexpected fear bubbled up.

"Will you and Huan have to go back?" he said under his breath.

Philip paled as he considered the question. "We won't have to worry about Huan. He'll be a veteran's exception with his prosthetic."

"But what about you? Do you think because you've served before, they'll let you off?"

"Unless they need trained medics." Philip's long fingers gripped the paper tight enough to crinkle it. "Maybe enough people will sign up that it won't be necessary."

Sebastian knew in his gut he should be worried about his own family, but at this moment, the thought of piano-playing Philip being carted across the ocean to war made his heart ache.

"I don't want you to go."

Philip sighed as if he was thinking the same thing. "I won't go if I don't have to, son."

It was all so wrong, so backward. Why couldn't the Romans and the Northern Alliance just let it go? Why did people have to keep dying in their stupid war? Another thought crossed Sebastian's mind. If Philip was recruited and shipped across the ocean, that would leave Huan here without either of his family members.

Sebastian swallowed. "Maybe it's time for Liam to come home."

The sad agreement in Philip's eyes was undeniable. "I think you're right."

Sebastian's phone buzzed on the table. Sebastian lifted it to see a text from Nessie.

Nessie: What are you up to today? Want to hang out?

Sebastian rolled his neck out from side to side. While he genuinely liked Nessie, he had too much on his mind today to make plans with her. He might have to leave this house and family soon, and he might not ever see them again. Sebastian typed out a quick reply.

Seb: Sorry, hanging out with my exchange family today. Maybe tomorrow?

Philip looked up at the clock, shaking his head. "I'm going to be late for work if I don't get going."

Somehow Sebastian knew the hospital was the last place Philip wanted to go right now.

"You could call in sick?"

Philip shook his head. "It'll be all right. I need to help those I can before the hospitals implement their war protocol and staffing gets even shorter. Then things will get really bad."

Philip must have read the worry in Sebastian's face. He reached out and squeezed Sebastian's hand, a gesture both Philip and Huan did so often that Sebastian had started to expect the contact. If he was being honest, he'd even started to like it.

"You know, even if Liam comes home early, maybe you could still stay the month."

Sebastian glanced up, surprised. "What?"

"We'd have to convince your parents and make sure Huan and Liam are okay with it, but… it's been nice having you here, Seb. And while it may be selfish, I don't want to send you any closer to the war if you don't have to go."

A wisp of relief softened Sebastian's tightening core.

I could stay.

But even as he basked in the thought, Sebastian felt guilty. Here he was, living in this expensive house with wonderful people while his and Gareth's families could be facing an invasion any day now.

Philip gave one last reassuring squeeze before turning back to his coffee. Sebastian couldn't help but notice how Philip's hand shook slightly as he turned the front page, which was plastered with the military news. Feeling useless, Sebastian did something he never did: he sent up a mental prayer to Vesta.

Please keep this family together. Let my family and friends back home be safe. And please, even if it's selfish to ask, let me stay here for at least a little longer.

Sebastian could have sworn the candle burning on the stove flickered as he cast off his wishes to the goddess of hearth and home.

CHAPTER L

BLAKE

Despite the ache in her tailbone, Blake refused to move from the wooden chair at Psyche's side. She layered a cool lavender-and-honey gel Jaylynn had mixed over the woman's fingers. Psyche's burns didn't seem to be healing as fast as her own. When Blake went to change the bandages, she was shocked to find Psyche's fingers withered, her knuckles swollen bright red and twisted with age.

"Hang in there, Psyche. It's only a couple more days."

The buzz of a saw quieted, and Blake twisted to peek outside. In his first few days here, Hunter had chopped enough wood to fill the covered firewood stack along the shed. Since then, the sawing and hammering was continuous when the weather allowed for it, and Blake idly worried how many trees would be left when Psyche finally woke up.

Hunter strode past the window and Blake shrank closer to the frilly curtain. The overcast day suggested the rain could come back at any time, but Hunter behaved like it was warm and sunny. His blue T-shirt clung to his chest and deltoids, darkening from sweat down his spine. As if he had a sixth sense, Hunter's eyes landed on Blake's window. She slammed herself back, embarrassed to be caught staring. She busied herself by adjusting Psyche's hair as the cabin door opened.

"You got a minute?" Tendrils of soft brown curls peeked out from under Hunter's ball cap.

Blake swallowed. "Sure."

The wet grass was slick under her sunflower rubber boots as Blake rubbed at her arms, following Hunter back to the shed. Since last night, Hunter had retreated to his reclusive self. When Blake had rolled out of bed this morning, he'd already been outside hammering away. Now, as he led Blake across the property, the hairs on her neck rose in worry.

What could he possibly need me for out here?

Hunter turned back to her, a touch of pink on his summer-bronzed cheeks. He held out his arms in display. "What do you think?"

Blake came to a stop in front of the toolshed.

"What— How did you...?" Blake froze in momentary shock. In front of her, a low table made of cream-tanned wood stood in the grass. Instead of classic peg legs, thick beams crossed in an X shape on each end, stabilizing the two-inch-thick top.

"I had some random tools in the back of my truck and got bored. I figured this would look nice in front of the couch." Hunter met her eyes, then dropped his gaze. "Do you think Psyche will like it?"

Blake didn't reply. She marveled as she traced her fingers over the perfectly smooth surface. It wasn't a saw she'd heard earlier. He'd been sanding the table smooth.

Hunter cleared his throat. "If not, it could also stay out here. Maybe we could put it by the firepit? It might be too big for inside anyway."

Blake fought the urge to smile, both at the thoughtful addition to the cabin and Hunter's apparent nervousness. She recognized the olive branch and decided she was due to extend one of her own.

"It's amazing, Hunter. Psyche will love it."

He couldn't have known Psyche's old coffee table was still abandoned in a clearing not far away, but somehow he'd noticed the empty gap in the otherwise cozy house and went and filled it. This was, of course, after he'd already sanded down the legs of Psyche's kitchen table so it sat more level and adjusted the bathroom door hinges so they wouldn't creak anymore.

Hunter's shoulders lowered in relief as Blake stood up. She reached out and squeezed his hand in appreciation. The invisible tension where neither of them knew what to do next resurfaced. Blake wasn't sure where to look. The gnawing sensation that she needed to do something beat incessantly, and Blake stuttered as she tried to figure out her next words. But what could she say to this boy who had no reason to stay but stuck around anyway?

"Why did you stay?" Blake finally asked. She wasn't sure if she meant that first day or after their fight last night, but the meaning was the same.

"At first, I think because I was curious," Hunter admitted. "I finally had a tattoo and I wanted to see what all the fuss was about." He adjusted his ball cap. "I almost left the night you told me about Venus—but I stayed because of my family. I don't want my mom and pop or Kennedy living without magic like I have to. I couldn't do that to them if there's a chance I could help fix things."

Blake could read between the lines. It wasn't only magic Hunter lived without. It was love. Their eyes met, both tentative and anxious.

I can't do this anymore.

Before she could think twice, Blake took the extra step to close the space between them, pushed up on her toes, and kissed him softly on the corner of his mouth. Hunter stood stock-still as she breathed in the fresh scent of sawdust and sweat on his skin, then she flitted back.

"Thank you," Blake whispered, uncertain if she was thanking him for the table or for still being here.

Then Hunter's hand wrapped around her forearm and tugged her closer. Blake practically collapsed with relief into his arms. His massive body curled around hers like a cocoon. A warm, tender touch tilted her chin up. Blake didn't fight it, instead blinking at the man who kept showing up no matter how hard she pushed him away.

"I don't want to fight anymore." The way he said it, it was more of a declaration than a request. Then Hunter's lips were on hers.

It was like a dam had been broken. The flood of desire she'd unconsciously been fighting pulled her under. Blake wrapped her arms over his shoulders, pulling herself higher to meet the growing urgency behind their connection. Hunter's hands dropped to her thighs, scooping her up so she could wrap her ankles around his back.

Without breaking their kiss, Hunter turned to the cabin, striding confidently with her in his arms like she weighed nothing.

"The door—" Blake hardly had the words out before Hunter readjusted his grip, lifting Blake higher as he pulled the front door open and then closed behind them.

"Bathroom or bedroom?" Hunter groaned between kisses.

As much as it seemed profoundly wrong to choose the bedroom, the bathroom was much too small.

Surely Psyche wouldn't mind if it meant getting compasses back and saving her life?

Blake tilted her head, letting the feverish kisses suppress any guilt she might have. "Bedroom."

Hunter closed the distance lightning fast, and Blake grasped the door as they went, shutting it just in case Psyche chose today to miraculously wake up. Blake's back hit the mattress and the flood of desire colored with a tinge of fear. Hunter tore his shirt off over his head, but as his eyes met hers, he paused, assessing the slightest shift in her breathing.

"Okay?" he asked breathlessly.

Blake nodded, not trusting herself to speak.

Hunter held his palms out. Blake took them, conscious as their pace slowed and the reality of the moment became crystal clear. He pulled her up to sit, her legs still framing his thighs. He curled down so his lips met the top of her head.

"Listen. If you need me to stop, just tap out, okay?" His hand found hers and he gently tapped her knuckles twice.

Blake nodded again as his fingers tugged at the hem of her shirt. Suddenly she felt a huge wave of gratitude that Jaylynn had forced her to wash all of her things, including her underclothes.

Both their shirts found a home on the floor. Hunter sat back against the headboard, guiding Blake to straddle his lap. The gesture seemed intentional, like he remembered she was afraid of being pinned down. Her heart hammered as the tension between them rose again even as Hunter's movements were slow.

She could do this. This was much easier than talking.

Blake let all her walls fall down as her eyes closed. She sighed as he kissed across her collarbones to her tattooed arms. He slowed when he got to her wrist before gently kissing each of her burned fingertips and cut knuckles.

When Hunter looked back up to her, his eyelids were heavy with desire.

Blake's whole body tingled as his hands ran down her ribs in reverence.

"It's still my time of the month…" she whispered, sparing a thought for Psyche's bedding.

Hunter kissed her hard once, and Blake took it as an acknowledgment to shut up and not ruin the moment.

Blake melted into Hunter's strong arms, not caring if this didn't go further than kissing. She couldn't remember the last time she'd felt so relaxed. If the hunger behind his lips was any indication of how badly he wanted her, it meant he'd forgiven her for running away, stealing his things, and their fight. And if Hunter was starting to warm up to her, maybe, just maybe, Blake might have a chance of falling in love with him after all.

CHAPTER LI

NYLAH

In a matter of twenty-four hours, Nylah's life had once again turned upside down, and not in a good way. Sure, it was a relief finding out the true meaning of the hourglass sands… but facing what it meant? That was something Nylah had no interest in dealing with. Especially now, as Jazz held their plaid jacket out. Nylah sighed before sliding each arm into a sleeve and turning to face him.

The energy between their bodies was like an electric current. Nylah didn't want to go. They didn't want to follow their mark. Everything Nylah wanted was standing right here, looking like a puppy tied to a stake in the yard.

"I'll meet you down in the truck." Jaylynn politely excused herself, giving Nylah and Jazz their first real privacy since her arrival.

As the latch clicked shut, they closed the distance, wrapping each other in a tight hug.

"I'm so sorry," Nylah whispered.

Jazz kissed the top of their head. "Don't be. It was just bad timing."

It felt worse than bad timing that Jaylynn had offered a chance to get their compass back right when Nylah didn't want it anymore. Nylah took a deep breath of Jazz's cardamom cologne.

Maybe I could say no and just stay right here. But even as Nylah wanted to say the words out loud, they knew they couldn't.

"You'll stay safe today? Promise?" Nylah asked. The fact that Jazz was going to help Fates' Followers crash the military protest worried Nylah. They'd agreed Jazz needed to make an appearance; their absence over the past couple days must have been noticed by now. They couldn't run the risk of him appearing like a deserter. So, Jazz would go and hand out flyers to all the people protesting like a good disciple, and if Nylah was lucky, their mark would lead them far from the rally and the eyes of the priests.

While the army conscription made Nylah vibrate with indignation, they put those thoughts on the back burner. If they succeeded with Venus' task and compasses came back, maybe the war would settle. All Nylah knew for sure was that their time was better spent now solving their hourglass marker than going to protests or getting friendly with Fates' Followers.

Jazz wrapped his palm around the back of Nylah's neck, pulling them closer. "Of course I will. You too, though. Okay?" He took an unsteady breath. "Do whatever you have to, okay? Remember the lives you'll save if the cult stops."

A pinching pain cut through Nylah's chest. Nylah unraveled from the hug, conscious that if they didn't leave soon, Jaylynn might come back. Or worse, Nylah might lock the door to try to preserve whatever happiness was left to be found here with Jazz. He must have read their mind, because his grip slackened as Nylah stepped back. They stared at each other.

Don't cry. Don't cry. Don't cry.

Jazz frowned. He'd always been good at reading Nylah's mood. Maybe that was why he looked so pained—he couldn't give Nylah the thing they wanted most.

"Go," he whispered. "I'll follow after you when I'm sure it's safe."

"Okay," Nylah replied, but their feet didn't move. They couldn't just leave, couldn't walk away from this. Nylah stood frozen, tears gathering in unshed pools. And then they were both moving, their lips crashing together and their hands weaving into each other's hair. Jazz was incredibly tall in comparison, and Nylah had to rise on their toes to meet his desperate last kiss. Because that's what this was—their kiss goodbye to what could have been.

Nylah didn't let the fierce embrace evolve to more. Instead, they let their heels fall, and they turned, trying not to make a sound so Jazz wouldn't know how hard they were crying.

After forty minutes of trying (and failing) to follow Nylah's mark, Jaylynn pulled her truck into Park. Around them, throngs of people wove between the gridlock of cars.

"Does your mark at least feel close?"

When Nylah had first seen the hourglass, the tiny stardust flecks streamed into the empty chamber below. Now, the bottom rolled with glittering sands like a mini desert, almost three quarters of the sand already fallen. There wasn't nearly enough time left, but they would have to work with what they had.

Nylah considered the metallic sands. "I don't know. It doesn't feel the same as Cupid's compass did."

"Charity said your body will feel hotter the closer you get, and when you make contact with your mark, the heat will all rush away."

It was too stuffy in the truck to know if the growing warmth under Nylah's skin was from the mark or just from wearing a jacket, but the coat had to stay. They needed to keep the mark hidden.

Oh, for the love of Cupid. Why didn't I just follow it the first day I got it? This was like their compass all over again. For years

Nylah would tell people they were waiting for their soulmate to come and find them. Now the truth couldn't be more obvious. Nylah was a coward. And facing the unknown terrified them.

"Let's get out and walk for a bit. Either way, we're not going anywhere fast," Nylah suggested.

As they exited the truck, a sign flickered in the sunlight above them, its words stark white.

UNIVERSITY AVE.

The street name slammed into Nylah's chest.

"No—"

"What is it?" Jaylynn rose up on tiptoe to see ahead.

The buzzing energy of people should have tipped Nylah off that this wasn't an ordinary traffic jam.

"It's the conscription protest… We're heading to the rally." The one Fates' Followers had asked disciples to attend to try to increase their own recruitment. Nylah stepped aside as a young group of students chattered by, dragging bundles of homemade signs scribbled in black marker on cardboard.

War is a choice. Freedom should be too.

Stop Canadian recruitment for the Roman war.

Endless War = Endless Deaths

Jaylynn sighed. "Well, it looks like we're joining the throngs. Maybe we'll get lucky and find your match quickly."

Nylah gave their sister a doubtful look before taking the lead. They tried not to think of the military recruitment as they wound back and forth, the sound of megaphones grating at their ears. As they walked, Nylah repeated the reasons they had to do this in their mind. If they succeeded, compasses would return. The cult would stop murdering people. If the cult settled, Jazz would be freed from their grasp. If compasses came back, the war might settle too, and Nylah wouldn't have to worry about recruitment. But first, they had to follow their mark.

And choose the right match.

After having Jaylynn repeat her task over and over again, Nylah had become hung up on that specification. It suggested there was an option, likely between Jazz and their hourglass target. Would it even be a choice, though? How could anyone ever compare to Jazz? What would happen if they hadn't reunited with their original soulmate by the time the last grain of sand fell?

Jaylynn trailed close behind as Nylah spiraled mentally. They both dodged as needed when a fist or a sign sailed into their vicinity. The edgy, frustrated crowd didn't help Nylah's nerves. While they were fairly certain Venus' mark would lead them to the dark-haired boy from the café, what if it was someone else? Would that make it better or worse? And was Nylah even ready to see him again? What could they possibly say?

As they were sucked deeper into the crowd, which spanned blocks, Nylah watched for Jazz's face, but there were far too many people. It was like trying to pick out a single runner in a marathon. The crowd was predominantly university students, though a persistent theme of black and scarlet clothes scattered the masses. Though they weren't the priest robes, Nylah could see the cult's colors infiltrating the group.

Shake it off. You're just being paranoid. If they confront you, you'll say you're here with the cause.

As Nylah took sneaky glances at their arm, Venus' mark led them deeper into the frenzy. Nylah's claustrophobia was creeping up to an all-time high, and they would have given anything to take their coat off.

"Okay," Jaylynn panted as they came to a stop. "Maybe I was wrong and this wasn't a good idea."

Nylah gave their sister the best I-told-you-so look they could muster, then turned their attention back to the tattoo. It was easier to watch the arrow than to face whatever they were walking into.

"Maybe we should—"

Nylah instinctively pulled Jaylynn close as a neon-yellow vest came up beside them. A police officer rode by on horseback, his wary but firm gaze landing on each protestor. As much as Nylah wanted to explain they weren't here for the protest, they bit down. Then, out of the corner of their eye, Nylah's attention snagged. A boy turned, not six feet away, his gray-green eyes pinned on the police officer, the corners of his mouth tugging down. Nylah's blood sang.

It's him.

Panic and relief crashed together as his eyes met theirs. Nylah's knees felt like they were being swallowed up by quicksand. He started to turn away, but Nylah surged forward, closing the gap between them.

"Hey!" Nylah grabbed his shoulder, pulling his attention back. The suffocating heat released its vise grip with a whoosh, and Nylah took a deep, relieved breath. His black leather jacket was soft to the touch, and Nylah's eyes flitted over the maroon shirt he wore underneath. Up close, his golden-brown skin gleamed.

He frowned. "Can I help you?"

This is it.

Thoughts and words tangled in a mound of mud as Nylah scrambled for what to say next. Other than freedom from the hourglass's heat, there were no sparks or the instant love people described when finding their soulmate. The air didn't feel light and breezy, and there weren't fireworks exploding in Nylah's chest.

Nylah glanced around, taking in the few people surrounding them sporting black and dark red as they tried to figure out what they were supposed to do. Some instinct drew their eyes back to his shirt. On a whim, they reached out and grasped the boy's arm.

"Fates be with you."

The boy cocked his head, his cool suspicion melting away with recognition. If Nylah had been better prepared, they'd have dressed in cult colors too. Either way, the greeting seemed to work.

"And with you," he replied. His accent was undeniably English, his gentle features young and bright. Nylah wondered how old the boy was. Eighteen? Maybe nineteen? If he truly was Nylah's soulmate, he seemed young. But Cupid didn't make mistakes, did he? Or was the reason Venus led Nylah to him a trap? Maybe this boy was never Nylah's soulmate chosen by Cupid, but Venus was playing on Nylah's doubt as a game.

"Could I talk to you quickly?" Nylah called over the crowd. "It'll just be a minute."

The boy glanced back at his companions as if unsure. "I don't—"

"I have a message from the priests," Nylah improvised. Everyone felt too close, including Jaylynn. Nylah gave her a stay-put glare and pulled the boy out of the crowd. He was slow to follow, glancing back at his comrades and offering a shrug. He shoved his hands into his pockets.

Based on the twenty-minute walk in, the privacy Nylah so desperately craved was unlikely to appear anywhere close, so instead they stopped in the shade of a tree. When they turned, the boy stared expectantly, and Nylah floundered.

What am I doing?!

Nylah wished they knew the exact combination of words that would make their story seem true and bring compasses back for everyone—even if Nylah didn't want the magic for themself anymore.

"You believe in the Fates above all else, right?" Each word came out breathy, and Nylah strained to look composed.

The boy nodded, glancing back to where they'd come from. Venus couldn't just want a greeting. Nylah needed to choose between him and Jazz, and if they were giving this an honest try, Nylah needed to get to know this boy. So far, Nylah had only one lead on something they had in common, but it was something that might work in their favor.

"What if I told you I had a direct mission from them? The Fates. To bring back compasses."

This caught his attention. Nylah took one glance around to make sure the police officer was gone, then took the gamble. They pulled up their sleeve. The hourglass tattoo glittered in its usual out-of-this-world way, the sands falling and shifting into a mountainous peak. The glittering arrowhead notch pointed directly down Nylah's wrist at the boy as if beckoning him closer.

"What in Terra Mater…?" The boy raised his hand, taking Nylah's wrist to inspect the tattoo more closely. The second he made skin-to-skin contact, the hourglass shifted, the silver arrowhead tracing counterclockwise. Nylah stared in a mix of fascination and horror as it settled into a new position, the arrow clearly no longer pointing to the boy in front of them.

"And you say you got this from the Fates?" His pale gray-green eyes cast up to Nylah. Nylah's mind spun, surprised the mark had changed. Would the hourglass point to Jazz now? Or was it pointing to someone else entirely? What kind of adventure was Venus' mark going to take them on?

"Who else would bless one of Fates' Followers?" Nylah lied, trying to focus on the task at hand. They paused for emphasis before continuing their improvisation. "I have a special mission, and I need your help. The Fates' mark is guiding me to the people I need to gather, and they have chosen you."

His cool eyes flickered back to the undeniable magic on Nylah's wrist. He was intrigued; Nylah just needed to sell it.

"What would you give to get compasses back for everybody?" Desperation fueled every word as Nylah leaned in. "I know it sounds crazy, but can you look at this mark and say it wasn't made by the Fates? And you saw for yourself, it pointed to you. It chose you."

But is there any world where I would choose this boy? It seemed highly improbable. The boy glanced back toward the crowd, doubt casting over the beauty marks speckling his cheeks.

"I know you don't know me," Nylah rambled on, "but I know we both believe in the Fates. Help me bring back compasses. It's my divine mission."

It was basically true. The only lie was the true deity acting as Nylah's puppeteer. The boy bounced on the balls of his feet, glancing between Venus' mark, the crowd, and Nylah's pleading eyes.

"What do you need me to do?"

Yes.

Nylah's mouth perked in a playful smile. "First, I need you to tell me your name."

The boy brushed back the black-brown curls that swept over his brow.

"Damien. Damien Diaz."

Nylah's heart thudded as they put one more piece of the puzzle together about this strange boy. This person who was supposed to be their soulmate. Maybe.

"I'm Nylah." They clasped hands in a formal greeting. "Nylah Clare."

Over Damien's shoulder, Nylah registered an impatient head of auburn hair pushing through the crowd.

"And I'd like you to meet my sister."

CHAPTER LII

Jaylynn leaned against the tree, its shade giving them a slight refuge from the crowds. "Tell me exactly what happened."

Nylah pulled out a cigarette, and Jaylynn furrowed her nose.

"It's that simple. I showed him the arrowhead pointed at him. He picked up my wrist to look closer, and then it moved and it didn't point to him anymore." Nylah coaxed their lighter to life, then adjusted downwind from Jaylynn.

"So, it wasn't him."

"I'm telling you it most definitely was. That was the boy from the café."

That was reassuring, though it wasn't great that the mark had changed. Would it lead back to Jazz? It hadn't occurred to Jaylynn that Venus might give Nylah more than two choices, making the *right* call even harder. And what was the right choice anyway? Would Venus consider her son's original love match to be the right one? Hadn't Venus said she wanted to prove love was fickle and easily manipulated?

Jaylynn wanted to pull her hair out. She scanned the crowd, realizing they didn't have many other choices.

"I guess the only thing we can do next is follow the new coordinates and see what happens."

Nylah looked miserable at that response, taking an extra-long drag and blowing the smoke out to the sky. "Fine."

Jaylynn huffed in equal displeasure. "Snub that stick of ash out and let's get to it."

Nylah didn't discard their cigarette but did plunge back into the crowd.

Jaylynn had to admire Nylah's method. Their sibling wove through the crowd with ease, their left hand extended up to cut between bodies with only a small fragment of the tattoo showing past their sleeve, guiding their course. Nylah was careful to keep their eye on the arrowhead as they pushed deeper into the crowd.

Then Jaylynn's vision blurred. The bottom of a stake cuffed Jaylynn's cheek under her right eye and she winced in pain, stepping away from the man pounding his sign in the air.

Jaylynn's back was met with an elbow as she staggered. She sucked in a breath through her teeth, ducking her head to avoid another white sign. This one was painted bloodred, the words dripping to the bottom of the plastic.

Cupid Is Dead! Long Live the Fates!

The tips of Jaylynn's fingers came away red as she touched her cheek where the wooden spike had struck her. Nylah grabbed Jaylynn's shoulder, pulling her closer.

"Jay! Are you okay?"

"It's fine. Typical struggles of being five-foot-nothing." Jaylynn tried to brush off the cut even as the pain made her eye tear up. "Let's just get where we're going."

At the front of the crowd, the microphones were thunderous. Nylah wove their fingers through Jaylynn's and led them deeper. Jaylynn's healing burns ached in protest, but she didn't let go. The smell of sweaty bodies made her miss Psyche's peaceful cabin more than ever.

"Oof!" Jaylynn came to an abrupt stop as she ran into her sibling's back.

"Jazz?" Nylah reached out with their left hand, taking the man's shoulder and turning him. Jaylynn wasn't sure if she was relieved to see him or not.

Jazz's face was plastered with confusion when he saw Nylah. "What are you doing here?"

Nylah dropped their cigarette in surprise, their freckled cheeks flushed dark. Jaylynn made a point of stomping the stick out. Before Jaylynn could ask Nylah if their mark led them to Jazz or if this was just a coincidence, Jazz took Nylah's hand.

"You two are going to get crushed like ants. Come on." Without pause, Jazz cut back out of the thick of the crowd. Nylah glanced back, but all Jaylynn could do was shrug. She wasn't opposed to leaving the mosh pit.

When the trio broke free of the worst part of the crowd, Jazz led them to a corner with stone benches. Jaylynn took out her phone and flipped her front-facing camera on to inspect the cut under her eye. It was already swollen, but overall nothing dire. The top quarter of her phone lit up with a new text message.

NESSIE: Can you come over? I need you. Now.

Whether it was Nessie's task, the puppy, or something with Charity, Jaylynn didn't know, but Nessie wouldn't have texted if it wasn't urgent. Jaylynn muttered under her breath as she weighed her responsibilities, her thumbs hovering over the keys.

"What is it?" Nylah asked.

"I don't know, I think something went wrong Ness' or Charity's tasks."

"What about Nylah's task? Did you find your mark?" Jazz asked.

Jaylynn glanced up from her phone. As usual, Jazz was dressed like a fashion icon. He must have gone home and changed before coming here today. His black pants and black shirt were fitted and simple, topped by a maroon dress shirt that he wore unbuttoned, the sleeves rolled to his elbows. Nylah's smile didn't reach their eyes.

"Yeah, but we can talk about that later. Jay was just dropping me off."

Jaylynn frowned. "I was?"

Nylah wrapped Jaylynn in a hug. "Go. Nessie needs you and this isn't your crowd anyway."

"I would argue it shouldn't be yours either."

Nylah brushed a thumb under Jaylynn's cut cheekbone and dropped their voice. "Go take care of this. Trust me to handle the hourglass."

"It led you back to Jazz, didn't it?" Jaylynn asked.

Nylah pursed their lips and nodded.

That was both good and terrible news. Jaylynn could see the stubborn set in Nylah's eyes, as if they'd already chosen. How could Jaylynn leave without knowing for sure, though? There were only two nights left before the supermoon. The underside of Jaylynn's eye throbbed as she squeezed her eyes shut. She couldn't be in two places at once, and her gut told her whatever was going on with Nessie was important.

"We'll meet up with Damien tomorrow, okay?" Nylah offered. "Just let me stay with Jazz for now."

I'll go to the McKenzies' and then come back, Jaylynn resolved. She let out an exasperated sigh and squeezed her sibling tight.

"You're sure?"

Nylah nodded. There was an unreadable look on their face that made Jaylynn's skin tingle.

"I'll be at Charity's until you call. Stay safe?"

"I've got Jazz." Nylah gave their best friend a playful punch, drawing him back into their conversation. "He's like a seven-foot bodyguard. I'll be fine. You're sure you can make it back to the truck okay?"

"I am not seven feet tall," Jazz protested, but the corner of his mouth perked, suggesting he was pleased at the comparison.

"Yet you make a spectacular bodyguard." Nylah grinned back. Whatever worry had cast over their features before eased in Jazz's presence. It made Jaylynn doubt everything. Was there any point in trying to change her sibling's heart if it already beat for Jazz? What choice did Venus want Nylah to make? Jaylynn leaned in for one last hug.

Stars, I sure hope Nylah knows what they're doing.

It took Jaylynn another two hours before she parked Gertrude at the McKenzie house. The key to the front door was hidden under a potted plant. Jaylynn followed the texted instructions, letting herself in. She hung her coat and slid out of her boots, the eerie silence of the home reminding her of a tomb.

"Hello?" Jaylynn's call echoed through the house.

Nessie came around the corner wrapped in a big blanket. The darkness under her eyes was worse than ever, making Jaylynn wonder how much the girl was sleeping.

"Hey," Jaylynn said, relieved to see her unharmed. "What happened?"

"Jupiter Almighty, what happened to your face?"

Jaylynn waved her worry off. "It's nothing, I'm fine. What happened? You're not working on your task today?"

Nessie shook her head. "Seb's busy with something, and honestly, I'm really worried about my mom."

Jaylynn gave the girl's shoulders a squeeze. "I'll go check on her. Why don't you start us some tea?"

She made her way upstairs to the last bedroom on the right as Nessie had directed. The door creaked as it opened slowly.

"Charity?" The room was blackout dark, and Jaylynn blinked as her eyes adjusted.

"Please... The door. I can't..."

Jaylynn quickly obliged and closed the door, shutting them back into darkness. She crossed the room to the far side of the bed. The sound of sniffing and wiggling came from somewhere in the folds of fabric, making Jaylynn smile. Ladybug must have fallen asleep tucked in with Charity. The puppy stretched and clumsily trotted over to Jaylynn. She caught the pup before she slipped off the side of the bed. Jaylynn held Ladybug up with one arm and went to Charity's side.

"What's going on?" Jaylynn murmured, resting a cautious hand on Charity's forehead.

"I made a mistake." The response was weak, and Jaylynn could tell Charity's voice was hoarse from crying. "I can't sleep. I can't eat. I cursed myself and ruined us all."

Jaylynn noticed the covered mirror. This was Venus' doing. "Charity, what happened?"

Charity's features became clearer as Jaylynn approached. Fear pleated the wrinkles at the corners of her friend's eyes.

"Jay, I met Apollo."

Jaylynn's eyes widened. "You what? When?!"

Charity winced, and Jaylynn immediately dropped her voice back to a hushed whisper. "Tell me everything."

There was a long pause as Charity gathered herself. Jaylynn sat at the foot of the bed, trying her best to ignore Ladybug as she chewed and pulled on the end of one of her braids. Charity took a shuddering breath.

"I took Lacey to Apollo's Temple for the Sunday service. Then, when I was sitting in the pew, it was like I slipped away to an alternate reality. I was still in the church, but it was empty, save one person."

Apollo. Jaylynn shuddered to think of facing another god, let alone on her own.

"What happened?" Jaylynn pulled her hair away from Ladybug and set the puppy down on the bed. She took Charity's hands with a reassuring squeeze. Ladybug pranced to the other side, turning her teething on a pillow with tassels.

"He was talking about the war and prophecies. How the gods were divided about the veil between realms falling. Then he asked what I wanted."

"What did you say?"

"Oh, Jay, I was so dumb. I should have said healing. I should have wished Psyche to be revived or to bring compasses back, but I wasn't thinking straight. I asked for a prophecy because I thought it would help us beat Venus. But now every time I close my eyes, all I see are flashes that make no sense. I don't know if they're of the future or possible outcomes. I think I'm losing my mind."

Charity burrowed deeper into her pile of blankets, her bandaged hands covering her eyes in shame.

"Shhhh, it's okay," Jaylynn cooed. "I doubt Apollo could have fixed the compasses anyway."

A sniffle of objection was the only response. Jaylynn leaned closer, her own curiosity burning.

"Tell me about the visions, Charity. Everything you can remember."

It took a minute for Charity's breathing to slow.

"They're so fast, it's hard to grasp what they mean before they change again. I see a full moon cresting over treetops. I see you screaming, your hands clawing at the air. Then I see Nessie, standing all alone with a twisted staff in her hand." Charity choked back a fresh surge of tears. "I see a wall of fire, an inky black-green river, and a black hole of whipping winds. I see rows of doors—giant ones that stretch taller than buildings—and a glowing silver box." Charity sucked in a breath. "And I keep seeing Luke. My Luke."

At this, Charity fell apart completely. Jaylynn reached out and pulled Charity's head to her chest. No visions of Psyche or Blake, Jaylynn noted. Whether that was good or bad, it was hard to say.

"I never should have asked for anything from a god. I should have known it wouldn't be a gift."

"It's okay. It might help," Jaylynn soothed her.

At this, Charity cried harder. "I don't want to do this anymore. I don't want to face gods. I don't want to be crazy."

Jaylynn cupped Charity's face, forcing her to meet her eyes. "You are not crazy. You are more than capable of facing this. And you are not alone."

Charity's tears soaked into Jaylynn's bandages as she steadied herself.

"It's only a couple more days until the supermoon. We've got this. I'm here."

UNTIL THE SUPERMOON

Jupiter's lightning and Cupid's great wings;
Add Pandora's box to Vulcan's crafted things.
The reclusive god masters flame and metal galore,
His blacksmith talents alter Terra Mater evermore.
Nestled deep in a volcano burns his undying torch:
Vulcan's forge stays forever lit by his lava's scorch.
—The Inventor

CHAPTER LIII

"Hey, Mum. Hey, Dad." Gareth's mind felt fuzzy from too little sleep, but he sat up taller as he answered the video call. He hadn't expected his parents to reach out so early in the morning, yet he knew it was only a matter of time. The worry in his parents' eyes was undeniable.

"Gareth, are you all right?"

A pit of yearning opened like a chasm in Gareth's heart at his mum's question. Since he'd returned from the Suns', his homesickness had only gotten worse. He'd tossed and turned in Dakota's bed all night. The news yesterday that the Northern Alliance had claimed Brussels hadn't helped one bit.

"I'm good. You?"

Elise gave a soft smile but it didn't reach her usually bright eyes. "We miss you, son. How was your weekend?"

Gareth filled them in on what he could, from boarding up the gallery to staying with the Suns. He tried to make it sound like he was having fun, but it was hard to smile when his heart was so clouded by worry. How much time did his family have before the Northern Alliance would be on their doorstep? And where would they go? They had nowhere to flee.

Kenyon seemed to share Gareth's dampened mood. He kneaded his forehead. "Son, I don't know how much news they're sharing about the Endless War in Canada, but… there are rumors here they might suspend travel soon."

"Gareth," Elise cooed. "Honey, we think it's time you come home. Before things get any worse."

Home. The thought of being back in his own room, of seeing his brothers and his parents in person, sounded like Elysium. But would Sebastian be ready to go? Gareth had never seen his best friend as relaxed and happy as he'd been the last couple days. And the gallery repairs had only just started. Some part of him felt bad leaving the Harts when they needed all the extra hands they could get.

"I—" Gareth struggled to reply. If he could have anything, he wished he could have his family shipped here, away from the war. "How are Dakota and Liam doing?" He knew he was deflecting, but he wasn't sure what to say.

The corners of his mum's usually wide smile tilted down. "They are also ready to go home."

Gareth's heart sank. Was the war really so bad that they didn't want to stay? Or was it just that they missed their families? Gareth glanced around the bedroom and realized once Dakota was back, there wouldn't be room for Gareth here.

"Because of the rumors, the price and demand on flights is skyrocketing," Kenyon explained. "I don't think we can afford to wait a few more days to see what happens. Son, please come home, before it's too late." It was the small plea, so unlike his father, that made Gareth second-guess everything.

Even though they were giving him the choice, Gareth could tell there was only one right answer. He took a long breath as he weighed the options. The reality was, he had nothing here. He stayed in a bedroom that wasn't his, with sisters who barely spoke to him, and parents so locked in their grief they could barely function.

The only real loss was his kindling friendship with Nessie, but even that didn't feel the same anymore. After she mentioned the idea of her and Sebastian dating, Gareth couldn't help but wonder if he'd misread all her smiles. Was she being nice to him just to get closer to Sebastian the whole time? Did he read too much into their brief kiss? And if that was the case, why did he feel so hurt by it? Gareth clenched the sheets in his hands. While he usually fought hard to see the bright side of things, now all he could see were reasons to leave.

"When's the next flight out?"

Elise's smile was sad, but Gareth knew she'd be relieved to have him home. His dad would relax without the expectation to feed and protect two exchange boys. Everything would go back to normal. Well, almost normal. Gareth rubbed at his chest and the unexpected pain that came with his resolve.

Home. Gareth was going home.

CHAPTER LIV

Because she didn't have a phone and couldn't leave the apartment, Lacey had resorted to using her dad's laptop to connect with the outside world. It had taken her all day to remember her Instagram password, but she'd eventually gotten onto the app and found what she'd needed.

Damien Diaz.

Lacey was desperate for some confirmation that they were okay—that Damien wasn't mad at her. The horror of her parents kicking him out ached like a fresh bruise. She would do anything to fix things. Unfortunately, finding her boyfriend on Instagram didn't mean he would respond to any of her messages.

Lacey toggled the refresh button at the top of the screen again, her eyes blurring. She had scrolled through the meager photos on his profile so many times over, she practically had them memorized, but she started from the top again. Under the very first picture, one username jumped out at her.

Liked by @alva-babes

Lacey paused, her curiosity piqued. Was this *the* Alva? The one Damien considered a sister and missed? Lacey clicked on the username and started her investigation.

Alva was, much to Lacey's horror, quite pretty. Every photo framed either her tiny waist or a plunging neckline of a shirt. Worse, Damien had "liked" every single one of her photos. Lacey's eyes raced over each photo's caption, her heart sinking as she scoured the comments for any proof she was worried about nothing.

They're just close friends. Of course they like each other's posts.

But then she came to a photo of the two of them. Alva had her arms wrapped around Damien's neck as he piggybacked her. They were both laughing, not paying any attention to the person behind the camera.

Lacey's heart wilted. Who was this girl in Damien's life before she'd shown up? And would he be mad if she asked more about her? Would it come off as jealous? Then a darker thought crept up. Did the reason Damien seemed so practiced at everything intimate have anything to do with Alva?

"Lacey?" Kade came around the corner, already pulling on his coat. "I have to go to the pharmacy. Will you keep an ear out for your mom while I'm away, please?"

She nodded, sitting up taller from her spot on the couch. "Of course."

Between being grounded and having no way to contact Damien, Lacey's life wallowed at an all-time low, but there was one win: her mom was home and conscious. There was no more wondering if Renee might relapse into a coma and never wake, and that glimmer of happiness kept Lacey afloat.

"Do you need anything while I'm out?" Kade asked.

Fresh air? A new phone? A chance to get out of this apartment for a while?

"No, I'm good," she said instead. Lacey pushed away the laptop. She needed a distraction, even if it wasn't leaving the house. "I was thinking I might make breakfast."

Kade stopped and gave Lacey a double take. "Oh? What did you have in mind?"

"I don't know. I figured I could probably make scrambled eggs and toast. Do you think Mom could eat that?"

The appreciation on her dad's face was undeniable. "That's perfect, sweetie. I'll be back as soon as I can."

This was the one unexpected thing that was working out this summer. Despite her mom's near-death experience, the totaled car, compasses disappearing, and the new military announcements, it finally felt like Lacey and her dad were on the same side of things. Caring for Renee gave them common ground. Usually, if the three of them were cooped up in the house, they'd be at each other's throats, but ever since the initial blowout, the apartment had been surprisingly peaceful.

Lacey waved as her dad left, refocusing her attention on the kitchen. She peeked once at the laptop to make sure there weren't any new notifications, then faced the stove.

When the plates finally made it to the table, it was a small wonder. The eggs were probably a bit too brown, but no one complained. Renee's wheelchair fit well at the table, and Kade shared a knowing smile with Lacey at her mom's progress as Renee took small bites.

"Is the temperature okay? Do you want me to cut the pieces smaller?" Kade brushed a piece of Renee's hair behind her ear.

"I'm fine, Kade." Her mom's voice still rasped, and Lacey tried not to flinch at the sound. "Were you able to get more painkillers?"

Kade glanced at the white paper bag on the counter. "Not the same ones you were on. They were out. The pharmacist gave me the best they had, though."

Every time Lacey's guilt began to ease, something like this would come up. If only she'd stayed in the car, or even in

Montreal, her mom wouldn't wince every time she tried to eat. She wouldn't need pain medication. Lacey could feel the depths of shame rising, and she swallowed tears. She couldn't cry anymore, not after she'd cried herself to sleep last night. Though they hadn't spoken the words out loud, Lacey knew her dad was leaving. It was only a matter of time. She forced away the thought, trying to find something positive to focus on.

"I was thinking," Lacey said, "whenever you guys feel ready for it, maybe we could invite Damien for supper so you could get to know him better." Lacey twirled her fork as she put out the idea.

Renee wiped her mouth with a napkin. The bruising from her broken nose was more green and brown today and made her look even worse for wear despite the fact she was talking better. "Can you give me a few more days, Lacey, please? I'm still so tired and I just can't handle more right now."

Lacey pinched her lips together in disappointment.

But Dad might be gone by then…

The two times he'd met Damien had gone horribly, and Lacey wanted nothing more than to prove she'd won the lottery in soulmates. But instead of pushing, Lacey bowed her head in submission. It was her fault her mom was in so much pain and was so tired.

"Of course."

"Maybe we can have a movie day today," Kade suggested. "Something light and easy."

"Sure." Lacey figured if all she was doing otherwise was waiting for a notification to pop up on her dad's laptop, it would help pass the time. She cleared the plates as her mind swirled from one bleak thought to the next. As she tucked the orange juice away, the heaviest thought of all hit her.

What if this is the last day we all have together?

Kade wrapped his arm under Renee's shoulder as he helped her onto the couch. He adjusted the pillows until Renee swatted him away.

"I'm fine. Stop fretting."

Lacey took a steadying breath and willed herself to think of anything other than the prospect her father might die in the war. She grabbed the remote and joined her parents on the couch. She gave her dad's hand a squeeze, and the way he looked at her made her want to cry all over again. He was thinking the same thing—she knew it.

CHAPTER LV

If bad decisions were a city, Nylah could run for mayor. Their lanyard swung as they wrestled with the lock on the café's door. In their manager's hastened firing, Nylah had dropped their apron and walked out without looking back, café key accidentally in tow. Based on the fact they hadn't gotten any texts, it was safe to say the manager had their hands full and had completely forgotten to retrieve it.

The red Closed sign swung as Nylah opened the door and welcomed their companions inside. Every business on the block had been shut down, giving the Toronto street a strange eeriness despite it being half past two in the afternoon. Jazz strutted in unfazed and went to one of the long, low tables with armchairs all around it. Jaylynn followed more slowly, her lip caught in her teeth.

"You're sure this is okay?"

"Relax, Jay," Nylah said. "No one will know we were here."

There were no cameras to catch them trespassing. As for the priests, Fates' Followers wouldn't have recognized Jaylynn's truck when it pulled into the underground parking this morning. Nylah and Jazz had curled up in the back seat, careful no one saw them leave, so they were as safe as ever.

"It's so quiet in here." Jaylynn wandered by the bulletin board pinned with posters and business cards. Nylah flicked on the lights and the espresso machine.

"Give me a couple minutes and the glorious sound of grinding metal and beans will soothe your ears."

Jazz smirked as he draped a leg over the arm of his chair. "I didn't realize we'd be getting personal service."

Nylah grinned as they dug out the open bag of coffee beans. "We'll leave cash in the tip jar to pay for whatever we drink."

There was nothing Jazz or Jaylynn could say to make Nylah feel bad about this. Even if it was a bad idea, coming back once more felt like payment for being fired unjustly.

Jaylynn took a seat next to Jazz, sinking into the oversized armchair. "So, when are you going to tell me how everything went last night?"

Nylah flipped a switch on the metal machine. The familiar motions helped ease their nerves. Jazz watched them with a knowing look, and it took everything in Nylah to stay on their side of the counter. That subtle smirk was part of Nylah's Bad Decisions city, and Jazz knew it. He knew Nylah's choice the minute they'd entered his apartment and their shoes came off, quickly followed by everything else. They had crashed together in equal parts pleasure and guilt, insatiable and undeniably *right* in every way. Now, Nylah had to prove it to their sister.

Hot steam curled up as Nylah frothed milk for each coffee. Once all the cups were poured, Nylah knew there was no more avoiding Jaylynn. They carried the cups over and sank into their own chair.

"Spill," Jaylynn demanded.

Sunlight flashed across the wall as the bells on the door tinkled. They all sat up straight. Nylah relaxed as Damien closed the door behind him. His dark curls were slicked back from his face, and he seemed a bit more at ease than he had at the rally. He glanced between the chairs, assessing the gathered company. Nylah hoped he hadn't expected more of Fates' Followers. To be safe, all three of them had dressed in different touches of crimson to keep up Nylah's lie. Nylah had their corduroy coveralls, Jazz had his suit pants, and Jaylynn had a dark red scarf woven into her braids.

"Hey, Damien." Nylah adjusted their glasses, trying to look more collected than they felt. "Come sit. I made you a coffee."

Damien sat in the chair to Nylah's left, directly across from Jazz. Though they'd agreed Jazz would be nothing but kind when meeting Damien, Jazz's stare was filled with animosity, as if trying to figure out why this boy had been paired with Nylah. It mirrored Nylah's own thoughts.

Damien sat in his chair and pushed the fourth steaming cup away. "I'm not much of a coffee drinker."

Nylah gave a polite smile and pulled the cup closer to themself. They had no qualms about drinking two cups. "Can I get you something else? Tea? Water?"

Damien eyed the cooler of cold drinks. "I'll take an energy drink?"

Jaylynn rose and went to the cooler, clearly over her previous issue with using the café as a rendezvous. She subtly flipped the lock on the door as she came back. Damien took the tall can with a nodded thanks.

It was now or never. Nylah was pretty confident their theory was right, but they had to know for sure. Pulling up the sleeve of their striped shirt, Nylah displayed their left wrist. The amount of sand left in the top bulb was horribly low. Nylah brushed the back of their free hand across their brow, self-conscious of how much of a sweaty mess they were. Damien stared mesmerized at the tattoo as if he was surprised it wasn't an illusion.

"Take my hand," Nylah coaxed him.

Damien's eyes flicked up, then around the room. Everyone was staring at him and the silver heart that pointed to his seat. He took a deep breath and placed his palm on Nylah's. For a beat, nothing happened. There was no cold relief from contact with the match. Then the mark moved, rotating one hundred and eighty degrees, exactly as they'd hoped. Nylah looked up expectantly to Jazz and held their other hand out to him.

Jazz's brow creased as he realized what Nylah was asking. For a moment he sat frozen, calculating. Finally, he took their hand.

Every nerve in Nylah's body went still as the heat in their core evaporated. They closed their fingers over each boy's hand, not letting either pull away as the magic shifted into something new. Jaylynn sat on the edge of her seat, her mouth open in awe.

The hourglass marker shifted again, but instead of pointing to Damien or Jazz, it turned a quarter of the way.

"It's you. It's pointing to you. Just like Nessie's compass pointed to herself," Jaylynn murmured.

Before Nylah could ask what their sister meant, Damien pulled his hand from Nylah's. "You know Nessie?"

Jaylynn cocked her head. "Yes… She's a close friend of mine."

While it was unlikely Damien and Jaylynn would ever have mutual friends, Nylah also couldn't imagine there were many people named Nessie in the world.

"Blond? Dimples? Doesn't take compliments well?" Damien took a sip from his can as he leaned back into his chair.

"Ha," Jaylynn coughed. "I guess you could say so. That's not really my experience of her, though."

Jazz gave Nylah's hand a gentle squeeze, then let go. As soon as the link was fully broken, the room temperature rose again. Nylah missed the touch, but there was a flicker of hope. They'd done it. Nylah had proven that their mark pointed to both Jazz and Damien. Now all Nylah had to do was choose. While Nylah already felt set, they knew what was at stake. The least they could do was get to know Damien better. Then, when Nylah still chose Jazz in the end, they'd be able to stand behind the choice wholeheartedly.

"Guys," Nylah interrupted. "Can we get back on topic?"

Jaylynn reoriented herself immediately. "Of course."

Nylah took off their glasses, rubbing away a smudge on the lens with their sleeve. "Damien, why don't you tell us a bit about yourself?"

"What do you want to know?"

Jazz leaned forward, his shoulders tight enough that Nylah did a double take. Was he intentionally flexing his arms or was he just that tense? "What made you join Fates' Followers?"

"At first, to piss off my parents." Damien smirked as he sipped his can, but Nylah got the distinct impression he was trying to play cool to hide his discomfort.

"Reminds me of someone I know," Jaylynn snorted and gave Nylah a pointed look.

Nylah rolled their eyes playfully.

"Were they atheists?" Nylah asked. They were conscious Jaylynn would use every opportunity to point out why Damien was the right choice, so if anything, this was Nylah's chance to prove how wrong they were for one another.

Damien scoffed. "No. My dad is a priest of Mars and my mum was a priestess of Venus."

They all stiffened at that. Jaylynn was the first to speak.

"That's an interesting pairing."

Damien crossed an ankle over his knee. "They both argued over whose faith I would choose. To make it easier, I chose another altogether."

"So, joining Fates' Followers wasn't just to find your soulmate, then?" Nylah clarified.

Damien shrugged. "The fact they offered answers no one else could helped. I wouldn't be here or have found Lacey without them."

Anger rekindled as Nylah zeroed in on the name of the girl with black hair. Jaylynn's face also darkened, but Nylah didn't understand why.

"You… are soulmates with Lacey?" Jaylynn's cup hung frozen at her lips.

Nylah scowled. "You know her too?"

Their sister nodded. The web of Venus' game only grew more complicated as Nylah tried to piece together why that was relevant.

Jazz cracked his knuckles, eager to move on. "And you're happy with who Cupid chose for you?"

Nylah nodded. That was an excellent question.

Damien took another gulp of his energy drink. "Why would anyone doubt the god of love?"

Maybe because he might have paired you and me?

Jaylynn gave Nylah yet another pointed stare.

"Well, here's to trusting in the gods." Nylah raised their cup. "May the Fates help us bring compasses back and return everything to how it was."

Their glassware clinked and they all settled back.

"So, what has to happen next?" Damien asked. "To bring back compasses."

Jaylynn sipped her coffee. "We all go to the ceremony tomorrow at sunset."

"How exactly are you involved?" Damien asked.

Jaylynn flipped one of her braids over her shoulder. "My mark was Nylah. Now that Nylah has you two, the group is complete."

"Why doesn't the hourglass point to you too, then?"

Jazz leaned forward and placed a protective hand on Jaylynn's knee.

"Listen, none of this will work without Jay. We wouldn't even have a chance to get compasses back without her."

Nylah wanted to point out it was also Jaylynn's fault they lost them in the first place, but they held their tongue.

Damien didn't look convinced. "I really don't know about all this. I thought there'd be priests here or something more official."

While part of Nylah didn't want to entertain Damien as an option, they also knew they needed to get him on board. To be safe, Jaylynn wanted to bring both boys to the ceremony. Which meant Nylah had to convince Damien to be there too.

"What's more official than a magical tattoo?"

"The hourglass literally points to you," Jaylynn added. "You can't deny that."

Damien stood and everyone rose in his wake. "Yeah, I saw whatever that was." He shot an unreadable look at Jazz and turned on his heel.

"Damien, wait." Nylah hated how desperate their voice was as he paused at the front door. "At the rally, you seemed invested in getting compasses back."

Damien's hand hovered over the lock. Sweat dripped down Nylah's back.

"It's because a part of you isn't sure," Nylah gambled. "You remember this café, don't you?"

Damien glanced around, his eyes tracing over the menus.

"I know that because I was here." Nylah stood up and walked to the counter, resting a hand on the surface. "I was here when you walked in. I saw you lose your compass, and I saw the girl who claimed you."

Wrongly. The word burned in Nylah's mind. They couldn't say it, but they did need to make sure Damien doubted his current match enough to want to bring compasses back and show up tomorrow. Then Nylah could choose in front of Venus, and everyone would get compasses back. Jazz would be freed from the cult. Where that left Damien, Nylah couldn't say. They pushed on.

"I know, deep down, part of you isn't sure she was meant to be yours." It was manipulative, but it was also the truth, and Nylah could see their reasoning was hitting its mark. Damien's brows knit together. "Lacey isn't what you were expecting, is she? If you haven't already started questioning it, you'll notice it now. All the ways she isn't right for you."

Jaylynn leaned forward, her grip on her mug tight.

Nylah held their sleeves in their fingers. They needed to seal this. "The Fates chose us to bring back compasses. Whether you do it for the world or for your own proof, it's up to you. But believe me when I tell you, we need you at that ceremony tomorrow."

Damien leaned his head forward and rested it on the doorjamb. "What do you need me to do?"

There was something in his answer, the sound of something worn down and broken, that made Nylah feel awful. All these truths, all these lies; all these games to appeal to one vengeful goddess. But they would do it, because now Nylah could see what their happily ever after was, and they were going to earn it by getting everyone else's compasses back.

A new thought hit Nylah. Could they be sure Jazz would still choose them too once compasses returned? Or would the chance to meet his soulmate change things?

"Just meet us back here tomorrow. The rest should be easy," Nylah instructed, even as a new seed of doubt wove itself into their heart.

CHAPTER LVI

"The meeting shouldn't run longer than an hour," Huan explained as he fussed with the sleeves of his suit jacket. It seemed too formal for the fun-loving Huan who Nessie had been getting to know.

"We'll be fine," she encouraged. "We'll meet back at Soldiers' Tower when you're done."

Huan sighed in agreement. He squeezed Sebastian's shoulder once, then turned to follow all the other veterans and army personnel. Next to the suits and uniforms, Nessie felt underdressed. She'd paired her worn jacket with a knee-length white dress and a pair of cute flats. Venus' lack of mirror appearances yesterday and today was making Nessie's anxiety worse, but right now she had to focus. She was finally alone with Sebastian and was going to make the most of each moment, even if it was in a stuffy old university hall.

"Want to see somewhere cool?" Nessie asked.

The corner of Sebastian's lips twitched up. "Lead the way."

Nessie had spent hours researching the university campus when Sebastian mentioned he'd be here with Huan today. Thankfully, Sebastian accepted her company without question, and Nessie knew exactly where she wanted to spend the hour.

Sebastian hesitated a step as Nessie guided him away from the building.

"Don't worry. We're not going anywhere near the protests," she said. Nessie had no plans of getting tear-gassed or Tasered.

He relented as she gave him her biggest smile, tugging him down the front steps into the courtyard. Tall leafy trees lined the stone walkways, not a student or protestor to be seen.

"Did Gareth say why he couldn't come today?" Nessie asked.

"No, but it was strange because at first he sounded like he really wanted to hang out, but after I told him where we were meeting, he said something came up." Sebastian scratched his temple. "Maybe the Harts needed help with something else at the gallery."

Nessie nodded. She couldn't help but wonder if Gareth was actually busy or if he was giving Nessie and Sebatian space. A subtle sadness paired with her endless guilt and Nessie tried to shake it off. She couldn't afford to waste this chance with Sebastian. She had only one more day to make him fall for her.

Nessie bumped his shoulder as he walked with unfocused eyes. "What's on your mind?"

Sebatian's hair tumbled over his brow as he waved her off. "Ah, it's nothing."

Steeling herself against the fear of rejection, Nessie wove her arm with his. She needed to truly connect with Sebastian if this was going to work. "No, it's not. You look like you're a million miles away. Tell me what's going on."

Sebastian sighed but didn't push her away. "I'm just worried, I guess."

A single beat of hope hummed in her chest. He hadn't stepped away, and he was opening up. Those had to be a good signs.

"About what?" Nessie urged.

"I don't know, everything? The war back home. The Suns. Liam." Sebastian scrubbed his free hand over his face. "I just don't know if I should go back home or stay here. Things were hard before compasses disappeared, but since then… everything keeps getting worse."

Nessie spirits fell with Sebastian's. "I get what you mean."

"I know Huan thinks this meeting will help," Sebastian explained. "He believes that if the army itself pushes back against the government, Canada will pull out of the Roman Empire," Sebastian said.

"But you're worried it's all for nothing?" Nessie guessed.

Sebastian nodded. "It's called the Endless War for a reason."

Nessie gave a sympathetic smile, even as his words hit somewhere deep inside of her. If they finished their tasks and compasses came back, would the war settle? Or had the damage already been done, and would the reignited war continue to burn hotter than ever?

"Well, I hope you stay," Nessie said. "I'm sure your family misses you, but I'd be sad if you left so soon."

What she couldn't say was that she desperately needed him to stay for at least one more day. Nessie glanced back at the map on her phone, choosing to focus on what she could control, and reoriented them. Ten minutes stretched under the sunny sky before Nessie found the building she was looking for.

"This is it."

"There's even more trees in here than outside," Sebastian said with a laugh as they stepped into the medical building. Tall bamboo trees and tropical plants covered the atrium.

"Come on." Nessie grinned and took his hand. Nessie led Sebastian deeper, to where the marble walkways gave way to wooden planks, to the hidden spot she'd discovered online. The small studying corner had a long bench and was completely surrounded by trees. It was the closest thing she could find to a romantic spot on campus that would steer clear of the protests, and she was pretty proud of her discovery.

Nessie sat on the bench and basked in the sun filtering in from the glass ceiling that stretched floors above them. Office windows framed the tall walls, but from what she could tell, the place was close to empty. Whether Sebastian thought the nature reserve was cool or not, she didn't know, but she was confident her mom would have loved it.

"Seb," Nessie said, pausing as she gathered her courage. "I wanted to say the other day, I'm sorry you missed finding your soulmate."

He shrugged as he sat beside her. "It's fine."

"Can I ask how long you had your compass before it disappeared?" Even as she asked the question, Nessie wanted to strangle herself. She was so curious, but she worried bringing up compasses would make things harder. She reasoned she had to know what she working against, though.

Sebastian sighed. "Two weeks."

"Oh." Nessie swallowed. That was a lot shorter than she'd expected.

"I got it on a Saturday morning." Sebastian threaded his fingers together. Nessie tipped her knees in his direction as he spoke, doing her best to relax her shoulders. "You know, at first I would have done anything to get rid of it. Compasses usually mess people up more than anything. But then I got on that plane and I came here, and for a second I actually wanted to know who Cupid had chosen for me—who he thought my perfect match was—then, as soon as I tried to follow my mark, it disappeared."

Nessie watched the way his jaw ticked and wondered if she should reach out or stay still. Sebastian kept talking, as if now that he'd started, he wanted to get it all off his chest.

"Twelve ten. That was the time I was fated to meet my soulmate. I was four minutes away when compasses vanished."

Nessie swallowed, the blame landing square between her shoulders. "I'm so sorry, Seb."

"It's fine. It's not like it was your fault."

But it was.

Tears pricked the backs of Nessie's eyes as she tried to recover.

"So, if compasses came back, would you be happy to have a linked soulmate again?"

"I don't know," Sebastian answered with a heavy exhale. His tone implied he didn't think that was an option anymore.

The information trickled through Nessie's mind as she considered the projected outcomes. If Sebastian was holding out for his one true love, it would be impossible for him to fall for her. She would fail her task, and he would never meet his perfect match. And yet, if she succeeded, if he did fall for her and then got his compass back, what then? Would he forgive her for playing with his heart when the goal was to get his chance at one true love back?

"And if compasses don't come back?" she whispered.

Sebastian thought for a long moment. "I spent years not wanting a compass tattoo but still wanting my own family one day. I guess… I hope I'll find someone who wants the same things as I do, even without compasses."

There was a sense of resolution in his statement as he sat up a bit taller. His eyes met hers, and they held a depth Nessie hadn't seen before, something raw and real from his confession. She finished weighing the pros and cons in her mind. There was no perfect outcome, so she would have to settle on the lesser evil. Sebastian would have his heart broken whether or not compasses came back, and Nessie's fate was ruined the day she got her compass. But all the people around them? They still had a chance at happiness.

Nessie leaned closer, butterflies of nerves snagging her breath. She needed to make her intentions clear. She couldn't afford to be shy or unsure. Sebastian didn't resist as she pulled his hands apart and wove her fingers with his. She'd taken to wearing her bandages only on her palms and wrists, and relief pounded alongside the pain of her healing burns as he held her hands back.

"Seb," Nessie said quietly. "I may not be your soulmate, and I don't know if compasses will ever come back, but I know one thing: you're a good person. You're kind, and funny, and sensitive, and to be honest, if I could choose who my compass had pointed to, I would have chosen you."

The truths and lies bled into one another, and Nessie's heart ripped as she saw understanding dawn in those sea-colored eyes. Her words were so much like what Gareth had told her, and she hated herself for twisting his confession to her own end. Now

Nessie was truly playing Venus' game, manipulation and all, and she had never felt further from the person she wanted to be. But the lies worked. Nessie didn't have to close the gap. Sebastian did.

His lips met hers with a curious, tentative kiss. She leaned in, desperate to sell how much she wanted this even as her internal shame threatened to strangle her. Sebastian's hand moved to her hip, gently pulling her closer. It was nothing like the way he'd kissed Lacey in the hot tub—all fire and no fear.

Lacey.

All at once, pieces fell into place in Nessie's mind. The basic facts stared her in the face. Lacey got her compass two weeks ago on the Saturday morning after their math exam. Her compass time was 12:10. Lacey met her soulmate right as compasses disappeared.

Or at least, she thought she did.

Nessie gasped and pulled back, her fingers falling over her tingling lips.

Damien.

Venus.

Everything clicked into place. Why Venus chose Sebastian as her task. Why Nessie couldn't find it in her to like Damien.

He was never meant for Lacey.

But had Damien lied? Or did he also believe, like Lacey did, that they were a destined match?

Sebastian froze, his fingers curling closed.

"I'm sorry," Nessie whispered. She knew she needed to rectify this, but the realization was a punch to the gut. "I know I started it, but…" Nessie trailed off, glancing over her shoulder for some kind of distraction, a solution, a moment to think.

I really am cursed, aren't I? And everything I touch gets ruined.

Gareth. Sebastian. Lacey. Maybe even Damien. She was personally responsible for all the heartbreak and drama unfolding.

A gentle squeeze of her fingertips brought her attention back to Sebastian.

"It's cool," he said. "We have all the time in the world to figure things out."

Sebastian gave her an easy smile, and Nessie tried to match it as she took a panicked breath. He couldn't know how wrong he was. The gods were literally playing with Sebastian's heart, forcing her hand to ruin him alongside her.

Lacey will never forgive me for this.

The dawning horror of just how big Venus' game was made Nessie's limbs go cold. But this was it: her ticket to saving her dad's soul and her mom's sanity. To Jaylynn's and Blake's happiness. To getting compasses back for the world and maybe stopping the war. She willed her heart to slow.

"No, I'm sorry. I was just surprised," Nessie confessed. "I wasn't sure you liked me that way."

Sebastian's eyebrow quirked up as if to say, *Well, obviously I do.* He rubbed his thumb over the backs of her fingers, the same way Gareth had in the bathroom. "Ness. You're one of the only good things that's come into my life since compasses disappeared. Of course I like you. I wouldn't be here if I didn't."

But was Sebastian admitting he liked her the same as Nessie claiming his heart as Venus demanded?

I belong in the Underworld for this.

"What about the Suns?" she teased, feeling more comfortable with playful banter than physical intimacy.

Sebastian stood and pulled her up with him. "Okay, you're the second-best thing in Canada."

But Lacey should have been the first.

"Come on," he said. "Let's go explore more."

Nessie forced herself to smile as she took his hand, their fingers weaving together again, but the weight of Nessie's new knowledge changed everything. She no longer felt proud of gaining traction on Venus' task. She felt positively awful.

CHAPTER LVII

BLAKE

"I'm just saying, a fence would keep animals out of the garden." Hunter leaned against the fridge, beer in hand.

"You're just looking for another excuse to build something." The corner of Blake's mouth rose with a knowing smirk as she washed the last dish from dinner. "While I'm sure Psyche will love her new coffee table, I'm not sure how she would feel about waking up to a fenced property. And I'd bet she leaves her garden open intentionally to feed the wildlife."

"I could make a gate to keep people from the highway wandering in."

Blake pitched an eyebrow. "Like you wandered in?"

At this, Hunter smiled. It wasn't a big, wide smile like Jaylynn might have. No, Hunter's smiles were subtle: a slight hitch at the corner of his lips, or the softening of his brow. He readjusted his ball cap, tucking soft brown curls out of his eyes.

"I'm just saying it would have more than one purpose."

Blake wrung out her cloth. "Why don't we talk about it after tomorrow?"

Tomorrow.

They both came to a lengthy pause. Venus' deadline was tomorrow. Between Hunter's hourglass running out of sand and the growing size of the moon, the conversation they'd both subtly avoided seemed to come up more often as the day came closer.

"Don't chop more wood." Psyche might not be around to need it afterward.

"Do we need more groceries?" We don't know how long either of us will stay when it's all done.

"Kiss me again." Who knows what will happen after Venus' tasks are over?

It was painful, all these partial conversations, dancing around the truth. Maybe that was why it was so easy for Blake and Hunter to coexist in silence. There were too many questions with unknowable answers.

Blake wiped her hands dry and opened the fridge. In the back corner, Jaylynn's pink love potion sat labeled *FOR BLAKE*. Jaylynn hadn't mentioned she'd finished the recipe—she'd just left it in the fridge for Blake to choose. Blake itched to grab a glass of whiskey, but Jaylynn's handwritten cursive stared at her poignantly.

Fine. While Blake doubted it would actually help her fall in love, Jaylynn had hand-counted two hundred and twenty-two tiny dried-up rose petals for this concoction. The last thing Blake needed was her showing up to the cabin tomorrow and seeing the jug still full.

They took their customary spots on the couch: Blake facing Psyche, and Hunter watching the door. The fireplace crackled, filling the cabin with warmth. To Blake's relief, the love potion was smooth and flat, more like a creamy tea, and while it wasn't particularly sweet, Blake deemed it bearable enough to drink.

"Blake. We really should talk about tomorrow."

She coughed. "What's there to talk about?"

Hunter took a long drink from his beer bottle, but his concentrated frown didn't disappear.

"What about you 'n' me?"

Blake ran a finger around the rim of her glass, unwilling to meet his eye. "What about it?"

"What's going to happen once compasses come back?"

"You assume we're going to succeed," Blake retorted. "We have no idea how the other girls are doing with their tasks."

But that wasn't the only problem. Every time the tasks came up, Blake was confronted with the worry that of all four of them, she was the one failing. She was trying, *really trying*, to love

Hunter. He was kind, patient, and helpful, yet Blake *knew* she didn't feel it. She wasn't sure what falling in love felt like, but it couldn't be this. This was comfortable and warm, but she wasn't about to take a bullet for this man, and to Blake, that's what love was: being willing to die for the person.

Hunter couldn't know that, though. Here she was, still lying to him. Telling him *he* had to fall in love with *her*. She took a large gulp of her drink.

"Okay, so two scenarios, then," Hunter offered. "What happens to us if compasses come back, and what happens if they don't?"

You leave.

The words caught in Blake's throat, but that was the only end she could see either way. Couldn't Hunter see that because Venus had orchestrated all of this, none of it was real? There was no relationship or future here. She breathed out heavily through her nose.

"I don't know. Can't we just wait and see how things go?"

Hunter didn't seem to like this answer. Minutes passed in a heavy silence.

"You know, I would build you a house if you asked."

Blake looked up from her frothy pink drink at a loss for words.

Hunter's plaid shirt strained against his chest as he took even breaths.

"Any way you wanted it. Whatever it took for it to feel like home to you."

Blake had never imagined owning a house, let alone building one. Psyche's cabin was the closest thing she'd found to a home in a long time, but that didn't even belong to her.

Hunter rolled his bottle of beer in the palm of his hand. "I left my home. I left my *country*, for Jupiter's sake." Hunter's grip tightened on the dark glass neck. "And I've spent the past week trying so hard to figure out what you want from me—what you need from me."

Blake swallowed and sat back, too stunned to reply.

"I keep waitin' for you to agree that we're good together. To say that no matter what happens tomorrow, we'll stick together. All I want is some confirmation that as soon as this mark is gone, you're not going to up and run again."

At this, Hunter looked up. Blake wasn't ready for the plea in those honey-brown eyes.

"So, I'm askin' you directly, Blake. Do you plan on runnin' as soon as you can? Because if you're playin' with me—if the stars and the Fates and the gods are all having a laugh—I wanna know now so I don't look like a fool tomorrow when you hightail it out of here."

Blake met his stare, a defensive wall rising inside her. "How can we even have this conversation when we don't know what's going to happen?"

Hunter clenched his jaw and let out a measured breath.

"Do you plan on runnin'? Yes or no?"

Blake hadn't outright thought about her plans, but now that Hunter had laid them out so neatly, wasn't that the most appealing option? Hadn't that always been her plan, even when she wasn't thinking about it?

"No." The lie caught in her throat. Hunter's gaze hardened as if he knew. Blake reached out and clasped his hand as he went to stand. He couldn't leave. Not now when they had only one day left.

"I don't know," Blake bit out, her words both sharp and fragile. "But what I do know… is that this has been nice."

Hunter watched her carefully, and Blake tightened her grip.

"Being with you has been nice. Kissing you has been nice. And I know you want me to open my heart and tell you everything in my head, but I just—" Blake scrambled for an excuse. "I'm not built that way. I'm not like Jaylynn. I don't wear my heart on my sleeve and cry because I feel sad. I don't tell people I care about them even when I do."

Blake's whole body trembled. She released Hunter's hand. "Talking isn't easy for me. Opening up is like cracking a mountain in two. It feels awful and I don't know why people do it."

Hunter didn't answer, but he also didn't leave. Blake sank her head in her hands.

"I see you trying," Blake continued. "And I'm trying the best I can. This is all just a lot. Too much, if I'm being honest."

Hunter cleared his throat. "Promise me you're not going to run when this is over. Or at least have the decency to have a conversation with me before you go."

Tears rimmed Blake's eyes, and she swallowed against the growing lump in her throat.

"I—I'll try," Blake said with as much honesty as she could muster. She couldn't promise. If they succeeded and compasses came back and Psyche woke up, where did she belong in that kind of aftermath? Would Hunter expect her to go back to the US with him? Would Psyche kick her out? Being homeless again, wandering streets and starving, was the last thing she wanted. But what Hunter was asking from her—a commitment, a promise—felt impossible.

Hunter huffed as if her thoughts were spelled out on her face. He didn't reach out to console her, instead he sat in silence as if weighing the unspoken truths. When Blake was sure she couldn't bear another minute, he shook his head.

"You know, you asked me to stay, Blake, when every bone in my body told me to go. Even then I knew all of this was bad news." Hunter stood, brushing his hands down his lap. "If you really wanna survive tomorrow, you gotta choose to stay too. Not tomorrow when it's almost too late. Now."

Blake's shoulders tensed as he came to stand by her side. He held out a patient hand. Blake set her empty glass down, her fingers trembling as she took his hand. She let him pull her up. The soft smell of wood and cologne blended together as she rested her face against his chest and wrapped her arms around his waist. Then Blake did something she'd never done in her life. She sent up a prayer to Cupid.

Please, Cupid, show me how to love this man.

CHAPTER LVIII

Ladybug tugged at the end of her leash, clearly delighted by the change of scenery. She snapped at the bushes lining the paved trail. Jaylynn and Nessie walked on either side of Charity, both a million times more relaxed than Charity felt.

"See, isn't the fresh air already helping?" Jaylynn beamed.

People losing their grip on reality shouldn't be in public.

Charity didn't have the energy to fake a smile. She hadn't slept since meeting Apollo, and her appetite had completely left her. She'd almost forgotten to feed Ladybug this morning, but Nessie had swooped in with her loving corrections. The subtle reminder was physical proof she was fading away again, but Charity knew this time was worse than before because she wasn't going into gray oblivion. This time, her mind was being reduced to madness. The only thing that brought her any solace was, surprisingly, Ladybug.

The feisty, playful pup helped pull Charity from her worst hallucinations. She coaxed Charity's rare smiles out by lying on her back and demanding belly rubs, as if that was the only reason humans existed. But despite the tiny happinesses the puppy brought, Charity's world had never felt so dark.

Any other week, the melting sunset would have been beautiful. Today, it looked like a wall of fire to Charity. Wait… it *was* flames. Charity stopped and grasped Jaylynn's wrist in alarm as black billowing smoke filled the horizon.

"What is it?" Nessie asked as Charity pointed with a trembling hand.

"The fires," Charity whispered. "They're burning the city down."

Jaylynn and Nessie swapped concerned looks.

"What fires, Mom?"

Perhaps it wasn't the rioters burning the city, but instead the gods. Maybe Vulcan was so close to crossing the veil that his volcanoes were bursting forth to meet him. But even as Charity stumbled, she realized that didn't make sense—there were no volcanoes around here.

"Why don't I take Ladybug?" Nessie offered, gently prying the leash away. It was her daughter's tone that made Charity sure something was deeply wrong.

"You don't see it? The flames in the distance?"

Nessie's brows creased in concern as she shook her head. "No."

"Let me keep her, please." Charity's grip tightened on the leash. "It... She helps."

Nessie obliged, but the worry in her face was stark. Charity had to face the truth. Apollo was breaking her mind further. Her feeble mind was collapsing under his weight, and all she had was a ruby-colored puppy keeping her sane.

"So," Jaylynn hedged, acting like this was a perfectly normal walk. "What's our plan for tomorrow?"

Nessie let out a heavy sigh. "I convinced Seb to come with us to the cabin for the evening. I told him we plan on doing a full-moon bonfire and wiener roast."

"And... do you think his heart is yours? Has he forgotten about his soulmate?" Jaylynn asked.

"I've known him for less than a week! Does he like me as a person? Sure. Does he love me? I don't see how he could. But I think I've done everything I can on that front." Nessie punched her fists deeper into her jacket pockets.

Charity fought to keep her attention on the dog and not on the flames in the horizon.

"You're a beautiful and smart girl, Nessie. He's probably more into you than you know," Jaylynn said as their path rounded a bend. Dark lake waters glinted ahead.

Charity could feel how much her daughter needed her reassurance too, but some instinct wouldn't let her look away from the water. Then a pair of slim and pale hands broke the surface, clawing and grasping for purchase. Charity stopped abruptly.

"Someone's drowning!" Charity gasped, but before she could make it a step, a hard hand gripped her arm. Panic surged in Charity's veins as she struggled forward.

"Mom," Nessie said firmly. "There's no one in the water. It's okay."

Jaylynn scoured the water in the direction where Charity's finger trembled.

"I don't see anyone either. Charity, breathe," Jaylynn murmured into her ear. "You are safe. There's no one in the water. I swear to you."

Nessie's eyes were wide as Charity forced her attention back to her companions.

"We'll head back soon, Mom. Just hang in there."

You're seeing things. None of this is real.

Jaylynn squeezed Charity's hand gently, a weight to keep her in the real world. "So, Seb is coming to the cabin and Hunter is already there."

"Hopefully Blake has her task underhand. How did it go with yours today?" Nessie asked.

"Well, Nylah's mark clearly points to two people," Jaylynn sighed. "And they're both on board to come to the cabin tomorrow, but I don't know how much more I can do. Nylah has always been stubborn, so even if I knew who the right choice was, I don't think I could change my sibling's mind if my life depended on it."

Nessie had on her thinking face. "Maybe you just need to trust that Nylah knows their own heart."

They came to a stop as Ladybug squatted. Charity had never been so relieved to see the dog do her business—it meant they could turn back.

Jaylynn's shoulders dropped as they pivoted back up the path. "My task just doesn't make sense. Why would Venus throw Jazz in the mix if not to distract Nylah?"

Charity kneaded her temple with her free hand. Her skull felt like it was going to burst open. She couldn't begin to guess what games Venus was playing at.

Jaylynn pressed her lips together in concern. "Charity, are you even going to be able to drive to the cabin tomorrow? You can barely keep your eyes open."

Nessie grimaced as if she'd already considered this. "I can drive as a backup if she can't. You'll already have a full car."

"You remember how to get to the cabin?"

Charity flinched as a shadow passed overhead, launching toward the flaming sky and swirling water. She knew it wasn't real, but there had to be a reason Apollo was showing her this. Was this the future if they failed and the veil continued to fall? Were the visions set in stone or just a potential outcome? Then a worse question arose: Would Apollo's curse continue to haunt Charity once the tasks were over? Or would they go away once compasses returned? A cool hand squeezed Charity's, and she glanced up to Nessie's worried eyes.

Nessie's face, bloodied and covered in dirt, clutching a twisted staff—

The vision doubled in a veil over the current moment.

"What if we're fated to fail?" Charity whispered.

Jaylynn shook her head. "I don't believe that. Look at Ladybug—she's smitten with you. Nessie's snared Sebastian. Nylah's going to do what Nylah does. We are so close to setting things right."

Charity couldn't tell if it was intuition or blind optimism that made Jaylynn so confident, but Charity had the oracle's gift. Whether they succeeded or failed, something bad was coming.

SUPERMOON DEADLINE

Who better balances light and dark than the Underworld's queen?

The radiant youth who strides between death and evergreen;

Her gentle nature brings comfort to dead souls who grieve.

Pluto's wife, darling Proserpina, mortal's winter reprieve.

For six months belowground she rules with gothic power,

Until the spring day breaks, when she's beaconed above to flower.

—The Reaper's Queen

CHAPTER LIX

"**What if we** were wrong and needed to do something more? Do you think Venus will count this as a task completed if we bring both of them? What if we're walking into a trap?" Jaylynn picked at the hem of her shirt while they waited for the boys to use the restroom in the gas station.

"It's too late, and it doesn't matter," Nylah replied, holding their hand up to block the afternoon sun. "All we can do now is show up and hope Venus is in a good mood after all the drama she's caused."

Jaylynn rubbed her eyes. She'd been up all night consoling Charity, whose visions were getting darker by the hour. If Apollo was prophesizing doom, was it even worth showing up to the cabin? Maybe the god of the sun would spare them?

Damien and Jazz came out of the convenience store at the same time.

"Stop second-guessing. Trust Psyche," Nylah said in their last moment alone.

"You know, you should invest in a taller vehicle," Jazz quipped from the back as he crawled into Nylah's yellow Volkswagen Beetle.

Nylah snorted. "You're welcome to buy me a new car anytime."

Jaylynn took a measured breath in through her nose, then out through her mouth.

Just another day of surrendering to the chaos that is my life.

The drive from downtown Toronto to the cabin stretched close to two hours. Jaylynn did her best to bait her companions into talking, but the oppressive weight of the upcoming evening quieted them all. When they finally parked on the familiar gravel driveway, Jaylynn could have sung with relief to escape the tense energy in the car.

"Blake? Hunter?" Jaylynn called out, slinging her backpack over her shoulder.

There was no answer.

Jaylynn spread her arms out, showing off the property. "Well, welcome to my beautiful home away from home."

Nylah took in the rustic house and surrounding trees with an appreciative nod. The boys followed suit, Damien being the last one out of the car. Jaylynn breathed in the fresh summer air and marched up the cabin steps. She gave the door a quick rap and opened it without waiting for an answer, surprised by how light it seemed. For some reason she remembered the door being heavier and creakier.

The sound of running water from the bathroom filled the cabin. Jaylynn peeked into the back bedroom, but no one was there. She shrugged, assuming Hunter was out gathering wood or something while Blake showered.

Jaylynn wove to her mentor's side, noting the new coffee table and tidiness of the space. The window was open, and a summer breeze ruffled the soft white curtains. In the sunlight, Psyche took Jaylynn's breath away. The woman had aged decades in a matter of days. Her entire head was covered in long white hair, and age spots painted her cheeks and chest. She'd lost weight, her usually toned muscles hanging slack. Deep curves settled into the hollows of her eyes and cheekbones.

"So, this is the famous Psyche." Nylah hovered at Jaylynn's elbow. "I honestly thought she'd be prettier. I don't see what Venus was so vexed about."

Jaylynn choked. She wasn't sure if the goddess was listening, but she didn't want to beckon Venus sooner than sunset. Damien passed a wary eye over Psyche before sitting with Jazz on the couch. Hearing a clatter and a muffled giggle from the bathroom, Jaylynn stilled.

Did Blake just… laugh?

Steam curled into the room as the bathroom door opened. Hunter and Blake both stepped out in towels, their faces flushed. They froze when they realized they had company.

"Blake," Jaylynn said on an inhale as she took in the pair's bright faces. Jaylynn couldn't help but grin. Blake had done it. The girl had actually completed her task. Whatever happiness flushed Blake's face disappeared. Blake's smile fell as she clasped her towel tight to her chest, her stare landing on the seated pair of boys. She raced to Psyche's bedroom.

Jaylynn tried to suppress a giggle as she nodded at Hunter.

"Hey, Hunter."

He nodded politely. His curls dripped water down his bare chest and his cheeks glowed bright red as he followed Blake into the bedroom. The door slammed shut.

Nylah gave Jaylynn a look that said they were equally entertained and impressed. Only a couple minutes passed before Blake came back out. She wore Psyche's shorts paired with a simple tank top. Her tattoos stood stark along her thin arms, but Blake definitely looked healthier. Whether she'd gotten some sun or was just eating better, there was a color to her cheeks that hadn't been there before.

Before Jaylynn could get around to introductions, Blake's stare settled on her. Then Blake stomped across the room.

Jaylynn took a step back as Blake came right up to her, lifting a hand to her face. Jaylynn flinched, half expecting a sharp slap to follow. Instead, Blake cupped Jaylynn's cheek and turned her chin.

"What happened? Did someone do this to you?"

Jaylynn had almost forgotten about her black eye. While the injury was tender and far from a pretty sight, she'd been too worried about her task and Charity to give it much thought. Blake turned suspicious eyes on Jaylynn's companions.

"It's nothing, Blake." Jaylynn gently pushed Blake's hand away, her cheeks reddening at the attention. She could only imagine her face looked awful if Blake was being this reactive about it. "I got hit by a protestor's sign. I'm fine, really."

Blake gave the cut under Jaylynn's eye one last unconvinced look.

"And who are these people?"

Jaylynn fought the urge to roll her eyes. Of course Blake was the opposite of welcoming to strangers she knew very well were coming. They rolled through introductions quickly. Blake refused to shake the boys' hands, giving them each a curt nod. Nylah gushed over Blake's tattoos, and Jaylynn smirked at the undeniable delight it brought Blake. Hunter shook each person's hand before excusing himself to start a fire outside.

As she followed Hunter out, Jaylynn took one last glance at Psyche, conscious that in a matter of hours the woman might wake up or never rise again. She blew out a breath. Blake stood in the doorway, jumping on one foot as she slid on a pair of boots. A small smile crept up the corner of Jaylynn's mouth.

"You know, of all the things I pictured coming back to, I never imagined you rocking my sunflower rubber boots."

Blake froze as Jaylynn's mouth twitched. Clearly Blake had thought they were Psyche's.

"It's fine," Jaylynn offered, sliding back into her shoes. "You can keep wearing them. You need them more than I do," Jaylynn said as a small peace offering. The last thing they needed was an even angrier Blake before the rest of the company, mortal and divine, showed up. Blake stomped away from the cabin in Jaylynn's boots to Hunter's side, and Jaylynn grinned.

CHAPTER LX

"Come on, Ness! We have to go." The afternoon felt too bright, and Ladybug's barking was driving an ice pick into Charity's brain.

"Just a minute!"

Please don't let this be another day of Venus messing with Nessie's wardrobe...

Charity picked up the bag of dog toys and extra clothes she'd packed and opened the front door. She was just pushing Ladybug back into the house with her foot when she saw it: Kade's car. The familiar sedan was coming around the corner, and Charity immediately ducked back inside and slammed the door closed. The bag fell to the floor as she drove the dead bolt into place.

Nessie came down the steps, her hair pulled up into a tight pony. She glanced at the door and her face softened.

"Mom, what is it? What did you see?"

Charity couldn't answer. Her mind raced. What could she say if Kade demanded the dog back? She couldn't give Ladybug over. Not now, not today. His text messages had been getting progressively more aggressive, and the last thing Charity wanted was to face his rage when she felt like her mind was splintering in two.

"Are you having visions again?"

Charity shook her head. "Kade is here," she rasped.

Nessie cursed. "Should we hide?"

Then, as Charity had expected, the doorbell rang. They both winced as Ladybug abandoned her bag inspection and barked in reply.

No, no, no… Charity gently shushed the puppy. Kade banged on the door repeatedly, and Ladybug barked louder. Charity raced to the fridge and pulled out the bag of shredded cheese. Ladybug's ears perked up, and she trotted over.

"CHARITY! Open up. Now!" The anger in Kade's voice carried through the door.

Nessie lifted her palms in an unspoken question: *What are you going to do?*

Charity scoured her fleeting thoughts, trying to listen to her own inner voice. *Steal a love.* Venus wanted to create drama when she gave Charity this task. If that was what the goddess wanted, Charity had to deliver, because they were only one day away from putting Luke's soul to rest, and Charity had never wanted something so badly.

Charity clasped Ladybug's leash to her collar and gave the puppy a small chunk of cheese before stuffing the bag into her hoodie pocket.

"You're packed?" she asked Nessie.

Nessie's nod was broken as the doorbell rang again and again.

"Grab what you need and follow me out. Go straight to the car. Say nothing."

Charity draped her jacket over one arm and picked up her bag. "Ladybug! Who's a good girl? Do you want more cheese?" She pulled a couple more strands of cheese out, and Ladybug came and sat at her feet.

"Yes," Charity affirmed, giving the puppy her reward.

In Charity's peripheral vision, the plants on the counter started to melt into pools of green tar. She pressed her eyes shut as the doorbell echoed again and Kade's fist slammed against the front door.

"You're okay," Nessie said. "Everything is going to be okay. Mom, you can do this."

Charity imagined herself as Venus portrayed her: a no-nonsense military woman. Someone who was brave and walked with square shoulders. Then she opened the door.

Kade stumbled forward, his cheeks beet red. "Charity."

"Kade. I'm so sorry, you're catching us at a bad time." Charity pushed forward using her bag as a shield and holding Ladybug in a heel with more cheese pinched between her fingers. "We are already late to pick up our friends. Can this wait until tomorrow?"

Nessie followed tightly behind, quickly locking the front door. Then she squeezed by, backpack on her shoulders and car keys in hand. Kade's head swiveled between them in angry confusion.

"I'm here to take Ladybug back." Kade reached for the leash, but Charity quickly sidestepped him. She held her shoulders back as he blocked the porch stairs.

"Kade, stop. Jupiter Almighty, look at yourself. When's the last time you slept? Or even ate? You look ready to be taken by Pluto." Kade did look like death, and Charity felt horrible pointing it out.

"Maybe if you answered my damn calls."

Charity stepped back to brace herself as he came closer, careful to avoid Ladybug, who was staring adamantly at her fingers. Charity dropped another pinch of cheese.

"Kade, you've sounded like a raving lunatic in all your texts and voicemails. Forgive me for waiting for you to cool down before trying to have a civil conversation."

His eyes bulged as he threw his hands up in the air. "Are you kidding me? You left my daughter unsupervised and have been dodging my calls for three days!"

Charity's eyebrows pitched up. "I dropped Lacey off at the hospital to be with you and Renee! You can't fault me for that. Maybe instead of trying so desperately to pin the blame on me, you should be having words with your daughter."

The sound of the car starting was her cue. Charity quickly sidestepped Kade, pressing against the banister to squeeze down the stairs.

"I'm sorry, Kade, but I don't have time for this. Ladybug, come." She held out a big wad of cheese, and the puppy bounded behind her as she trotted briskly down the concrete path. Charity kept her attention on Ladybug, not the threat of violence in Kade's flabbergasted stare or the giant shadow lurking on the roof of the house.

It's not real. It's not real. It's not real.

"Charity, stop!" Kade yelled, his fists curling. "Give me my dog back."

Charity opened the back door and set her bag on the floor. She grabbed more cheese out of her pocket and turned to face Kade as he stormed down the front steps.

"Ladybug!" Kade's voice hardened. "Come."

The puppy looked toward Kade.

"Ladybug," Charity said, cool and controlled. "Sit."

If there was anything Charity had learned about Ladybug, it was that Sit was her favorite command. Charity rewarded the puppy instantly. Charity gave Kade her best version of a dispassionate once-over.

"I have somewhere to be, Kade, and it's clear you're in no shape to look after a dog. Ladybug is healthy and happy. When you get control of yourself, then we can talk."

It was ridiculous that she was suggesting Kade was losing his mind when a massive lurching shadow was creeping over the roof behind him.

Charity scooped Ladybug up and quickly thrust her into her open crate in the back seat. She closed the grate and the car door before turning back to Kade. When she did, he looked absolutely shattered.

"You can't—"

"I just did, and will continue to," Charity cut in, feeling terrible. A few days ago, she'd promised to help him and lighten his stress. Now here she was intentionally pushing him even further. "Go get some rest, Kade."

CHAPTER LXI

"Sebastian. Can we have a word with you before you go?"

The heaviness in Huan's tone pierced Sebastian's chest like a knife. He knew it was bad news. Why did today feel so strange? Maybe it was the full moon, or maybe it was because he was going to be hanging out with Nessie on his own again, which, if he was being fully honest, he felt a little nervous about. Sebastian liked Nessie—that wasn't the problem. He just wasn't sure what she wanted from him.

Gareth was going to be busy all evening at a full moon ceremony with the Hart family. Sebastian hadn't had a chance to talk to Gareth since he'd kissed Nessie, and he needed to catch up with his best friend more than ever, but all of Gareth's texts had seemed short and distant recently. Sebastian tried to ignore the feeling that something was off about this day and focused instead on the person right in front of him.

"Of course." Sebastian sat at the table, giving him a clear view outside in case Nessie arrived. She'd texted earlier to warn they were running late, but her last message reassured him she would arrive soon.

"We've made a decision," Philip said, his eyes trained on Sebastian's as if ready to gauge his reaction.

All at once, Sebastian knew what this was about. They were going to send him home. Philip was going to be drafted again, and Liam was flying back. They'd changed their minds and couldn't house Sebastian when their family was going through such a tough time.

"Okay." Sebastian swallowed hard, trying to guess how many days he had left. Would his last night in Canada be spent with Nessie? If they were going to send him home first thing tomorrow, he would have to cancel his plans with her. He'd choose to spend his last hours here with the Suns in a heartbeat. And what about Gareth? Would he go back home at the same time?

"Liam and Dakota were able to get flights home this evening. So, we need to chat about the best options for our family."

Sebastian forced down the storm of emotion building like a hurricane in his chest: the fear of going home, back toward the war; the sadness of leaving the Sun family; the hurt that Philip had suggested he might be allowed to stay the month and was now taking it back.

Philip gave Huan's hand a reassuring squeeze.

Is sending me away as hard on them as it is for me?

Sebastian resolved he wasn't going to get mad. He wouldn't even cry. He was going to be strong and not make this family feel guilty for sending him away when their lives were being turned upside down.

"You know we've absolutely loved having you stay with us," Philip added. His tall, willowy frame seemed extra frail since the call from medical chief came yesterday. Sebastian couldn't fathom how the army could classify this man as fit to go to war. After numerous calls back and forth, the decision was final. Huan got out of reenlisting because of his prosthetic foot, but Philip had little in terms of physical ailments to hold him back. Philip Sun was destined to return to the war where he'd first met Huan.

Despite his best intentions, Sebastian's hands trembled. He wasn't sure what he was more afraid of—going home himself, or Philip going overseas. Huan squared his shoulders, taking on the burden of delivering Sebastian's sentence.

"We wanted to ask if you'll stay anyway."

What? Sebastian glanced between them, confused. Huan's and Philip's hopeful eyes bored across the table in military-grade attention.

"At least until the month's end when your original flight was scheduled to leave," Philip added. "Liam has already agreed. He thinks it's a great idea."

"You will be safe here, and your parents—" Huan cut off as if trying to figure out what to say.

They won't care. No one was going to voice the unspoken truth, though.

"You would be safe here," Huan rectified. "I'm sure they would be grateful if we kept you just a little longer."

"If you want to stay, that is," Philip added.

Sebastian's mind whirled at the revelation. He and Liam would properly meet and live together for the summer, their rooms across the hall from one another. He wouldn't be shipped back to his parents and sister, or the worsening war. But Philip… Philip would be leaving soon. And he wasn't the only person Sebastian had to worry about.

"What about Gareth?"

At this, the Sun men shared an uneasy glance.

Huan grimaced as he leaned back. "His flight home is already booked."

"Seb, we can't make this decision for you. If you want to go home and be with your family before things get worse—"

"No." Sebastian spread his palms on the table as he interrupted Philip. He knew he wanted to stay, even though the news that Gareth was leaving surprised him. Why wouldn't Gareth have texted? Did he assume Sebastian was flying out at the same time?

"You'll stay? At least, for now?" Philip's fingers wrapped around Huan's biceps like a vise.

"I would be grateful if you let me," Sebastian answered.

The men surged up at once, crossing the room. Sebastian stood, letting them crush him in a hug. The surge of emotions he'd been trying so hard to curve surfaced, but instead of hurt or fear or anger, it was gratitude that pricked his eyes.

They wanted him to stay, even as their lives were equally falling apart. The high-pitched horn of a car broke up their moment, and they all turned to see Charity and Nessie waving from their car.

"I—I guess I have to go. Do you want me to stay so I can come pick up Liam with you?"

Huan ruffled Sebastian's hair. "Nonsense. Go enjoy your night out. We won't be leaving to pick him up until the morning anyway. Say hi to Nessie for us, and text when you're on the way home."

Home. At least until the end of the month.

Sebastian slid into the back seat of the car and broke into an unexpected smile as a small red puppy bounded against the door of her crate. The dog's excited yapping suggested she was delighted to have company.

"Hey, pup." Sebastian threaded his fingers between the grate, letting the dog lick him. Then she started to chew his hand, so he pulled away.

"That's Lacey's dog, Ladybug. I hope you don't mind—we're dog sitting," Nessie said, tossing her ponytail over her shoulder as she spoke. The puppy barked at hearing her name, and Sebastian smiled, his mood lightening.

Then Sebastian realized he hadn't thought about Lacey once since his and Nessie's day at the university. All his thoughts had been consumed by worry about the war, the Suns, and going home.

"Is Lacey's mum doing okay?"

"Oh, yeah!" Nessie exclaimed. "She's actually back home from the hospital now. That's why we're watching Ladybug."

He pulled on his seat belt, then paused as he did a double take between Nessie and her mom.

"You drive?" he asked.

Nessie shrugged with a grin that sharpened her dimples. "I like to practice whenever we go out of the city." Today she wore a tight-fitted top with a simple white-and-blue flower pattern. Her jean jacket lay discarded in the back seat to his side.

"Cool." Sebastian pulled out his phone. "I just need to text Gareth quick, if that's okay."

"We've got a good drive ahead to the cabin, so it's no rush," Nessie answered.

He leaned back, his thumbs hovering over the buttons. Sebastian wasn't sure where to start. Was it wrong to open with the news that the Suns invited him to stay?

Sebastian let out a huff of breath, staring at his phone. How could a single text be so hard to send? He wished they were bringing Gareth to the cabin too. This would be so much easier face-to-face.

"You okay?"

Sebastian glanced up and caught Nessie's worried eyes in the rearview mirror.

"Great, actually." Sebastian dropped his phone back into his lap. "Huan and Philip are flying Liam home tonight, and they asked me to stay for the month."

That was so easy. Why can't I say the same thing in a single text?

Nessie smiled, turning her attention back to the road. "That's great news. So, why do you look miserable?"

Sebastian let his smile fall. "I'm afraid to tell Gareth. His flight home is already booked."

Nessie swallowed. "Oh… I didn't know. When?"

Sebastian shrugged. "I don't know. He never told me. I found out through the Suns."

There was a heavy silence as they mutually grieved Gareth's imminent departure.

Charity raised a shaky hand, speaking for the first time since Sebastian had gotten in the car. "Ness!"

"It's okay, Mom." Nessie grabbed Charity's hand, returning it back to her side. "I've got this."

Sebastian strained to see what had panicked Charity, but nothing stood out.

"Why don't you send a general text to get a feel of what he knows?" Nessie leaned forward, her eyes on the road. "Say something like… 'Hey, mate, apparently Liam's coming home early.'"

Sebastian laughed at her exaggerated British impersonation. "Is that what I sound like?"

Nessie grinned. "Listen, I never said I was great at accents. I'm just great at problem-solving." Her eyes sparkled, and Sebastian couldn't help but smile back.

"I guess it'll do."

Without giving himself time to think twice, he sent off Nessie's vague suggestion of a text.

"So, where exactly are we heading off to tonight?"

Charity leaned forward, massaging her temples as if she was fending off a headache. Nessie glanced at her mom, clearly worried.

"A friend of ours has a beautiful cabin just a bit out of town." Nessie pulled a pair of sunglasses out of a compartment. "Here, Mom. Maybe these will help."

"Will there be a lot of people there?" Sebastian asked. He wasn't sure what he'd signed up for when he agreed to this. All he knew was it seemed important to Nessie, so he'd said sure.

"Yeah, probably a few. You'll meet Jaylynn and Nylah. They'll be the redheaded siblings. Nylah goes by nonbinary pronouns, by the way. They're both really, really nice. I think they're bringing a couple of guys."

Nessie leaned forward as they came to a turn, glancing both ways for cars before proceeding.

"Then there's Blake and Hunter. Blake's really cool and acts meaner than she actually is. Hunter is her beau of sorts. I think we're going to have a hot dog roast and play some games by the fire. It should be really chill." Something about Nessie's tone had changed, but Sebastian wasn't sure why.

"Will Lacey be coming too?"

"No."

Before he could ask why, his phone dinged. Sebastian drew in a sharp breath.

GARETH: Yeah, Dakota's coming home too. I also have my flight booked now. I leave tomorrow morning.

Sebastian sank in his seat. Was he making a mistake by staying? If he wasn't already in this car, he would have canceled his plans to spend tonight with his best friend.

"Was that Gareth? What'd he say?"

Sebastian glanced back up to Nessie. "Just that he leaves tomorrow morning."

"Oh." The sadness in Nessie's face was crystal clear. "That's so soon."

Sebastian nodded.

Nessie hummed as she took another turn, merging smoothly with highway traffic. "Ask him what time he leaves. Maybe we can surprise him by meeting him at the airport for a big send-off. He is not getting away without saying a proper goodbye."

Sebastian leaned back in his seat, his thumbs hovering over the keys.

This was never how our trip was supposed to go.

CHAPTER LXII

Gareth's stomach turned despite the drool-worthy scents coasting on the warm evening breeze. Smoked jalapeños, buttered potatoes, rich beef stew, and wild rice filled the outdoor Pow Wow grounds. The potluck dishes were tucked under pavilions in case it rained, but based on the clear full moon rising opposite to the setting sun, rain seemed highly unlikely.

Along with the rich aromas, the air was abundant with chatter, jingling dresses, and upbeat drumming from the Hart family's local tribe. Dozens of people had gathered, each taking time to pay their respects to Winona. Gareth stood with Mikom a couple feet back, quiet sentries as they witnessed the wholesome feast.

Winona's face was solemn as she shook hands. Her ornate ceremony dress was an array of brightly woven yellows and blues. Tokala had shucked her hoodies and baggy pants for the evening, adorned in similar garments in dark patterns of violet and cranberry reds. But while both Harts were lovely, Dyani stole the show.

"She's spent so long working on those moccasins and sewing sequins into her shawl," Mikom murmured, his proud eyes on his daughter.

"They turned out beautiful," Gareth agreed.

Dyani's regalia was by far the brightest of the three, vibrant in fuchsia and magenta fabrics. Her dark braids were tucked under a glittering headband featuring plumes of white feathers. Her shawl, which Gareth now recognized as the project she'd been fretting over since he'd arrived, was draped over her shoulders, the bottom half of carefully sewn ribbons hanging like rainbow tassels to her calves. But it was her smile that took Gareth's breath away. Her eyes sparkled the whole drive over as she spoke of dancing tonight.

Now, watching the three Hart women surrounded by their community being crushed in hugs with tearful smiles on their faces, a deep pang twisted in Gareth's gut. He missed home so much it hurt.

"You doing okay, son?" Mikom frowned, and Gareth realized he'd let his careful mask fall.

Gareth tried to smile but found it harder than expected. "Yeah. This is brilliant."

Dyani and Tokala skipped up arm in arm, their plates stacked with food.

"Gareth!" Tokala called out. "You should try the tacos if you haven't already. They're made with Bannock and they're to die for."

Dyani grinned. "Oh, and the frybread! If there's one thing you have to eat, it's the frybread."

Gareth nodded, though he knew he couldn't stomach much more than the few bites he'd already had. Whether it was nerves or stress, the uneasiness in his gut turned anew. Why was it that as soon as he was leaving, everyone finally started talking to him? He tried once more to pull on a more cheerful smile as an elder across the bonfire called Tokala and Dyani over.

"I'm sorry your time here wasn't what you'd hoped for," Mikom said, his voice low.

"No, you were all great. Thank you for everything. And thank you for bringing me tonight. It's a cool send-off."

Mikom nodded, but a sadness cast over his features as he watched his wife. In the stretched silence, Gareth thought of Sebastian's last text.

SEBASTIAN: Huan and Philip offered to let me stay.

Was that what was making this extra hard? That Gareth would be going back home without Sebastian? He figured if

Sebastian chose to stay, that was his choice. Gareth knew the Suns would be good to Sebastian, but Gareth was going home—for better or for worse. Idly, he wondered if Sebastian and Nessie were enjoying their night out, and a pang of jealousy hit him square in the chest.

At least when I go, Seb will still have Nessie. And who knows, maybe they'll end up dating after all.

He pictured two years from now Nessie and Sebastian standing in Juno's Temple of marriage, swearing lifelong vows as if compasses never existed. He could see the rose petals showering their heads, then the two of them hugging Gareth in celebration of their found love. All as if Gareth and Nessie hadn't shared a midnight kiss—one he wasn't sure he'd ever forget.

CHAPTER LXIII

Time was ticking, or rather, trickling by slower than ever. It was as if the last grains of stardust swirled leisurely now, with no haste to join the rest of the sand in the hourglass's bottom. Nylah nibbled at their hot dog bun. They were both too hungover and too sober for this.

The campfire meal was tense. Jazz stayed by Nylah's side, his arm always touching theirs. Damien sat across from them, his foot tapping rhythmically as he stared into the flames. Maybe he was starting to figure out that this wasn't organized by Fates' Followers, or maybe he just felt like an outsider. Either way,

Nylah didn't know what to say. The three of them had made it, and their trial would soon be complete.

Ten feet away, Blake picked up a long branch and settled herself against a tree trunk. She pulled a knife out of her pocket and went to work carving the blunt end to a tip with long, graceful strokes.

Within the first five minutes of arriving at the cabin, Nylah had made a few definitive observations about Blake. One, the girl had a defiant side that Nylah instantly loved. Two, despite her divine pairing with Hunter, Blake was most definitely crushing on Jaylynn. Three, Jaylynn—as expected—was entirely clueless.

Nylah couldn't explain how they knew. It was something about the way Blake watched Jaylynn. There was a protective gleam in her eye coupled with a wariness. All Nylah knew was it didn't bode well for the girl's task. Even when she was at Hunter's side, Blake was always tracking Jaylynn.

Nylah had kept the realization to themself but couldn't help but worry. Did this mean she'd failed her task with Hunter? Jaylynn seemed happy, as if everything was going as planned, but Nylah wasn't convinced. If they, as a complete outsider, were picking up on Blake's mixed emotions, how could a goddess miss it?

The last car of guests arrived and Nylah stood, curious to see who else Venus had summoned through her trials. Two teenagers got out first, hauling a crate with them. The girl— Nylah assumed her to be Nessie—opened the crate, and a little red puppy bolted out. Based on Jaylynn's debriefing, the boy must have been her mark. He raced to pick the puppy up, turning back to Nessie with a huge smile on his face as he captured the struggling tuft of red.

Well, at least her task looks like it's going okay.

From the passenger seat, the last woman got out of the car. Jaylynn skipped to greet her, and they sank into a deep hug.

"Did you guys get lost? I thought you'd be here forever ago!"

Nylah ticked off the last name in her head. This had to be Charity.

Blake put her stick-spear down and strolled up to Nessie. They bumped fists, then Nessie introduced her friend.

"This is Seb." Nessie tossed her long blond ponytail over her shoulder. Sebastian tilted his head to say hi to Blake, then turned to Nylah. Before they could say hello, the boy's eyes focused on something behind them.

"Damien?"

"What are you guys doing here?" Damien stood up. He shoved his hands in his pockets as Nessie and Sebastian both froze, clearly surprised. Nylah glanced between them, remembering now that Damien had mentioned knowing Nessie. Apparently he knew Sebastian too.

Nessie's face drained of all color as she looked between the group members, as if trying to figure out whose task Damien was.

"Same thing as you, I'm guessing?" Sebastian filled in.

Nylah clasped Damien's shoulder. It felt weird to touch him, to feel their hourglass spin back to point to Jazz, but they smiled. "Damien and Jazz are friends of mine."

Jazz nodded as he joined them, resting a hand on the small of Nylah's back. The minute he did, Venus' magic settled. Nylah took a steadying breath. There were too many lies being woven tonight to keep straight, and they'd just dodged a bullet. Jaylynn had laid it all out this morning.

Damien was only here because he thought he was chosen by the Fates. Hunter thought his job was to fall in love with Blake when it was actually the reverse. And poor Sebastian was the only person here who didn't know that a goddess would be crashing their party at any moment. One glance at the burnt-orange sky told Nylah they were out of time.

The group loosely gathered around the fire as greetings were exchanged, and Nylah glanced down at their hourglass tattoo. The last piece of starlight fell from the funnel, landing on the peak of the sand below it. It winked, and Nylah's eyes shot up to the sky, where the supermoon already hung in all her glory.

"It's time," Nylah whispered.

CHAPTER LXIV

Emotional resilience Blake could manage any day, but the minute Hunter's entire weight collapsed in Blake's arms, she knew she was physically outmatched. The bulk of his height and muscle crashed down on her as Hunter's eyes rolled back into his head.

"Hunter?!" The cry came out high-pitched as Blake scrambled to hold his dead weight, but she was no match. Her ankle gave out, and as she fell, Hunter's limp body followed. Others echoed her cry of alarm, but Blake couldn't see anything.

"For the love of Cupid—" Blake grunted as she pushed against the soft muscles of Hunter's shoulders. He remained unresponsive. Her lungs shuddered in desperate and shallow breaths as she realized she was completely pinned. Grinding her teeth, Blake shoved harder, her bent ankle aching in protest. Then Hunter's weight eased ever so slightly. Blake scrambled, clawing the ground for purchase. With a final wrench, Blake pried her leg free, gasping as Hunter's body slumped back down.

Charity stood above her, hand outstretched. Blake took it, her heart in her throat as she gasped for air.

"Thanks."

The woman nodded, her attention already moving on to the next crisis. Blake followed Charity's gaze. Nessie knelt beside Sebastian's unconscious body, delicately cradling his head, her face tight. Damien and Ladybug both sprawled on the grass completely knocked out. Nylah had collapsed beside the long horizontal log next to the fire, but Jazz had fallen forward and Jaylynn scrambled to pull his body back and away from the crackling blaze. Blake took one last glance at Hunter before launching over to help Jaylynn.

They pushed Jazz into a seated position together, resting his back against the log. His head lolled worryingly to the side. Jaylynn turned to check on Nylah, but Blake grabbed her by the arm. The eerie sound of someone *tsk*ing made her blood run cold. Every instinct in Blake's core screamed at her to run. No birds chirped and no frogs croaked. Even the soft crackling of the fire sounded subdued. Slowly, Jaylynn and Blake turned in tandem.

Venus strolled across the yard. As the goddess had before, she wore Blake's body—her hair thick and healthy, her body muscular and toned. In her arms, Psyche's limp form drooped like a wilted flower. The edges of Psyche's dress dragged across the dirt, and a small whimper escaped Jaylynn's throat. Blake held her shoulder, willing her to be still.

Based on Blake's best guess, Jaylynn was probably seeing herself in her wedding dress again. Jaylynn's expression was haunted, her freckles washed away in the shock of seeing Psyche's head tipped back, throat exposed to the sky.

By Hunter's side, Charity dropped to a knee, her lips moving in a rapid, incomprehensible manner. Opposite to her mother, Nessie's eyes were not wide in shock or fear. They radiated fury. The girl planted herself between Venus and Sebastian. Seeing her rage grounded Blake.

It's time to end this.

Venus' strides were slow and intentional, and she carried Psyche with minimal effort. She looked like a pallbearer walking a casket to the hearse. Blake clenched her free fist, grateful for the tiny bite of her healing hands to keep her present. The goddess stopped beside Nylah's body, nudging their head so it tilted upward. Cracks splintered Nylah's glasses and dirt smeared the left side of their cheek. Under Blake's hand, Jaylynn stiffened.

"I really thought some of you might succeed, but this?" Venus chuckled, her musical voice clawing the insides of Blake's ears. "This is humiliating. No, this will not do."

"We did as you asked. All our tasked people are here," Blake spat. "It's time you hold up your end of the bargain."

Venus pinned Blake with her golden eyes. "*You* do not demand things of *me*."

The goddess's graceful demeanor hardened, and she dropped Psyche. Jaylynn cried out, jumping forward to catch her. Psyche's long hair had hardly grazed the ground before her body stilled in midair. It was as if a string connected Psyche's chest to the darkening sky. Her body rose throat-first, her head still hanging limp and wrists slack at her sides. Blake stumbled back as she saw the other unconscious bodies rise into the air. Nessie grasped Sebastian's arm as he levitated up, only letting go when his body crossed over the campfire, drawn to Venus' side. Even little Ladybug's limp body floated toward her.

Nessie glared at the grinning goddess, cautiously moving to her mother's side. Charity remained on her knees, her hands clasped in prayer at her chest.

Is she seriously praying right now?

Blake wasn't convinced there was anyone left worth praying to. All gods did was mess with your life. This had proven that. Jaylynn's hand reached out to Nylah, but Blake pulled her away from Venus so the four of them stood together. Open grass spanned the distance between the two lineups, like teams facing off.

Venus walked in front of the levitating bodies like a war commander might before sending the front line of an army to battle. "We made an agreement, and you failed." She stopped in front of Psyche, whose levitating body was centered in the row. Venus slowly lowered her. Psyche's bare feet had just grazed the grass when Venus' hand reached out to grasp the woman by the chin.

"It is delightful to see the gift of time finally ravaging you, Psyche. What would Cupid say now if he could see you? Wasting away in this decrepit body." Venus let out a huff of a laugh.

Blake itched to step forward and tear away the goddess's fingers tracing Psyche's cheek.

"Venus." Jaylynn's voice hardened. "We completed your tasks to the best of our ability. Please." Her voice broke slightly. "Let Psyche go. Give compasses back to the world. Let things return to how they were."

"You gave us impossible timelines." The sharp tone of Nessie's accusation caught Blake off guard, but she was glad for it.

Anger is better than fear.

Venus scoffed. "I told you to prove how fickle and easily manipulated love can be. It's not my fault you couldn't do it within the deadline." She turned and Psyche's floating body followed her like a lifeless shadow. Venus turned her judgment on Charity. The murmuring woman shrank even smaller under the goddess's attention.

"I will say, I was impressed with you. Watching you crush Kade's heart like that—I didn't know you had such a cruel streak, Charity. You must be so pleased to have succeeded in your task."

Pain streaked across Charity's features. Blake didn't care if Charity felt guilty, though. She just wanted this to be over. Whatever she'd had to do was worth it if it meant they'd be free.

Venus leveled her hard golden eyes at Nessie next. "Yet, you, darling… While you certainly kept me entertained, why is it Sebastian still hopes he'll find his soulmate?" The goddess *tsk*ed. "I guess you just weren't lovable enough."

Nessie parted her lips, torn between shock and arguing. Before she could say anything, Blake bristled as Venus turned to face her head-on. The goddess stepped forward, her thin lips in a haunting grin. Blake had never realized just how punchable her own face could look.

"Blake." A stick snapped as Venus stepped closer, and Blake bared her teeth, every nerve in her body aching to lash out. "You were the only one who had complete control over the outcome, and yet, you somehow fell in love with the wrong person."

No. Blake wanted to object, to scream that Venus was wrong, but there was no air in her lungs. Her heart hammered in her chest as everyone's stares turned to her. Blake didn't dare look at Jaylynn. Instead, she scrambled for a lie to explain Venus' taunt. That the goddess was wrong, or maybe she meant Blake loved Psyche. Blake's compass had led her to River in the first place. But as Blake tried to gather her wits, the open question in Nessie's and Charity's eyes flooded Blake with a new fear.

If Venus knew the truth of Blake's heart, what extent would the goddess go to in order to break it?

Blake knew it was a mistake—Jaylynn would never feel the same way—but she instinctively shifted her stance as the goddess turned her hateful glare on the redhead who'd captured Blake's heart. She wasn't about to let the bright and honest girl suffer this psychotic goddess's games alone. Venus' eyebrow pitched up in an entertained arch before she continued.

"Then we have the biggest disgrace of all. At least the others *tried* to do their tasks. You did nothing to prove Damien was Nylah's soulmate. You spent more time managing everyone else's tasks than completing your own."

"Who Nylah loves was never for me to decide," Jaylynn said between clenched teeth.

Venus huffed in contempt. "All in all, this whole trial looks like a failure to me."

"Maybe you just don't know what love really is," Nessie retorted with a cool voice.

Blake's spirits sank.

That was probably not the right thing to say to the goddess of love.

"Excuse me?" Venus choked on a laugh.

"You gave us these tasks to prove love is fickle, but *you* failed. *You* gave unrealistic timelines, and in your haste to make us fail, *you* picked impossible scenarios. If anything, you've proven you're not as gifted at matchmaking as your son is."

Normally, Blake would have praised Nessie for being so bold, but the molten lava in the goddess's eyes made Blake's knees tremble. She ducked as the goddess's temper cracked.

"Insolent!" A violent burst of wind tore free from Venus as she spread her arms. Blake barely had a chance to brace as the tornado hit her head-on, thrusting her down to the grass. Her tailbone throbbed as it struck the hard ground.

"Petulant!" Venus screeched as she spun, her arms twisting as her feet rose off the ground.

"Mortals." The last word came out like a low growl.

Blake used her heels to push back from the goddess's growing wrath. To her dismay, Nessie didn't back down. She'd been knocked back but kept one foot planted in a partial kneel.

"We may be mortal, but at least we know what it is to love and be loved."

Jaylynn met Blake's eyes in a desperate plea. Angry Nessie was no longer helping.

"Ness." Jaylynn pulled at Nessie's shoulder, but the girl shrugged her off. Then Nessie stood, putting herself between the goddess and the rest of them.

"You think you know what love is?" Venus snorted. The wind unnaturally lifted her hair as Venus approached Nessie like a predator ready to strike. Blake stood, putting her hand on Nessie's back to let her know she wasn't alone. A warmth pressed against Blake's back, and she knew without looking that Jaylynn and Charity had risen with her.

"I do. If you had given me a possible task, I could have completed it," Nessie challenged.

At this, Venus smiled.

Oh, stars, no.

The malicious grin on Venus' face terrified Blake. "You know, you remind me of Minerva. All boldness and pride—convinced you can solve any problem if you put your mind to it. Nessie McKenzie, it's time you learned to properly fear the gods." Venus turned, gesturing to the unconscious hovering bodies. "You say you know what love is, so why don't you show me. Pick three sacrifices, Nessie. Pick who will pay with their life for your impudence. Cast three of your tasked matches to the Underworld, or you can say goodbye to your mother, Blake, and Jaylynn as they find their early graves instead."

Blake's knees buckled.

CHAPTER LXV

All the blood in Nessie's body ran cold.

"Three deaths on your conscience would help you remember what happens to those who disrespect the divine. Perhaps the lesson will help you survive when the veil falls once and for all."

Venus' dimples sharpened and her long blond hair cascaded in perfect curls over her shoulders. For the first time since seeing Venus' beautified version of herself, Nessie became acutely aware of how much she didn't like the way she looked. She loathed the graceful twirls of Venus' wrists. She hated who she'd become to try to appease the goddess. Every step Venus took in this form revolted Nessie with the wrongness of the warped reflection.

"That isn't fair." Nessie bit her lip, grateful for the steady weight of Blake's shoulder holding her up. Nessie had wanted another task about love, more time to complete what she'd started, but this? This was more than cruelty. It was insanity and bloodlust.

"You wish to appease me, then we will do it like the days of old. Choose three human sacrifices, Nessie, to pay for your disrespect."

Pick three. Nessie balked. How could she possibly pick three? Even if the cabin crew shared the blame for ending up here, Nessie couldn't imagine living in a world without her mother, let alone Blake or Jaylynn. Nessie's pulse raced as she considered the row of levitating bodies. But how could three innocent deaths be fair? They were blameless. It wasn't their fault that compasses disappeared.

"The choice is yours, Nessie McKenzie. Who will it be?"

I am the stupidest mortal alive.

The horror of the decision was crippling. Did she have it in her to be a killer? What would happen if she refused? Would Venus instantly kill her closest friends? Or would more than three souls end up in the Underworld because of Nessie's cursed existence?

At Venus' side, Psyche's elderly body hung delicately. The woman to blame for all of it. Nessie's eyes watered. Wouldn't it make sense for her to be one of the sacrifices? It would free

Psyche of her curse, which the woman had said she wanted more than anything.

"Not her," Venus said as if she read Nessie's mind. The goddess flicked a finger, and Psyche's body was drawn away from the lineup. "And not the dog either."

Nessie glared at the distorted version of herself as Ladybug and Psyche floated to hover by her sides.

Nessie's heart hammered as her choices went from seven to five. If three had to die, that meant she could save only two. Venus steepled her fingers, drawing them up to her mouth in delight. Nessie glanced down the line. At the end, Hunter's bulky form sagged, his callused palms open to the sky on each side.

Can I take the one person Blake has a chance at love with? Even if Venus thinks she's in love with someone else? Nessie couldn't explain the deep-seated loyalty that made her want to avoid hurting her friend. But then she looked at Nylah's bright curls and broken glasses. Jaylynn was her friend too. Nessie couldn't take away her sibling.

Her eyes flicked to her next choice, and she instantly knew she would save Sebastian, no matter the cost. Nessie's gut twisted as she realized she would have to kill one of the people she'd already mentally saved.

"Tick tock, wise one."

Nessie's frantic eyes landed on Damien next. What would Lacey think if Damien disappeared? If she got her compass back, would she forgive Nessie if Sebastian still lived? The only other choice was Jazz, who Nessie didn't know the first thing about.

Charity had started to murmur prayers again, and it was making Nessie's skin itch. She stepped forward, shaking free of her pack. Nessie had to make this choice without them. If she tried to account for their personal feelings, they'd never leave this clearing. Guilt gnawed at her core as Nessie walked toward the bodies, pausing in front of each of them.

This was a puzzle that had no right answer, which meant she had to figure out what the lesser evil was.

"Nessie, you don't have to do this. This is madness. Venus, please, there has to be another way." Jaylynn's voice cracked.

The smell of roses and mint curled in the air as Venus came to stand at her side, ignoring Jaylynn's pleas.

"Tell me, Nessie, who will you choose to punish in Tartarus for all time?"

"Tartarus? I thought they'd go to the Underworld," Nessie choked out.

Venus smirked. "Tartarus is but another layer of the Underworld, as are the Elysium fields."

Nessie glanced back down the line, desperate for a better answer to appear.

Three deaths and this will be over. We will all be free of Venus' games and can move on.

Knowing what she had to do didn't make it easier, though. Nessie's mistake was looking back at her friends. Her mom's eyes were pressed shut, praying as tears trekked down her face. Jaylynn shook her head, her fingers threaded together, begging for another option. Even Blake looked horrified, her eyes darting between the five bodies.

Nessie turned away, unable to face them. There was no other choice. Dread and terror pounded in her heart, yet another anxiety attack building in her chest. Sweat slicked her brow, and it was as if Venus' fist was crushing Nessie's windpipe. The first name slipped from her lips before she lost her nerve.

"Damien."

The boy who had taunted her endlessly and who Sebastian and Gareth despised. Of everyone in the lineup, he was the easiest choice, though the thought of Lacey's inevitable grief made Nessie's hands tremble.

She'll have Seb. She'll be okay.

As the whispered name slipped from Nessie's mouth, a violent crack split the ground. Nessie stumbled, falling hard on one knee. All the air in Nessie's lungs fled as a fissure widened under the floating bodies. The smell of sulfur poured out as the earth stopped moving. Then a thin line of black smoke curled up. Nessie blanched as it took the shape of massive, gnarled knuckles with black talons. Time slowed as the hand struck, grasping Damien's hanging body, then ripped him down into the hole. In the matter of a heartbeat, he was gone.

Jaylynn screamed. Sheer panic filled Nessie's chest as her breathing grew rapid and ragged.

Tartarus. I just cursed Damien to die in the darkest realm of punishment that exists.

Shame blacker than any storm cloud hit Nessie square in the chest, and new questions surfaced in quick succession. Would Damien die quickly down there? Or would his soul be tortured for all eternity, unable to leave the realm of monsters? Nessie's hands shook as nausea slammed into her. Her knee buckled, and she fell back in the grass and dirt as she heaved.

"Nessie, stop," Jaylynn cried. "It shouldn't be them. You know we're the ones to blame. Please, please—"

A muffled, choking sound made Nessie glance back. Blake's arms were wrapped around Jaylynn's body as she flailed, one hand clamped firmly over her mouth. Jaylynn clawed at Blake's forearms, but when Blake didn't let go, Jaylynn's nails raked the empty air instead, her eyes bulging. Nessie's mom had curled up even closer to the ground, her prayers now coming through as outright sobs. But it was the firm understanding in Blake's eyes that made Nessie refocus on her new task. Damien was gone. Two more names. If she could sacrifice two more people to Tartarus, this would all be over.

Save who you can.

She glanced once more down the line, her heart tugging at each option left. Sebastian would live, so that left Hunter, Nylah, Jazz. Nessie could feel her will crumbling, her mind clouding with fear and grief. Before she could overthink her instinct, she forced the next name out of her mouth.

"Jazz."

The muffled wail that came from Jaylynn was like a spear through Nessie's back. She pressed her eyes shut, but the cool pressure of Venus' wind tipped her chin up. The goddess's unspoken command was clear—Nessie would watch each sentence unfold. There was no stopping Nessie's tears as the ghastly hand returned like a cobra and struck, snatching Jazz's unconscious body into the gaping hole.

"No!" Jaylynn screamed. There was the sound of a scuffle, and Nessie was sure Blake was full on fighting to hold Jaylynn back.

Nessie felt as if the weight of the sky was about to crash down on her as her heart ripped into shreds. She was an awful person. Every choice she'd made in the past week was wrong. She'd helped compasses disappear, she'd manipulated Sebastian, and now she'd just murdered two innocent souls. Nessie wished she could take it all back. She wished she didn't ruin everything she touched.

What did I do to earn this cursed life?

Jaylynn wept as she cried out. "Nessie, please stop! Stop, stop, stop!" The desperation in her voice gave Nessie chills. Her shoulders shook as her own sobs escaped.

I deserve Tartarus for this.

Guilty tears raked over her cheeks. Nessie clawed the neckline of her shirt.

"Please, Venus!" Jaylynn cried. "There has to be something else you want. Isn't there anything else you could ask for?"

But Nessie was almost there—she'd almost freed them. She couldn't let Jaylynn wrap them up into yet another one of Venus' cruel games. Nessie could hardly breathe as she settled on the last sacrifice.

Venus' grin stretched wider as Nessie's eyes cleared.

This is the lesser evil. Nessie's whole body shook with violent tremors as her anxiety attack reached its peak. All she could see was the black void where dirt tumbled behind the two souls Nessie had already traded to Tartarus. Her final sentence came out as a shaky whisper.

"Me. The last one needs to be me."

Venus' grin faltered, but before the goddess could intervene, the black gnarled hand of smoke returned. Nessie hardly had a moment to brace before it struck, clamping her arms down. Nessie screamed as the air whipped out of her lungs. She had no chance to apologize. No last hug from her mother. She'd never know if Lacey and Sebastian would figure out they were meant to be together. She wouldn't get to see Gareth again and apologize for what she'd said. But her chosen family would live.

The last thing Nessie saw was curling black as Tartarus claimed her soul.

CHAPTER LXVI

"Nessie!" Charity screeched. She launched forward, one hand outstretched to the spot her daughter had knelt a second before. A sinister groan echoed in the forest, and the dirt under Charity's bent knees vibrated. Then, just as the fissure had arrived, it snapped shut with a booming crack. Hunter's, Nylah's, Ladybug's, and Sebastian's bodies all dropped from the air.

"No!" Jaylynn sobbed. She thrashed, her elbow catching Blake in the jaw. With her sudden freedom, Jaylynn raced past the jagged scar in the grass. She gathered Nylah in her arms and held her tight.

Nessie is gone. Charity couldn't breathe. The gods had finally done it—they'd taken everything from her. Her husband, her sanity, her daughter.

"Bring them back!" Jaylynn cried out as she cradled her sibling. "Bring them back right now, Venus."

The goddess didn't move. She stood in her military uniform, eyes glowering at the place where Nessie had been. There was no love or remorse in her glare. If anything, the goddess looked livid.

Blake staggered to Hunter's side, her face pale and eyes wide with shock like she didn't know where to go.

Apollo's visions pounded alongside Charity's haunted reality. As they had for the past hour, dead trees burned and the sky bled red. The grass under her feet shifted to black sands. Charity willed herself to ignore the visions. She knew they couldn't be real. But Nessie getting snatched? Every bone in Charity's body knew that was real. Charity flinched as a dark wraith dove above her head, its claws missing her head by a hair.

Not real. Not real. Not real.

But then Charity paused. Why would Apollo send her these visions if they weren't relevant? What if the visions were real— just not here? All the hallucinations, the horrifying landscapes— what if Apollo wasn't torturing her needlessly? Was she seeing Tartarus?

"Wait," Charity whispered, her words feeling like a far-off echo. She stood on wobbly legs, calling out louder. "I said wait."

Venus turned her venomous stare on Charity.

"You once said there was a task for each of us to earn back compasses, but you never gave one to Psyche."

The goddess cocked her head and turned her golden eyes on Psyche's frail, aged body.

"This crone? There is nothing more I want from her but to see her rot," the goddess spat.

Charity's vision blurred as the glowing silver box spun in her mind's eye.

"You want Pandora's box." The voice that came out of Charity's mouth was not her own, but she didn't shrink from it. There was a resonance and unquestionable truth to it.

Venus turned sharply, her nostrils flaring. "How interesting. Apollo, darling, how nice of you to come and play." Her lip curled as she assessed Charity. "Of course *you* know that I have coveted it for millennia."

Jaylynn stared up at Charity in open terror. Charity longed to reach out and tell her friend not to fear, but the grasp Apollo had on her kept her standing firm. Blake stood frozen, as if she could make herself invisible to the godly presences if she didn't breathe.

Venus pressed her lips together in a coy smile as she glanced back to Psyche—the only body still floating. Venus brushed back Psyche's gray hair as she spoke. "If you want to play, Apollo, I'll play. If Psyche wants to try, I would take Pandora's box in exchange for our original deal: the return of compasses."

Charity felt the moment Apollo's presence slipped away, as if he too felt like her skull wasn't big enough for the both of them. The visions still swam around her, black sands and dead trees, but the weight of the god was gone.

"You want Psyche to steal from Proserpina?" Jaylynn's whisper caught between hiccups. "The goddess of spring and flowers, the wife of Pluto and death, the queen of the Underworld?"

"Yes," Venus preened.

Before anyone could change the course Apollo had set them on, Charity broke the silence.

"She'll do it."

It was her own voice that rang out, not Apollo's. Jaylynn turned to Charity in shock. Blake stared at her with hostile betrayal. Charity wished she could explain, but she could see now what her visions meant. They were always going to have one more task. Apollo had said, "*The goddess's tasks are but the beginning… all must repent for the hope of winning.*" Psyche was there the day they first called Venus. She needed to repent too.

The goddess's dark smile glinted.

"Then we have a deal." The scent of rose petals and mint leaves filled Charity's nostrils as the goddess marched forward to stand in front of them. The bands of metal pins on her shoulders glinted in the last rays of sunset. "But if Psyche fails, all of your bodies will build the steps of my returned reign when the veil finally falls. Psyche will stay in the Underworld, and

Cupid will stay in the stars. And no one will get compasses back, ever."

Wind swirled around the clearing, and Charity knew there would be no more bartering. The contract was sealed. She could feel it lock in as Venus' hourglass magic bled from her arm, joining the mystical breeze that swirled around the goddess.

"Don't dally." Venus gave a sultry wink before vanishing into thin air.

When Venus disappeared, so did her spell work. Sebastian sat up abruptly, his eyes darting around. Ladybug and Hunter were slower to move, both blinking as the magic faded.

"What happened?" Nylah groaned, holding their splintered glasses up to the darkening sky.

Blake rushed forward to take Psyche's hands, gently stabilizing the woman as her eyes opened. Psyche grasped at her chest like she couldn't quite believe she was breathing.

All Charity could do was sit and watch, stunned. How could anyone explain what had happened?

The moment Jaylynn had thrashed screaming in Blake's arms, clawing at the air, Charity knew everything was happening as her vision foretold. But there were no flames or rivers of poison. There were no doors. The greater prophecy wasn't complete. Apollo had known they would face Venus again, and he had known they had yet another journey to undertake. The four tasks were only the beginning; the fifth would end it all.

And I have the key to fix everything.

Charity searched her mind for any solid proof they would be successful, but she found none. All she saw were the doors, the rolling sands, and a chance.

We have a chance.

One shot to bring back Cupid's magic, one unimaginable journey, and in her head, Charity had the answers. For once, her scattered mind could save the day.

A single other fact made Charity confident they had to go to the Underworld. In her visions, Nessie had been holding a twisted staff. No such thing had happened, *yet*. That meant her daughter was alive and fighting in Tartarus. Charity could only hope Nessie could hold on long enough that they could save her, because now, that was the only thing Charity wanted. Compasses and Luke's restless soul didn't matter when her daughter's life hung in the balance. And maybe, if they were lucky, they could save Damien and Jazz too.

They would go to the Underworld and retrieve Pandora's box, and they would stop in Tartarus along the way. Charity would find her daughter if it was the last thing she did, and then they would set everything else right.

Jaylynn's fingers traced the jagged seam in the grass where the fissure had been. Her eyes watered as she looked up at Charity.

"You're sure that was the right thing to do?" Jaylynn whispered.

Charity nodded. They had a prophecy to fulfil.

Stay tuned for book three of the Soulmate Seekers Series:

JUPITER'S

JUDGMENT

Find more information at www.ashleyweisswrites.ca

CHARACTER APPENDIX

Addi Williams: Gareth's younger brother

Alva: Damien's friend back in the UK

Blake: Aliases J.B. or Jordan Blake | tattooed over her compass | soulmate link led her to Psyche

Boots: Nylah's rescued kitten

Charity McKenzie: Nessie's mother | was married to Luke, who died in the military five years ago | newest compass link pointed to Jaylynn Clare

Dakota Hart: Gareth's exchange partner

Damien Diaz: Teammate and rival of Sebastian and Gareth

Dyani Hart: Twin sister of Tokala | part of Gareth's exchange family

Elias: Jaylynn's deceased fiancé | died in fire

Elise Williams: Gareth, Emmet, and Addi's mum

Emmet Williams: Gareth's younger brother

Gareth Williams: Sebastian's best friend | had a compass that constantly changed who it pointed to

Huan Sun: Father of Sebastian's exchange family | works as a counselor

Hunter Brooks: From Pennsylvania | never had a compass-clock

Jaylynn Clare: Nylah's younger sister | compass link changed from her fiancé, Elias, to Psyche

Jazz Singh: Nylah's best friend | part of Fates' Followers

Kade Baker: Renee's husband | Lacey's father

Kennedy Brooks: Hunter's sister

Kenyon Williams: Gareth, Emmet, and Addi's dad.

Lacey Baker: Renee and Kade's daughter | Nessie's friend

Ladybug: Kade's soulmate-linked puppy

Liam Sun: Sebastian's exchange partner

Luke McKenzie: Charity's husband | Nessie's father

Mikom Hart: Father of Gareth's exchange family

Natalie Clare: Jaylynn and Nylah's mother

Nessie McKenzie: Charity's daughter | Lacey's friend | had a frozen compass

Nylah Clare: Jaylynn's older sibling | Jazz's best friend | didn't find their soulmate before compasses disappeared

Philip Sun: Father of Sebastian's exchange family | works as an anesthesiologist

Psyche: Alias River | Cupid's soulmate | friend and mentor of Jaylynn

Renee Baker: Kade's wife | Lacey's mother | compass link changed from her husband to her daughter

Richard Clare: Jaylynn and Nylah's father

Sebastian Evans: Gareth's best friend | didn't find his soulmate before compasses disappeared

Tara Blake: Blake's mother

Tatiana: Blake's ex-girlfriend from New York

Trevor: Coach of the soccer/football team in Toronto

Tokala Hart: Twin sister of Dyani | part of Gareth's exchange family

Vee Evans: Sebastian's older sister

Winona Hart: Mother of Gareth's exchange family | runs an Indigenous art gallery

ROMAN MYTHOLOGY APPENDIX

Asphodel: A neutral region of the Underworld where souls who are neither heroes nor sinners go to rest

Apollo: God of the sun, archery, prophecy, and healing | twin of Diana

Capitoline Triad: Jupiter, Juno, and Minerva | purist believe these three gods are the primary figures

Cupid: God of love | Psyche's soulmate

Decuma: One of the three Fates | decides the length and quality of the thread of life

Diana: Goddess of the hunt | twin of Apollo

Elysium fields: A region of the Underworld where souls who were heroes go to rest

Fortuna: Goddess of chance and luck

Hekate: Goddess of magic and dark arts

Janus: God of doors, gates, and transitions

Juno: Goddess of marriage and childbirth | queen of the gods

Jupiter: God of the sky and thunder | king of the gods

Mars: God of war and agriculture

Mercury: Messenger of the gods | god of interpreters and translators

Minerva: Goddess of wisdom and defensive warfare

Morta: One of the three Fates | the one who cuts the thread of life

Neptune: God of the sea and horses

Nona: One of the three Fates | the one who spins and creates each thread of life

Pantheon: The Roman temple dedicated to all Roman gods and goddesses

Purgatory: A region of the Underworld where souls who have not properly crossed over into death roam

Pluto: God of the Underworld

Proserpina: Goddess of spring and queen of the Underworld

Psyche: Cupid's soulmate

Tartarus: A dark region of the Underworld where condemned souls are sent to be tortured | realm of monsters

Terra Mater: Goddess of the earth | "Mother Earth"

Three Fates: Nona, Decuma, and Morta

Underworld: The place passed souls go to rest | realms include Elysium, Asphodel, Purgatory, and Tartarus

Venus: Goddess of love and beauty | mother of Cupid

Vesta: Goddess of the hearth, home, and family

Vulcan: God of fire, the forge, metalworking, and volcanos

ACKNOWLEDGMENTS

Oh my goodness, I can't believe another book of this series is printed and out in the world. My darling book baby, *Venus' Vengeance*, wouldn't be the heart-wrenching chaos and drama it is without my amazing family, friends, and community.

First, I need to praise my epic beta reading team. To my summer betas—Laura Pinkasavage, Sabrina Ulicki, Ashley Stevens, Krystin Jacob, Angeline LeTourneau, and Sam Wiancko—you helped this book earn her title, and I will always remember you as the beta book club that called for blood. Thank you to Krystin for being my Indigenous sensitivity reader. I could never have a book set in Canada without the Harts' presence. Ashley, thank you for making sure this book stayed PG-13 for my younger readers and school libraries. Sam, thank you for all your advice to keep the medical plots accurate. Laura, Sabrina, and Angeline, thank you for your fantastic catches and advice on how to make the pacing stronger and the structure better. This book would have been such a different vibe without all of you!

To my fall beta team—Aleisha Cloutier-Parcels, Casia McLeod-Weiss, Cindy Ferrige, and Rachel Bryant—I changed this ending five times over, and I will forever be grateful you were the group that helped me figure out the perfect way to finish it. Aleisha, thank you for being my beta who left the most comments. It's every author's dream to have 2000 reminders you have no idea how to spell certain words or use commas and desperately need editing services—haha. Thank you, Cindy and Rachel, for all the love you gave this manuscript and for helping me guide the political tone around the Endless War. And thank you, Casia, for being the person who ultimately inspired me to go big or go home on the ending. I'm not sure Nessie thanks you, but I do.

And lastly, to my winter beta team—Zanne Klingenberg, Kim Sandle, and Rose Parker—the last people to see this before I sent it off to copy editing. After months of this story gradually getting darker and grittier with each rewrite, thank you for helping me weave some light and hope back in. Bonus thank-you to Rose for fangirling over the manuscript and making me laugh out loud with all the Gen Z comments. It warms my heart to know this story means as much to my YA audience as it does to me.

While *Venus' Vengeance* was born in my brain, the emotional ride of this story wouldn't be the same without any of my betas, so thank you all.

To my parents: Rob, Cindy, and Mike. Thank you for giving me so many tools to create this book. For teaching me what love is, and isn't; for encouraging me to read and write; for pushing me to keep dreaming; for helping me pay for the occasional publishing costs; and for continuing to show up to my book events. This passion of mine wouldn't exist without your belief in me. I love you all to the stars and back.

To my love, Brendan Marquis, thank you for standing beside me through this entire process. I'm sure it's no easy feat to live with a creative soul, and I'm grateful for your continued patience while I strive to make my author dreams come true. Thank you for letting me talk through my big vision, my publishing frustrations, and for giving me reliable advice whenever you can.

To my office supervisor, our darling fluffy-butt Jackson, thank you for all the hours you kept me company as I typed away and for always reminding me to go for walks when I've been staring at the computer for too long.

To my cover designer, Franziska Stern, I can never thank you enough for creating yet another book cover of my dreams. Your gift at finding the balance between magical and moody is divine, and I can't wait to wrap the series up with Book Three.

To my editors, Leah Mol and Beth Attwood, thank you for all the hours you put into this novel to ensure it's grammatically correct.

And of course, thank you to all the readers who finished *Cupid's Compass* and fervently demanded Book Two be released immediately. While it took me two years to deliver, the unanimous push for the next part of the story was the fuel that made this book special. I hope it was everything you hoped for, and I promise not to leave *Jupiter's Judgment* on another cliffhanger.

ABOUT THE AUTHOR

A natural storyteller with a flair for the dramatic, Ashley Weiss lives in Alberta, Canada. Her debut novel, *Cupid's Compass*, began as a 2020 quarantine project and grew to be an irreplaceable passion. When she isn't writing, Ashley can be found cuddling her dog or watching movies with her love.

Find her on Instagram @ashley.weiss.writes